FATES OF VEILORE BOOK THREE

AF486422

# FATE OF LORDS

## IRELAND LYDON

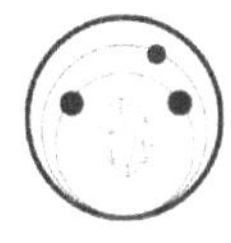

AN IMPRINT OF VEILORE PRESS

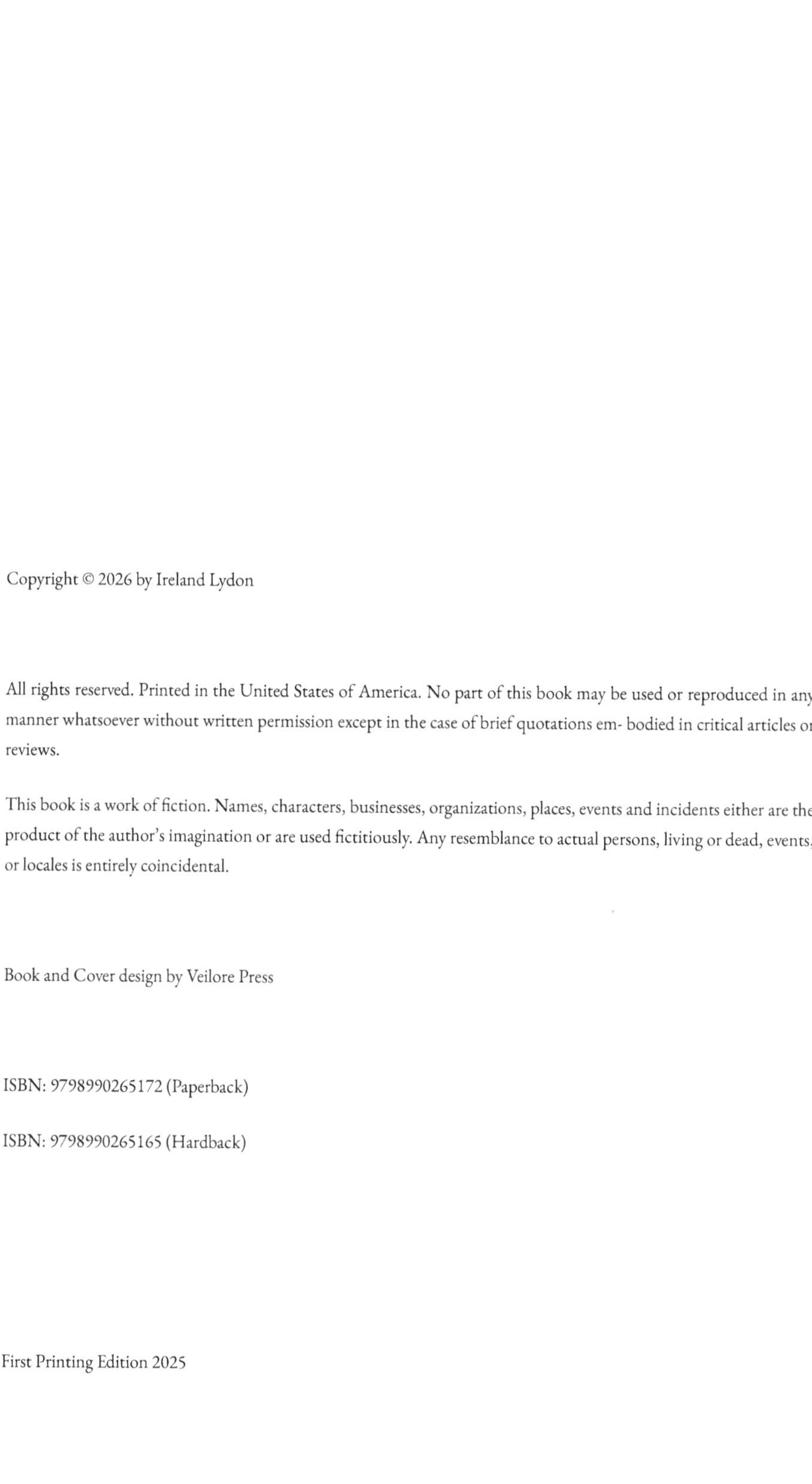

Copyright © 2026 by Ireland Lydon



This book is a work of fiction. Names, characters, businesses, organizations, places, events and incidents either are the product of the author's imagination or are used fictitiously. Any resemblance to actual persons, living or dead, events, or locales is entirely coincidental.

Book and Cover design by Veilore Press

ISBN: 9798990265172 (Paperback)

ISBN: 9798990265165 (Hardback)

First Printing Edition 2025

*'Yet do not cast all hope away. Tomorrow is unknown. Rede oft is found at the rising of the sun.'*

J. R. R. Tolkien, Legolas in The Two Towers

### *Veil of Shadow and Flame*


*Beneath a cold and watchful dome,*
*where silence carves the soul to stone,*
*soft-spoken vows in darkness lie,*
*half-truths beneath a breaking sky.*


*A sovereign forged in ash and flame,*
*a blade that trembles at her name,*
*one dares to stay, one dares to flee—*
*two hearts at war with destiny.*


*A promise draped in gilded thread,*
*unspoken words, a path misled,*
*she walks the line where duty binds,*
*a steadfast gaze, though fate unwinds.*


*A love once bright now veiled in night,*
*a fragile pull, a fading light,*
*she whispers where the shadows creep,*
*to ghosts of all she could not keep.*


*Three souls adrift on tangled strands,*
*longing lost in quiet hands,*
*yet when the dying daylight falls,*
*love endures—though silence calls.*

JORN
MONSELT
PORT OF NORD
BRAC
HILVAER
JORN CITY
DEN
EIR
FOREST OF DERN
DERN
AUGUSTA
FOREST OF AAVIN
AAVIN
R'HUN
THOURNS
FIELD OF THOURNS
ALNWICK
WESTERN GAP
SANCIA
LEJAL
FELOUR
SIG
MVORS
DIVNA

eacherous Seas
ENTHEAS
TAUF
THELGH
LEDENJOUR
PORT OF
GHELFIN
TAASTRA
TAUDREN
CITY OF
CORAD
CORAÐ
EHLMOR
EHLMOR ISLES
NIHTAR ISLA
VEILORE

# FATE OF LORDS

*Fate of Lords* is a fantasy romance novel part of a series include elements that may not be suitable for all readers. Such as RAPE, death, murder, blood, mentions of suicide and suicidal notions, SA and descriptions of past SA, captivity, and sexual acts are all mentioned within the series. Readers who are sensitive to such elements please take note.

# BEFORE

*Beneath the Field of Thourns. West Rhun. 2004.*

SUNLIGHT FLICKERED LIKE WHISPERS over the waves of lavender that lined the river's edge, planted long ago by hands now forgotten. Concealed within a shroud of ancient magick stood the cathedral, its spire piercing the clouds, unseen by the war torn lands that sprawled beyond the hills. The cathedral, lost to the memories of those old enough to recall its presence, remained a sanctuary for one who could peer into the fabric of magick, discerning the hidden truths that lay between certainty and the unseen.

Centuries passed in solitude, unnoticed and unremembered by the western realms, where the name Sanna held no meaning. Trapped in youthful vigor when she began her payment to Ehnarea.

Beneath the protective shield of magick, she wandered through her garden, a place where the warmth never waned, and blooms flourished in perpetual sunlight. Her hands, delicate and purposeful, tended to plants and herbs, harvesting what she needed for the potions she had her familiars deliver at the gates of Rhun. These offerings, marked for the Blessed Lady of Light, Blaihr, sustained the city behind its stone walls that surrounded Castle Caerh, curing ailments and concocting powerful balms, though the true source of this aid remained a mystery to those who sought the goddess of light, Ehnarea.

Sanna's movements were fluid, her basket resting in the crook of her elbow as she walked along at the garden's edge. Her gown, once a garment of fine craftsmanship, had faded and softened with the centuries, hanging loosely from her thin willowy frame. She reached out to a bush of roses, her fingers brushing over each velvety petal with practiced care. Though blind, a sacrifice made to the goddess long ago, Sanna's world was vivid in her mind's eye, shaped by magick and a deep connection to the life around her. Each snip of the shears was deliberate, her touch guiding her to the perfect bloom before it joined the others in her basket.

But as she reached for the last rose, something shifted—a ripple of unease coursed through the magick that bound her world. The sky beyond the shroud darkened, clouds twisted ominously, and a chill wind, foreign to her garden, threaded through the air. Sanna's smile faded, replaced by a rare tremor of uncertainty, her fingers hesitating as the familiar gave way to the unknown.

Sanna gasped, her head falling back as a vision came, grasping her body in a force that paralyzed her. Her milky white eyes shifted as the vision began.

*Brendolyn wept openly, her hands grasping the curve of the dead king's hand. Unable to perceive the man with dark hair crouched beside her. He was soothing her, whispering to her,* Sanna could just hear the eager words of Pavan as the Ehlfern helped the princess to stand.

*Trembling, the princess was unwilling to leave the king, her agony crippling the room with despair. Her emotions are agonizing and cruel. But Pavan was firm, grasping the princess by the hand, guiding her with hastened steps to the window. Cold blistering in through the room as rain began to mist their faces. Pavan heaved his frame into the window, grasping firmly to the jagged stone and twisty vines that grew along the wall.*

*"Hold onto me," Pavan spoke calmly, easing his large frame towards the window, reaching in at the princess.*

*Brendolyn's breath hitched, but did as he asked. Pavan eased the princess around his neck, magick shifted.* Sanna felt the warmth envelope her as her sights flickered, watching the Ehlfern descend into the depths.

*Now, deep in the dark shroud of night. Pavan set the princess on a bench under the shelter of the gazebo within the quiet gardens of Jorn Castle.*

*"Brendolyn," his hands gently grasped her shoulders. Her thin frame shook under his touch, looking directly into her golden eyes so wrought with fear it made Pavan tremble.*

*Pavan clenched his jaw, forcing away the grief that began to claw through him. The princess sighed into his touch.*

*"Listen to me carefully...you must return to the castle on your own. Can you find your way unnoticed?" He spoke, but Brendolyn could not answer, her chin trembled. She shivered, agony gnashing through her body. He melted, grabbing her cheeks delicately. His heart was beating faster.*

*"Bren." He spoke, gentler.*

*Fresh tears fell, it broke Pavan to see her, to feel Brendolyn so terrified. "I can't...he is there...I can't." She shook her head.*

*"He cannot hurt you, Brendolyn, I promise. You are so brave, you are strong, fearless. Now, return to Lahrs. You must return to him now."*

*She nodded, her body shaking under his hands. Vulnerable. He was sickened by the pull, being drawn to her then. Keenly aware of the connection between them, Pavan pulled his hands away. Pavan stood, taking a step back.*

*"You will not return with me?" She asked, looking up to him desperately. Her eyes wet with fresh tears.*

*"You must return, I cannot stay here..." he began to say, his magick festering, growing rampant.*

*"Don't leave me," she begged.*

*Brendolyn rushed forward, wrapping her arms around his middle, as she had done beneath the alcove of the steps. Pavan felt his heart beat wildly. Holding her for but a moment, then, yanking her arms free of him. Letting her go.*

*"I am so sorry..." He disappeared into the darkness.*

Sanna gasped, her breath catching as the vision tore through her mind, leaving her trembling. Her basket slipped from her arm, roses scattering across the garden path like crimson tears. She reached up, her fingers trembling as she wiped away the blood that traced a thin line down her upper lip, her gaze scanning the once vibrant garden now cloaked in shadow.

Above the shroud of magick, dark clouds churned, casting an ominous gloom that seeped into the very air. Ignoring the scattered petals beneath her feet, Sanna moved as if drawn by an unseen force, her steps unsteady as she approached the edge of her sanctuary. The shimmering boundary of magick pulsed before her, a barrier she had not crossed in centuries. Her hand lifted, trembling as it neared the shroud, but something deep within recoiled.

A surge of pain exploded in her mind, a sharp, searing agony that brought her to her knees. Sanna's body convulsed, her vision blurring as tears of blood welled in her milky white eyes, the color slowly shifting to a vibrant, unnatural green.

The second vision struck without warning, more violent than the first, leaving her paralyzed by fear. She clutched her head, desperate to quiet the screams that echoed in her mind, to silence the voices that howled in her ears. The taste of blood filled her mouth, and the acrid stench of burning fires and death invaded her senses.

Sanna crumpled, the weight of the visions pressing down on her, her body trembling as she fought to resist the overwhelming terror. The garden around her faded into the background, replaced by the horrors that flickered behind her eyelids, vivid and unrelenting. The vision held her captive, a harbinger of the darkness that loomed just beyond the veil.

*"Blessed be," Arienne gasped, her body convulsing, blood spilling from her pale lips.*

*"Arienne," Pavan soothed her, holding the woman in his arms, even as the chapel burned around him. As the screams of the Blessed Sisters dying echoed in Sanna's mind. Pavan remained at Arienne's side.*

*Arienne was burnt, her once magnificent hair blackened, burned away to one side, the side of her face bubbled with burns, Pavan held her, shielding them with what little magick he could command.*

*"It is too late," she spoke, Arienne's final words tearing from her smoke heavy lungs. Shaking away the attempts that Pavan wished to heal her. Pushing away with a turn in hand.*

*"I can save you..." Pavan argued, hoisting the woman further into his arms, but he winced, the woman cried out in agony.*

*Arienne's hand clenched tightly to her chest, the skin was raw, but extended it out to Pavan, feeling the weighty pendant and chain fall into his open palm.*

*Pavan grimaced, the weight of the pendant mirroring the grief that now anchored itself deep within him.* Sanna's empathetic sorrow echoed in her chest, the connection between them magnifying the pain that surged within Pavan's heart. *As the realization sank deeper, his tears fell freely, unbidden, tracing a path down his cheeks.*

*"Thad," Arienne whispered, her voice a faint gasp that seemed to echo in the stillness. Her body convulsed violently, each breath a desperate struggle, her eyes wide with terror until, suddenly, she went still.*

*Pavan gently laid her down on the cold stone beneath them, his body shivering as the magick around him tightened its grip. The pendant in his hand felt like a burning brand, the weight of it too much to bear. His teeth ground together as he fought to contain the surge of magick rising within him, clawing at his throat, threatening to overwhelm him. The protective barrier he had clung to shattered, leaving him exposed to the searing fire that raged around him, the air thick with the heat of his own grief and power.*

Sanna screamed, *her voice a silent echo lost in the chaos as Pavan's agonizing cry filled the air, a sound so powerful it seemed to shake the very foundations. The stone walls around him trembled, cracking under the force of his unleashed magick, which burned with an intensity far greater than the flames that flickered around him. The sheer magnitude of his power engulfed the chapel of Denorn, reducing the sacred space to a scene of utter devastation, the remnants of the Blessed Light of Jorn lying in ruins.*

In that moment, Sanna felt the bond between them snap, a sudden, jarring severance that left her gasping. The connection that had linked their hearts, their pain, was gone, leaving her isolated, her senses reeling from the abrupt void. The silence that followed was deafening, a stark contrast to the raw destruction that still lingered in the air.

# CHAPTER

## 1



PAVAN SHIVERED, PULLING THE collar of the warped leather jacket higher to shield his neck and face from the cold. In his haste, he had taken the jacket from a merchant stall in Denorn. There had been a scramble to close the shops when the rain began to drown the city in a haze of pelting sleet.

In the cacophony of villagers rushing for the nearest homes and shops, Pavan tucked himself into a narrow alleyway, crouching in the growing darkness until the cover of night would conceal him.

He had awoken from a toxic sleep, his body raw and exposed after expelling so much magick. The fire had consumed everything, leaving only carnage in its wake. Pavan shivered, silently walking the long road to the wreckage of the chapel of light. Returning to the place where he had been not many hours ago.

He looked to the south, knowing there was danger in the wind. Pavan could feel the pull calling to him—a thousand whispers in his mind that he needed to return.

It was the sound of a horse that drew Pavan back, dropping in a hurry to bound behind a fallen pillar, and breathing slowly as the hooves drew near.

"Blessed be," came a low voice. "I see you there, stranger."

In the silent darkness the voice was carried clearly. Pavan shivered, his magick coiling in his gut. Willing himself to remain silent, his arms, blistered raw, burned against the tension as he clenched his fists tight as footsteps approached.

"You needn't show yourself..." The voice was soft, and a hint of something stirred in Pavan as he listened. Something familiar etched itself into his heart. "You mustn't be afraid, for I knew your father."

His breath stilled. Peaking around, Pavan saw the man standing not far from where he hid, horse at his side, and in the darkness Rhys was illuminated briefly by the light of the moon. Pavan grimaced, his wounds beginning to stretch and weave closed. But with his burns so deep, and his magick weakened, he dared not move any further.

"I have brought my fastest horse from the royal stables in Jorn City. Ciar shall take you away from here. And I have brought bandages..."

Pavan lurched, his haste causing the horse to start and step away.

"That horse does not belong to you." Pavan frowned, eyeing the elf who watched him with tentative grey eyes.

"You know many things that have truth." Rhys smirked, his riding jacket tight around his body to stave off the cold. "Ciar will return home when you have reached Rhun."

"I do not intend to run to Rhun."

Now it was Rhys who frowned, stepping closer to Pavan, "Heed your fathers warning...his sacrifice shall not be in vain."

Pavan clenched his jaw. "Beaumont was not my father, Rhys."

A warm hand pressed firmly against his shoulder. "He told me who you were, Isaac. I know of your birth as I knew your mother and your brother. Let those loyal to your kin keep their duty, my prince."

Sneering, Pavan turned up his collar, wincing against the burn beneath the leather. "I am not a prince."

Offering him the reins, Rhys scanned the ruined cathedral beneath the glow of the moon. "Do not take the main roads. I heard whispers in the great castle of men in Bannon's pocket that patrolled the streets and crossroads from Denorn to the southern coast."

Pavan watched in helpless wonder as the elf turned to leave, disappearing into the darkness that shrouded the cold damp night of Denorn. At his shoulder the horse nudged him, feeling the hot breath upon his neck, he tentatively rested his hand upon the beast's nose, gliding his hand up to the dark hairs that fell between perked up ears.

"Your lady shall miss you terribly should she be in need of a quick escape." Pavan let his hands fall, looking deep into the dark black eyes. "Come, Ciar, we must find Arienne. Her death must be honored in a proper way."

He walked the great length of the fallen outer wall, and into the rubble that was now the great chapel of light, returning to the spot where he had laid Arienne. Taking the bandages from the saddle bag, Pavan began to wrap the white linen around the stiff limbs and body, making quick work through the pain.

Darkness swallowed his journey, a relentless pull in his chest guiding him back to Eir. Ciar followed close behind him as he walked ahead, occasionally looking back to secure the wrapped linen corpse of Arienne. At daybreak, just as the shift of blue began to creep over the eastern skies, Pavan stopped. His heart sank, confirming the dread that had taken root within him. The once formidable stone structures were now skeletal remains, standing defiantly against the early morning sky as smoke billowed high above.

Releasing the reins, he hurried forward, his footsteps falling hard on the cobbled steps as he rounded the main street, coming to an abrupt halt at the center square. Pavan's legs gave out, collapsing to his knees. Grief tore through him, a consuming force that left him numb. He knelt before the corpses piled carelessly like a grotesque monument.

"*Ehnarea bless them...*" he rasped, his mouth dry. Pavan could feel the flames licking at his spirit, threatening to drag him into the abyss along with everything he had ever loved. He knelt there, until the sky grew pink, and the fire had dwindled.

Behind him, Ciar emerged, pressing the flat of his nose into the curve of his neck so Pavan could both smell and feel him there.

Pavan worked in silence, the burns that marred his forearms, the pain a distant echo in his mind now heaving an empty hollow in his chest. Pavan leaned forward, picking up the shovel he had set aside, and returned to the shallow grave he had started in the grove just south of the village. The grove was untouched by the fires, a peaceful refuge where the air was clean, untainted by smoke and ash. Here, he could breathe again, and here he vowed to finish her grave.

Arienne's body lay wrapped in the tattered bandages given to him by Rhys. Pavan had carefully tucked ferns against her cold skin, laying her gently on a bed of stone until his work was done. The weight of the pendant around his neck pressed heavily against his chest, its presence an inescapable reminder of what he had lost. Every movement brought his attention back to it, the burden of its significance growing with each passing moment.

For so long, Pavan had managed to push aside the thoughts that now clawed at the edges of his mind, distracting himself with the necessity of survival, the relentless need to keep moving. But there was nothing left now to stop the storm that was brewing within him, a storm that threatened to consume him whole.

Thad was dead.

The thought hung in the air, undeniable and suffocating, a truth he could no longer ignore. A finality settled over him like a shroud, as heavy as the soil he would soon lay over Arienne's body. Pavan's hands tightened around the shovel, the weight of his grief pressing down on him as he continued to dig, his heart breaking with each shovelful that fell into the grave.

Pavan's soul shattered as he collapsed, his body crumpling. His hands shook uncontrollably, the tremors a cruel reminder of the magick simmering just beneath the surface, ready to erupt. He flexed his fingers, desperate to keep the power at bay, feeling the searing heat and electric tingling that threatened to break free. Somehow, he managed to suppress it as a single tear slipped down his cheek, a silent acknowledgment of the unbearable truth.

Thad was dead. They were *all* dead.

The thought tore through him, each word a blade that cut deeper than the last. Anger surged, a fierce, consuming fire that hurt less than the grief gnawing away at what was left of his core. The grief was a void, endless and suffocating, but the anger gave him something to hold onto, something to fuel the darkness that had begun to take root in his heart. Thoughts intruded, unwelcome and relentless, breaking through the wall he had tried to build around his emotions.

He could feel the pain seeping into his bones, radiating from the soft soil beneath him, as if every living thing around him was crying out in agony, mourning the scar that now marred the realm. The weight of their collective sorrow pressed down on him, feeding the anger that burned hotter with each passing moment. Pavan's jaw clenched, his entire body coiling with the effort to contain the magick pulsing behind his eyes, throbbing in time with the rage that consumed him.

But it was a losing battle. The grief, the anger, the magick were all too much. The storm inside him raged, unstoppable, threatening to tear him apart from the inside out. And yet, all he could do was kneel in the grave, his hands buried in the cold dirt, as the world he had known crumbled around him.

*Isaac*, the voice called, pulling Pavan toward its soothing melody, a balm to his raw nerves. But Pavan sneered, his fist clenching as he fought against the pull, refusing to yield to the voice's seductive call.

He forced himself to stand, muttering an old prayer under his breath, one he had learned long ago. Gently, he eased Arienne's wrapped body into the shallow grave, making the sign of the cross out of habit, a relic from his childhood spent attending mass. With a final look, he crawled out of the grave and began to fill it with earth, whispering a blessing as he did. Arienne would rest now, her soul free to journey to whatever awaited the women of her order.

The sound of approaching hooves snapped Pavan from his reverie and his eyes darted toward the remnants of the outer wall. Panic surged through him, and he scrambled from the grove, moving swiftly and silently through the trees. He hoisted himself over the wall and dropped into the rubble of the village, finding a hiding spot beneath a collapsed roof.

He listened intently as the soldiers rode in. The horses were uneasy, their riders discontent. But it was the slither of magick in the air that made Pavan's skin crawl. Peering through the gaps in the caved-in roof, he saw a man sitting tall on his horse, only fifty yards away. Leuthere, Captain of the King's Guard. Twenty soldiers in Lord Bannon's armor flanked him, their presence ominous.

Leuthere shouted, sweeping his arm in a wide arc, signaling a search. Though Pavan couldn't make out the words, the intent was clear. The men dismounted and began their grim task, sifting through the wreckage of Eir.

Pavan slid deeper into the shadows, moving like a wraith along the darkness. He crept along the remnants of the stables, keeping to the shadows, his heart pounding in his chest.

As he reached one of the larger stalls, he pressed himself against the wall, listening for approaching footsteps.

There was a rustle by the outer hedge, a tingling on his tongue as he sensed the presence of someone he had not noticed before. Crouching low, Pavan watched the entrance to the stall, every muscle tensed.

Sir Eero emerged, pulling back his hood as he surveyed the shadowy interior of the stables. His eyes skimmed over the darkened corners, and Pavan saw the knight was alone, the soldiers elsewhere.

"Ehnarea bless me," Sir Eero murmured, placing a hand over his chest and bowing slightly. He spoke as if to the room, his voice reverent in the old elven dialect. "There was malevolence done here, what cannot be undone..."

From his hidden place, Pavan watched the knight touch a stone pillar, one of many that supported the stable's roof.

Eero continued speaking in the elven tongue, his words a prayer. "Take the souls of the lost, guide them...it is into your arms they are now welcomed." The knight's steps were soft, his voice a soothing counterpoint to the tension thrumming through the air.

Suddenly, Sir Eero halted, just outside the stall where Pavan crouched. The silence between them was thick, Pavan held his breath, afraid that even the sound of his heartbeat might give him away.

"It is unforgivable," Sir Eero said softly, his gaze drifting into the darkened stall before shifting toward the entrance. "But what is done cannot be changed. Do not let this shape your path..."

Pavan's glare burned from the shadows, knowing the knight couldn't see him, yet feeling as if the words were meant for him alone. His fist clenched tighter, his anger a cold flame as he sank further into the darkness.

Sir Eero sighed, resting his hand on the stall door. "Go to the ruins, just south of Jorn... leave this realm at nightfall. You must be ready to run... I can only buy you time. Beyond that, I am without power to aid you."

Eero's eyes flicked toward the corner where Pavan hid, acknowledging his presence without forcing him into the light. Without another word, the knight turned and left, his footsteps fading as he retraced his path through the doorway.

Crawling from his hiding place, Pavan shifted to the outer wall, peering through the shattered remains of a window, now blocked by charred wood crumbled from the fire.

His eyes tracked Sir Eero as the knight crossed the open yard, maneuvering through the rubble of what had once been homes. With a measured pace, Eero examined the closest ruins before disappearing around a curve and buying Pavan the precious time to escape that he promised.

Pavan's fist clenched again as the anger within him coiled tighter.

Thick globs of rain began to fall from the gray clouds above, the first drops heavy and cold. Pavan lifted his gaze, watching as the sky darkened further, casting a deep shadow over the village. A flash of lightning split the sky, followed by a thunderous rumble as the heavens opened and rain poured down, turning the ash-covered ground into a muddy mess.

He opened his palm, feeling the icy rain against his skin, a sharp pain coursing through him as it touched the burns on his arms. His skin, still raw and healing, stretched painfully with each movement. Another flash of lightning lit up the sky, the accompanying thunder loud enough to shake everything beneath him. Over the din, Pavan heard the shouts of the soldiers, their voices urgent as they scrambled to mount their horses, eager to escape the storm.

Pavan stood motionless, his clothes growing damp as he walked into the square of the village of Eir. Through the misty haze, he watched the horses gallop away, their riders hurrying to leave the desolate ruins behind. But one lingered longer than the rest, the rider turning his head to catch sight of Pavan.

Sir Eero's gaze met his, the knight's expression unreadable in the downpour. For a moment, the two stood connected by that fleeting look, then Eero turned and spurred his horse, galloping after the other soldiers.

# CHAPTER

## 2

*Jorn City, Realm of Jorn.*

BARROW SAT MOTIONLESS, HIS gaze drifting over the sea of veiled faces, a blur of figures lost in their collective mourning. The court seemed a distant, hollow echo of itself, each sorrowful countenance blending into the next. The words of the Bearer of Light—an aging man with graying hair—reverberated in the air, but they held no comfort for Barrow. Bitterness gnawed at him, a cold creeping presence in his heart.

His mind wandered, unbidden, to memories of another funeral, another day of mourning. He could still hear the solemn chants that had filled the air when Queen Eleanore was laid to rest, the same songs that had echoed through Jorn City on the day his mother, Aletta, was buried. The streets had been adorned with lavender and wreaths of fern crowned the heads of mourners as they watched her coffin descend into the catacombs. That day, too, had been shadowed by loss, but his father's mourning cut deeper.

He had stood among the men as they carried his father's body into the catacombs beneath the royal cemetery—the final resting place of the family of Aubin. The mausoleum loomed large and cold, a reminder of the fate that awaited him as it had claimed his forefathers.

"Your Majesty." A soft voice interrupted his reverie, pulling him back to the present. Barrow looked up into the pale weathered face of the Bearer of Light, Amadeus Astor.

The older man's kind, brown eyes were tinged with an unspoken understanding. "It is time."

Amadeus had known Barrow since childhood, his presence here a bittersweet comfort. He had traveled from Brac to offer the prayer, and to bring news of Barrow's sister, who had been wisely kept in Brac for her safety. Amadeus's watchful gaze lingered on Barrow, staying close throughout the mourning processions, his hand resting firmly on the chair as if anchoring Barrow in place.

Barrow frowned, the weight of the moment pressing down on him. "Continue," he muttered.

With a respectful bow, Amadeus turned away and descended the marbled steps to address the courtiers. Barrow's eyes followed him, but soon his attention was drawn to the front of the gathering where a bowed head beneath a veil caught his eye. The figure was unmistakable—Brendolyn, sitting beside her father, who looked as lifeless as the stone around them. Yet Barrow's gaze lingered on Brendolyn, her eyes cast downward, refusing to meet him. There was no solace in her presence, only a painful reminder of all that was lost and all that could never be.

"At first of the sun…" Amadeus began the prayer. His voice carried aloft throughout the great hall.

In unison, Barrow heard the voices of the hall echoing the faithful prayers phrase, his own lips forming over the formidable prayer. His chest ached with every utterance, listening as Amadeus went on.

"As the day is done…" Again, every voice followed in the prayer. Barrow felt the chill creep in at the base of his spine.

Barrow's gaze swept the room, each flicker of his eyes betraying the deep unease gnawing at him. The chill in the air grew more pronounced, a subtle shift in the atmosphere that only he seemed to perceive. His eyes darted to the courtiers' lips, to the princesses of Corad, to the king's stony face. The hue of their skin had taken on an unnatural bluish tint, yet none seemed perturbed.

The icy tendrils were undeniable now, he could see them creeping across the chairs, a frosty sheen beginning to crest the pillars that soared to the room's vaulted ceiling. The cold seemed to pulse with an almost sentient malice, spreading silently but insidiously through the chamber.

Barrow's fists tightened, knuckles white against the growing chill. He held his breath, his heart pounding in his chest, desperate to remain motionless. The frost continued its relentless advance, an ominous herald of something unseen and unknowable. Barrow's eyes, wide and unblinking, fixed on the encroaching ice, his mind racing to make sense of the impending dread.

"In triumph or in sorrow..."

Barrow shivered, drawing a slow, agonizing breath as he watched the Bearer of Light amidst the encroaching ice. The frost spread like a spectral shroud, creeping along the floor and up the pillars, a chilling tableau that seemed to freeze time itself. His gaze locked onto Amadeus, who moved with a purposeful grace despite the growing cold.

Silence was overwhelming, punctuated only by the relentless beat of Barrow's own heart, echoing in his ears like a drum. He blinked, struggling to push away the disturbing visions that plagued his mind, but the scene before him grew more surreal by the moment.

Amadeus turned, his mouth moving in silent prayer or incantation, though no sound reached Barrow's ears. The old man approached with deliberate steps, each movement accentuated by the oppressive silence. In his hands he carried a golden circlet, encrusted with deep red gems that seemed to catch and magnify the eerie glow of the ice.

Barrow felt a pang of bitter recognition—this was his destiny, thrust upon him. The throne, once a distant concept, was now his to inherit. A fate he would never have chosen, but one that had come to claim him, nonetheless. He would hold the title for a year, when they would come again to the ceremony to cast the votes with the Lords of Jorn, a final judgement if Barrow would be worthy to hold the crown.

As Amadeus ascended the steps towards Barrow's seat, the weight of the moment settled heavily upon him. He was to take his father's place, to assume the mantle of king. The realization was suffocating, a cold, heavy burden pressing down on him. The crown loomed closer, a grim reminder of the responsibilities and expectations now tethered to his reluctant ascent.

"Many years of tomorrow," Amadeus spoke, placing the crown upon Barrow's head.

It sat heavy, cold to the touch. Barrow swallowed hard, letting out the breath he did not know he had been holding. Looking out to the courtiers, the princesses, the king of the south. Looking out to the vibrancy of their life. No longer did the visions of death cloud him, nor did the icy sheen that threatened to overcome him. Barrow took in the approving looks of his people, of the people closest to his heart.

"Favor find you," they all said in unison. Their voices joined as one, following after Amadeus, who bowed to Barrow in dutiful resignation.

"Long may your reign forever be blessed by the goddess!" Amadeus spoke loudly. "May your reign under The Veil's eyes be just. And shall your heart be guided by the memories of your forefathers. Let the call of our people be your guide, and the righteousness of your mind be forever true."

Amadeus bowed, his fist resting over the flat of his chest, over his heart. Behind him, the room filled with courtiers and knights that stood guard, did likewise.

"King Barrow!" The cheer erupted, a rising tide of voices that reverberated through the grand hall.

"Long live, King Barrow!" The call was echoed, gaining momentum until the entire room was awash with the sound of his name, a tumultuous roar that seemed to shake the very foundations of Barrow's resolve. The din rattled through him, a physical weight pressing down on his chest, making the golden crown feel like a leaden burden.

Barrow closed his eyes, attempting to shut out the overwhelming noise. He drew a deep breath, but the pounding of his heart drowned out the echoes of his name. Bitterness churned within him; he was not a king. He was not meant to succeed the greatness of his father, Beaumont, who had been a towering figure, a monarch revered and beloved by all. The man who had ushered in an era of peace and prosperity.

"Barrow." The voice pierced through the tumult, drawing his attention sharply.

His eyes flew open, and he found himself standing at the entrance of the balcony, overlooking the sprawling city below. The bells of the castle began to toll, a resonant proclamation of his new title.

Simeon Bannon stood beside him, a stoic figure draped in dark woolen garments adorned with intricate silver filigrees. His silvery hair was neatly styled, and his gray eyes gleamed with a penetrating light against the backdrop of the sun.

"They cannot see you, but your people know you stand here, for them," Simeon said, his voice firm, cutting through Barrow's disquiet.

Barrow trembled, struggling to swallow the lump lodged in his throat. He turned away from the balcony, and the two attendants closed the massive doors, muffling the relentless clang of the bells.

"In time, Barrow. In time you shall be great," Simeon spoke with a sigh, his words carrying the weight of practiced reassurance.

Tears welled in Barrow's eyes, but he blinked them away, lifting his gaze to meet Simeon's. The lines of wisdom etched into the lord's face spoke of experience far beyond Barrow's own.

"Will I be as great as my father?" Barrow asked, his voice tinged with a mix of hope and fear.

"You shall be greater, Barrow. With my aid, you shall rise above and conquer," Simeon replied, exuding a confidence that felt almost too smooth, too practiced. A smile, unfamiliar and unsettling, touched his lips.

"I do not wish to conquer... I wish to—" Barrow's voice faltered as his eyes drifted across the hall. He saw Princess Brendolyn being escorted by Sir Lahrs, heading towards the royal guest suites. The sight stirred a pang of guilt that raked through him like searing coals.

Realization of his new reality, the weight of his responsibilities, and the lingering connections from his past coalesced in his mind, leaving Barrow adrift in a sea of turbulent emotions.

"It is only natural to have reservations, My King. Give yourself time to reflect upon the misgivings this realm has endured." Simeon spoke as they walked in the opposite direction of the exit Barrow saw Brendolyn leave from.

Barrow's heart burned with a relentless ache as he recalled his obsession with Brendolyn, the fierce, consuming desire that gnawed at him. The longer he stayed away, the more it festered, a torment deep within his soul. Love had clouded his judgment, leaving him vulnerable to memories he wished he could erase. He could still see Thaddeus's orange eyes, feel the revulsion of his unwanted touch, and the way Thaddeus's presence had poisoned every facet of his life.

"You have a desire for the young Coradian girl," Simeon observed, a mirthful undertone lacing his words. His chuckle rolled through the room, cold and mocking. "She is indeed beautiful just like her mother. It reminds me of an old tale. Have you ever heard of King Sabian's enchantment by the faie in Hana of Augusta?"

Barrow's gaze narrowed as Simeon's eyes slithered towards him, a predatory glint in their depths. Barrow swallowed hard, unease gnawing at his insides.

"No, I have not heard," he replied, his voice steady despite the turmoil inside.

Simeon continued, leading Barrow into the map room where a detailed chart of the three realms lay sprawled across a grand table. His fingers traced the mountainous lines, following them to the sea.

"She was a striking woman—well acquainted with your late mother, Queen Aletta. It was said Hana bewitched the King of Corad himself, and from their union came Brendolyn, a creature of uncommon blood kept in her father's favor." Simeon's voice carried a touch of admiration as he stepped toward the shelf, retrieved a slender bottle and poured a dark, amber spirit into a glass. "But she is not as she would have you believe, Barrow. Though raised beneath the banner of Corad, under the watchful eye of that elven knight Sir Lahrs, the fire of her kin still burns within her. She bears the blood of Augusta, the last of the flame wielders, a line both ancient and dangerous. And now, here she captures the fair of face, beguiling of heart... yet born of traitors."

Barrow's jaw tightened. "She is not like them. She was not raised with the heart of a traitor."

"It is her kin standing beside the magick of Eir, cloaking defiance in the guise of peace, that has taken the heart of your father."

Barrow's eyes scanned the map, from the fortress of Hilvaer to the port town of Denorn, lingering on the small city of Eir nestled near Augusta. The vibrant city of faie now reduced to a shadow of its former self.

"What happened to Eir?" Barrow's voice was hoarse, a tremor betraying his controlled demeanor. He reached out to touch the bumpy ridges of the map as if seeking answers from the very terrain.

Simeon sighed heavily, approaching Barrow with the glass. He offered it with a gesture that seemed almost too deliberate. Barrow accepted the drink, the licorice and mint flavor burning down his throat as he swallowed, the bitterness only adding to his growing discomfort.

"Eir was an unfortunate loss," Simeon said, his tone laden with a feigned sympathy.

Barrow hissed against the burn in his throat, slamming the glass down on the table. He glared at Simeon, his eyes wrought with rage. "You told me there would be no bloodshed. You promised me you would find him without unnecessary violence."

"They would not give him up," Simeon countered, settling into a chair with a resigned sigh. "He was like a king to them, rescuing them from despair, opening trade routes with Corad and Entheas. I instructed Leuthere to search every home, to find the man who murdered your father. Was it wrong to command my most trusted men to seek out the traitor at all costs?"

Barrow's chest tightened, tears blurring his vision as he glared at the map. "*Children... women...*" His voice cracked with the weight of his anguish. "Your men slaughtered them in their sleep, burned their remains in the square. That is not justice."

Simeon leaned forward, his sharp grey eyes fixed on Barrow with an unblinking intensity that made the air feel frigid. "These were faie-touched traitors who would have rallied against you. They were forming an alliance with a powerful magick user. Pavan's actions are evidence of his terrifying power. He could stop a man's heart with a single touch. Do you not understand the threat he poses?"

Barrow felt the cold seep into his bones as Simeon's words echoed in his mind. The realization of the cost of power, the price of vengeance, and the heavy burden of leadership weighed down upon him.

Barrow felt the significance, felt the heavy weight of the truth in what Simeon spoke. Surely, if Pavan was capable of killing his father, who was skilled in so much, that he could have raised an army of magick users to destroy his kingdom. His temple spasmed, his headache growing more steadily, pounding behind his eyes.

"You are certain they are all gone?" Barrow breathed, hesitation flooding through his lips. "Can you tell me without question they are all dead... even that companion of his... the orange eyed one with the copper hair?"

A snarl peeled back Simeon's lips, exposing his teeth.

"You speak of the faie, the one closest to Pavan?" he snarled, unmistakably loathing at the mention.

"Thaddeus..." Barrow nodded, affirming. "He spoke to me, whispering terrible slander against my father."

Standing so close to him, Simeon raised a hand to touch the edge of Barrow's jaw. Looking deep into those grey eyes, Barrow was afraid.

"He was working with Pavan, to ensure you would not interfere. Do not linger on the thoughts that faie puts in your mind. His magick was born of deceit to trick you, Barrow." He searched Barrow for more remnants of thoughts and the room became hot as his touch lingered on the pulse of his throat. "He was dealt with... along with that meddling elf. Arienne."

Barrow looked up harshly. It was a great wickedness to do harm against the women who spent their lives devoted to the goddess. He looked up to the far wall, where the statue of Ehnarea stood looking down at them. His heart began to beat madly in his chest, heat dripping in sweat along his brow. It was wrong to derive so far from her light, to act so against her blessed ones.

"The Chapel of Light has fallen?" It was but a whisper.

"Her wickedness had turned from Ehnarea's path, Barrow." Simeon stood now, approaching to stand so close to Barrow he could feel the warmth of his breath. "She wished ill of your kingdom, Barrow, she wished for the fall of your father. She plotted with those traitors. Now, she is ashes beneath the rubble of that once holy place. Along with the traitors that would conspire against you."

Barrow trembled. "Thaddeus is dead?"

"Yes."

He felt the pressure of Simeon's hand upon his shoulder. His lips so near to Barrow's ear, it felt as though he heard the whisperings of death beneath his breath. Barrow trembled, suddenly afraid.

"What about Pavan? How will we find him?"

A smile creased the lines of Simeon's mouth. Showing his teeth, his gums red and bleeding. "He has lost everything. Give it time, Barrow, he shall give himself to you willingly."

# CHAPTER

## 3

Brendolyn sat in the cool shade of a canopy, the delicate rustle of leaves overhead mingling with the gentle chirping of birds. The king's garden, usually a sanctuary of tranquility, now seemed a place of quiet mourning. She sipped her tea with a sense of duty rather than pleasure, her eyes wandering over the meticulously arranged blooms and the well-tended greenery that had once been a source of comfort.

Elsa, seated beside her, appeared more at ease, her auburn hair catching the sun's rays and gleaming against the soft green of her gown. She scanned the garden with a practiced eye, ever vigilant for the approach of any unwelcome courtiers. Elsa's presence was a balm to Brendolyn's grief, a steady anchor in the sea of her sorrow.

Brendolyn's own attire was a stark contrast in a gray linen gown that felt as scratchy as it looked, a constant reminder of her mourning. The color seemed to absorb the light rather than reflect it, mirroring her inner turmoil. She cast a glance at Elsa, her friend's vibrant appearance only amplifying the dullness of her own garb.

"This is the first time I've ventured out since..." Brendolyn whispered, her gaze drifting to the garden's edge where shadows mingled with sunlight. "I wish I could find solace here, but it feels... too soon."

Elsa offered a comforting smile, though her eyes remained alert. "The gardens were his favorite place," she said softly. "Perhaps it's fitting that you return here, even if it's not quite in the way you imagined."

Brendolyn nodded, though her heart remained heavy. The garden's beauty, once a haven, now felt like a stage where every leaf and petal was a reminder of what was lost. She sipped her tea slowly, trying to find a semblance of peace amidst the bittersweet memories that lingered in the air.

"I wish we could have returned to Corad, by this time…" Brendolyn spoke, after a long moment to reflect.

Elsa placed her cup down with deliberate calm, her eyes narrowing slightly. "It was unwise to venture out with the threat still looming," she said, her voice carrying an edge of concern.

A flush of irritation colored Brendolyn's cheeks. She sighed heavily, her gaze fixed on the dappled sunlight filtering through the canopy. "Pavan is innocent," she stated in elven, her tone flat but resolute. She cast a sidelong glance at Elsa, who was scanning the gardens with a mix of vigilance and anxiety. The courtiers, a constant presence, seemed to drift around them like restless shadows, their whispers ever present despite their best efforts to ignore the princess.

Elsa's grip tightened on Brendolyn's hand. "Yes, we know the truth, but we must not ignore the real dangers," she replied softly, though her eyes betrayed a flicker of unease. She was well aware of the treacherous currents beneath the surface.

Brendolyn's body tensed. The thought of Simeon Bannon made her tremble. Elsa, sensing her discomfort, reached for the plate of fruits and bread, her movements practiced and insistent. "You should eat," she urged, though Brendolyn's appetite was as faded as her grief.

"I cannot." Brendolyn shook her head, her voice a mere whisper against the backdrop of the garden's tranquil sounds.

Elsa, undeterred, placed a plum in one hand and a slice of bread in the other. Her look was both gentle and firm. "You must," she said, her tone brooking no argument. Brendolyn nibbled reluctantly at the bread, the sweetness of the plum barely masking the ash like taste in her mouth.

She frowned, her gaze falling away as her hands lowered to her lap.

"Perhaps a turn in the orchards would be refreshing," Elsa suggested, her tone even as she glanced towards a group of ladies strolling nearby. Their presence seemed to heighten Brendolyn's tension. The whispers, carried by the light breeze, were impossible to ignore.

Brendolyn's heart quickened, her cheeks flushing as the voices of the ladies reached her ears. She could feel their eyes upon her, even as they attempted to avert their gazes. Elsa's hand reached out, a comforting anchor in the swirling sea of courtly gossip.

"They'll be gone soon," Elsa whispered, her voice a soothing murmur. Laughter from the group of ladies echoed around them, a cruel soundtrack to their discomfort.

Brendolyn's eyes darted across the garden, searching for Sir Lahrs, but he was too distant to offer immediate aid. Her gaze flicked back to Elsa, who could sense her growing agitation. With a nod, Brendolyn allowed Elsa to guide her away from the ladies, though the need to escape was palpable.

As they moved, the whispers followed, biting into Brendolyn's resolve. "Pity, really… it's a shock that blackheart didn't do more damage…" one voice jeered, dripping with contempt.

Another added, "Such a shame. Now they rush Lisetta's marriage with the prince… but she is ruined."

"Ruined and tainted by the faie filth. It's shocking Barrow would want to have her after what the king slayer did, leaving her like that in the library."

The words, sharp and insidious, stung Brendolyn deeply. Anger flared within her, and she turned abruptly, her eyes locking onto the source of the slander. Lady Rosalind, tall and imperious in a mustard yellow gown, caught her gaze. The woman's eyes widened, a mixture of surprise and guilt crossing her powdered face. It lasted but a moment and in the company of the other courtiers, her mask of perfection resurfaced.

"Blessed be, the other one is looking at us…" Lady Rosalind whispered hurriedly to her companions, her voice laced with a thinly veiled scorn.

Brendolyn's anger boiled over, her voice cutting through the garden's quiet. "If you had no intention of being overheard, Lady Rosalind, perhaps you should avoid lingering where the whole court can hear."

The taller lady chuckled, fanning herself, the sweat already pooling at the edge of her curled hair pinned beneath the small hat. Beside her, her companions also fanned themselves, clearly embarrassed.

"There is not a restriction to speak within the king's gardens, Brendolyn." Lady Rosalind smirked, looking around her pointedly.

Coolness flickered deep in Brendolyn's gut, glaring harshly at the ladies who stood before her. Brendolyn straightened. "Of course."

This submission appeased the ladies, and Lady Rosalind chuckled, fanning herself again as she whispered to her companions. Elsa pulled on Brendolyn's arm, but she was resistant to leave.

"Perhaps you can enlighten us all, Lady Rosalind, of your opinions of my sister," Brendolyn said loudly, catching the ladies off guard, and also bringing attention to them by a few of the gardeners and lords who walked arm in arm with their lady companions nearby.

Lady Rosalind smiled but it was forced to keep her features demure.

"It is of private matters, Bren—"

Stepping forward, Brendolyn felt the magick begin to grate under her tongue, glaring at the woman who challenged her.

"Do not forget whom you address. We are not intimately acquainted, nor are you of my inner circle. You forget yourself, and to whose court you belong, Lady Rosalind." Each word felt easy and gladly spoken.

Lady Rosalind colored and her fanning quickened as she chuckled again to hide her discomfort. Brendolyn felt the shudder of fear in the woman and the unease of the other women, equally unsettled.

"Princess," Lady Rosalind curtsied slightly.

Brendolyn sighed. "You slander your king speaking as you do. Taking liberties in his kingdom, in his very garden. King Barrow is gracious allowing such obscure families to remain here under the protection of his guard."

Elsa gripped Brendolyn's arm, cautioning her.

She took notice of her heightened emotion. The magick that began to build beneath the surface, but she had no intention of surrendering to this woman.

"We speak only of what has happened..."

Brendolyn sneered. "You have no right to discuss the matter of my sister. Not one of you has the right to whisper behind her back... those I have seen flatter her, those who attempt to become her friends."

The ladies turned away in shame, unable to look at Brendolyn anymore. Only Lady Rosalind was brave enough to face her.

"We only have her best thoughts—"

Brendolyn prickled in irritation. "She will never bring you forward again, Lady Ros-alind. It is clear how ill you truly think of my sister. Yes, *my sister*, a known fact very few seem to regard. She shall know of your slander as will King Barrow. They shall be married before the new moon, before the turn of the tide... do you believe they would continue with your patronage, that they would invite you here in the next season with the way you speak?" Brendolyn began to heat, her cheeks growing hot as her eyes stung with unwanted tears.

"My family has given centuries of patronage to his majesty..." Lady Rosalind looked affronted.

"You are but one of hundreds of great families, Lady Rosalind," Brendolyn snapped, her body singing with magick as her words tightened in her mouth. "There are many bannerman in Jorn who would gladly give themselves to support King Barrow, ones who would not slander his new wife nor provide ill contempt in the presence of those in highest standing within the realms."

"This is absurd, you cannot persuade me that King Barrow would toss my family aside for a mere fact that is spoken from every servant within this castle." Lady Rosalind fanned herself, starving off the musk of fright that permeated from her pores as sweat beaded along her pristinely powdered face. "That Silveran of Eir contrived his way into this castle, making them all swoon. I heard from all of their mouths how charming the magick he wielded is. Your sister was no better... he was pure eloquence. It was not a wonder he hadn't raped half the women in the castle had Leuthere not swooped into the library in time to save your sister from having her throat cut."

Brendolyn clenched her fist, magick dancing on her tongue.

"Bren." Elsa grabbed her hand.

It faded away almost as quickly as it had begun. The burning in her chest retreated as the consciousness of where she was and in what company she belonged cautioned Brendolyn to use her magick.

"Well, perhaps it is true what they say about you, after all..." Lady Rosalind's voice was a pitch of laughter, yet her amused expression was tangled with malice.

Elsa was quick to retort. "You fare better with keeping your tongue Lady Rosalind."

Those sharp eyes shot to look at Elsa.

Lady Rosalind's fine lips curved into a smile. "Don't try to defend her, Lady Elsa. Her mother was a faie, and we all know what ill-bred ilk that heats the blood. I am surprised Brendolyn has not been sent far south to Divna, that is where she belongs, after all. They whisper about the crimes of the faie in Eir, a long known fact that every one of them deserves a traitor's death."

Brendolyn felt the heat rise within her, her blood pulsing with a seething magick. But instead of unleashing her power, she stepped forward, her movements precise and controlled. She closed the distance between herself and Lady Rosalind in a heartbeat and delivered a swift, forceful punch.

The impact was jarring, silencing the garden's ambient sounds. Lady Rosalind's smug expression shattered as Brendolyn's trained fist collided with her delicate features. Lady Rosalind staggered, her composure unraveling as the blood trickled from her nose, dripping down her chin, and creating a stark contrast against the elegant fabric of her dress.

The other ladies gasped and recoiled, their faces a mix of shock and horror.

Brendolyn stood her ground, her breath steadying.

"It was not my mother's magick which taught me that, Lady Rosalind, but I cannot promise to restrain myself should I hear slander upon your lips again about my sister." Brendolyn looked hard at the affronted woman and then the other ladies. "Do not speak of my kin with such ill contempt."

"You can't threaten us!" Lady Rosalind's voice was shrill.

"That was a promise." Brendolyn glared hard at the ruined pretty face.

In a hurried flurry of rustling skirts and anxious whispers, the ladies fled from the scene, their retreat marked by a cacophony of hurried footsteps and dismayed murmurs. Brendolyn stood resolute as the commotion receded, her anger still simmering beneath the surface. Elsa's eyes were clouded with concern, though she masked it with a veneer of calm.

"She is horrid," Brendolyn huffed, her voice tinged with frustration and lingering rage.

From behind Elsa, Lahrs emerged, his tall figure commanding immediate attention as he descended the steps towards them. His sharp, grey eyes took in the aftermath of the confrontation—the retreating figures of the ladies and the lingering tension in the air—before settling on Brendolyn.

Brendolyn, feeling a wave of self-reproach, cast her gaze downward, her cheeks flushed with a mixture of anger and shame. "Forgive me, Lahrs. I should watch my temper," she began, her voice softening with remorse.

There was no immediate retort, no disapproving lecture. Instead, Lahrs closed the distance between them and enveloped her in a firm, reassuring embrace. The warmth of his chest against her cheek was a grounding comfort, and the steadiness of his presence eased the firestorm within her.

"You held your form in excellence," Lahrs said, his voice low and reassuring. "I have taught you well."

Brendolyn lingered in Lahrs' embrace, her breathing slowly steadying. The unrest of the moment began to recede, replaced by a somber reflection on the recent events that had unfolded. She pulled back slightly, her eyes searching his face for some hint of honesty in the familiar grey eyes.

"How is Lisetta?" she asked, her voice trembling slightly as she sought reassurance.

Lahrs's jaw tightened, his eyes clouded with a storm of emotions he struggled to conceal. "She is recovering," he said, his tone clipped. "But the wound she bears is not merely physical."

Brendolyn's heart clenched at his words. "Do you know who was truly behind the attack?"

Lahrs remained still, his silence louder than any words. The tension in his expression was palpable, his anger barely contained. His gaze shifted towards the distant grove where the trees stood silent and imposing, a backdrop to their somber conversation.

"We don't have definitive proof," Lahrs finally admitted, his voice low and tense. "But there are whispers that have reached me from the maids. Audry was there to aid your sister. Lisetta was beside herself, as she rightly should be. By your sister's words it was Pavan. But Audry has certainty that Pavan had fled the castle long before the attack took place. The possibility that someone from Corad might be involved is... unsettling."

Brendolyn's brow furrowed, a mix of concern and disbelief crossing her features. "You think someone from Corad could be behind this?"

"There is disquiet in the possibility," he said finally. "To have one of our own turn against us is... a betrayal we are not prepared to face."

The three of them began walking through the lush grove, the gentle rustling of the leaves providing a quiet counterpoint to the gravity of their discussion. A quiet haven where none of the courtiers walked for fear of dirtying their feet on the unpaved paths. Elsa trailed behind them, her pace deliberate and respectful of the weight of the conversation.

Brendolyn's mind raced with the implications of Lahrs's words. "What are we to do if it turns out to be true? How can we trust anyone if the possibility of betrayal is so close?"

Lahrs's expression hardened, a mixture of resolve and frustration etched into his features. "Trust is a fragile thing, and once shattered, it takes more than time to mend. We need to uncover the truth, but we must do so without compromising our position or falling into panic."

Brendolyn nodded, her thoughts aligning with Lahrs's words. The grove, bathed in dappled sunlight, offered a momentary reprieve from the harsh realities they faced.

Brendolyn paced her room restlessly as evening fell, the silence of her chambers pressing in on her like a tangible weight. Elsa, oblivious to her friend's unease, slept soundly on the bed, her peacefulness starkly contrasting with Brendolyn's internal storm.

Unable to bear the confinement any longer, Brendolyn's thoughts churned like the darkening sky outside. The wind began to howl, rattling the window with an ominous energy. Brendolyn's eyes darted to the open window, and without hesitation, she moved toward it. A storm from the southeast blew cold air, chilling over her skin.

In a moment she decided, pulled herself up into the frame and then leaned out to grasp the vining. Hastening as the wind began to shake around her, she made her descent below. Once on the ground, she looked around to ensure she was alone before making her way through the shadowed labyrinth of the gardens. The chill of the storm from the southeast cut through her gown as she navigated the twisting paths, her breath forming faint clouds in the cold air. Her steps brought her to the familiar haven of the gazebo.

She collapsed onto the seat, feeling the bite of the evening wind as she wrapped her arms around herself. Brendolyn's composure cracked, and she began to weep, her sobs muffled by the sound of the storm. The urgency of her emotions surged like a tempest, recalling the horrors of the night when Pavan had saved her from the clutches of that dreadful room. The chilling memory of Beaumont's death and the fear of being discovered by the Kings guard, the thought of what might have been had she not been rescued, surged with relentless intensity.

They had seen Pavan at the window.

Her throat tightened, swallowing back her cries of agony, grasping the soft fabric of her gown, trying to collect her thoughts, to not become overwhelmed. The gazebo, a sanctuary in daylight, now felt like a prison of sorrow. Brendolyn wiped her tears and took deep, shuddering breaths, trying to pull her fragmented thoughts together. The weight of hopelessness pressed down upon her, and for a moment, she felt utterly lost.

Pavan was innocent, but there were so many now against him. Barrow hunted him, he wanted Pavan to be killed. Brendolyn wished to speak with him, to plead with her love that the man was innocent, but she knew Barrow would not listen. He would not listen to what she said with Lord Bannon so close to his side, whispering falsehoods into the young king's ear.

It was hopeless.

Movement in the shadows made her pause. She stood as a man approached. Her breath stilled for a moment, seeing the man who had saved her before her again. But her moment of glee turned to hidden fear. This was not Pavan.

Brendolyn's heart pounded as she froze, the shadows around her seeming to pulse with the storm's energy. Her moment of unexpected joy at seeing a familiar figure quickly turned to dread as the man stepped into the light. His resemblance to Pavan was uncanny, but his eyes darted nervously, and his posture was unnaturally hunched. The vibrant, corrupt aura that clung to him was a stark contrast to Pavan's usual presence.

"How did you find me?" Brendolyn demanded, her voice trembling despite her attempt to sound composed. Her gaze swept around the darkened garden, searching for any sign of a retreat. But the two of them were alone, the wind and rain the only witnesses.

"I wished to see you again," the man replied, but the voice that emerged was unsettlingly different—an echo of Pavan's voice but tainted with an undercurrent of falseness. The tone was sickly sweet, like overripe fruit, and it made Brendolyn's stomach churn. The magick that shimmered around him was foreign and corrupt, disguising the truth beneath a veneer of deceit.

Brendolyn's breath hitched as she took a cautious step back, her eyes wide with alarm. "Liar," she hissed, the word sharp and cutting. Her instincts screamed at her, the very essence of her being recoiling from the twisted form before her. The man's eyes flickered with a disconcerting gleam, and the magick around him seemed to writhe confirming her worst fears.

The man's face contorted into a mockery of a smile. "Why so suspicious, my dear? Is it so hard to believe I'd come to find you? To claim you?"

Brendolyn's mind raced, trying to grasp the full extent of the deception. Her thoughts began to run wild with the imaginings of Leuthere beneath the glamour, after what Elsa had told her, but there was something less powerful than the man who stood beside the deceitful lord. This figure was not cunning, nor powerful, but cruel.

"Where is Pavan?" she demanded, her voice firm despite the rising fear. "What have you done with him?"

The man's eyes flickered, and he took a step closer, his presence growing more menacing. "Pavan is of no concern to you anymore. You should be more worried about yourself."

Brendolyn's hand subtly pressed against the flat of her bodice, feeling the hidden hilt of a blade beneath the edge where her busk would be, her gaze never leaving the impostor. She knew she had to remain sharp, every instinct telling her that this encounter was fraught with danger. The man's presence, his unnatural demeanor, and the stench of deceit were all warning signs that she knew to protect herself against. Knowing Lahrs had taught her well, she did not shrink away.

The imposter stepped closer. "I am sincere, I have cared about you for so long, little pigeon," he said, his voice tempered and calm.

"You have cared not for me… I have heard what you have done. I know what you did to my sister." Brendolyn felt her throat tighten, wanting the truth from his lips.

He sighed. "It was a misunderstanding."

"You raped her," she said, forcing her words to pass her tongue. She knew what they said about that night, how the maids found Lisetta. It made Brendolyn sick, knowing it could not have been Pavan, knowing it was some plot against him.

The illusion face of Pavan sneered, stepping even closer to Brendolyn. She felt the glimmer of magick recoil in the man as the glamour began to waver, unable to keep the facade as the man's emotions faltered.

"Stay away from me." Brendolyn warned, her hot tears angrily running down her cheeks. She knew who he was and fear rippled in her calm.

He outstretched his hands. "You can trust me."

Brendolyn's breath quickened as she took a step back, her eyes scanning for an escape route. Standing between her and the gazebo's exit, his posture blocked her way. "Trust you?" she spat out, her voice cracking with intensity. "I could never trust you, *Varick*."

His expression softened, a pretentious mask of concern settling over his features. "I am doing this to protect you," he said, his tone dripping with feigned chivalry. "It's for your own good."

Brendolyn's anger flared, her eyes blazing. "Protect me?" She scoffed, her voice trembling with indignation. "There is nothing you offer but betrayal. You have broken your vow of protection and committed crimes against the crown. You will answer for them."

Varick stepped closer, looking down his nose at Brendolyn.

"I am well protected, Bren... but *you*... perhaps there is a chance he will spare you." The knight's hand trailed up the length of her arm, resting along the line of her collarbone, his touch rough against her skin.

Brendolyn frowned. "I don't need your protection."

Her words were bitter and when Varick sneered, the illusion of Pavan's fine features distorted on his face, his brown eyes flaring in anger. His hands were strong and restrained her where she stood.

"He won't take you. Barrow is king now, there is no use for you anymore." Varick smiled, leaning closer.

Brendolyn felt her skin itch with magick, her cheeks growing hot.

Trembling against the rough touch, his lips kissed the curve of her ear all while feeling Varick's hot breath on her neck. Nausea crept into her throat, shutting her eyes as he pressed her back into the smooth stone behind her. Brendolyn trembled under his hands as his lips journeyed, eager to taste what he could.

There was a breeze whispering through her hair, chilling her flushed skin. Remembering the night in the gazebo when Pavan rescued her, she was afraid then, as she was afraid now. But Pavan was there. Brendolyn remembered his green eyes, his gentle touch.

*He cannot hurt you, Brendolyn, I promise. You are so brave, you are strong, fearless. Now, return to Lahrs. You must return now.*

"I shall not be yours."

Brendolyn's kick landed with precision, forcing Varick to stumble back. The grimace that twisted his face revealed the pain behind his veneer of control. He growled under his breath, his hand reaching out again as if to reclaim his hold on her. Brendolyn darted around him, her heart pounding as she bounded down the gazebo steps. The chill of the wind whipped her gown around her legs, amplifying her fear.

Her breath hitched as she felt a strong grip on her arms. She spun around, her fist connecting with her assailant's cheek in a solid thud. The force of the punch made him recoil, cursing loudly. But before she could make a clean escape, Varick's hand swung in a vicious arc, backhanding her across the face. The impact sent her crashing to the garden path, her lip splitting open with a sharp sting.

Varick was relentless. His rough hands grabbed her, turned her onto her back and pinned her down. He knelt, his weight pressing heavily onto her legs, his eyes cold and unyielding. Brendolyn thrashed wildly, her fingers clawing at his face in a desperate bid for freedom. Her nails scratched his cheek, drawing blood, but Varick's grip only tightened.

He looked down at her, hissing, "You will be mine."

Brendolyn tried to scream, but Varick's left hand clamped down over her mouth, muffling her cries. His weight bore down on her, making her punches and scratches feel futile against his overpowering presence. The glimmer of his façade faltered, his true intentions becoming sickeningly clear as he began to push up her skirts, his hand creeping along her bare thigh.

Desperation surged through her. She bit down hard into his hand, sinking her teeth into the flesh. Varick shrieked in pain, his grip loosening as he pulled back. The glamour around him flickered, revealing glimpses of the true malice beneath the guise of Pavan.

Seizing the moment, Brendolyn fumbled beneath her bodice, retrieving the hidden dagger. The cold metal felt reassuring in her hand as she grasped it tightly. Her heart raced as she prepared to defend herself, her mind focused on the need to escape and end the threat before her.

"I will never be yours," she hissed and with force, she thrust the dagger up.

Varick reeled back with a gasp, the blade of her dagger embedded deep into his side, beneath his armpit, and penetrating through flesh and muscle. Blood seeped from the wound and dripped onto her hand. Brendolyn's gaze was fixed on the wound, then lifted to meet his eyes.

He staggered, Varick's form wavering as the glamour shattered under the stress of the injury. His body shifted unnaturally, revealing his true self beneath the illusion. With a guttural, pained moan, Varick reached for her with a bloodied hand, his movements unsteady as he attempted to rise.

Brendolyn scrambled back, her breath coming in ragged gasps. She kept her distance, eyes locked on him, her heart pounding with both fear and resolve. She was ready to strike again if needed, but for now, she watched as Varick's form grew weaker, his attempts to reach her faltering with each staggering step.

Varick's eyes were wide with shock and pain as he stared down at his blood soaked hands. Deep red trickled from his side, staining his tunic.

His voice, strained and filled with disbelief, croaked, "What have you done?"

Brendolyn held her blade steady, its edge catching the moonlight with a cold gleam. Her voice was unwavering despite the tremor in her hands. "You may overpower my strength, but Lahrs taught me how to fight. Follow me, and you will feel my blade again." She stepped around him, her face set in a determined frown.

She walked the garden paths, her breath coming in ragged bursts, her bare feet pressing into the damp, muddy ground.

Each step felt heavier, burdened by the weight of her fear and the adrenaline still coursing through her veins. She glanced down at her bloodied gown and hands, the dagger still coated in Varick's blood. The stables loomed ahead, their warm light a stark contrast to the cold night. Brendolyn approached the end of the garden, her thoughts a whirlwind. The threat was gone for now, but the night's events had left her raw and shaken. She sought the stables for refuge, hoping the warmth and security of the place could offer some semblance of peace amidst the chaos of her thoughts.

She began to shake.

Panic seized her, and the dagger clattered to the stone, its echo a chilling reminder of the violence she had just endured. Brendolyn's hands shook violently as she wiped at the blood on her skirts, her own sobs muffling her cries. Each breath was a ragged gasp, the weight of her fear and guilt pressing heavily upon her.

Footsteps intruded upon her despair. She looked up through her tear streaked vision to find Rhys, the stable hand, his eyes wide with shock and confusion.

"Princess..." he started, his voice trailing off into silence.

Brendolyn's instinct was to retreat, curling into herself as she pressed deeper into the shadows. She could feel her heart thudding in her chest, a relentless drumbeat of terror. Rhys hesitated, his gaze darting between her and the approaching sound of a horse.

"Stay there," he urged, his voice trembling with unease. He glanced back at her one last time before retreating quickly from the stable, leaving her in the darkened corner.

The sound of footsteps grew closer again, and Brendolyn's muscles tensed in fearful anticipation. She squinted through her blurred vision to see Sir Eero, his face a mask of worry and dread.

"Brendolyn…" he began, his voice gentle yet strained. "Are you injured?"

Rhys lingered in the doorway, his posture rigid and alert, as if bracing for any threat that might appear.

Brendolyn fought to draw a steady breath, her chest heaving with the weight of her grief. Tears flowed freely as she choked out her confession, "I stabbed him… he attacked me, but I didn't let him… I couldn't."

Her gaze dropped to the dagger, its presence now a source of unbearable guilt. She crouched down, her legs trembling uncontrollably. Sir Eero knelt beside her, his eyes soft with concern as he sought to understand her turmoil.

"Stabbed who, Bren?" His voice was strained, almost pleading.

"Varick," she sobbed, her voice breaking into a heart-wrenching cry.

"Bren, you are so brave," Sir Eero said, his voice a mix of admiration and anguish.

Brendolyn's tears continued to flow, her hands slick with blood as she tried to wipe them on her once blue gown that was now stained crimson. She felt lightheaded and weak, her body succumbing to the emotional and physical toll.

"Brendolyn, I beg you," Eero's voice took on a desperate edge. "Let me take you to Lahrs. Allow me to carry you to him."

The need for Lahrs was overwhelming; he was her anchor in this storm. With a nod, she gave her consent, her voice failing her. Her senses were overrun with the metallic scent of blood, her stomach churned, and her limbs grew numb.

Sir Eero gently gathered her into his arms, his movements careful and reverent as he cradled her against him. "I've got you," he murmured, his tone soothing despite the gravity of the situation. Brendolyn clung to him, her fingers weakly wrapping around his neck as he lifted her.

"I wanted Pavan to return… I hoped he was in the gardens," she whispered, her voice barely audible against the soft murmur of his breath.

"Shhh, don't speak," Eero urged softly, his voice a distant echo as he navigated through the unlit servants corridors. The warmth of his embrace was a small comfort in her disorientation.

Brendolyn blinked, struggling to stay awake as the world around her swirled. Her breathing slowed, and she felt her consciousness slip away. "Do not be alarmed, Eero," she murmured, her voice growing faint. "I am only fainting."

As her vision blurred and her grip slackened, Sir Eero's reassuring presence was the last thing she felt before the darkness claimed her.

# CHAPTER

## 4

VARICK'S VISION BLURRED AS he staggered forward, each step a struggle against the searing pain that shot through his side. The wound, deep and vicious, continued to bleed profusely, staining the stone floors with every faltering step. His hand, slick with his own blood, pressed desperately against the gash, but it did little to stem the flow.

His breath came in ragged gasps as he approached the dimly lit corridor that led to Lord Bannon's chambers. Shadows danced along the walls, flickering as the torches struggled to stay alight against the draft that whispered through the hall. Varick's senses were dulled, every sound and movement muted by the throbbing in his head and the weight of his injury.

Just as he reached the final turn, his body nearly giving out from exhaustion, Varick noticed a figure standing ahead of him. The figure was cloaked in darkness, features obscured by the shadows that clung to them like a second skin. They stood unnaturally still, as if waiting for him, exuding an air of quiet menace that sent a chill down Varick's spine.

Varick's vision wavered as he extended his bloodied hand toward the figure, desperate for any sign of help or recognition. His fingers trembled in the cold air. But the figure remained motionless, shrouded in darkness, not even flinching at Varick's feeble attempt to reach out. His body, braced against the stone wall, began to slump down.

In the dim light, the shadows began to peel away from the figure, revealing the sharp, cruel lines of Lord Bannon's face. His sneer twisted his features into an expression of disdain, lips curled in amusement at Varick's suffering.

"Lord Bannon..." Varick's voice faltered as he struggled to stay upright, the pain from his wound searing through him like fire. The mocking gaze of Simeon bore into him, every inch of his posture exuding cold, calculated malice.

"Did you truly think you could stumble here, drenched in your own blood, and garner my sympathy?" Simeon's voice was low, almost a whisper, but the venom in it was unmistakable. He made no move to help, but instead, reveled in Varick's desperation.

Varick's outstretched hand slowly fell to his side, fingers brushing the cold stone floor as his strength waned. He could barely keep his eyes open now, the weight of his injury dragging him closer to unconsciousness.

"Why..." Varick croaked, his voice barely more than a whisper, "Why... betray me?"

Simeon's sneer deepened, eyes narrowing as he took a step closer, towering over Varick's crumpled form. "Betrayal, you say? You were simply a pawn in a game far beyond your understanding. Your usefulness has ended, Varick. And now, so shall you."

Varick's pleas fell on deaf ears as Lord Bannon's hand closed around his throat, lifting him effortlessly off the ground. The pressure on his throat was immediate and unforgiving, cutting off his breath and forcing a strangled gasp from his lips. His vision darkened, and panic surged through him as he clawed desperately at Simeon's hand, his nails scraping against unyielding flesh.

Simeon's eyes turned an eerie, glowing white as he muttered incantations under his breath, words twisted with power and malevolence.

Varick's body convulsed, his own blood bubbling up and choking him, as he felt something being ripped from within—a vital essence, his very life force, pulled inexorably into the hand that held him. The pain was excruciating, and Varick's eyes rolled back, his strength draining away with every pulse of magick that Simeon siphoned from him. He could feel his life slipping through his fingers, no longer his own, as Simeon fed on it with a cruel grin.

As Simeon's strength surged, a twisted satisfaction settled on his face. The moment stretched into an eternity, until at last, with a final squeeze, Simeon snapped Varick's neck with a sickening crack. Varick's body went limp, his head lolling to the side as the last remnants of his existence vanished into oblivion.

Simeon released the lifeless body, letting it fall unceremoniously to the cold stone floor with a dull thud, followed by the crack of bones. He didn't spare a second glance at the corpse as he stepped over it, his steps deliberate as he made his way down the corridor.

Reaching the stairs that led to his chambers, Simeon's eyes still glowed with stolen magick as he locked the doors behind him. Darkness closed in, a cloak of shadow and silence that Simeon embraced. With a practiced motion, he retrieved a dagger from his side, slicing across his palm. The pain was fleeting, a small price for the power that surged within him.

As his blood dripped to the floor, it ignited a spark of magick, a hot red fire that flickered to life in the candles around the room. The flames cast a hellish glow, dancing in the dark as if beckoning something forth.

*Simeon.*

His lips curled into a smile.

Lahrs jumped to his feet as the door burst open, Sir Eero carrying an unconscious Brendolyn, entered the private apartment seating area. His stomach rolled to see her covered in blood.

"She was attacked," Eero huffed, placing Brendolyn down on the nearest chaise chair.

"Don't tell me she was—" Nausea built in Lahrs' stomach.

Eero shook his head. "No, she stabbed her attacker. This is his blood."

Kneeling, Lahrs began to wipe the blood from her face. "Good girl," he muttered, but his hands soon began to shake. He looked up at Eero, eyes stinging with tears. "Is he still there, did she tell you who it was?"

"Varick."

Fury boiled in Lahrs' chest but cooled sufficiently as he looked down at Brendolyn again, his hands pushing back the bloody strands of her hair.

"You are not surprised," Eero stated.

"He always wanted her... I warned him for years to stay away. I cautioned Sabian, but he would not listen... I had trained her to defend herself against any attack."

Lahrs began to unpin the front of her bodice where the blood had seeped through the layers, it was ruined. They would need to be set to flame, immediately.

"It was Varick that raped Lisetta..." Eero spoke in a low, hushed voice. "He wore Pavan's face, he found her... I saw her most recent memory."

Lahrs swallowed back the hate. "Please, Eero... find him."

"I will, he can't have gone far with a wound like that. If he is not dead, I will end it with my own hand," Eero spoke readily and then turned to leave at once.

"Thank you." Lahrs nodded.

Lahrs hurried across the hall, beckoning Elsa to come quickly. He did not wait for the lady as he returned to his own chambers to retrieve the water basin, and set to work wiping away every trace of blood.

Elsa emerged, frantic. "Ehnarea, help us!"

"She is unharmed," Lahrs spoke, hurriedly pulling at the bodice. "She stabbed her attacker... Eero has gone in search of him."

Lahrs handed the bodice to Elsa, now frantically working on her skirt. When the last layer of blood coated garments was removed and handed to Elsa, Lahrs spoke again.

"Throw them into the fire."

She hesitated and Lahrs noted the distress on the girl's face.

"No one can know she was attacked, Elsa. Do it now, please."

Doing as she was told, Elsa threw the gown into the fire, watching it slowly burn.

"Shall I run a hot bath?" She turned to the elf, who was scrubbing his hands in the basin. Elsa approached him, placing a hand on his arm. She had never seen him this emotional.

He pulled his hands from the basin, "Yes... yes, run a bath."

While she rushed into the small joined room, Lahrs turned to Brendolyn. Wiping her face with a dampened cloth, before lifting up her light frame in his arms. She was unresponsive as he maneuvered her to his bed, depositing her safely beneath the covers. Elsa returned to his side, wordlessly.

"Did she say anything to you... why did she leave the room?"

He was deliriously calm.

"We did not talk much, she was very lost in thought. Even when I asked her, she didn't say anything. Earlier today, in the gardens, she was so angry I could feel it in my very heart. Had I not fallen asleep maybe I could have..." But Elsa's voice broke off. Her emotions grew as tears began to fall.

Lahrs sighed. "She would have left even with you awake, Elsa... she is very tenacious when her mind is made up."

Elsa nodded.

"I will go see if Eero has found anything, sit with her. If she wakes, she must bathe."

He left them safe in his rooms.

Rounding a corner, he gasped when he saw Prince Barrow walking up the corridor towards him. He was in shock—pale, sallow skin and dark circles around his eyes that made him look ill.

"Your Majesty, are you alright?"

Barrow started, his mouth set in a firm line, and when he offered nothing, Lahrs put a hand on the man's shoulder.

"Barrow."

"They have just discovered Sir Varick... he was stabbed in the chest and his neck was snapped." His firm mouth frowned.

Lahrs felt dread fill him, but he could say nothing.

Barrow looked up to him with strikingly harsh eyes. "Forgive me, I was not in my right mind earlier..." he uttered, his brows knitting together.

"Where is Eero, has he found anything?"

Barrow stepped back, running a hand shakily through his hair. "I have not seen Eero since this morning..." The prince was lost, looking around before his eyes settled again on Lahrs. "Is she safe?" he whispered.

Lahrs gave a small nod. "She is in my own chambers now, finally asleep... she is fearful, Your Majesty."

Barrow frowned again, looking to be on the verge of tears. "I will right this, Lahrs... when I catch him, I shall kill him."

Lahrs grabbed Barrow's arm. "Do not let anger and hatred poison your mind, Barrow. Think with a level head. If you kill this man or the ones he shares company with without a trial, there could be heavy consequences."

Barrow grimaced, pulling his arm free. "His only consequence is the fact that he murdered my father, is that not a fair price to pay for the life he has taken?"

Lahrs was pained to see the fear and anguish within the prince.

"Find him out, Barrow. Do as you must to the man, but do not punish those who are innocent." Lahrs willed the man to see through the haze of his anger.

"You cannot command my hand, sir. You may be in line for your own throne but do not assume you have the right to govern what I accomplish in mine." He turned and strode away.

Lahrs called out, "If you kill innocent people, Barrow, she will never forgive you."

This made the prince stop. He did not turn to look at Lahrs but stayed rooted to the spot.

"Let them alone. I say this as one who believes in the good of your heart. I have known you to be kind and reasoning, Barrow. But if you do this... if you begin your reign with tyranny, there is no going back. If this is the path you choose, she will not follow. No matter how much you say you love her, Brendolyn will not remain at your side."

# CHAPTER

## 5

Lahrs entered through the narrow passage, his senses immediately assaulted by the musty, stale air that clung to the attic rooms. The heat was oppressive and sweat beaded on his brow as he navigated the cramped space. He hadn't expected to find himself in such a forgotten corner of the castle, but the maid's cautious whisper had piqued his curiosity.

She had approached him with hesitance in the lower gardens, her eyes darting around as she relayed her tale in the common tongue. *The southern king*, she said, had *slipped into the attics hours ago and had yet to return.*

Lahrs hadn't known the attics were even accessible anymore. They had been abandoned for years, left to gather dust and memories of a time long past. He stifled a cough, the thick air tickling his throat, and fought back a sneeze as he reached the end of the passage. The narrow hallway before him was dimly lit, and the floorboards creaked ominously underfoot.

As he reached the small door at the end, he hesitated only briefly before pushing it open. The door groaned on its hinges, revealing the shadowed, cluttered room beyond.

"Your Majesty?" he called out, peering into the small room now settled in dust. His eyes scanned the linen shrouds of furniture until his eyes befell the king.

Sabian sat slumped among the exposed shelves along the outer wall, the flickering light casting long shadows across the attic. In his lap rested a small, ornate box, its lid open to reveal a collection of letters, their edges yellowed and brittle with age. He held one of them delicately, his fingers trembling slightly as he read the faded words, lost in memories.

Lahrs approached slowly, his steps careful and measured, not wanting to disturb the somber atmosphere. As he drew closer, he could see the traces of dried tears on Sabian's cheeks, etched like scars into his weathered skin. The once vibrant features of the southern king had dulled, his illness and sorrow carving deep lines into his face.

Sabian's frame was gaunt, his body thinned by weeks of suffering. Dark circles rimmed his eyes, evidence of countless sleepless nights, and his once dark hair was now peppered with white, a stark reminder of the toll the years and his burdens had taken on him. Lahrs hesitated for a moment, pained by the sight of his king in such a fragile state, before finally speaking, his voice low and gentle.

"I spent years regretting the choices I have made, Lahrs."

Easing himself around, Lahrs sat upon the seat beside Sabian. Glancing down at the letters, he recognized the insignias sealed into the aged parchment.

Sabian chuckled. "You speak not. I know you are angry with me, I have been less than favorable, Lahrs."

"You are grieving."

"I have never stopped grieving." Sabian sighed heavily. Looking down at the letters he held in his hand, his touch lingered over the wax seal of green with the insignia of a feather.

Lahrs nodded. "Kryana was beloved by all."

"It was meant to be easy, the alliance that would build an empire. We were young, delighted with the world and the possibilities," Sabian began with a smile, but it faded too soon. "I remember the summer we arrived here. Kryana was delighted with the beauty of the forests, the gardens... but it was Monty she fell in love with. He was captivating, kindness itself. So full of life and happiness... how he danced."

Sadness darkened the happy memory, and Lahrs saw the twist of Sabian's frown as his fingers tightened on the letters in his grasp and the glare at the letters between his sister and the man they both loved. Lahrs remained silent, listening to each heavy breath.

"It was wrong to love him in the end. We were wrong to follow the paths of our hearts that pulled and yearned for each other. If I had not insisted, if I had not begged, then my sister would not have died. She was ill with a broken heart... broken by my foolishness. It was my duty to protect her and I was her ruin."

Lahrs kept his voice low. "Kryana died of a fever that spread from an infection of the liver. Since she was young, she suffered seizures that weakened her blood. My mother treated her at the end of her illness, Sabian. She was there with her to the last and Kryana only ever spoke of your goodness in the end."

Fresh tears dripped along the southern king's nose.

"How ill I have treated her memory. How ill this castle has shadowed my kin with darkness. No more, I say, Lahrs. We shall be free of this place, we shall be free of this blasted realm to our own shores."

Lahrs nodded. "Of course, as soon as the road is clear. I have sent a letter to the Duke of Rhun, begging him for safe passage through his realm."

"Is it wise to leave by the king's road? Would we not encounter danger?" Sabian breathed, his eyes glossing over.

"Eero has promised an escort whenever we need his services. But I can assure you the king's road through Rhun is safer than the coast. There is unrest in Denorn..."

"Have they found him, the man responsible for all of this?" Sabian hissed.

Lahrs lowered his gaze. "He remains in hiding, Sabian. But the man who killed Beaumont shall be dealt with soon enough."

Satisfied, the southern king nodded. Placing the letters safely back into the box, he stood to return them to the shelf at the far wall. A drop in his great shoulders, Lahrs was aware of the uncertainty in his king.

"This was our sanctuary... a place we would come to in order to get away from the duties of our realms," Sabian said without turning around. He touched the shelves, his eyes scanning the trinkets that lined the dust.

"The servants speak of it, but dare not venture here... now, it shall be forgotten. Now that Beaumont is gone, this place shall be shut away and never opened again," Lahrs breathed.

Sabian was quiet, taking in the many books that lined the shelves, the little statues of marble, the boxes of letters, pens, and parchment. But his hand paused over a stone the size of his palm. Lahrs could see the hesitation in the king, not daring to pick up the opalescent stone from its perch.

"Was it a gift?" Lahrs asked, his own eyes taking in the familiar gem. The gleam of the edges catching in the light that streamed in through the window.

"An heirloom." Sabian shrugged, noticeably quieter. "He treasured it above all the jewels crafted on these shores. Beaumont told me it belonged to their ancestor. Aubin, the first of his name, received this as an offering from Entheas... now a gift passed from father to son. I suppose it belongs to Barrow now."

Lahrs trembled, his eyes glinting over the stone, then to the king. Sabian rested his hand at the corner of the shelf, waiting, thoughtful. But at last the king turned, his face serious and cold.

"I think it best that it remains hidden..." Lahrs watched Sabian for a moment and then magick flickered to life at his fingertips. "You cannot tell anyone about the stone or where it is hidden."

Sabian blinked, his lips falling lax before blinking it away. He glanced at Lahrs and then took in the room.

"Blessed be, are we still up here, Lahrs? I think it is about time we return to my chambers for tea."

Sabian was out of the small room in a moment, leaving Lahrs to gaze at the flickering stone. It hummed as he drew nearer, and the breath caught in his throat as he looked down at the purest stone fragment he had ever seen.

His hand raised, desperate to take it, but he stopped, hissing as pain radiated through his bones. He quickly withdrew his hand as magick whispered in his ear. *Not right*, it seemed to say. *Not right, by your hand, or your design.*

Lahrs frowned as the magick wards placed over the stone and around the room began to pulse hotter, pushing him back.

It was safe, for now.

Brendolyn blinked, her head throbbing.

A hand went to rub it and  as she began to sit up, she started, looking out around her. She woke to an open glade, surrounded by hundreds of unmoving trees, each one frozen but it was not cold. Brendolyn shifted in the long grass and as her bare feet touched the ground, it felt warm and soft, as if walking upon the sand.

She smelled it then, the sea, it called to her, beckoning her forward. This was a dream, she decided and a delight calm washed through her frame. Brendolyn never remembered being so awake within her dreams, but she was never so alert as she was now.

Her eyes took in the landscape before her sights set upon the ruins of an old temple. She had seen these before on one of the many rides she took with Eero into the Forest of Dern. Everything was quiet, eerily so without the normal shift of the wind or the voices of the forest. Magick, vibrant and warm, drew into her with every step.

*"Bren."*

She turned suddenly at the voice that echoed in her brain.

There he stood, tall as she remembered. His eyes glimmered like the sea. His dark hair lay about his shoulders while he looked upon her with such concern, she became breathless.

Pavan.

*"What are you doing here?"* he asked, his voice shifting around them like a crashing of waves upon the shore.

"Am I dreaming?" Her own voice made him take a step back.

*"You should not be here,"* he whispered, looking around the woods but there was nothing there. His eyes settled on her again.

"He has done terrible things, Pavan... that man." Brendolyn paused, visibly seeing the fear in Pavan's face.

*"You shouldn't be here."* Turning from her, Pavan returned to the entrance of the ruins but stopped. Retrieving a dagger from his belt, the silver blade glinted as Pavan examined the sharp point with the edge of his thumb.

Brendolyn watched him kneel before the ruins, raising the dagger to press the tip of the blade to the exposed skin of his chest above his heart. Blood running cold, Brendolyn raised her hand, unable to stop the force of magick that forced her out. Her brain hurt, her vision shifted, and brightness surrounded her as heat burned through her skin. She winced, covering her eyes, and opening them again when she was back in Lahrs bedchamber.

Elsa was immediately at her side.

"Oh, Bren," she exclaimed, her dearest friend pressing a cold damp cloth to the curve of Brendolyn's neck.

From another part of the room Lahrs came into view. His eyes were tired and Brendolyn felt the strain of worry fluttering in the air. A terrible headache began building behind her eyes.

She thought her memory was fuzzy, but the gardens quickly came to her, and the sickening vision of Varick wearing another's face made her stomach churn. She grimaced, looking up at Lahrs.

"Is Varick..." She couldn't finish, her throat felt tight.

"He was found in the corridor sometime after you were brought to us by Eero. But he died not from the wounds you inflicted, Bren... his neck was broken. They believe he fell from the upper balcony."

She was shocked, her mouth agape as she looked at Lahrs, who sat on the bed near her, taking her hand in his. *When did Lahrs become so tired*? Brendolyn gripped him tighter, touching the calluses of his hand.

"No, that can't be. He was skilled, he wouldn't have—it must have been Simeon," she breathed, her eyes filling with tears. "It was that man, he has that kind of power. He will find out. He will find out I have seen him!"

"He cannot hurt you here, Bren. I have utilized the magick I possess to safeguard this room, at least for now. But it will not hold forever. As soon as we are able, we must return to Corad. We will return home from this place and there you will be safe."

But Brendolyn felt helpless. "We cannot leave... not now. I cannot let Barrow remain here alone with that man."

"As long as Barrow believes Pavan is the one who has killed the king, he is safe from Simeon."

Brendolyn let her chin tremble, still holding tight to Lahrs hand.

"Can you tell me anything more about that night? Anything that could clarify."

But Brendolyn was shaking her head. There was so much that had happened since then, it felt like her mind was forgetting.

"Beaumont was angry..." she began, her heart beginning to hurt thinking of the king right before his death. Lahrs was patient, holding her hand. "They argued... I was so afraid, I can't remember what he said... Beaumont was trying to stop the black market..."

She paused, looking at Lahrs as a tear fell from her eyes. "Beaumont saw me, Lahrs... I was hiding from them, because I should not have been near that part of the castle. But Beaumont saw me when Simeon did not."

Lahrs squeezed Brendolyn's hand. "We can stop if you wish."

But she shook her head. "No, I should tell you everything I can... but it hurts." She closed her eyes for a moment, letting tears trail along her cheek. She could now feel Elsa's hand on her arm.

"When you're ready," she encouraged.

Brendolyn shook her head again, finding herself back in the room.

"It was more than that... there was something Beaumont was feeling, I remember it here." She pressed a hand to her chest, and beneath it, her heart was racing. "Beaumont knew something about Simeon, a secret. I think he kept Bannon by his side, let him believe he was powerful, to watch his movements, to be sure of one thing...

"He was the king slayer... Beaumont called him Charles Maison. That is the man who had killed King Broderick. But that is not what broke Beaumont, what drove him to such extent..." Brendolyn felt flush, her tears forming in her eyes, remembering the words spoken. Her chest heaved, wrenched by the pains in her heart and the memories of Beaumont's agony. "He killed her... it was Simeon who had killed Eleanore. What he did to her, what I have seen... I can't, I'm so sorry—"

Elsa immediately held Brendolyn while Lahrs stood and rubbed his face.

A gentle knock came to the door, Lahrs hastened to it, unlocking the bolt and greeted a small servant.

"A letter for you, sir." She curtsied. Lahrs took it, turning the letter over in his hand. It was addressed to him but only by name.

"Who delivered this?"

She shrugged. "It was left at the door early this morning."

Lahrs turned from the door, now shut, and looked down at the letter in hand. It was sealed, but lifting it to his nose, it smelled of sap. Lahrs tore into the parchment, letting his eyes take in the contents.

He grew faint and then hurried from the sitting room, stashing the note in his pocket as he grabbed his jacket. He needed to see Eero immediately.

"Do not leave this room," Lahrs instructed, looking in at the girls. Brendolyn watched him closely.

"Where are you going?" She sat up, drying her eyes on the back of her hand.

"I need to see Eero immediately. Please, I shall return shortly but lock the door."

He was gone in a flash, and as the door shut behind him, Elsa hurried to bolt it. Turning back to Brendolyn, she stepped on something.

"I think he dropped this." She looked down at the note.

Brendolyn sat up, outstretching her hand.

"I don't think we should read it." Elsa sniffed the wax seal. "It smells of pine."

Brendolyn snatched the letter from her friends' hand, ignoring the throbbing of her head as she stood there. Her eyes scanned over the words within and Brendolyn felt sick.

*Dear sir,*

*I write this in the most explicit terms of my intended surrender. From this moment forward I give myself over at your nearest convenience. Without delay, consult Eero upon the matter of my whereabouts as he knows the forests to locate me. Know that I have resigned, I am done.*

*Faithfully yours,*

*P.*

"He means to turn himself in?" Elsa read the letter over.

Brendolyn's throat tightened, gulping back her tears as lowered the letter. "He can't," she gasped.

Elsa hurried to the bedchamber, returning with Lahrs's trousers and tunic. "Wear these, you will travel faster without a skirt."

Brendolyn looked at her friend in shock. "You aren't going to stop me?"

Elsa smirked. "I could try, but would you listen?"

Brendolyn dressed in haste, tucking the tunic into the trousers as she synched up the sides with a belt. Unceremoniously, she plaited her wild onyx hair, before forcing her feet into the little tattered boots she nearly always wore.

# CHAPTER

## 6

Bღ RENDOLYN LOOKED SIDEWAYS TO her friend with compassion.

"You do not need to follow, Elsa, but this is something I need to do." Brendolyn made her way through to the silence of the stables. They snuck into the stall where her horse stood grazing, the mare that Barrow had given to her long ago. The horse twitched, sniffing, nudging Brendolyn with her nose as she approached.

"What if we are caught? Or what if—" But they stopped, looking at one another.

"Are you stealing a horse?" A voice called which made them stop. Brendolyn slowly turned, taking in the sight of a stable hand.

"Technically, she's mine." Brendolyn felt her cheeks going hot, looking at the stable hand who was carrying his leather bag of tools. His eyes rounded, recognizing her at last.

"You are the princess of Corad."

"I only need her for an hour, I shall bring her back unharmed." She felt the soft nose of her mare nuzzle at her shoulder.

He looked at her, then to her horse, the stable hands eyes flickered with emotion.

"Are you going after the traitor?" His voice was soft.

"He's not a traitor," Brendolyn snapped. Elsa quickly grabbed at Brendolyn's sleeve but she ignored her friend's warning. There was something about the elf before her, something about his look that puzzled Brendolyn greatly.

The elf lowered his gaze "I saw him... that night." Brendolyn felt the pang of guilt, the heart wrenching pain emanating from the elf.

"He is not a traitor..."

Those eyes locked on hers making Brendolyn's magick shiver. He was stern, unyielding in determination.

"Beaumont was afraid. He was afraid for his family... find him, Brendolyn. Find him and tell him not to lose hope. His father loved him."

Brendolyn blinked rapidly. "Beaumont is Pavan's father?"

"There is no time, princess. I cannot explain..." Rhys looked back over his shoulder—there was someone approaching. He turned to Brendolyn with wide eyes. "Go. Go now, I shall stall them as long as I can."

Rhys retreated away from Brendolyn's horse.

"Perhaps I should remain here, and keep a lookout..." Elsa whispered suddenly, timidly walking around the horse. "I'm not a very good horseman after all."

Brendolyn nodded, pulling herself onto the bare back of her mare. Holding tight to the mane, she looked down at Elsa.

"I shall be no more than an hour."

Elsa nodded, watching her friend as she maneuvered the horse to the gate.

They walked slowly to the door which lead to the hills and a slow rolling fog speeding over the ground. A silence chilled the air.

"Ride with speed, Bren... and please, be careful," Elsa pleaded, grasping Brendolyn's hand for a moment.

Brendolyn nodded before taking the reins in her hands and guiding the mare forward. In a moment she was off as quick as the legs of her horse would go until they reached the edge of the forest. Coming to a slow walk, she took a glance back but the rolling fog covered her vision. Turning now to the forest, she entered the silent woods, her vision obscured as she went, tracking back to the familiar trail she took when Eero and she rode.

It was just before the clearing of meadow, before the ruins, that Brendolyn's mare canted back, refusing to move any further. Brendolyn cursed the stubbornness of her horse.

Dismounting, she tied the mare to a nearby tree before continuing on foot. She walked through the thick wood and entered the meadow. She advanced on the ruins, now clearing into view, and her heart began to race.

Suddenly, she stopped as a shadow moved before her. Her breathing stilled as her palms began to sweat. Then he stood before her, his expression surprised.

"You shouldn't be here."

Relief filled her, letting out a shaken breath to see him standing there. Not an apparition, but *real.*

"It is dangerous for you to be out here alone," he told her.

Brendolyn shook her head.

He breathed out, his face written in torment. "I have hurt people before, Brendolyn. I have brought pain and suffering wherever I go. You shouldn't be here. Not with me."

She furrowed her brow. "You would never hurt me, Pavan."

He looked angry. Hurt filled his eyes and Pavan shook his head.

"You don't know me, Brendolyn. Nor do you understand what I could do... I am a monster."

Brendolyn dared to take a step closer to him, her breath hitching as she crossed the threshold of his guarded space. This time, he didn't pull away. Her trembling hand reached out, gently closing around his. Her lips felt dry, and she swallowed her unease as her fingers drifted to the flat of his chest. Beneath her touch, she could sense the fleeting beat of his heart—a rhythm that matched the subtle tremor of his anxiety.

Her hand smoothed over the front of his tunic, feeling the familiar ridge of the deep scar she had seen before, one that marred his skin like a bitter memory. There was no fresh wound—Pavan had not pressed a dagger to his heart as she feared. Yet beneath his silence, Brendolyn could feel the ache, the gnawing grief that twisted in his chest, a sorrow so deep it resonated within her own. It sank like a stone in her stomach, heavy and relentless. Her hand lingered, her touch an unspoken plea for connection, a fragile offering in the midst of his pain.

"Pavan, what happened?" she breathed.

He stood in silence, his gaze drifting away from her as if distance might shield him from her touch. But Brendolyn couldn't shake the grief tightening her chest; it clawed at her, sharp and unyielding. She winced, her mind suddenly ablaze, as if something within her was being pulled toward him, drawn across a threshold she had not meant to cross.

Images flashed in her mind, vivid and terrible—scenes of fire and ash, the stench of blood and charred flesh. She blinked rapidly, trying to clear them away, but they only grew more intense. In one instant, she saw the elf in Denorn dying in her arms, her breath catching as despair threatened to drown her. She tried to look away, but every turn showed her more horrors, visions that seared her thoughts. Shutting her eyes against the onslaught did nothing to muffle the agonized screams, a wail so piercing it left her throat dry. Rage tore through her veins, a fire so fierce she felt it might consume her entirely.

Her scream was raw as she was suddenly pushed back, breaking free from the visions. When her eyes fluttered open, Pavan was stumbling away, grasping his arm as if recoiling from her touch. His face was turned from her, ashen with grief and fury. But the burning in her mind lingered, the flames licking at her senses, the memory of the fire still vivid—the building engulfed in flames, the ground sodden with blood, ash drifting down like mocking snowflakes.

The agony overwhelmed her and her knees buckled as she crumpled to the ground. Tears streamed from her eyes, desperate to silence the echoing screams.

At last, there was quiet. Brendolyn dared to look up and found Pavan kneeling before her, hands trembling as strange markings twisted along his skin. His eyes, clouded with white mist, slowly cleared as the fire in her vision smoldered out. His gaze met hers, now a familiar shade of emerald, a coolness that steadied her frayed nerves.

"You should not have come," he murmured, standing as if retreat was his only option. The distance between them felt colder, more final.

Brendolyn felt a tear burn its way down her cheek. "Denorn... that was the chapel on fire... it was Eir, burning..." Her voice was strangled with disbelief, the truth seeping into her heart like poison.

Pavan's face twisted with bitterness as he looked away. "Your prince was thorough... Leuthere searched for me there. He sent his guards to root me out. What they found... it was enough."

"It was burning... why was it burning?" Her voice trembled, barely holding onto the question as she pushed herself to stand.

Pavan's snarl cut through the tension like a blade. "I saw what he's truly capable of, Bren. Eir is destroyed—my people slaughtered in the square."

"He couldn't have... he wouldn't..." Her protest wavered, the words choking in her throat as memories of bloodshed and death surged forward. Arienne's death flashed before her eyes, a sickening wave of nausea rising as the magnitude of loss clawed at her heart. Through her tears, she saw the ice hardening in Pavan's demeanor, a bitter coldness that left her breathless.

"He has taken everything from me," Pavan breathed, his voice low, simmering with pain.

Brendolyn trembled, a name falling from her lips like a plea. "Thad."

"Do not speak his name." The words came out as a hiss, sharp and edged with pain. The air around them grew heavy, stifling, as Pavan's anguish seemed to seep into every breath Brendolyn took. His eyes darted away, refusing to meet hers. "Go back to your prince. Go back to your books and your gardens... I have no spirit for childish games."

"I am not a child," she whispered, her voice trembling yet determined.

Pavan scoffed, bitterness lacing his tone. "Then why have you really come? What do you want from me, Brendolyn?" His voice was raw with despair, his agony palpable, fluttering through the air like a dying breath. Without waiting for her answer, he turned away, dropping heavily onto a slab of stone as though the weight of his grief was too much to carry. Above them, birds shrieked, their cries echoing in the stillness.

Brendolyn swallowed hard, struggling to find her voice. "I... I can't be rid of his voice," she admitted, the words catching in her throat. "I felt his heart stop, felt his pain like it was my own." Her voice cracked, the tightness in her chest unbearable. "I see Beaumont every time I close my eyes."

She searched his expression for something—anything—that might give her hope. But there was nothing from Pavan, only the cold, bitter sting of sorrow. She forced herself to bridge the gap between them, kneeling in the damp grass despite the chill that seeped into her legs as desperation clung to her every word.

"Please," she begged. "Take it from me. I know you have the power to stop it—I've seen you do things that defy reason. Take my pain, take away the memory."

He sneered, a flicker of frustration tightening his jaw. "You know not what you ask of me."

"I cannot think of anything but his pain, anything but his death, Pavan..." Her voice was choked with tears, the weight of grief threatening to drown her. She could feel his turmoil, the despair bleeding from his soul, heavy and suffocating. But then something changed—his green eyes shimmered with unshed tears, his hard glare softening as he reached out with a tentative hand. His touch, even through the fabric of her jacket, sent a chill down her spine.

"I cannot take it from you, Bren..." he whispered, his voice so gentle it nearly broke her. "I cannot take away your burden. Forgive me, but you've seen far too much for one person to bear. You are no longer a child—you're seeing the world as it truly is, in all its cruelty and darkness."

His words, tender and laced with sorrow, made Brendolyn quake. The realization that her innocence was gone—that she was now a witness to the world's harshest truths—felt like a wound that would never heal. Pavan's touch, though cold, was the only comfort she could find in the storm of her emotions. She closed her eyes, letting the tears flow, wishing she could forget, even as she knew some things could never be undone.

"You are going to give yourself over to them."

"Enough blood has been spilled in my name..." Pavan's voice was weary, his broad shoulders slumping under the weight of his decision. "I said enough. This will end it. Let them take me."

Brendolyn's heart pounded as she pulled the crumpled note from her pocket and held it out toward him. "You cannot hand yourself over, Pavan. Don't give in to Simeon. Surrendering now won't bring peace—it will only strengthen his hold. You can't give up without trying to clear your own name."

Pavan's frown deepened as he reached for the note, but Brendolyn jerked her hand back, holding it out of reach. "So naive, still clinging to stories of heroism and fantasy, Bren... This is not a storybook. If I run, more innocent lives will suffer. Your prince will burn the world down to find me. But if I turn myself in to Barrow and give him what he wants... the world will move on."

Tears pricked Brendolyn's eyes as she crumpled the note in her fist. "You've done nothing wrong, Pavan. Beaumont died trying to protect you—to protect his kingdom, and to protect me..."

"Beaumont is dead, Brendolyn," Pavan said harshly, bitterness tightening his voice. "He was the only one holding back Bannon's darkness from poisoning your prince. Now, with him gone, it's inevitable. This has to end."

A wrenching pain twisted in Brendolyn's chest as Pavan's magick surged, thickening the air between them. Her chin quivered, her emotions tangling with his. The letter slipped from her hand, landing forgotten in the damp grass as she drew herself closer to him, desperate to make him stay.

"You can stop Simeon," she whispered, voice trembling with urgency.

Pavan shook his head, his expression hollow. "I am not strong enough."

"There has to be another way," she pleaded, touching his arm, so close now that she was enveloped in his scent—citrus mingled with the arcane essence of magick. It coiled around her, tightening beneath her skin, as if binding them together. "There must be books, magicks we haven't discovered yet. You can learn, Pavan. Please, there has to be something."

But his eyes remained downcast. "There is no other way," he murmured, barely audible.

"Barrow will see the truth," she insisted. "He'll understand once he knows what's really happening."

Pavan's gaze turned dark. "Your prince is already poisoned by the lies of a madman. Lord Simeon craves power more than anything. He'll destroy anyone in his path."

The memory of Varick's lifeless form flashed in Brendolyn's mind, her stomach twisting with nausea. Tears brimmed in her eyes, spilling over as she choked on her words. "You can't give in, Pavan. You're good—you saved my life, you saved my father's... We can't let Simeon win."

Pavan's voice was hollow, resigned. "He already has control of Jorn, princess. Soon, he'll have Entheas, then Corad, and after that... nothing will stand in his way. It can't be stopped. This is the only way."

"Wouldn't it be worth trying?" Brendolyn's voice broke as she fought to hold onto hope. "To stop him before the world burns?"

Pavan looked shattered, the last flicker of fight draining from his eyes. "If I fail, Bren..." His words trailed off as he leaned closer, his fingertips brushing through her dark hair. The scent of citrus and magick surrounded her, and her heart hammered in her chest.

"Don't give yourself over," she pleaded, her voice shaking. "Your magick is strong—I've felt it. If Simeon takes you, if he siphons your power like he's done with others, he'll become unstoppable. The world will die."

Pavan shook, his despair seeping through his mask of resolve. "I can't save them," he whispered, voice breaking under the weight of hopelessness.

Anger flared in Brendolyn, raw and consuming. She grabbed his face with both hands, forcing him to meet her gaze. His skin was smooth beneath her trembling fingers as she desperately searched his emerald eyes.

"I forbid you to give yourself up. I forbid you to die," she commanded, her voice slipping into her faie voice, resonant and otherworldly.

The power in her words startled him, making him reel back as if struck. He quickly pulled her hands away, eyes wide with disbelief.

Standing abruptly, he left her there in the dirt, untying the ribbon from his wrist and throwing it to the ground between them. "Take it, so I may be rid of you."

Brendolyn's breath caught in her throat as she watched him retreat, his silhouette fading into the shadows. Gulping back a sob, she stared at the ribbon lying on the grass, a bitter reminder of how close she had come to losing him entirely. It was faded and tattered but she still tenderly wrapped it around her hand. A small part of her crumbled, a piece of her heart withered. Clinging to the ribbon, she pressed it to her chest.

Hoofbeats thundered behind her, jolting Brendolyn from her thoughts. She spun around, her heart lurching as a familiar rider approached. Lahrs pulled his steed to a halt, his expression a mixture of disbelief and concern. He dismounted swiftly, eyes scanning her face.

"Bren, what are you doing here?" he muttered, his voice tight with worry.

She held up the crumpled note in trembling hands, offering it to him. Lahrs took it, frowning as he glanced over her shoulder toward the ruins. Without a word, he strode toward the shattered remains of what once was a sanctuary, Brendolyn trailing closely behind.

"Pavan!" Lahrs called out, his voice echoing against the crumbling stone walls. He halted a few feet from the ruins, waiting with measured patience until Pavan emerged from the shadows, the weight of the world etched on his features.

"Lahrs," Pavan greeted him with a solemn nod.

"You cannot turn yourself in... That's exactly what he wants," Lahrs warned, his expression hard to read.

"Clearly." Pavan's scoff was laced with bitterness as he turned his back, dismissing the warning.

"He's dragging Barrow down a path of darkness," Lahrs continued, undeterred. "If you surrender to Simeon's demands, you'll be handing him the very power he craves. The grip he already has—"

Pavan's voice cut through, sharp as a blade. "Barrow ordered the attack on Eir."

"It was an order to question the men at the gates, nothing more. He instructed the guards to find him."

A dangerous tension crackled in the air and Brendolyn's breath caught in her throat as she sensed Pavan's seething rage. "You're a fool if you believe Simeon allowed free men to walk into that throne room unscathed. There was no such arrangement."

"Barrow would never permit such atrocities," Lahrs countered, disbelief clouding his eyes.

Pavan's snarl was fierce, a wave of magick radiating off him. "Then you don't know him, Lahrs. You don't know what a man is capable of when he's fueled by vengeance, when he's desperate and alone. Barrow's been led by Simeon Bannon's lies since he was young, and now those lies are etched in blood. He'll carry the scars of Eir's massacre until the day he dies."

Lahrs's voice softened, nearly a whisper. "You went there, to Eir..."

Pavan's jaw clenched, his eyes distant. "They were slaughtered in their sleep. Men, women, children—my kin. Burned in the square like cattle. They weren't warriors; they had no magick to defend them. I have no use for your empty assurances. It's done—leave me to the fate of the court."

"We cannot let him rule Barrow's throne," Lahrs pressed. "More blood will be shed if he does."

"I can't help Barrow. He's beyond saving now." Pavan's gaze flickered to Brendolyn, before turning back to Lahrs. "I don't have the strength to stop Bannon's lies from spreading."

"You can learn," Lahrs urged. "You can still harness your power."

Pavan's face twisted with grief, tears brimming in his eyes. "I never wanted this," he hissed, his fists trembling. "Even if I did master it, it wouldn't be enough. He siphons magick from others—he answers to something far darker. And even if we somehow killed Simeon, at what cost? How many more souls would you send to the Veil for the sake of this?"

An uneasy silence fell between them, heavy and suffocating.

"You must leave, Pavan. That is your path now." Lahrs pulled a letter from his pocket and extended it toward him.

Pavan stood still, defiance burning in his eyes. "I won't seek her out."

Brendolyn's pulse quickened as she caught the contempt in Pavan's sneer. Her hand tightened around the ribbon in her grasp, holding onto a sliver of hope.

"She can help you," Lahrs insisted, his tone unwavering.

At last, Pavan took the letter, though he did not open it. Instead, he lifted his gaze, locking eyes with Brendolyn.

"Pavan," she whispered, her voice trembling with unsaid words.

"Favor find you," he murmured. Raising a hand, his fingers barely grazed the fall of her hair as they brushed against the ribbon she clutched.

"Until we meet again," Brendolyn breathed, her senses buzzing with the pulse of magick that hung thickly in the air.

Pavan's eyes shifted back to Lahrs, hardening. "Keep her safe," he commanded, before stepping back and raising his hand in farewell. A thick mist rolled in, shrouding him from view, widening the distance between them with each passing second. Lahrs grasped Brendolyn's arm, pulling her away as the fog deepened, swallowing Pavan's figure whole.

"Come, Bren... we must return with haste," Lahrs urged, his voice steady despite the turmoil swirling around them.

Brendolyn's eyes stung with tears. "I commanded him away, Lahrs. I used my faie voice to forbid him from surrendering..."

Lahrs rested a hand on her shoulder, his sigh heavy with understanding. "Then you saved his life, Brendolyn. Don't doubt the choices you made."

"He's gone," she whispered, her gaze lingering on the vanishing mist. "He's gone from this place forever."

Arriving back at the castle, Brendolyn's feet take her through the guest suites to find the rooms where she was told to stay away from. Lahrs had warned her to not venture there, but it was the room she desperately wanted to see.

Entering the chamber that had belonged to Pavan, it smelled like him. There was a lingering scent of sandalwood, of the scented oils that adorned the man's hair. Looking about the untouched room, her eyes fell upon the tunics that hung within the open wardrobe and all of the silken shirts.

Cautiously reaching up her hand, she touched the fine garments and her chin quivered. Pavan had never left, he did not return to Eir as she had been told. What remained of Pavan's clothes, the oil slicked leather he wore when breathing fire, it was a lie to protect him. To protect them all from the truth of what happened, but Brendolyn's heart was grieved.

Feeling the silk shirts that were dyed in blues and oranges, her heart began to beat wildly. Thad wore these shirts, the faie was here. Brendolyn turned seeking the shelves to the left where trinkets of hair combs, bottles of oils, and boots lined the wall beneath the window.

"Brendolyn?" Sir Eero's voice startled her. She turned to see the knight standing in the doorway.

"I'm sorry... I know I shouldn't be here, but..." Brendolyn wiped her eyes. Glancing at the bed, rumpled from sleep, but never made, her eyes settled on the night table where a red leather book was left.

Eero approached, but stopped, his hand touching the wardrobe door that still held clothes collecting dust.

"We have been forbidden to remove any of the items left by him..."

Brendolyn nodded. "But Thad... is it true? Eero, please tell me, is it true?"

She felt the sadness rolling from the knight, his eyes unable to meet hers. Grasping her stomach, she winced at the sharpening pain settled deep within at the remembrance of losing Beaumont in her arms.

"He loved him, Eero..." Brendolyn gasped. "Pavan loved him... I felt his pain. There was so much pain."

Those eyes sharply turned.

"You saw this... how?" he asked, his voice above a whisper.

"I followed the letter he wrote to Lahrs. You told Pavan where to go... you helped him escape to the ruins of Dern Forest." She took a deep breath, trying to calm her tears.

"But you saw Eir, you saw the fall of the chapel?" Eero looked horrified, stepping closer to Brendolyn, there was hardly a few feet between them now.

Brendolyn shook her head. "When I touched Pavan's arm, I saw—I felt his grief."

He relaxed, if only slightly but she could still feel the unshakeable sadness that dragged in the knight's heart. Resolved at last, Sir Eero reached out, extending a hand to her.

"Come, it is best we leave this place."

She couldn't. It was wrong to leave what was meant to be put away, to be righted and returned to the family of the dead. But Brendolyn lowered her head. There was nothing left of their family. Nothing for these sacred items to be placed to rest.

"Bren, please," he begged. His hand was so close to her, and she desperately wanted to take it, to leave this room and forget her heartbreak.

"I can't," she breathed. Her eyes searched the room as it was, remembering everything that remained. She would never forget every piece that remained. She would remember it all.

"Please." His soft fingers touched her hand where he brought her forward, guiding her out of the room.

They moved away, together. Eero walked with her down the steps, leading them towards the western library.

"Here I must leave you... they shall be changing the guards soon and I have my duties, princess," Eero spoke softly and brought her hand to his lips, brushing a tentative kiss there.

"Thank you, Sir Eero..." Brendolyn curtsied, watching the knight turn away. He descended down the stairs leading towards the stable yards.

Brendolyn turned at last, her steps heavy as she made her way back toward her chambers. Rounding a dimly lit corner, she gasped, colliding with a broad chest clad in bronze. She looked up, startled, only to be met with the cold eyes of Leuthere.

"You are out of place," he sneered, his grip like iron as he clamped down on her arm.

"I-I was just in the library," Brendolyn stammered, her voice catching in her throat. His fingers dug painfully into her skin, unyielding, as though intent on leaving a mark.

"Little pigeon's strayed from the nest," he drawled, his other hand sliding up to trace the curve of her neck. His touch made her shudder, and fear clawed at her chest.

Leuthere yanked her roughly down the winding steps, leading her to the great hall and through the towering doors of the map room. The echo of their footsteps died as they entered the chamber where the flickering candlelight cast shadows across stone walls.

"She was caught outside the west wing, sir," Leuthere reported with a smirk, shoving her forward.

Barrow, now seated near a grand map table, turned to face them. His gaze softened as he saw her, waving the guard away. "She's fine, Leuthere. You may go."

Leuthere bowed and exited, leaving Brendolyn standing alone before Barrow and Lord Bannon, who watched with calculating eyes from the edge of the room.

Brendolyn's heart raced, but she forced herself to speak. "I was looking for you," she said at last, her voice wavering slightly as she glanced uneasily at Bannon's looming presence.

Barrow's expression warmed with a smile as he took her hand in his. Yet there was something off—a roughness in his touch, a callousness that hadn't been there before. "You are always welcome here, Bren." His thumb brushed a tear from her cheek. "I want us to be together, just as we once dreamed." His tone was gentle, almost pleading. "If we wait until my thirtieth birthday, it could be possible with the new will my father left."

Brendolyn blinked, startled by his sudden mention of his father's will. "I don't understand," she murmured, searching his eyes.

Barrow's cheeks flushed. "You haven't heard, have you?" He took a steadying breath, excitement glinting in his eyes. "Your mother, Hana DeFay, was a great lady of Jorn in Augusta. My father reopened the heraldry in the old city, restoring the title and lands to the last descendant of the DeFay line. That's you, Bren."

He squeezed her hands, his smile broadening, eyes alight with hope. "You're a Duchess, Brendolyn. You come from one of the most revered families in all of Jorn. There's nothing standing in the way of us being together now."

But his words brought no comfort. Brendolyn pulled her hands free and stepped back.

"What's the matter?" Barrow asked, confusion clouding his expression.

"Is it true?" Her voice quivered, barely above a whisper. "Did you order the city of Eir to be destroyed?"

Barrow's face blanched. "The men have been apprehended. They'll tell me where the traitor is hiding."

"No one was brought to the castle," Brendolyn shot back, her voice rising. "They all burned in their homes, Barrow. While they slept. The Blessed Light, Arienne—she was among them! Tell me there's no truth in it, that you didn't command such a slaughter." Her stomach churned with dread as she watched him struggle to respond.

Barrow's eyes darkened, shame briefly flickering across his features. "It... it had to be done," he stammered. "They harbored the traitor who murdered my father."

"The women, Barrow. The children," she pressed, her voice breaking.

Barrow's gaze hardened, his resolve steeling. "Perhaps this isn't the time to discuss this," he said, his tone clipped. "I have matters to attend to with Lord Bannon."

"Can't you see that he's leading you down a path you cannot return from?" Brendolyn cried out, desperation lacing her words. "This is not the way to rule, Barrow."

Barrow whirled on her, fury blazing in his eyes. "I am king now, Brendolyn. The people are under my rule, and they will bend to my will, just as they did under my father."

A wave of dark magick rippled through the room, the air thickening with Barrow's anger. Brendolyn felt sickened and bile rose in her throat.

"Your father never ruled through fear or cruelty," she said, her voice shaking with emotion. "The people of Jorn won't fall in line when they learn what you've done."

"They will do as I command," Barrow snarled, his voice cold and unfeeling. "Or they will hang as traitors."

Brendolyn's heart broke as she gazed at the man before her, realizing with a sinking dread that the Barrow she once knew was slipping away, consumed by darkness.

"This is not you, Barrow," Brendolyn whispered, stepping closer, her fingers lightly brushing his arm as she searched his eyes—once clear and bright, now muddied with flecks of darkness that deepened them to a near-violet hue. Magick hummed beneath her fingertips where she touched him, pulsing with a twisted, unsteady energy. "Don't let him cloud your judgment," she pleaded, pushing aside a stray lock of his golden hair, desperate to reach the man she once loved. Barrow's frown deepened, but he did not pull away.

"Lord Bannon has revealed the weakness in our defenses," Barrow replied, his voice resolute, though cold. "For centuries, unchecked magicks have been allowed to fester at our borders. But no more. With Leuthere commanding our forces and Eero securing this city, Jorn will be safe again." The chill in his words sent shivers down Brendolyn's spine.

She drew her hands back as if burned, pain swelling in her chest at the cold betrayal woven through his intentions. "You plan to be rid of them... to murder those with magick?" Her voice quivered, tears shimmering in her eyes as she searched his face, praying for some sign of remorse.

"They're dangerous, Bren," Barrow insisted, though uncertainty flickered in his gaze. "They conspire against the throne. I will not allow them to endanger this realm or you. This is the legacy of my forefathers—the courage to do what must be done. To keep this kingdom safe... to keep *you* safe." He reached for her hand, but his touch felt foreign, wrong. *He* was wrong.

"No," she said, shaking her head as tears slid down her cheeks. "The only way to keep the realm safe isn't by slaughtering that which you do not understand. Your father tried to correct the pain that the faie have suffered in retribution to our grandfathers sins against Ehnarea."

"They have done nothing but rob us of our resources, centuries of unchecked magick is dangerous if you leave it to fester."

Brendolyn could not believe what he said. "A small handful of rogue magicks—they have taken nothing that did not already belong to them, Barrow. They have fought to survive in this world that wishes to separate them from freedom. Yet we have slaughtered thousands of them, enslaved them... *ridiculed* them."

"Bren, if we let them free, they shall take control of the kingdom," Barrow's voice cracked as he reached out to caress her cheek, but she recoiled, disgust and sorrow twisting inside her. "Stand by my side and right the balance of what is right. We cannot let them rule us."

"Do not fall down this path, Barrow, not to depths of where I cannot follow you," Brendolyn whispered, keenly aware of the slithering form of Simeon Bannon not far away. "Can you not see he has corrupted your ideals, Barrow?"

"I have seen the truth, Brendolyn. Pavan used the forbidden magick, hidden from even Bannon's sight. Trusting them in our kingdom was a mistake, one I do not intend to make again." Barrow was hardened, but his eyes softened looking down at her. "Please, Brendolyn, stay with me."

"I cannot remain with a monster."

The words stung, cutting through the air like a blade. In a flash, the darkness within him surged, and before either of them could grasp what was happening—*slap!*—his hand struck her across the face. The sharp sting radiated through her skin, her cheek aflame as her wide eyes met his.

Barrow froze, horror dawning in his expression as he realized what he had done. His features crumbled, tears brimming as his trembling hand reached out toward her, but she stepped back, her breath shallow as she retreated out of his reach.

Slowly, Brendolyn straightened, lifting her chin, though her voice trembled. "Tomorrow, I am taking my father and sister back to Corad."

"Brendolyn, please, forgive me," Barrow's voice cracked with desperation as he stepped forward, but she took another step back, cold resolve hardening in her gaze. "You can't leave—it's dangerous beyond Jorn's borders."

Her jaw clenched. "You have no right to prevent King Sabian of Corad from returning to his own lands. And you certainly have no claim over me, Barrow. Keep your whispers of love. I don't want them."

The anguish in Barrow's eyes was palpable, tears slipping down his face as he reached for her one last time, but she was already pulling away.

"Brendolyn, please," he rasped, the guilt and sorrow rolling off him in waves, crashing futilely against her resolve.

She curtsied with a cool precision, her voice steady. "Goodbye, Your Highness." With that, she turned and swept from the room, leaving him standing alone in the shadow of his own regret.

As Brendolyn walked down the empty corridor, her steps slowed, the pain and tears she'd held back now surging forth. She clutched her side, her body shaking with sobs as she braced herself against the wall. Tentatively, her fingers grazed the tender swell of her cheek where Barrow had struck her. The reddened mark was stark against her olive skin, and she winced at the touch, letting her hand drop away, tears falling silently down her face.

"Princess," the voice slithered down the corridor, chilling her spine.

Brendolyn's heart lurched as she spun around to find Lord Bannon closing the distance between them with unnerving speed, his steps eerily light for such a towering figure.

"Lord Bannon," she managed, hastily wiping away the remnants of tears from her cheeks, forcing her shoulders back in a display of poise. Her heart pounded in her chest, but she kept her expression guarded, watching the man approach with a false calm.

"I come offering you tea," he said with a smile that was all teeth and no warmth, a serpent's grin that made her stomach twist.

She swallowed hard, dread pooling in her chest.

"No, I should return to my room," she said, turning away, but his hand shot out like a viper, seizing her upper arm with an iron grip. His fingers dug into her skin, forcing her to wince as he leaned in close, his breath carrying the sickly-sweet scent of anise.

"I insist," he hissed, dragging her down the corridor. Brendolyn's pulse quickened, but she kept her chin lifted, refusing to let him see the fear gnawing at her. They reached an open door leading into a small sitting parlor, and with a swift motion, he shoved her inside, slamming the door shut behind them with a resounding thud.

The room was thick with tension. Brendolyn stood tall, her hand resting on the hilt of her dagger, though she knew it offered little comfort against a man like Simeon.

He chuckled darkly, the sound low and mocking. "I would forget the little toy, child. It serves no purpose here."

She met his gaze with defiance, clenching her teeth until she felt her jaw strain. His eyes gleamed with dark amusement, every bit of him exuding a twisted sense of control. "You know why I've brought you here," he purred, his voice silky with malice, each word a calculated trap.

Brendolyn refused to speak, refused to give him the satisfaction of watching her squirm. Her silence only fueled his growing impatience. "Come now, insufferable girl, there's no need for this pretense of bravery. You know you're outmatched."

The anger that had been simmering within her now flared, hot and wild. "You killed him," she spat, her voice teetered with both rage and sorrow.

Simeon's smile broadened, satisfied with the crack in her composure. "Yes," he replied simply, as if discussing the weather.

His nonchalance struck her like a blow. She stared at him, momentarily stunned by his brazenness, but he only laughed—a cold, hollow sound that echoed off the walls.

"Why?" she demanded, her voice breaking, the lump in her throat threatening to choke her. "Why would you do that?"

With an elegant flourish, Simeon glided to a nearby chair, lowering himself with a practiced grace. He leaned back, resting comfortably as if they were discussing idle gossip. His gaze flicked back to her, assessing every nuance of her reaction. "Because I can," he said, the casual cruelty of his words slicing through the air.

"Liar," she hissed, her grip tightening on the dagger's hilt. His eyes flicked to her hand, the faintest twitch of his lips betraying his amusement.

"Did you not hear the mighty king beg for mercy?" he asked, his tone dripping with mockery. "Or were you too busy trembling in your little hiding spot?" His words were a taunt, a deliberate stab at her pride.

From within the folds of his sleeve, he produced a letter, holding it delicately between two fingers as though it were a trifling thing. His expression remained as stony and inscrutable as ever, the mask of indifference never slipping.

Brendolyn's gaze locked onto the letter, her breath hitching.

Simeon's voice dripped with mockery as he echoed Barrow's words. "*Every moment apart from you is agony. Let me express my love to you one final night before the end.*" The sickly sweetness in his tone made Brendolyn's stomach churn, bile rising as the lord's twisted smile grew.

"He is a poor poet," Simeon sneered, relishing her discomfort.

Brendolyn's fingers tightened around the hilt of her dagger, the metal warming against her palm as if responding to her mounting fury. She refused to let her gaze waver from the man before her. "He will see right through your façade, Lord Bannon," she spat, though her voice quivered despite her efforts to remain resolute.

Simeon's expression darkened with a predatory gleam as he leaned closer, his voice a low, insidious whisper. "That is where you're mistaken, little princess. Who better than I, to whisper dreams of power into his ear while tightening the reins of this kingdom with the other?"

The temperature in the room seemed to rise, the very air thickening with dark magick that clung to Simeon like a shroud. His presence was suffocating as he rose to his feet and approached her, his aura a heavy, oppressive force that sapped her strength with every breath. His eyes were a hideous swirl of bloodshot red and putrid gray, a reflection of the rot festering within his soul.

Brendolyn instinctively retreated until her back slammed against the door, her knuckles white around the dagger's handle. She was trapped. There was no escape. Her only choice was to fight.

"Kill me then," she dared him, her voice raw with both fear and defiance. "I know your secrets."

Simeon's smile twisted into a snarl as his hand shot forward, his fingers clamping around her throat like a vice. Brendolyn gasped, her left hand clawing at his wrist as her right hand jerked the dagger free from its sheath. With a cry of desperation, she drove the blade into his chest, aiming for his heart.

The blade sunk deep, but Simeon didn't flinch. He merely glanced down at the dagger buried in his flesh, his expression was one of mild amusement. Brendolyn's eyes widened in horror as he chuckled—a low, sickening sound that reverberated through her bones.

"You cannot kill me," he whispered, his voice rasping with dark mirth.

His grip on her throat tightened, crushing the air from her lungs. Panic flared in her chest as she clawed at his hand, her kicks growing weaker with every passing second. Simeon's sneer deepened as he leaned in close, his cracked lips splitting open as he dragged his tongue along the side of her face, savoring her terror.

"You'll stay alive," he murmured into her ear, his breath hot and vile. "Because I allow you to be alive. I don't understand what he sees in you, but you've captivated him. Barrow will claim you as his on his thirtieth name day. He'll be satisfied." His words burrowed into her mind like venom, searing her thoughts with agony and despair.

Brendolyn's vision blurred as she struggled for air, her nails raking against Simeon's hand in a desperate bid to break free. But his grip was unyielding, his magick seeping into her throat like acid, burning her from within. Tears streamed down her face as she felt her strength draining.

Simeon's face twisted with cruel delight as he watched her suffer.

"You will no longer be captivating with your words. No longer shall you sing your traitorous song. Your body belongs to Barrow, your cunt shall satisfy him."

Simeon's magick was a venomous thing, laced with a darkness that clung to her like tar, poisoning every breath she struggled to take. The foul scent of rotting flesh, anise, and decay invaded her senses, making her stomach churn. Her voice was strangled as she tried to scream, but only a pitiful wheeze escaped. Tears blurred her vision as she clawed at his hands, her nails digging into his skin, but it didn't matter—his grip was iron, and the magick that coursed through him only tightened its cruel hold.

When he finally released her, she crumpled to the floor, her knees hitting the cold stone as she gasped desperately for air. Each breath scraped her raw throat like shards of glass, the burning still lingering even though his hands were no longer there. She clutched at her neck, trembling as the lingering echoes of his magick left her in agonized shudders.

A sharp clatter made her flinch. She looked down to see the dagger—her dagger—lying at her feet. Simeon had tossed it there, its blade glinting uselessly in the dim light. The letter fluttered beside it, an afterthought to the torment he'd just inflicted. She barely registered it as he leaned down again, his presence a looming shadow that made her skin crawl.

"Shut yourself in Corad," he hissed, each word laced with venom. "Reflect upon your misery and misfortunes in solitude. He shall collect you when the time comes. His reward will be your undoing..."

His breath was hot against her ear, and she flinched instinctively, recoiling from his closeness. But he only smirked, enjoying her fear.

"I shall have undone his mind," he continued, savoring each word like a twisted lullaby. "To create a man worth a thousand wars. He will use you, brutalize you in every possible manner before I let him see the true beast he has become. When you are on the brink of death, he shall slit his own throat. Then, oh my dear... then you may die."

The finality in his voice sent a chill down her spine. Straightening his tunic, he resumed his air of civility, a sharp contrast to the cruelty in his eyes. He sneered down at her, a predator reveling in the suffering he had caused.

"Tell him, Brendolyn, and I promise you shall see my cruelty. Any whisper of warning, and I shall carve the skin from his flesh. I shall castrate him, carve out his heart, and feed it to his dogs."

His words were a death sentence, and Brendolyn could only watch in numb terror as he turned and strode out of the room, his footsteps echoing down the corridor until all that remained was silence.

She knelt there for a moment, the world spinning around her as she tried to gather her strength. Her throat spasmed, each gasp a painful reminder of Simeon's magick still lingering like a toxic residue. Her hand shook as she reached for the letter, her fingers brushing against the cold metal of her dagger before wrapping around the paper. The dagger felt like dead weight in her grasp, its once reassuring presence now reduced to a hollow memory.

The door creaked open behind her, and Brendolyn jolted, her heart pounding in her chest. She spun around, wide-eyed and quivering. Relief washed over her as she saw a maid slip in through the servant's entrance—a young woman with corn-yellow plaits and warm hazel eyes. The maid froze upon seeing Brendolyn's state, her own eyes widening in horror. The cloth and pan she held clattered to the floor.

"Blessed be!" the maid gasped, clasping her hands to her mouth.

Brendolyn stumbled back, pressing herself against the wall. Her throat was raw with pain, tears streaming down her cheeks as she shook uncontrollably. The maid rushed forward, her voice dropping to a hushed whisper as she glanced around the empty room.

"Princess, are you alright?" she asked, her tone edged with both worry and fear. She leaned in closer, her gaze sharp with concern. "Were you... forced upon?"

Brendolyn shook her head frantically, her tears falling faster. Every movement sent searing pain through her body, and a broken whimper escaped her lips before she could stop it.

"You've been attacked, look at you." The maid's voice softened, and she took Brendolyn's hand with a gentle touch. "Don't worry, I can help. My name is Jenne... I was a friend of King Beaumont."

There was sincerity in the girl's voice, but Brendolyn's mind was clouded with confusion and exhaustion. Her magick flickered weakly within her, disoriented and drained. Blinking back more tears, she tried to focus on the maid's face, but the words wouldn't come.

"I won't tell a soul," Jenne promised on a whisper, her fingers brushing a lock of Brendolyn's disheveled hair. Her eyes lingered on Brendolyn's neck, where the dark imprint of a hand was likely forming. "Let's get you upstairs, and I'll bring hot water and an herbal paste to ease your pain."

With a steadying arm, Jenne guided Brendolyn away from the grim scene, leaving her cleaning supplies forgotten on the floor. The maid's voice remained soft as they moved through the castle's dim corridors. "Beaumont trusted me with many secrets in times of distress. I'm here to help you too, Princess. You can rely on me."

Brendolyn could only nod, her voice choked by lingering terror. They ascended a narrow flight of stairs, the steps winding up and up until they reached the familiar corridor that led to her room. The walk was agonizingly slow, but Jenne's presence was a fragile lifeline, one Brendolyn clung to in her weakened state.

As they neared her chamber door, Jenne's voice dropped lower, though it carried an undercurrent of urgency. "Whenever you need me, ring for me directly. Use those stairs whenever you must, my lady. We all know what's happening—we carry on with our duties, but we know."

Brendolyn glanced sharply at the maid, catching the flicker of fear in those hazel eyes. The words unsettled her, but she didn't have the strength to question them. Instead, she simply nodded.

"I'll bring the hot water right away," Jenne promised, her voice fading as she hurried off down the stairs.

Brendolyn stood for a moment at the threshold of her room, clutching the door handle as she tried to steady herself. Inside, she knew Elsa would be waiting. Drawing in a shaky breath, she pushed the door open and stepped inside, fighting to hold back the tears that still threatened to spill. The safety of her chambers offered little comfort, but it was the only refuge she had left in this castle full of shadows.

# CHAPTER

## 7

Brendolyn's hands paused mid fold as her fingers brushed against the edge of a familiar parchment buried among her belongings. The letter. Barrow's letter. Her breath hitched, and a tear threatened to fall as she quickly stashed it at the bottom of her trunk, tucking it beneath layers of stockings and chemisettes. But not before catching Elsa's curious gaze.

"I really wish you would tell me..." Elsa's voice was gentle, almost pleading.

Brendolyn shook her head, raising a hand to her throat. The ache in her neck was still there, a constant, painful reminder. She swallowed against the roughness, wincing at the gravelly scrape that seemed to mock any attempt to speak.

Elsa's frown deepened. "You believe it's gone... forever?"

Brendolyn nodded, biting back the tears that threatened to resurface. Speaking was more than just painful now—it was a torment. Every attempt to force words through her damaged throat brought nothing but frustration and agony. It was easier to remain silent.

With a resigned sigh, Elsa turned back to the wardrobe, retrieving the last of Brendolyn's gowns and carefully folding it. The air was thick with unspoken worries, neither woman willing to break the fragile silence when a light knock at the door pulled their attention.

Lahrs entered, his expression grave as he crossed the room, arms laden with a stack of books. "You're nearly done, I see," he said, his gaze shifting between the two of them.

"This is the last of it," Elsa said, forcing a smile that Lahrs did not return.

He placed the books on a nearby table, pulling a smaller, red leather-bound one from the top of the pile. "I found this while sorting through my things," he said softly, turning to Brendolyn. "Eero left it in my room. He said it's meant for you."

Brendolyn's eyes flickered to the book, instantly recognizing it. It was the one she'd seen in Pavan's chamber. The sight of it sent a pang through her chest, and she quickly looked away, unable to bring herself to reach for it.

"You should take it, Bren," Elsa urged gently.

Ignoring them, Brendolyn busied herself with repacking the letters she'd hidden earlier, ensuring they were safely tucked away, but Lahrs wasn't fooled. He could sense the tension humming beneath her movements, the way her fingers were unsteady as she smoothed out the fabric.

"Something's wrong," he said, a note of concern sharpening his voice.

Panic surged in Brendolyn's chest. She stepped back, instinctively raising a hand to her throat. The ribbon she'd tied there to hide the marks shifted beneath her fingers, a flimsy barrier against the truth. But Lahrs was already moving, his eyes narrowing in realization as he gently brushed her hair aside. The room seemed to still as he took in the faint but unmistakable bruising dark shadows in the shape of a handprint marring her skin.

Brendolyn shuddered, her chin quivering as she met the elf's gaze. The anguish in his eyes mirrored the guilt she carried. His fingers traced the bruises with a tenderness that made her want to break down all over again. He would try to heal the mark, if he could, but Brendolyn knew the magick was unchangeable. It must fade with time.

"Did you know about this?" Lahrs asked Elsa, his voice tight with barely restrained anger.

"She asked me to wait," Elsa replied, her voice small and filled with guilt. "Until we got back to Corad. Her voice is gone, Lahrs... she thinks it's gone for good."

Lahrs's jaw clenched. "Simeon?"

Brendolyn's breath hitched as the name alone sent a sickening shiver through her. The memory of his words, dripping with cruelty, coiled around her thoughts like a venomous snake. Tears slipped down her cheeks, unbidden and bitter as she nodded.

In an instant, Lahrs pulled her into his arms, holding her tight against his chest. Brendolyn clung to him, her fingers fisting in the fabric of his tunic as she let the tears flow. It was a small comfort, but in that moment, she needed it. He held her as though he could shield her from every horror she'd endured, murmuring a silent prayer to Ehnarea.

After a moment, Lahrs gently pulled back, his eyes filled with both sorrow and resolve. He placed the red leather book in her hands. "Eero meant for you to have this, Brendolyn. It was a gift for you. We both know who it once belonged to, but now it's yours."

Brendolyn stared down at the book, her fingers brushing over the soft, worn leather. She could still sense the faint traces of Pavan's presence within it, a lingering warmth that made her chest ache. Holding it felt like a connection to a time before everything had shattered the fleeting comfort in a world where darkness now threatened to consume her.

With trembling hands, she clutched the book to her chest.

A brisk wind swept in from the bay, carrying with it the salty tang of the sea.

Eero turned up the collar of his woolen coat, bracing himself against the chill as he strode along the length of the docks. The creak of mooring ropes and the muffled voices of sailors mingled with the rhythmic lap of water against the hulls. The port was alive with activity, as it always was during the arrival of ships bringing goods from far-off lands. Jorn's trade lifeline pulsed here in Denorn, and it was Eero's duty since returning—after delivering the Royal Family of Moreau to Corad—to ensure that every vessel entering and leaving carried proper documentation and only legitimate cargo.

This task was never simple, especially with the influx of ships during peak trade seasons. The meticulous inspection of manifests and cargo weighed heavily on Eero, not because he doubted the officers' abilities but because of the lingering unease that crept over him whenever he thought about the king's decree.

"Everything seems in order, sir," came the steady voice of Officer Harden, climbing up from the lower deck of the latest merchant vessel. His boots thudded against the worn planks as he saluted.

Eero gave a curt nod, his eyes scanning the smaller sloops moored at the auxiliary docks. Their sails, now furled, swayed slightly in the growing wind. On the horizon, dark clouds gathered, a thunderhead promising imminent rain.

"Thank you, Harden. Return to the garrison with the others. I'll follow shortly," Eero replied, turning away from the ship and its bustling crew.

As he made his way back through the city streets, a shadow seemed to hang over Denorn. The air felt heavy, the streets quieter than usual, save for the occasional clatter of a wagon or the hurried steps of those eager to escape the coming storm. The city had changed after Beaumont's death. The late king's final decree had swept through Denorn like a cleansing fire, rooting out corruption but leaving behind a void, a city haunted by its sins.

Eero's steps faltered as he approached the charred ruins of the Blessed Chapel of Light. The skeletal remains of its stone walls rose like a ghostly sentinel against the darkening sky, the once-beautiful gardens now a scorched wasteland. Lavender lingered faintly in the air, a cruel reminder of what had been. His chest tightened, grief and guilt intertwining as he stared at the devastation.

The Blessed Lady, Arienne, had not deserved such a fate, nor had the women of her order. Eero closed his eyes, the weight of his failures pressing heavily on his shoulders. He had tried to protect her, tried to prevent this tragedy, but in the end, it hadn't been enough.

A shift in the breeze sent a shiver up his spine, and his thoughts drifted to Thaddeus. The faie had vanished after the fire, and despite Eero's efforts to track him, no trace of him had been found. The ship he was meant to board had departed without him, the captain and shipmaster both swearing they'd seen no faie among their passengers. Was it possible Thad had escaped the flames? Eero wanted to believe it, though doubt gnawed at him.

"Sir," a soft voice broke through his thoughts.

Eero turned to find a young elf girl standing before him. Her long, ashen-blonde hair framed a pale face, her violet eyes shimmering with a mix of fear and determination.

"Hello," he said gently, offering her a small smile.

She hesitated, wringing her hands before finally speaking. "Are you going to rebuild the chapel?"

Eero's smile faded, replaced by a sorrowful sigh. "It is forbidden."

Tears welled in her eyes, spilling over as she tried to contain her heartbreak. She wobbled, her grief almost palpable. Eero reached out, resting a hand lightly on her silvery hair, meeting her gaze with quiet empathy.

"Don't let him take away our magick," she whispered, her voice barely audible over the wind.

Eero frowned, glancing around the desolate square. The traitor. Even in death, the whispers of his betrayal lingered, casting long shadows over Denorn. He crouched slightly, taking her small hand in his.

"Do you fear the man?" he asked, feeling the quickened beat of her heart beneath his touch.

She nodded, her voice shaking. "They say his magick is dark, but I've seen him. I've seen the man they claim killed the king."

Eero stiffened. "Where did you see him?"

Her gaze drifted to the ruins of the chapel, her eyes haunted. "He was kind to us, sir. He protected us." Her voice broke, her words tinged with a desperate need to be believed. "I don't think he could've killed the king. He—forgive me, sir. I shouldn't—"

Eero placed a steadying hand on her shoulder as she turned to leave. "I knew him," he said softly. "Not well, but enough to know his courage and his goodness."

She gasped, bowing her head in reverence. "Blessed be. Have we all fallen from Ehnarea's light? We failed Arienne's teachings." Her small frame shook as she clasped her hands in prayer, her whispered pleas carrying an air of despair.

Eero knelt beside her, shielding her from the eyes of the bronzed guards patrolling nearby. "Do not be afraid, little one," he murmured. "Ehnarea does not abandon those who have hope in their hearts."

Her tears fell freely now as she kissed his hand in gratitude. "Thank you, sir... Thank you."

The heavy rain drummed against the windowpanes as Sir Eero approached Barrow, whose gaze remained fixed on the scene below. The carriages of the southern realm were lined up in neat rows, the guards surrounding them resolute in their duty despite the downpour. The gloom of the storm seemed to echo the atmosphere within the room, heavy with unspoken words and frayed tensions.

Barrow stood silent, his posture rigid, a blend of sorrow and resentment etched into his face as he watched the final preparations for departure. Down below, Sir Lahrs handed Lady Elsa into the last carriage with a practiced courtesy, the fleeting gesture lost amidst the rain. Then Brendolyn emerged, her pale gown trailing as she stepped out into the wet, her face momentarily lifted in their direction.

Sir Eero's heart tightened at the sight, an involuntary reaction to her familiar features and distant gaze. She did not wave, nor did she acknowledge them beyond that of a brief glance, and the emptiness of it struck him harder than he expected. He turned to Barrow, who hadn't moved, his fists clenched at his sides, the tension radiating off him like the electric charge before a storm.

"We are ready for departure." The air in the room was heavy with remorse and regret as Sir Eero's words fell into the silence.

Barrow's face was pale, drawn with an ache that ran far deeper than any wound he had suffered on the battlefield. The young prince's usual composure was fraying at the edges, barely held together by a thin thread of pride and shame.

Eero's eyes didn't leave Barrow, gauging every nuance of emotion flickering across his features. "We could not hold them here, Your Majesty," Eero said quietly, his voice steady. "And they have safe passage through Rhun. My men will ensure the road is clear. They'll be safe on their way home."

Barrow gave a small nod, the movement stiff and almost mechanical, as if acknowledging the facts was all he could manage. "It would be safest in Corad after all," he muttered, his voice rough, thick with the tears he fought to suppress. He turned abruptly, as though unable to bear the weight of the conversation any longer. "I let my anger get the better of me, Eero. And now... now I can't undo it."

The knight remained silent, letting the prince's admission hang in the air. Barrow's shoulders sagged, the burden of regret almost breaking him. "Sir Lahrs was right," Barrow continued, his voice distant. "She won't have me now. Even when there was nothing truly holding us apart. I told her about my father's will, that she was the Duchess of Augusta. But none of it mattered."

Eero shifted, choosing his words with care. "She never loved your title or the title you could give her, Barrow. I believe she still loves you, despite it all."

Barrow's eyes flashed with frustration as he spun to face Eero. "Don't be absurd. I don't want to hear comforting lies. As my friend, I ask that you never coddle me."

Eero's grip on Barrow's arm was firm, forcing the prince to meet his gaze. "I speak only what I believe to be true. Let her grieve, let her mourn. She cared deeply for your father as well. The loss is not only yours, Barrow."

The prince's defiance crumbled, leaving only exhaustion in its place. "You're right," he whispered, almost to himself.

Eero noticed the sudden flex of Barrow's right hand, a nervous habit that hadn't gone unnoticed. The motion made the knight's stomach twist as he observed the prince's distant stare. His voice was cold when he spoke, cutting through the uneasy silence.

"You struck her."

Barrow flinched, the truth laid bare in Eero's flat tone. His face twisted with a mix of guilt and self-loathing as his eyes welled up. "It was so sudden," Barrow choked out, his voice breaking. "Eero, what have I done?"

Eero's body tensed with anger, every fiber of his being recoiling at the confession. It took everything in him to swallow the surge of fury that threatened to boil over. He had seen the misery in the young prince, but nothing could excuse what had been done. Brendolyn was fragile, already plagued by enough terror and unrest. Eero bit back the words he longed to say, knowing they would be of no comfort now.

He straightened, giving a curt bow. "I shall see them home safely, Your Majesty." With that, Eero turned and left, his thoughts a storm of conflict as he walked away from the man he had sworn to protect. The rain outside continued to pour, a mirror to the unresolved emotions swirling within the castle walls.

Simeon Bannon's bedchamber was suffocating in its darkness, every trace of light banished behind the heavy, drawn curtains. The air was thick with the stench of decay, old vials of failed potions cluttered the floor, mingling with scattered notes and remnants of his latest twisted experiments. In his haste, Bannon had knocked over a table, sending glass shattering across the stone floor. He had barely managed to tear off his sweat-soaked tunic before collapsing into bed.

The heat within him was unbearable. His head pounded as if a hammer was striking directly against his skull, searing pain flooding every thought. He clutched at his chest, trying to rein in the wild surge of magic coursing through his veins, but it was slipping away, leaving him hollow and trembling.

*Foolish man.*

The voice slithered through the darkness, cold and unforgiving. Bannon's breath hitched, his cracked lips parting in a desperate gasp. His eyes darted wildly, but he could see nothing, only the shadows pressing in, thick as tar, while his heart raced in terror.

"Mistress..." His voice was little more than a whimper. Panic gripped him as he clawed at his chest, the spot where his magick once burned bright now chillingly empty. Without her power, he was nothing.

*Silence.* The voice cut through the air like a blade. *You have squandered too much of my gift, Simeon. You drain what is not yours to command.*

Bannon howled in pain, the sound choked as his throat tightened under an invisible force. Agony radiated behind his eyes, a white-hot fire that sent tears streaming down his gaunt cheeks. He twisted in his bed, the sheets tangling around him as his body convulsed.

"Forgive me," he begged, his voice ragged, shuddering as sweat drenched his brow. "Mistress, have pity on your servant."

The only response was a low, contemptuous hiss. *You pitiful creature. You dare cling to me when you've reduced yourself to this? There is nothing left for you but ruin, unless you sleep... recover... before you collapse entirely.*

"No..." His breath hitched as he struggled to speak, the remnants of his once-commanding magic slipping like sand through his fingers. "Do not leave me... I cannot... be without you..."

But the voice grew faint, retreating like smoke in the wind. *You have brought this upon yourself. Now, suffer in the silence you created. Sleep... or die.*

The room fell deathly quiet, the echoes of her words fading into nothingness. Bannon's shivering grew worse as the cold gripped him, his teeth chattering uncontrollably. He curled into himself, a pitiful, shivering figure wrapped in darkness. The last of his strength ebbed away, leaving only exhaustion in its wake.

Alone, with only the fading whispers of his mistress and the gnawing emptiness where his power once thrived, Bannon's eyes fluttered shut. His body went limp, succumbing to a restless, haunted sleep. The shadows held him tight, offering no comfort, only the chilling reminder of the depths he had sunk to in his pursuit of power.

And in the darkness, a single whisper lingered, echoing in the recesses of his tortured mind—*You are nothing without me.*

# CHAPTER

## 8

THEY HAD PASSED BEYOND the bridge of Rhun, delving deeper into the untamed wilderness of the middle realm, when Sir Eero suggested they halt for the night. The road was generally safe, especially with his men stationed at key points to provide protection throughout the hours of darkness. But there was magick that buzzed beneath Eero's boots and into his fingertips, a transfer of old whisperings which told him of the great despair that still marred the ground beneath them, reminding Eero of the war, and the sorrow that lingered over the land.

King Sabian remained ensconced within his tent, immersed in his letters and books, while Princess Lisetta had not ventured far from her richly adorned green canvas quarters, which was strategically placed close to her father's. Though the two tents were separated by only a short distance, their proximity was maintained for convenience and security.

Eero had assured them of their safety, and Lahrs had reinforced the knight's assurances to the southern king. With the camp established, Eero's twenty men patrolled the perimeter, their vigilance unwavering as the night progressed.

Eero made his way across the encampment, passing from the warmth of the communal fire to the cooler, more shadowed area where the tents were pitched. He found himself approaching the smaller of the three tents—the one belonging to the youngest princess. The air around it was tinged with the faintest scent of lavender and a whisper of magick that made him pause. He cleared his throat softly.

"Beg pardon," he began, standing at the entrance of the tent.

To his surprise, Lady Elsa emerged, her auburn hair gleaming softly in the dim light. She tucked a stray lock behind her ear, her expression one of mild surprise.

"Sir Eero, I did not expect you. Is there something amiss with the canvas?" she asked, her tone polite but tinged with curiosity.

Eero shook himself, feeling foolishly flustered. "No," he began. "Everything is settled. I came to inquire... how is she?"

Elsa's expression faltered, her features paling slightly. She glanced around for eavesdroppers before responding, "She is as to be expected, sir. Your concern is appreciated." She gave a slight bow and started to retreat back under the canvas door.

Eero stepped forward, his voice low and intense. "I know what happened."

Elsa bristled at his words, her eyes darting with a mixture of fear and urgency. She grabbed his arm and pulled him into the tent, ensuring they were alone. Lahrs and Brendolyn were nowhere to be seen.

"Where have they gone?" Eero asked, sensing something was amiss.

"Lahrs took Brendolyn to gaze upon the stars," Elsa said, her gaze sharp and penetrating. "How long have you known?"

Eero could smell the oils in her hair and noticed the flecks of green in her hazel eyes. He blinked, momentarily caught off guard by his admiration, but quickly refocused.

"Barrow told me."

Elsa's confusion deepened, her brows knitting together in a frown. "What are you talking about, Sir Eero?"

Eero took a deep breath, realizing that Elsa might not be aware of everything he knew. His face flushed with the realization that he might be discussing a matter she didn't fully understand.

"Barrow expressed his regrets about this abrupt departure... he divulged an act that was unforgivable." Eero spoke slowly, carefully gauging Elsa's reaction, but her confusion was turning into alarm.

"Eero, you're not making sense."

Eero's confusion mirrored Elsa's. There seemed to be a misalignment between what he knew and what Elsa was perceiving. He spoke of one matter, but Elsa's reaction suggested there was more to the story.

"Barrow struck Brendolyn in a fit of rage," Eero said, his voice laden with disbelief. "I couldn't have imagined it, but the guilt in Barrow's eyes made it undeniable."

Elsa's anger flared, but she remained silent. Her hands were clenched tightly, as if she were fighting to contain her fury. Eero waited, sensing her internal struggle.

After a tense silence, Eero asked, "Did something else happen, Elsa?"

Elsa's anger morphed into tears. Her face contorted in a way that revealed the deep pain she had been hiding. She wiped at her tears, struggling to maintain her composure.

"Brendolyn is cursed," Elsa hissed, her voice wavering. "Her voice has been taken by the one who does unspeakable things. It is agony to attempt the use of her voice."

Eero's heart sank. He nodded, reaching out to place a comforting hand on Elsa's arm. She didn't recoil, though he could feel the tension between them. His heart ached to ease her suffering, but he knew he lacked the power to undo what had been done.

"I see," Eero said quietly, letting his hand fall away.

Elsa crossed her arms, trying to shield her emotions. She glared at him with a mix of gratitude and defiance. "Thank you for escorting us home, Sir Eero. Your kindness and regard are deeply appreciated. Brendolyn would express her thanks if she could, and I would speak on her behalf to extend her gratitude for your assistance..."

Eero felt a wave of shame wash over him as he watched Elsa's composure crack. Her tears flowed freely, revealing the tender heart beneath her strong exterior. Even the strongest souls could be brought to tears. Unable to find the right words, Eero wished to embrace her, but remembered the brand that bound her painfully to another.

"Anything for her, Elsa," he whispered. "I vow to protect her at all costs, Ehnarea as my witness."

"There is nothing that can save her, Eero. A curse of this magnitude cannot be undone without its master..." Elsa's voice cracked as she brushed away tears with trembling fingers. Her sorrow hung thick in the tent, an unspoken agony shared between them. "You must not speak of this, not even to Barrow," she urged, her tone low but firm.

A soft rustling at the entrance of the canvas caught their attention. "Sir Eero," came a voice, stirring the heavy air.

Both turned to see Sir Lahrs stepping into the tent, his presence commanding yet understated. Brendolyn stood close at his side, her golden eyes catching the dim light like firelight flickering in shadow. Her gaze met Eero's, brimming with sorrow so profound that his heart ached as though a hand had reached inside and gripped it. She clutched a worn red leather book tightly to her chest, its edges softened with use, while a heavy cloak draped over her small shoulders, warding off the creeping cold.

Eero quickly dipped into a bow, his expression tightening with restrained emotion. "Forgive me, princess, Sir Lahrs. I came to inquire—We are well-guarded for the night. You shall sleep in comfort tonight; my men stand watch and are prepared to protect you."

Lahrs acknowledged him with a measured nod. "We are indebted to your service, Sir Eero."

Brendolyn said nothing, her slender fingers gripping the edges of the book. Eero's throat tightened as he watched her, searching for words but finding none. The princess's silence, combined with the weariness etched into her features, made him feel unworthy of intruding further. Instead, he addressed Lahrs directly, his voice steady but quiet. "Sir Lahrs, might I request a word?"

The elf glanced at Brendolyn, then at Elsa, who moved to guide the princess deeper into the tent's interior.

Lahrs inclined his head in agreement. "Very well."

Eero followed him outside, where the crisp evening air wrapped around them. The camp was bathed in shadows, the faint glow of distant campfires illuminating the outlines of tents. The two walked in silence to the edge of the encampment, their boots crunching softly against the rocky terrain. Beneath the sheltering canopy of trees, they paused, facing the dark silhouette of the southern banks of Rhun. The chill was biting, but Eero paid it no mind, his thoughts heavier than the cold.

"I must ask you something, Lahrs," Eero began, his tone low but carrying urgency. "Did Thaddeus fall in the ruin of the Chapel of Light?"

For a long moment, Lahrs was silent, his sharp elven features unreadable. When he finally spoke, his voice was careful, almost mournful. "I must warn you, Eero. The truth is a burden not easily borne."

A flicker of hope stirred in Eero, fragile as a candle flame in the wind, flickering amidst the sea of doubt and dread within him. He searched Lahrs's stormy grey eyes, trying to decipher the emotions buried deep within the elf's stony exterior.

"In all of this, Lahrs," Eero whispered, his throat tight with emotion. "Let there be peace at last for his soul with Ehnarea."

Lahrs exhaled deeply, his shoulders heavy with invisible weight. "Thaddeus is safe," he said finally, his words measured and deliberate. "He is with the kin of Audry upon the shores of Tauf. He delivered the faie-touched girls to Meilyr's care."

Eero's breath caught, his eyes widening. "Dahlia lives?" he asked, his voice barely audible.

"She is in health." Lahrs grasped Eero's arm suddenly, his grip firm and his eyes sharp as daggers. "They must not discover the truth, Eero," he warned, his tone heavy with urgency. "If Simeon learns that Thad still lives, the wrath it would unleash would cost Entheas dearly to shield him."

Eero nodded, though unease lingered. His thoughts drifted to another name. "And Pavan..." he began hesitantly.

Lahrs's expression hardened, the weight of his knowledge aging him further. "He must remain ignorant of this truth," Lahrs said, his voice steady but burdened. "It is better for Pavan to stay on his path. The truth would be the fall of the Realms."

Eero's chest tightened with conflicting emotions, but he bowed his head in agreement. "I shall bury the truth," he vowed, the words laced with quiet determination.

# CHAPTER

## 9

*Forest of Dern, Realm of Jorn.*

P AVAN SAT UNDER THE blanket of night, the stillness around him broken only by the soft crackling of the small fire made of the cold remnants of a broken tree. The flickering flames gave off a faint warmth, just enough light to push back the encroaching darkness. He could feel the pulse of his enchantment, weaving around him like a cloak, hiding him from prying eyes.

The ruins seemed to breathe with the darkness, a hollow, echoing void that matched the emptiness in Pavan's heart. He could feel the weight of the past crushing him. The ache in his chest was more than just the wound left by Brendolyn's absence, it was the unbearable guilt that dragged him deeper into despair. He had pushed her away, not out of malice, but out of a twisted sense of protection. Yet that knowledge did nothing to ease the torment. When the ribbon gifted to him was gone, the scar once hidden beneath on his wrist was a constant reminder of what he had lost long before this, when hope had been more than a fleeting thought.

Pavan's fingers traced the jagged scar with a kind of numb reverence, as if hoping to draw strength from the pain it once masked. Losing Thad left a deeper wound than any blade could cut. The faces of his fallen companions haunted him, ghosts lingering in every shadow that flickered beyond the firelight. They would still be alive if not for his choices, if not for the path he had forced them down. Hatred coiled in his gut, a venomous presence that refused to let him forget, that whispered accusations with every breath he took.

A sharp wind rattled through the trees and he clenched his fist, willing himself to focus, to shove the torment back into the recesses of his mind. But magick thrummed beneath his skin, wild and unrestrained, responding to his pain and growing hunger.

*Isaac.*

The wind howled again, as if the very elements sensed his turmoil. Cold tendrils of magick seeped into the soil beneath him, chilling the air, and making every breath sting. The dagger in his hand felt like the only thing anchoring him to reality, its edge gleaming wickedly in the dim firelight. He stared at it, the blade holding a kind of grim allure, a promise of silence and an end to this endless torment.

His tunic slipped from his shoulder as he exposed the scar above his heart, the one place where his past and present pain converged. The magick in him stirred violently, sensing what he intended, but he forced it back, forcing his thoughts to quiet, even as his body tensed against the unnatural chill snaking up his spine.

Kneeling before the fire, Pavan raised the dagger, holding it steady against his chest. His breath hitched as the cold steel pressed into his skin. His fingers shook, but he pressed harder, willing the blade to break through and grant him release. Pain flared, sharp and real, but his magick, that cursed force he could never fully control, flared to life. It rebelled against him, tightening around his heart, blocking the blade's passage.

Pavan's frustration twisted into desperation. He gripped the hilt with both hands, shoving with all his strength, but the magick held fast, a cruel guardian that denied him even this act. He could feel it seeping into his bones, the cold creeping through him like icy fingers. His breaths came in ragged, visible puffs, each one a testament to his body's refusal to let go.

Tears pricked at the corners of his eyes. He had lost control, lost everything he had fought to protect, and now even death was beyond his grasp. The blade slipped from his hands, clattering to the stone, leaving him kneeling there, shivering and broken.

The wind stilled, leaving a silence that felt heavier than before.

Alone in the ruins, Pavan slumped forward, hands still clutching his chest as if he could tear the agony out by force. But all he could do was let the tears fall, let the pain consume him, because nothing else would.

Despite the calm around him, a gnawing unease twisted in Pavan's gut as he drew a sealed letter from his pocket. The seal's opalescent sheen shimmered in the firelight, its shifting colors holding his gaze longer than he intended. His finger hovered over the wax, tracing the intricate design as doubt and tension tightened in his chest. Finally, with a slow, deliberate breath, he broke the seal, the wax snapping under the pressure of his fingers. The parchment unraveled with a whispering sound, delicate and smooth in his hands.

It revealed— nothing.

His breath caught, eyes narrowing at the blank page in disbelief. Anger surged as he crumpled it in his fist, scoffing at the mocking emptiness. But the fury quickly ebbed, replaced by a flicker of doubt.

Pavan smoothed the paper out over his knee, his fingers running along the creases. He leaned closer, searching for any hint of hidden script. His frustration lingered as he gazed at the blank page, but a whisper of magick tugged at his senses—a delicate thread just beneath the surface. Closing his eyes, letting his awareness stretch out until he felt the faint residue of enchantment woven into the parchment. It was subtle, almost elusive, but it was there. Holding his hand above the letter, Pavan channeled the dormant magick to respond.

Slowly, tendrils of pale light spiraled up from the page, wrapping around his fingers. The hidden spell began to unravel, responding to his touch as faint words started to take shape. A smile played on his mouth as the shifting essence swirled and embraced his hand. It was gentle, kind. Unwavering and eager to reach him.

Pavan sighed, letting the magick come to him, allowing it to flow through him. He blinked, looking at the fire where the flames flickered slowly. His movements began to slow to a crawl, his eyelids growing heavy. The note fell to the ground beneath him and his body began to fall back as the magick that entranced him, shifted him so he fell back gracefully.

Falling back into the stupor of sleep.

He gasped awake, but he knew he was still sleeping. Standing, Pavan opened his eyes to the dream, allowing it to take hold of each movement as he looked around the field of purple flowers. As far as the eyes could see, he saw them flowing in waves—lavender. His hand grazed the silky flower pedals as he walked through them.

Drawing in their scent as he stepped forward, he sighed heavily and gazed upon the miles of fields before him.

*Pavan.* A voice in his ear sent shivers down his spine, he turned, but there were only fields.

"Hello?" he called out. His voice a shimmering chime throughout the air. He felt a warm breeze, wrapping around him.

*Find me, Pavan. Find the field, find your destiny.* The voice softly whispered and Pavan leaned into it, welcoming it. But it pulled away, along with the warm wind.

"Wait... I don't know how to find you." Pavan glanced around, the lavender field undulating as though stirred by an unseen wind. But as he watched, the scene shifted, rippling away like a reflection on disturbed water. His gaze was drawn upward as a towering structure materialized before him. A weathered cathedral, ancient and imposing, its stone walls scarred by time.

Unease prickled at the back of his neck, yet something compelled him forward. Pavan stepped toward the heavy wooden doors, their iron hinges groaning softly as he placed his hand on the handle. The door yielded with surprising ease, swinging inward to reveal the dimly lit vestibule. The air was thick with the scent of dust and decay, as if the place had been abandoned for ages.

Pavan's footsteps echoed sharply as he crossed the cracked marble floor, each step a sharp reminder of the emptiness that surrounded him. The entrance gave way to a grand hall where rows of pews should have been, but only vast emptiness greeted him. Shadows clung to the high vaulted ceiling where fractured beams of light filtered through shattered stained-glass windows.

He walked on, drawn deeper into the eerie silence until he reached the transept. The void stretched out before him, and where an altar might have stood, only a single object caught his attention. On the raised platform, a lone ribbon lay draped across the floor.

Intricately woven with delicate patterns, the ribbon was out of place in the desolation of the cathedral. Its rich colors shimmered faintly in the dim light, hinting at hidden magick. Pavan knelt, fingers grazing the smooth fabric. It felt impossibly soft, as if it carried the memory of silk spun by unseen hands.

Without thinking, he brought the ribbon to his lips. The fabric's cool touch sent a shiver down his spine, a pulse of magick flowing through him, stirring the air around him. A whisper, distant and indistinct, fluttered at the edge of his awareness. The sensation lingered, delicate yet haunting, as though the ribbon held a forgotten story, a warning perhaps, or an unspoken promise.

Pavan's breath caught, realizing that this ribbon was more than just a remnant left behind.

*Your destiny is here, Pavan,* the voice echoed around him.

"Who are you?" Pavan asked, the ribbon clutched tightly in his fist.

*I have seen many things. Here it has been that I wait to meet you, Pavan,* the voice soothed,  and a gentle caress was felt across Pavan's cheek.

He gasped, stepping back. "I'm not anyone important," Pavan breathed, shaking his head as the dream shifted around him.

*Find me, Pavan... follow your guide, but do not fear.*

Pavan felt himself being pulled back. The ribbon sifted out of his hand, his eyelids growing heavy as he fell backwards.

Darkness surrounded him.

Hot breath shifted over him, smelling of rotten flesh and magick.

Pavan's eyes shot open and standing over him, nose close to his, was a Vohlgrum. His blood ran cold. Locking eyes with the creature, Pavan wanted to run, but his limbs were frozen in place. Pavan let a shaky breath fall from his lips. The beast before him growled in her throat, exposing sharpened teeth. As Pavan looked into the large black eyes, he felt the connection of magick developing from within.

He gasped, the familiar roll of magick flooding through him. Memories emerged from the beast into his own mind—a small pup. The Vohlgrum pup that he pulled from the trap now stood before him, fully grown.

"You are my guide?" he whispered, reaching a tentative hand to the flat crest of her head. His palm rested there, letting the magick and electricity buzz through him. He smiled, but his heart began to race.

"You are welcome." Pavan nodded, feeling the beast shock him as she pressed her head into Pavan's touch, her coat of fur shivering beneath it.

Slowly he stood, marveling as the great creature raised her head, reaching the curve of Pavan's shoulder. Those dark, uncanny eyes watching him closely.

"Do you have a name, my friend?"

Those large dark eyes blinked.

Pavan smiled. "In time. I can wait."

Pavan nodded and then looked out over the ruins as the sun began to rise. Glancing at the Vohlgrum, he bowed. "Upon your lead."

They walked side by side in the downpour of rain, winding through the forest, headed west towards the mountains that towered high into the skyline. Pavan shivered but did not stop as the Vohlgrum led the way, traveling along the base of the mountain, heading south until they reached a river that traveled east.

Pavan sat at the river's edge, removed his boots only to wince at the raw skin of the base of his foot, his heel and his ankle. Pavan reached out, concentrating to heal his skin, but the Vohlgrum nudged him with the bridge of her nose, knocking Pavan off the rock where he sat.

Pavan growled. "They hurt, I need to heal them."

Large black eyes stared back at him but Pavan stuck his foot out, showing the raw blistered skin.

"I cannot walk if I bleed," he said pointedly.

The Vohlgrum sniffed and then her large bluish purple tongue lapped at the skin. Pavan hissed, pulling his foot away. But when he looked down the skin that was raw and broken began to heal. Pavan said nothing, reaching a hand out, but the Vohlgrum turned away, showing her back. He shook his head, pulling on his boot to stand.

Standing beside the Vohlgrum, looking out over the river and to the trees beyond, he leaned in to feel the warmth rolling off of her large body. "We shall be on this journey for many nights at least, perhaps you can share your name with me, if you have one."

The large creature shifted Pavan a glance, blinking.

Pavan smirked. "I see... so there are no names among the beasts. You know who I am, but perhaps you have no words for my name. I am called Pavan."

To this the Vohlgrum huffed, a snap of the jaw and a very deliberate exhale of breath, looking to Pavan.

With a smile, Pavan placed a hand tentatively upon the shoulder of the beast where waves of electricity tickled his skin.

"Would you be offended if I gave you a name? Our secret, of course." The Vohlgrum did nothing.

Pavan nodded. "How do you feel about Delilah?"

The Vohlgrum growled and Pavan laughed. "Alright. Alright. Arn... Max... Rose..." The Vohlgrum shifted, pushing Pavan over, and knocked him back into the grass. Pavan chuckled to himself, looking up at the large creature who sat without giving him a glance.

Thinking for a long moment, Pavan said, "Órlaith ." When there was no reaction, he sat up straighter. "Órlaith, is that a name you like?"

The Vohlgrum looked to him, those black eyes unmoving. Pavan smiled, kneeled up onto his knees and lifted his hand up, palm outstretched. Wishing a simple shift, the large creature contacted the outstretched palm with the flat of his head.

Pavan followed Órlaith for many miles, until they reached a great river, one that raged and ran fast from west to east. Pavan hesitated as Órlaith padded through the bank, edging her way into the icy water. Pavan stood with his feet on the edge, hesitating to look at the dark raging waters.

Órlaith growled, catching Pavan's attention.

With a heavy sigh, Pavan stepped in, following in the great Vohlgrum's steps; gasping as the cold water sent a great chill through him. Wading, now waist deep, the current pulled him slightly, but he pushed forward, determined to follow the large beast. But as the waters rose to his chest and his breathing came short, his bones began to ache from the cold. The rocks beneath his feet began to shift, slippery with moss and Pavan lost his footing, plunging into the depths.

Reaching out with his hands to swim up, his hands grasped for the surface as he broke through, gasping and spitting out water, before the current swept him under. He tried again, thrashing for the surface, gasping for a moment before his head went under. His lungs burned and arms began to grow numb as he kicked to lift himself above the surface.

Pavan scrambled, trying to bring himself up, until his hands grasped thick fur, the large body swimming alongside him. Pavan held on, pulling himself above the surface of the river to cling to Órlaith's back.

Coughing, Pavan held tight. "Thank you, Órlaith," he spluttered, his limbs beginning to shake.

In a moment, Órlaith clawed at the bank of the other side, pulling up onto the thick lush grass as it brought Pavan along, water pouring over its thick fur.

Pavan collapsed onto the ground, breathing heavily. His limbs tingled as the breeze gave him such a chill, he began to shiver. Trying to concentrate, Pavan began to work through a spell to dry him, but his brain was muddled while his hands shook.

Beside him Órlaith shook the water off a few yards away, returning to Pavan's side where he lay. The Vohlgrum sniffed at Pavan's hair, but he couldn't speak, his lungs burning as he breathed in the cold air.

He winced, when Órlaith grabbed him by the arm with an open jaw, the sharp teeth scraping against his flesh through his wet jacket. The large beast dragged him a short distance away from the river's edge, finding a soft place within a patch of moss beneath a large cover of brambles and trees.

There Pavan lay shivering until Órlaith plopped down over him, shifting her body in a way to cover Pavan, with a large arm and paw on either side of him.

Pavan breathed in the wet fur stench but said nothing as Órlaith lay her head beside his, listening to the soft rhythmic purr vibrate through the large creature's chest. Within minutes the creature heating Pavan through. His eyes began to close, fighting sleep, but exhaustion overtook him. Pavan fell into a restless slumber, between waking and dreaming.

The morning was clear and bright, birds chirping in the distance, their songs a stark contrast to his weary state. Pavan's eyes were heavy with fatigue as he groaned.

He awoke alone, his gaze darting around in search of Órlaith, but the Vohlgrum was nowhere to be seen. The patch of ground where they had rested was bent and disturbed, a sign of the previous night's rest.

He moved slowly to the river's edge, kneeling to dip his hand into the frigid waters. As he brought his hand to his face, the cold splash invigorated him momentarily, the chill cutting through the haze of sleep.

Looking out at the tranquil, untouched world around him, Pavan found a brief moment of peace. The stillness was soon broken by a splash and his eyes widened as he saw a woman with pale skin emerge from the water, her long brown hair plastered to her body. Her black eyes met his with a chilling familiarity, making him shiver.

As she stepped forward, her form shifted. The woman's appearance dissolved into that of the beast Pavan had followed—Órlaith. The creature's black eyes locked onto Pavan, and he remained silent as he extended his hand. Órlaith met his gesture, pressing the wet fur of her head against Pavan's palm.

Pavan sighed, a mix of relief and confusion in his breath. "You are Athrun?" he asked, but Órlaith gave no reply. Instead, she nudged his side with her large nose. He knew the Athrun to be shifters of the faie, creatures of living magick. But their magick had rules. "You remained too long in this shape, you forgot who you once were."

With Órlaith's help, Pavan slowly rose to his feet. He followed the creature through the dense forest, his body aching with each step. As the day wore on, his exhaustion mounted, causing him to fall further and further behind. Órlaith stopped frequently, circling back to check on him, offering support with her body. Though Pavan was grateful, his determination to keep moving remained strong.

Despite his resolve, the pain in his limbs intensified. At one point, Órlaith, sensing Pavan's struggle, clamped her teeth gently around his forearm, not piercing the skin but pulling him back to safety. Pavan placed his hand on her head, feeling the warmth and magick emanating from her fur. He blinked, trying to clear the fog of delirium that clouded his mind.

"I cannot rest," Pavan muttered, his voice barely a whisper. The forest path before him blurred, and he felt lightheaded. Grasping Órlaith's fur for balance, he willed himself to continue, but his body was betraying him.

With a final, desperate push, Pavan fell to his knees. He clutched at Órlaith's thick fur, the warmth comforting yet not enough to stave off his exhaustion. "Curse my body," he gasped, "we must go a little further."

Órlaith settled down beside him, gently pressing her head against his back. Pavan clung to her, hiding his face in her dark coat as he wept in agony. The tears fell freely, mingling with the fur beneath him. Overcome by sheer fatigue, he soon succumbed to exhaustion, his body giving way as he lay against the comforting presence of the Vohlgrum.

# CHAPTER

## 10



*City of Corad, Realm of Corad*

GOOD NIGHT UNTO YOU *all. Give me your hands, if we be friends, and robin shall restore amends."*

Elsa stopped reading and looked to Brendolyn, who had sat unmoved as they finished the most recent readings in her little red book.

"Shall we start again, or would you like to begin with the two lovers?" Elsa flipped through the pages, seeking the next story.

A hand reached out to rest upon her own.

"I see." Elsa nodded, closing the book instead, watching it slip from her fingers.

Silently, Brendolyn stood from their seat in the outer gardens and walked towards the bubbling fountains. Clutching the red book to her chest, she gazed out over the vibrant gardens. This was how the days had become, after returning to Corad. Brendolyn wrote less on parchment, no longer engaging in expressing her desires. She would sit for hours looking out into the gardens or listening to Elsa as she read from the little red book.

Corad City was warm, shaded by canopies of vines that blossomed sweet smelling flowers. It reminded Elsa of her home in Signe and her brothers. She missed them more than anything, but she dared not write. Fear always catching her at times.

Elsa felt the stiffened bodice at her side, anger welling up inside her at the memories that intruded on her when she had time to think of them. Remembering a rough hand grabbing her made her flinch. Blinking away the tears, she calmed her breath.

She mustn't think of him now, he was far off, on the great seas with Eugene. Alaric would not dare enter the castle.

"Elsa, am I interrupting?" Lahrs broke her concentration.

Standing up, Elsa started with a gasp, searching the fountain for Brendolyn. "Lahrs, I was—Brendolyn was there—"

"Be calm." Lahrs smiled softly. "I instructed Brendolyn to take a turn of the gardens along the eastern wall."

"Oh." Elsa blinked, surprised.

"It was you that I have come to speak with," Lahrs went on, offering his arm. Elsa took it and they began to follow the path leading towards the palace.

"You are hoping to inquire as to Brendolyn's habits of late, since returning home?" Elsa offered.

Lahrs was silent in thought, before he replied. "My duties have been extended beyond always being in her care. King Sabian has appointed me with the task of inquiring to our men within the king's guard. He has learned from his mistake of trusting explicitly with Varick, whom he blames for Lisetta's attack."

Elsa gulped, her throat going dry. "Does he know..."

"No." Lahrs shook his head. "But he is paranoid that there are spies among the knights. I have interviewed them all but have not found any fault. A few more days, and it shall be done."

They walked further along the path, listening to the bright song of the doves. Across the lawn, Elsa could hear the boisterous singing of one of the gardeners as he pushed a cart of tools.

"I have only read from that book," Elsa began, reverting back to Lahrs' original inquiry. "She keeps it near, and when she is not crying, Brendolyn only reads from that book."

Lahrs said nothing but Elsa could see the tense crease on his brow, how his jaw was set hard. Elsa rarely ever saw this side of the elf.

"She's cursed, isn't she?" Elsa asked.

"There are very few references to the type of curse that has afflicted Bren. I have looked through my own library and have only found a few notes that describe the strength of power needed to take a voice." Lahrs frowned.

It felt as though Elsa had been punched, a tight agonizing pain wrenched through her.

"Ehlfern?" she breathed, barely able to utter the word. She remembered the stories her brothers told her about the ancient deities that walked the edge of the Veil.

"Bannon has dwindled Bren's magick by silencing her, but it is not merely her silence that worries me..." Here, the elf became more distant. They stopped walking, standing beneath a large statue surrounded by overgrown dahlias.

Elsa touched his arm.

Roused from thought, Lahrs sighed. "Bren is dying."

"Dying?" Elsa was alarmed as she searched the grey eyes of the elf. "How can a curse be so powerful?"

Lahrs shook his head. "Her soul is tarnished. I believe her heart is broken."

Elsa scoffed. "Soul mates. You believe Barrow was her soulmate? Don't be absurd, Lahrs. That man has no hold upon her heart after what he has done..."

"Barrow loves Brendolyn, I cannot deny that, but he is altered somehow. There's an obsession with his love, an unnatural bond..." Lahrs shook his head again and then stared hard at the statue they stood before. As Elsa looked at it, she understood it was a statue of the late queen, Natalia. "No. They are not soulmates."

Elsa frowned. "She gave her heart too soon."

"I thought it impossible, at first," he began. "It *should* be impossible, but it was unmistakable their bond. She first sought him on our first voyage to Jorn, when he was just a slave... then I saw him in Entheas. He was a free man but dangerously exposed to his magick. But it wasn't until now, when the world burns around them, their bond has been shaped by torment..."

Her eyes grew wide, listening to him speak.

"You believe Pavan to be Brendolyn's soulmate?"

"It is impossible for them to be together." Lahrs sighed, drawing his eyes away from the statue. "But beyond the sights of the greatest Seers, they are meant for each other."

"It cannot be so impossible then if it Ehnarea's blessing."

Elsa hated the idea of soul mates. It was only a story they told their children to guide them towards the reaches of the stars. Elsa knew heartbreak was real. She believed it was possible to be heartbroken by someone who claimed to love you.

"What could be so wrong if they should find happiness in each other? I do not think it right to say she belongs to any one man, should one of them treat her as refuse." Elsa felt her cheeks flush, anger tightening in her belly. "Barrow is monstrous in what he has done. Pavan has saved Brendolyn as well as King Sabian, I do not consider them anything but friendship or regard."

Lahrs gave her a smirk. "Your experience with watching them proves valuable."

"You think I am prejudiced?" Elsa crossed her arms defiantly.

"I believe you to be just in your premonitions, Elsa. You side with caution in regards to your friend because your own heart has been broken by the blackhearts of the world."

Elsa scoffed, rolling her eyes, but felt the little sharp tug of pain in her side, feeling more vulnerable under the stony grey gaze. Lahrs knew so much, it was insufferable.

"Pavan is amiable, Lahrs. But he is a traitor against the crown of Jorn. It is impossible for Brendolyn to love such a man as that," Elsa cut sharply.

"Yes, I believe that is also true…"

Elsa scoffed again. "What could you have possibly meant? What other impossibilities could have kept them apart?"

"Pavan is Ehlfern."

"Is that supposed to mean something? I have known plenty of faie to have married elven kind, and humans, as well… what would make an Ehlfern any different?"

"He has the capability of taking Brendolyn's soul. He may not want to, it would madden him, but he would take her soul if he was too close…"

Elsa gasped. "He would kill her?"

"Killing her would be easy… taking her soul… she would be barred from walking the Veil, Elsa. Her body would wither away and there would be nothing left."

Brendolyn wandered the gardens, the familiar paths lined with memories of a life both cherished and lost. The air was thick with the scent of late summer blossoms, yet she felt the coolness of the approaching autumn in her heart. She paused, her gaze drifting over the vibrant petals, when the crunch of heavy footsteps on gravel pulled her from her reverie.

Turning, she saw her father approaching. King Sabian moved with the weight of years upon him, his once youthful stride now a measured pace. His brow was furrowed, deep lines cutting into his once smooth dark skin. His hair, once a crown of deep ebony, was now streaked with rivers of gray, marking the passage of time that had left him aged and wearied.

Sabian halted abruptly when he finally noticed her standing there, a flicker of surprise in his dark eyes. But as recognition dawned, the harsh lines of his face softened, the stern ruler replaced by a father's tender gaze.

Brendolyn dipped into a graceful curtsy, her silence a testament to her respect and love.

"You are well, *mi amore*?" His voice was gentle, almost hesitant, as if he feared the answer. She nodded, a delicate motion that carried the weight of her unspoken emotions. Sabian's frown deepened, his concern palpable. "Your vow of silence continues, I see."

He knew the truth, of course. Lahrs had explained it to him—the vow Brendolyn had taken in honor of the late King Beaumont, a tradition among Felourian women who mourned the loss of their kin. Sabian had respected her wishes, though it pained him to see his daughter cloaked in such anguish.

"Walk with me," he offered, extending his arm to her. Brendolyn slipped her hand into the crook of his arm, finding comfort in the solidity of his presence. They moved together down the garden path, the silence between them thick with unspoken words.

For a while, they walked in quiet reflection. Brendolyn cherished the rare closeness with her father, a bittersweet joy tinged with the knowledge that such moments were fleeting. Sabian, however, was lost in a darker contemplation, the burdens of the past few months etched into his very being.

Finally, he broke the silence, his voice strained with regret. "You must forgive me, *amore*, that I have not been kinder to you these long years." His confession hung in the air, raw and vulnerable.

They stopped, and Brendolyn grasped his hand, her touch a balm to his troubled heart. "I know... you are so good," he murmured, his voice thick with emotion. He cupped her cheek, his rough hand gentle against her soft skin. Brendolyn saw the sorrow in his eyes, but beneath it, she also glimpsed a spark of hope—faint, but enduring.

She couldn't speak, but she conveyed her forgiveness with a kiss to his hand, her lips warm against his cool skin. Sabian's expression softened further as he nodded. "You were strong in Jorn." His voice grew firmer, pride lacing his words. "Lahrs told me of your determination to see us home. He was proud of your strength... and *I* am proud of your strength."

Tears welled in Brendolyn's eyes, her heart swelling with a mixture of love and regret. She wrapped her arms around her father, holding him close as if to anchor him to the present. Sabian returned the embrace, holding her tightly for a long moment before he pulled away, straightening his tunic as if to regain his composure.

"Now, now, enough of this," he said, though his voice was still soft. They resumed their walk, her hand slipping back into his. As they strolled through the garden, Sabian stole a glance at Brendolyn, a small, hidden smile playing at the corner of his mouth.

Brendolyn caught his eye and smiled back.

As they continued to walk, the garden seemed to close in around them, a cocoon of verdant green and vibrant flowers. The sunlight filtered through the leaves, casting dappled shadows on the ground, but neither noticed the beauty around them.

Sabian's grip on Brendolyn's hand tightened as they approached a stone bench nestled beneath a tall willowy branch of olive trees. "Let's sit for a moment," he suggested, his voice betraying a fatigue that went beyond the physical.

Brendolyn complied, easing onto the bench beside him, her hand still resting in his.

For a while, they sat in silence, the only sound the rustling of leaves in the gentle breeze. Sabian stared ahead, his gaze unfocused, as if lost in a distant memory. Brendolyn watched him, her heart aching at the sight of her father so burdened by grief and regret.

"I think of Hana often in this place," Sabian said suddenly, his voice a mere whisper. "She loved these gardens... it was her sanctuary, just as it is yours."

Brendolyn's breath caught in her throat at the mention of her mother, a woman whose memory lingered within the walls of Corad with a sad melancholic song.

"She worshiped these gardens," Sabian continued, his voice thick with emotion. "She spent so many hours walking these hedges with Natalia, so many summers they admired the bloom of the gladiolus lily."

Brendolyn's eyes shimmered with unshed tears.

"It was Hana's love of the flower that once thrived within this realm, a gift to her by a past lover. But I could no longer look upon the beauty that it once represented." There was so much resigned despair in the king.

A sad sort of laugh escaped his lips, looking at her then.

"She named you after that lily," he acknowledged at last. "*Brendolyn's* they called them in Nihtar. A rare bloom that became the symbol of their province."

She squeezed his hand, wishing she could convey her gratitude, her love, but all she could do was look at him with eyes full of everything she could not say.

Sabian turned to face her, his expression softening. "I've been a fool, Brendolyn. So consumed by my duties, by my grief, that I failed to see what was right in front of me. I failed to be the father you deserved."

She shook her head, but Sabian continued. "No, it's true. But I want to make amends, if you'll let me. I want to be here for you, *truly* here, for whatever time we have left together."

Brendolyn's tears finally spilled over, tracing silent paths down her cheeks. She leaned in, resting her head on his shoulder, and Sabian wrapped an arm around her, holding her close. The world seemed to pause, the garden falling into a hush as father and daughter sat entwined in their shared sorrow and newfound resolve.

After a long moment, Sabian spoke again, his voice gentle. "I don't know what the future holds, Brendolyn. The shadows on our horizon are dark, and I fear there is much we cannot foresee. But I promise you this—I will do everything in my power to protect you, to protect our family, and to ensure that your mother's legacy lives on through you."

They sat for a while longer, the garden around them a witness to their quiet reconciliation. And as the sun began its slow descent, casting the castle in hues of gold and amber, everything seemed to hold its breath, as though even time dared not disturb the quiet beauty of the final hour.

# CHAPTER

## 11

Lahrs stood before King Sabian, the weight of the conversation settling heavily between them. The king's chambers were dimly lit, shadows flickering along the walls as a fire crackled softly in the hearth. The air was thick with unspoken tension but Sabian's gaze was steady, though a hint of reluctance darkened his eyes as he addressed the elf.

"You are aware of your father-in-law's health, I assume?"

Lahrs nodded, his expression composed despite the unease gnawing at him. "Yes, Your Majesty. The last time I saw him, he was declining."

The king's hand moved to his chin, fingers brushing through his facial hair in thought. Sabian's frown deepened. "Your presence here has been invaluable, Sir Lahrs. As the Guardian of the Rose, your service has never faltered. Corad has relied on you more than you may know. *I* have relied upon you."

The words struck a chord deep within Lahrs, who fought to maintain his calm demeanor. Beneath the surface, melancholy churned. Leaving Corad, leaving the kingdom and duty he had devoted himself to for so many years, felt like tearing away a piece of his soul. Yet he knew this moment would come when the call of family, of a duty long bound to blood, could not be ignored.

"It has been my greatest honor to serve you, Your Majesty," Lahrs replied, his voice steady though his heart ached. "I have no wish to leave Corad, but I understand the need to return to my duties in Entheas."

Sabian's gaze softened, sensing the sadness behind Lahrs' composed exterior. "I do not ask this lightly, nor do I wish to see you go, but I respect your sense of duty. Entheas needs you now, just as Corad once did."

Lahrs inclined his head in silent acknowledgment, hiding the conflict within. He had grown to care deeply for Corad and the people he protected. To leave Brendolyn would be the hardest thing he has ever done. Leaving was not just a matter of duty, but a quiet heartbreak. He could not afford to show that despair now, not before the king. His loyalty to Sabian demanded that he remain resolute, no matter the personal cost.

"I will see to the transition smoothly," Lahrs assured, keeping his voice even. "But know that Corad and her people will always hold a place in my heart."

King Sabian placed a hand on Lahrs' shoulder, the gesture both comforting and final. "You've served this kingdom with honor, Lahrs. May your path forward be one of peace. Take the letter, so you may show it to Brendolyn shall she prove difficult to persuade of such change."

Lahrs bowed deeply, the weight of his misery barely contained beneath the surface. As he straightened, his face transformed into a mask of calm composure meticulously crafted to reflect the dignity expected of a knight of his station. Yet, beneath that veneer, a torrent of emotion churned, making each step toward the door a struggle.

The gardens outside were bathed in the soft glow of the evening light. Seeking the comfort of the gardens to clear his thoughts, Lahrs wandered among the blooming flowers and manicured paths. Each step seemed to echo with the memories of Brendolyn's laughter, her youthful delights, and the undeniable bond they had shared. Within the tranquil beauty of the gardens a sense of melancholy deepened within him, the serene beauty was a stark contrast to the inner confusion he felt.

After what felt like hours, Lahrs found himself standing at the entrance to Brendolyn's private library. The sight of the grand wooden doors brought a pang of resolve. He had to speak with her one last time, to say something more than what had already been uttered in the cold, harsh light of duty.

Lahrs entered the quiet of the library, and his grip on the letter tightened as he tried to calm the anxiety he fought to maintain. His breath came in heavy, uneven bursts, each one a struggle. He watched her for a few tranquil moments, seeing Brendolyn quietly at work in transcribing the little book given to her by Thad. She was studious, more so than she had ever been before.

"Brendolyn," he said, his voice cracking as he tried to catch her attention.

"*Lahrs.*" Her fingers moved in the language of the Silent Sisters of Divna. Brendolyn's eyes locked onto his, sensing that this conversation was different from their usual lessons.

Lahrs studied her, his gaze lingering on the woman she had become. Yet, in his mind, she was still the child he had cherished through every stage of her life. His heart ached as memories surfaced—the restless nights when he soothed her cries, the triumph of her first wobbly steps, the delight of hearing her first words. He remembered the way she clung to his leg for comfort, the times she begged to be carried in his arms, the mischievous sparkle in her eyes when she played her innocent pranks. Though she stood before him now, no longer a child, those moments were etched into his soul with painful clarity.

He had made a promise to her mother, a vow to protect her, to care for her every step of the way. And he had kept that promise, even when it meant burying parts of himself to ensure her safety and happiness.

But now, his heart twisted with emotions he could barely contain. Anger at the cruel hand of fate that demanded he leave her, shame at abandoning her when she needed him most. And beneath it all, a deep, gnawing guilt he had hidden the truth for so long, believing it was for the best. Now, as he faced the inevitability of their parting, that secret made the weight of his departure almost unbearable.

"There will be no lesson today." Lahrs's voice wavered, and he took a deep, steadying breath, preparing for the pain his next words would bring. "I have been summoned back to Entheas before the autumn months. I am to marry Duchess Kristjana of Tauf. My time here in Corad is ending, and so too is my role as your guardian."

The room seemed to still, the weight of his words pressing down like a silent gale. Brendolyn stood frozen, her golden eyes shimmering with unshed tears. Her chin wobbled as she fought to hold herself together, but her clenched fists betrayed the storm inside her. The hurt and confusion in her gaze cut through him like a blade.

"I'm sorry," Lahrs whispered, his voice breaking under the weight of his own anguish. The letter in his hand quivered as the composure he'd clung to crumbled.

Brendolyn's grief erupted in a burst of motion. She struck his chest with a closed fist, then another, each blow laced with her pain. Lahrs stood firm, absorbing her hits as if they might lessen the burden of her anguish. Finally, her hands clutched at his tunic, her tears falling freely despite the curse that silenced her cries. Without hesitation, he pulled her into a fierce embrace..

"Forgive me," he murmured against her hair, his voice quivering. "Forgive me."

She pulled back, desperation etched in her hands as she tried to form words. The language of the Silent Sisters aiding her muted voice, but her pleading fingers spoke louder than any voice. "*Don't leave me,*" she begged. Her hands stumbled over the sign for friend, frustration evident as she searched for the right term.

Lahrs gently cupped her cheek, his heart breaking anew. "If it were in my power, you would sail with me to Tauf and remain at my side. But you must stay here with your father."

Brendolyn's head snapped up, her expression darkening. She fiercely shook her head, forming the words with her trembling fingers. "*He is not my father.*"

"Brendolyn…" Lahrs shook his head, his own tears falling. "He is your father."

She stepped back, anger flaring as her fingers moved with sharp, deliberate motions. "*He has never comforted me, never loved me. You have been my father in all but name. He cannot claim me—he is only my king.*"

Lahrs staggered under the weight of her declaration, his pain bubbling into anguished anger. "I have no claim upon you," he cried. "I love you, Brendolyn, more than life itself. Above every reach of these realms, I love you. But I do not hold your birthright. It is his name that binds you, it is his power that keeps you from being mine."

Her shoulders shook as silent tears streamed down her cheeks, each one a testament to her shattered heart.

"You're leaving?" Elsa's voice was sharp, her teacup clattering against the saucer as she set it down with more force than intended. Her glare fixed on Lahrs, who stood unmoving by the hearth, as if rooted in place. He appeared calm and composed, but there was a tension in the set of his jaw, and a flicker in his grey eyes that betrayed something deeper.

It had started like any other when Brendolyn slept in the early evening—tea shared between them, the comfort of routine. But today, Lahrs had revealed something that shattered that sense of normalcy.

"It is not my choice of timing, Elsa," Lahrs said, his voice rough, as though he were speaking through clenched teeth. "Duke is gravely ill; he will not survive beyond the coming months. My oaths to that family bind me, and I cannot break them."

Elsa felt the words like a punch to the chest, leaving her breathless. "What about your family here? What about Brendolyn?" Her voice cracked as she fought to keep her emotions in check. Anger simmered beneath the surface, but it was the fear that was threatening to spill over. She clutched her mouth, trying to stifle the tremor that gave her away, but the tears welled despite her efforts.

The silence stretched thin until Lahrs finally moved, crossing the room to kneel in front of her. He took her hands in his, the warmth of his touch both familiar and infuriating. She hated him at that moment—for the betrayal she felt, for the abandonment she knew was coming.

"I will not abandon you, Elsa," Lahrs said, his voice low, tinged with a tenderness that almost broke her. "I made a promise to your brother that I would keep you safe, and I intend to uphold that promise. Once I am married, I shall find a way to bring you and Brendolyn to Entheas. There, under my protection, you will be safe."

But his words only deepened her fears. She shook her head, tears spilling freely now. "I can't leave this realm, not while my bond is still in place. Alaric will find me, he'll track me down, no matter where I go."

Lahrs reached up to touch her cheek, his thumb gently brushing away a tear. The warmth of his hand was meant to be comforting, but it sent a sharp, stabbing pain radiating through her chest. She winced but didn't pull away.

"He will never find you, Elsa. Whatever threats Leuthere made, they hold no power here."

She forced herself to take slow, steady breaths, letting his words sink in. When her shudder subsided, Lahrs shifted to sit beside her on the small couch, his expression distant, lost in thought. Elsa noticed the weariness etched into his features, lines that seemed deeper now, eyes that looked more tired than she'd ever seen them. For all his stoic strength, Lahrs carried a weight that was slowly breaking him.

"Do you believe this is Lord Bannon's doing?" Elsa asked, her voice hushed, as if fearing the answer. "Is he behind this, pulling you away from us?"

Lahrs remained silent for a long moment, contemplating. "The Duke has been unwell for some time... but perhaps. Lord Bannon's reach is long, and I cannot dismiss the possibility. Still, I cannot say for certain."

Elsa nodded slowly, pressing her lips together to hold back a fresh wave of tears. "Brendolyn will miss you, Lahrs," she murmured, her voice thick with emotion. "You've been more than just her guardian, you've raised her. I've never seen a knight so devoted to their duty as you have been."

A shadow crossed Lahrs' face, dark and unreadable, before it softened into a small, melancholic smile. He glanced at Elsa with a quiet fondness. "She is the single most important creature in all the realms," he said softly. "I delivered her into this world, and from the moment her cries filled the air, my life's purpose was clear. I swore an oath to her mother, a promise that I would protect the last part of her that remained. I've done everything in my power to keep that vow."

Tears glistened in his eyes, the rawness of his grief laid bare for only a moment. Elsa wiped away a tear that escaped down her cheek, her own heart breaking for the man who had given so much. She reached out and took his hand in hers, ignoring the sharp sting it sent through her ribs. "She's lucky to have you, Lahrs," she whispered.

Lahrs didn't respond immediately. He only squeezed her hand in silent acknowledgment, a quiet promise that even as he prepared to leave, his heart would remain with the ones he was leaving behind.

# CHAPTER

## 12

*Jorn City, Realm of Jorn.*

THE MOON CAST A pale glow over the city as Sir Eero patrolled its shadowed streets, the faint clink of his armor blending with the muted hum of nighttime activity. His movements were deliberate, his gaze sharp as he scanned the alleys and doorways for any signs of trouble. It was meant to be another routine patrol, until he spotted a familiar figure moving swiftly through the crowd.

Alaric.

The sight of the knight in this part of the city, especially at such a late hour, sent a ripple of unease through Eero. He narrowed his eyes, watching as Alaric disappeared into one of the city's most notorious dens, a haven for vice, magickal hallucinogens, and illicit dealings. Without hesitation, Eero followed.

The entrance was dimly lit, the air thick with a haze of smoke that clung to the narrow hallway. A woman draped in gaudy silks lounged by the door, her sharp eyes narrowing as she noticed him. "A knight wandering here? You must be lost," she said, her tone a mix of suspicion and amusement.

"I'm looking for someone," Eero replied, his voice cold and commanding. "Alaric. He came in here."

Her smile faded into a guarded expression. "I don't meddle in the affairs of paying customers," she said evenly. "What he does is of no concern to me."

Before Eero could retort, a scream pierced the air, a sharp, panicked sound that cut through the din. Instinct took over as he pushed past the madam and down the corridor, following the echoes of distress. Twisting halls led him to a room where a group of young women huddled, one clutching her bloodied nose as tears streamed down her face.

Eero's gut twisted, anger flashing in his chest, but he didn't stop. He pressed onward, shoving open the next door with such force it nearly splintered on its hinges. The room was shrouded in blue smoke, the sweet yet sickly scent of magickal incense clinging to the air. Dim lanterns cast shifting shadows across the walls, warping the figures within.

In the center stood Alaric, his once proud bearing now reduced to a drunken sway. His eyes, wild and unfocused, darted about as he shouted for a girl with red hair. His voice, slurred and full of arrogance, grated against Eero's ears.

Crossing the room, Sir Eero seized Alaric by the collar and dragged him out. Alaric thrashed and cursed, but Eero's grip was unyielding. He hauled the knight through the smoky corridors and into the cold night air, shoving him into a filthy alleyway behind the building.

"What in Ehnarea's name are you doing here?" Eero snapped, his voice sharp with barely contained anger.

Alaric sneered, his laugh a harsh, mocking sound. "Living my life, Eero. What's it to you?"

They stood face to face, the tension growing between them like a bow string pulled too tightly. "You're a disgrace to your oath, to the Brotherhood. You think wallowing in filth makes you free?"

Alaric spat at the ground, his lips curling into a bitter smirk. "You cling to honor, the loyalty to that cult as if it means anything. You're just like the others, blind to the truth."

Eero's hand flew to his dagger, the blade flashing as he pressed it to Alaric's throat. "You've already disgraced yourself enough. Don't make me end it here."

For a moment, fear flickered in Alaric's eyes before it was smothered by defiance. He tilted his head back, exposing the faint scar that marred his chest, a brutal reminder of his past betrayal, a wound inflicted by Thad. Eero remembered the encounter, shaking his head free of the memory.

"You think you're better than me?" Alaric hissed. "I've found a new master, Eero. Someone who offers real power. Not the empty promises of honor by the Brotherhood or duty from a simple king."

Eero's stomach sank as Alaric's next words landed like a blow.

"Lord Simeon Bannon," Alaric whispered, his eyes gleaming with a twisted satisfaction. "He has given me true purpose, he has shown me what true power reveals to those that wish to seek its truth."

Rage warred with a cold, creeping dread as Eero wrestled with the weight of the man's words. He wanted to strike Alaric down, to make him pay for his betrayal, for what he had done to Elsa, but he knew violence here would only play into Simeon's schemes. Lowering the dagger, Eero fixed Alaric with a steely glare.

"You've made your choice but know this—Lord Bannon's power is a shadow. It will crumble, and when it does, you'll fall with it."

Alaric chuckled darkly, the sound devoid of warmth. "We'll see who crumbles first, Eero, when this kingdom trembles to behold what storm is coming from the northern seas."

Eero turned and walked away, his mind a tempest of anger and determination. The city was no longer safe, not with Bannon's influence spreading like a disease. But Eero knew one thing for certain—he would not let the darkness consume everything he held dear. Even if it meant standing alone, he would fight until his last breath.

The chill of the night clung to Eero as he ascended the castle steps. Alaric's words echoed in his mind, each syllable a dagger of doubt. Simeon's shadow loomed larger than he'd feared, spreading like rot through the very foundations of the realm. And now, Alaric was another pawn in the lord's twisted game.

The guards at the castle gates saluted as Eero passed, their movements sharp but tinged with unease. The castle halls, usually a haven of order, felt different tonight—stifling, as if the walls themselves whispered of darkness. Servants moved hurriedly, their heads down, while courtiers whispered in corners, glancing nervously over their shoulders.

In the map room, Barrow sat slouched in his seat, his crown no longer on his head but resting on the large oaken table at the center of the room. He looked thinner than the last time Eero had seen him, his face pale and his eyes rimmed with red. A map lay spread across the long table before him, weighed down by goblets and daggers. Around it stood a handful of advisors, their expressions grim as they exchanged hushed words.

Barrow's gaze snapped to Eero the moment he entered. "Sir Eero," he called, his voice sharper than usual. "You've returned late."

Eero knelt, bowing his head. "I was patrolling the city."

Barrow waved a dismissive hand at the advisors, who grumbled but were quiet as they left the map room. "The seas are swarming with pirates. They've blockaded our merchant ships." He slammed a fist against the table, causing the goblets to rattle. "I want them dealt with immediately."

Eero stood close to the young king, noting the agitation in the air. "I will see to it. But there are other matters I wish to discuss—"

"Nothing is more important than restoring our trade routes!" Barrow barked, his voice cracking. Looking at Eero, his eyes blazed. "Or have you forgotten the King Slayer who roams the Realms in dark shadows?"

Eero met Barrow's gaze evenly. "I have not forgotten. But there is more at play here than pirates. Lord Bannon's influence grows unchecked, there is unnecessary bloodshed."

Barrow's jaw tightened. "Bannon," he muttered, his tone venomous. "It was Lord Bannon who put an end to the heresy of conspiring magick in the wretched city of Eir." He leaned closer, his voice dropping to a whisper. "They helped the King Slayer escape your clutches."

Eero's throat tightened. The king's paranoia was worsening, and it was clear that trust was a rare commodity in this court. "Barrow," he said carefully, "we must tread cautiously. If we act rashly, we risk playing into his hands."

Barrow sneered, stepping back. "Caution," he repeated bitterly. "You knights always speak of *caution*. Where was the caution when my father was murdered?" His voice cracked, and for a moment, the mask of anger slipped, revealing the grief beneath. "Where were *you*, Sir Eero, when he needed you most?"

Eero swallowed hard, guilt gnawing at him. He couldn't tell Barrow the truth, not yet. Simeon's treachery and Pavan's innocence were secrets that could shatter the fragile balance of the kingdom and threaten the safety of Princess Brendolyn. "I was where I was ordered to be, Barrow," he said quietly. "And I will remain steadfast until justice is served."

Barrow turned away, his shoulders slumping. "Justice," he murmured, almost to himself. "I want justice for my father. Find the man who killed him, Eero. Bring me his head."

Eero bowed. "As you command."

But as he left the throne room, his heart was heavy with conflict. Simeon's betrayal was a poison that could destroy the kingdom but revealing it would put Pavan in even greater danger.

In the quiet of the corridor, Eero paused, his hand brushing the hilt of his sword.

It was still dark when Sir Eero was roused from sleep, the soft knock of a maid breaking the hush of morning. His limbs ached from yesterday's drills, but the urgency in her voice left no room for delay. He dressed swiftly, pulling a tunic over his shoulders and fastening the last of his leather bracers with a practiced yank. The chill of the stones followed him as he bounded down the narrow spiral steps, his strides echoing in the hall as he made his way toward the training rooms tucked beneath the far wall, near the stables.

The sound reached him before the doorway, metal clashing with metal in dull, sloppy rhythms, and voices sharp with forced exertion. Then came the curses. Eero's brow knit as he crossed the threshold into the chamber, already breathless from the sprint.

There, beneath the high arched ceilings of carved stone, three knights stood in a loose ring around King Barrow. The king was clad in a padded doublet that sagged at the shoulders and arm, of which guards must have strapped on crooked. Padded leathers wrapped his legs like borrowed armor—ill-fitting and awkward.

Eero stilled in the shadows between the thick pillars, watching. The knights rotated turns against their young sovereign, engaging him in mock combat, though it was little more than choreographed defeat. Each one, at the last second, pulled their strikes, letting Barrow win with clumsy lunges and overextended blows.

Disgust rose in Eero like bile.

He stepped forward, boots striking the floor with a sharp finality that cut through the chamber. The knights turned at once, startled, but none so much as Gwayn, whose eyes went wide as Eero snatched the training sword from his hand.

"Sir Eero—" Gwayn stammered, already palling.

The others fell into an uneasy silence as Barrow turned, still panting, a pleased grin splitting his face.

"They've volunteered to assist in my training," he said proudly, lifting his sword with both hands, swinging it awkwardly side to side. "I asked for the finest swordsmen available. Leuthere claims these are the best."

Eero's gaze swept over the knights, each one stone silent and avoiding his eyes.

"You have been lied to, Your Majesty," Eero said, voice low and tight. He held the dull sword aloft, testing its weight. It was light. Too light. "That is a blade for a child. The same is given to squires when they first set foot upon the dueling square."

Barrow's smile faltered. "But I've bested them—"

"You've bested *ghosts*," Eero snapped, taking his stance with practiced calm, though fire stirred beneath his skin. He raised the blade, and the knights around them backed away.

Barrow hesitated, then mirrored the motion, his knuckles whitening around the hilt.

Eero moved with practiced speed.

Like a shadow at full gallop, he lunged forward, his blade colliding with Barrow's with a crack that echoed against the stone. The force of the strike jarred the young king to his heels, but Eero gave no pause, he swept again, driving forward three quick steps, pressing the attack without mercy. Barrow struggled, staggered, his arms shaking as he tried to parry. His defense was sloppy, slow.

And then, with a sharp twist and a step, Eero disarmed him. The dulled sword clattered across the chamber, a deafening clang that was swiftly followed by silence.

Barrow stumbled backward, chest heaving. The tip of Eero's blade hovered at his throat, unmoving. Eero didn't lower his sword. He turned it instead, pointing it at Gwayn with a glare that could cut steel.

"You shame your king with deceit," he spat.

Gwayn's lips trembled. "We—we only wished to please him—"

"To please him?" Eero's voice darkened to a growl. "You've pleased his vanity. And risked his life. Had he faced a true enemy, he would already be bleeding at your feet."

Gwayn shrank back, shoulders hunched in shame.

Eero's gaze flicked to the next knight, an older man with pepper-flecked hair and a jagged birthmark blooming across his neck like a burn. "And you, Sir Vorren," he said coldly. "You wear your insignia like a crown, but your command is a disgrace."

None spoke.

Only the sound of Barrow's ragged breath filled the chamber. Eero stepped back at last, lowering his blade, but not the fury burning in his chest.

"Train him," he said, voice cutting the silence, "or leave the sword to men who will."

Each man left, taking with them their swords, their guilt and shame, leaving Eero to stand in the room with the young king. There was a breath of a moment before he looked at Barrow, seeing the pitiable misery that befell him. Slowly Barrow strode the distance to pick up the fallen sword, hefting the dull thing in his grip.

"I shall find another." Barrow let his shoulders slump.

Eero straightened and holding his ground, raised his sword to Barrow in turn. "I shall train you, Barrow. As I should have done many years ago had it not been for your fathers request to not let you handle a sword."

Barrow's jaw clenched, holding the sword with a deadly grip.

"My father prevented me from doing a lot of things." Barrow's voice was soft, despite the hard glare he held with the knight. "It was his command that kept me from keeping my marriage with Brendolyn. I could have kept her as my wife, and we wouldn't have any need for the celebrations of my name day. My father would not have been murdered."

"It would have started another war to break the treaty."

Anger burned hot in Barrow's eyes, as the young king raised his sword and stepped forward, his free hand sweeping out in a dramatic gesture. "It would be worth it in the end to have her, Eero."

"In your heart you may believe that, but we both know that is not what your father would have wanted for you. *This* path is not what he wanted for you."

"You don't understand!" Barrow shouted, his sword sweeping in a halfhearted arc, coming in contact with Eero's in a loud reverberating clang. "I burn for her, Eero! Every time I close my eyes she is all I dream about, she is an ever consuming fire that drives me to act!"

Shifting his stance, Eero blocked a second weak thrust, knocking Barrow off balance where he stumbled. Remaining on guard, Eero watched Barrow grit his teeth, growling.

"I understand your grief, Barrow. But you must fight the enchantment that consumes you... you must let her go."

Barrow screamed, his eyes darkening as he hurled himself forward, swinging the sword in wild thrashing movements. Eero parried, moving on swift feet to defend himself. Each clash of the dull swords echoed off the walls, accompanied by the sounds of panting breath. Three more swipes and Eero swung with a downward stroke, sending Barrow towards the nearest pillar.

"I cannot let her go." Barrow was winded, his hands quaking as he pushed the sweaty locks of blond from his dripping face. "I cannot forget the faie's words for they slither in my mind. I can feel his mouth, his thighs around my hips... it is torture to desire it, that forbidden embrace."

A breathy silence, Eero stepped closer, seeing Barrow crumbling under his grief.

"Thaddeus was wrong to manipulate you, Barrow. It is unforgivable and his intentions were selfish." Eero stopped, leaning in to take the practice sword from the young king.

Barrow whimpered, wiping his running nose on the back of his hand. "But I wanted him..." Shame closed the blue eyes that swam in glistening tears. "I wanted him to make the ache recede, if only for just a moment. To forget the pain. Thaddeus showed me what it would be like with Brendolyn, he gave me thoughts of her while he touched me..."

Eero tossed the swords aside, resting a hand on Barrow's shoulder.

"He was wrong, Barrow."

"I am glad he is dead." Seething, the young king hissed, "He was closest to Pavan, Eero. It was by his design that he kept me distracted so the King Slayer would have ample time to seduce my father."

A part of Eero crumpled, but he knew of Lahrs' words in truth to Thad's life. He hardened himself to it, holding Barrow's shoulder more firmly. "Let his actions die with him, Barrow. Do not hold onto the guilt.

"I will have Brendolyn, Eero." Barrow grabbed hold of Eero's doublet, bringing them closer. "Even if I must send my greatest ships to storm the shores of Corad and take her by force. *I will have her.*"

# CHAPTER

## 13



PAVAN JOLTED AWAKE, HIS breath catching in his throat as he shot up, eyes wide with disorientation. His body, heavy with fatigue, sank into the soft, enveloping warmth of the bed, its covers comforting yet unfamiliar. The room around him was dim, shadowed by dark wallpaper that seemed to absorb what little light the flickering candles offered. Books lay scattered across the floor and crowded the shelves, a testament to years of neglect. Pools of old wax clung to surfaces, remnants of long burned candles, marking the passage of time in a space that felt both lived in and abandoned.

He scanned the room, heart pounding, and a sense of dread creeping up his spine.

"It is good to see you awake."

The voice was calm, almost soothing, yet it sent a shiver through him. He turned toward it, finding a petite woman standing in the doorway, her presence almost ghostly. Her hair, white as freshly fallen snow, cascaded past her waist, and her clothes were of a dull, ashen cotton, simple and unadorned. She smiled gently, but those clouded, milky eyes hinted at something far more complex, something that both intrigued and unsettled him. Her face, beautiful and serene, was young, but the look in her eyes was unmistakably old and ancient.

"Who are you?" he asked, his voice barely steady as she approached, her movements unhurried when she came to stand beside him.

"I am Sanna. I have been waiting for you, Isaac Maison." Her voice was soft, striking a chord that made his chest tighten. It was a voice he knew, a voice that carried memories he had long tried to bury. His breath caught as the floodgates of his mind opened, and with it came a torrent of memories, each one more vivid and painful than the last. He blinked, trying to center himself amidst the chaos inside him.

"I prefer to be called Pavan," he managed to say, his voice sounding distant even to his own ears. He watched as she reached out, her fingers brushing against his hand, then tracing along his wrists and arms, as if she were searching for something unseen.

She didn't respond immediately, seemingly lost in her own thoughts as her eyes, unseeing yet intent, traveled over his face. He held still, his breath shallow as she touched his hair, his forehead. There was an intimacy in her actions that both confused and comforted him, as if she were trying to memorize every detail of him through her touch. Finally, she stepped back, her hands raised before her, her lips moving in a silent prayer or incantation. The room seemed to hold its breath as the candles flickered and the shadows around them danced as if alive.

Pavan felt the tension in the air, the weight of something he couldn't quite understand pressing down on him. And then, just as suddenly, the candles steadied, and the smile returned to Sanna's lips, though her eyes remained as opaque as ever.

"Why have you been waiting for me?" Pavan asked, his voice shook slightly, a mix of fear and curiosity lacing his words.

"There will be time to tell you all, Pavan, but now is a time of rest. You have used so much magick... I am told you nearly killed yourself in the woods just three days ago." Her voice softened, and for a moment, she looked distant, as if lost in a memory of her own.

"Órlaith." He tried to sit up, his mind racing, but Sanna's hand pressed firmly against his shoulder, holding him back with a strength that belied her slight frame.

"Have peace, everything is as it should be," she murmured, her touch radiating warmth that seeped into him, easing the tension in his muscles.

His gaze dropped to the hand on his shoulder, then lifted to meet her eyes and those clouded orbs that seemed to see more than they revealed.

"Please don't enchant me," he whispered, a note of desperation in his voice. The last thing he wanted was to be manipulated, to lose his sense of self when everything around him felt so precarious.

Sanna hesitated for a moment, but drew back, turning her attention to a nearby table cluttered with small bottles, papers, and trinkets. She busied herself with them, her back to him, the air between them thick with unspoken tension.

"You call my guide Órlaith... she is very fond of your journey together."

"She is faie, of the old line of Athrun." Pavan rubbed his eyes, pain radiating behind them as his mind raced with rampant thoughts. "But she has lost herself to the magick that transforms her to the beast of the forest."

"She has lived amongst the Vohlgrum for so long, she has forgotten what it was like to be faie." A smile formed at the edge of Sanna's lips. "But she remembers you, Pavan."

"She was the cub Vohlgrum I rescued all those years ago..."

Sanna turned to face him, her expression unreadable. "It is exactly why I chose her for the task of bringing you here to me. She has longed to repay you for your kindness, Pavan..." She stepped closer, offering him a small cup, her movements graceful and deliberate.

Pavan nodded, his mind still swirling. "I have so many questions," he said, looking up at her, searching her face for answers that she seemed unwilling to give just yet.

She smirked, a hint of amusement in her expression. "I had not expected any less. When you are strong again, everything will become clear. For now, you must drink." She gently took his hand, guiding it to the cup, the warmth of her touch steadying him.

He stared into the cup, watching the small flowers swirl in the honey-colored liquid. He sighed, the scent of the tea bringing back memories of simpler times, times when the world hadn't felt so heavy. Slowly, he lifted the cup to his lips and drank, the warmth spreading through him and soothing the ache in his chest, if only for a moment.

Slowly his head lulled back, his mind ebbing on the brink of sleep as Sanna took the cup again in her hands. Tucking his arms close to his chest, Pavan found himself falling fast asleep.

Pavan's days blurred together, a haze of pain and restless dreams confined within the small bed. The room, with its dim light and heavy air, felt like a cocoon, both protective and suffocating. By the second day, he had grown accustomed to the soft creak of the door opening, expecting to see the white haired woman enter with her quiet presence and unreadable smile.

But when the door opened this time, it wasn't her. Instead, a tall elf stood in the doorway, his dark hair catching the faint light as he moved silently into the room. He carried a tray with practiced grace, his steps light and fluid, but what caught Pavan's attention was the magick that surrounded him. A warm, honeyed scent that filled the space that was familiar and it made Pavan's heart race with a mixture of fear and yearning. He instinctively shifted away, despite the sharp pain that lanced through his bones with the movement.

"Forgive my mistress, she is resting... but I have brought you nourishment," the elf said, his voice rich with an accent that tugged at Pavan's memories. It was the accent of Entheas, a voice from the southern regions of the elven realm. Pavan had heard it before, in the bustling markets of Taudren, where tradesmen spoke in melodic tones that hinted at distant lands. The realization sent a shiver down his spine.

"I am not hungry," Pavan lied, though his eyes betrayed him, lingering on the tray. His stomach clenched at the sight of the tea, the plate of fruits and cheeses, and the thick slice of bread. He felt a deep hunger gnawing at him, but his wariness was stronger, keeping him on edge.

The elf didn't budge, his expression firm. "You must replenish your strength."

As the elf stood over him, Pavan took in his features of the pale, almost luminous skin, the strong, square jaw, and the striking violet of his eyes. There was something achingly familiar in his face, a resemblance that stirred something deep within Pavan. It was in the curve of his mouth, the intensity of his gaze, a shared lineage that Pavan felt in his very bones.

"You are from Taudren," Pavan said, in awe of the elf.

A sad, distant smile graced the full mouth. "It was once my home. But that was many moons ago. Now, I am in service to my mistress."

Pavan frowned, but the elf offered no further explanation, instead, he gently urged him again. "Eat, my lord. Tomorrow is a new day." With a respectful bow, the elf left the tray beside the bed and retreated, leaving Pavan alone with his thoughts.

As the door closed behind him, Pavan felt a small measure of the tension leave his body. The elf's presence had unsettled him, but it was also strangely comforting, like a thread connecting him to something long lost. Slowly, he pushed himself upright, wincing as his body protested the movement. His eyes fell on the tray once more, then shifted to the small stack of books on the nightstand. The hunger gnawed at him, but curiosity won out, and he reached for the first book, his fingers tracing the worn leather cover before he opened it.

The handwriting was meticulous, so neat it almost seemed printed, but the occasional ink splotches and hasty sketches revealed the human hand behind the words. Pavan found himself drawn into the pages, losing track of time as he absorbed the information, the act of reading soothing in its simplicity.

*In the closing years of the Second Age, when the rivers yet sang with the voices of the Firstborn and the light of the Ehlfern shone in every corner of Veilore, there came she who is named in the old tongue as Vey'nora, the Breath that Unmaketh. She was the great harbinger of chaos, a being of hunger without end, who descended upon the realms not to reign but to consume.*

*It is told that she smote that of Ehlfere and from their sundered forms drew forth their magick as a thief drinks from a chalice. The Ehlfern fell, their power flowing into her until her form burned with stolen light. As the world teetered toward unmaking, the last of their kind gathered before the great marbled stone. There they spoke the Words Before Time and poured their own life force into the Banishment, casting Vey'nora beyond the Veil to the Outer Dark, where no lamp of our world may shine.*

*Yet their victory was no triumph, for in her fall the harmony of Veilore was sundered. The Great Temples, living vessels of magick and guardians of the Tomes, were broken or hidden away, entrusted to others in desperate secrecy.*

By the third day, his mind awash with the knowledge of ancient rituals, rights and magick. He closed the book with a sigh, looking up just as the door to the chamber creaked open again.

Sanna entered, her figure draped in a soft shawl, the light of the candle she carried casting a warm glow over her white hair. It shimmered in the dim light, golden hues catching in the strands, reminding him painfully of Lilja. He could see her so clearly in his mind, the way her hair had glimmered in the candlelight when they lay together, the soft intimacy of those moments filling him with both warmth and wretchedness.

The memory brought a flush to his cheeks, and he quickly averted his gaze, unwilling to let Sanna see the vulnerability in his eyes as she approached with a cup of tea. The past and the present collided within him, the familiar ritual of the tea bringing comfort, even as his heart ached with longing for what he had lost.

Sanna paused beside him, offering the cup with that same gentle smile, her presence both soothing and enigmatic. As he took the cup from her, his hands jerked slightly, but he managed to return her smile, a silent acknowledgment of the strange, fragile connection forming between them in this place of healing and hidden truths.

Pavan's heart throbbed painfully, each pulse sending waves of agony through his body. His chin twitched, betraying the sadness he tried to suppress. As Sanna reached the door, her hand hovered over the handle. She paused, sensing his uneasiness, and turned slightly, her gaze finding him even though her eyes were clouded. Pavan could feel her attention on him, a gentle pull that made him lift his eyes.

"Meet me in the gardens when you wake. There is much we need to discuss," she said softly, her voice a balm to his aching heart.

The next morning, the sun's first rays filtered through the window, casting a warm glow over the room. Pavan rose slowly, his body still weary but his mind focused. He moved with care, washing his face in the cool water from the basin, feeling each drop as it traced a path down his skin. The clothes left for him—a pair of dark breeches, a crisp white tunic, and a maroon quilted jacket with brass buttons—felt like a ritual as he dressed. But the absence of footwear left him hesitant, his feet bare against the cold floor.

Emerging from his room, Pavan was confronted by a long corridor, its many doors hiding unknown secrets. The narrow stairs spiraled downward, and he bent to fit through the passage, emerging into a small parlor filled with chaotic beauty, plants bursting from their pots and glass boxes teeming with life. The air was thick with the scent of earth and growth, a stark contrast to the sterile corridors above.

Navigating through the verdant maze, he found another door. The creak of its hinges seemed to echo his own uncertainty, but as he pushed through, a dimly lit corridor greeted him, lined with melted candles that flickered weakly. He hesitated, unsure of which direction to take, until a sudden, loud meow startled him. Looking down, he saw a thin cat with spotted fur weaving through his feet, its eyes the same milky hue as Sanna's.

Pavan sighed, a small smile playing on his lips as he followed the cat down the darkened corridor. The creature led him to a slightly ajar door, through which a stream of light beckoned. Pushing it open, Pavan was met with awe as he stepped into a vast cathedral. Light poured in through stained glass windows, casting vibrant colors across the marbled floor. The sheer height of the space made him feel small, yet it was a space devoid of the usual trappings of worship with no pews, no altars, only the purity of light and shadow.

The cat meowed again, drawing his attention to a sun dappled spot where it sat patiently. Pavan followed as the cat led him through another door, this time into a cobblestone corridor lined with windows that allowed glimpses of the wild gardens beyond. The greenery called to him, the vibrant colors promising life and peace. As he reached a large room, the sound of water splashing greeted his ears, and he saw a fountain feeding a clear pool. The space was open, merging seamlessly with the gardens outside.

He stepped into the garden, the sun's warmth caressing his face as the sounds of birdsong welcomed him. The lush greenery and the intricate dance of shadows and light, the beauty of nature was a balm to his soul. Pavan walked deeper into the garden, his steps slow and measured, until he found himself in its heart. The cathedral loomed behind him, its stone shimmering under the sun, but it was the magick of the garden that held his attention.

"There is a magick cast over the cathedral. It is not visible to those who are not invited here by me," Sanna's voice broke through his thoughts, gentle yet firm.

He turned to see her approaching, her white hair pulled back into a braid, her earthy clothes dusted with soil. She held a basket of lavender, the scent mingling with the garden's rich aroma. Her feet were bare, caked in mud, yet she moved with grace, smiling up at him.

Pavan forced a small smile in return. "You are a magick wielder?" he asked, his voice hesitant as he took in the living beauty around him.

Sanna laughed softly, a sound like the rustling of leaves. "Magick flows through everything we see and touch. It is the thread that weaves life together, binding us to each other."

Pavan followed her as she moved through the garden, her presence as soothing as the lavender she carried. The question that had been lingering on his tongue slipped out before he could stop it. "Do you see the magick in others?"

His cheeks flushed with embarrassment, but he couldn't avoid her gaze. Sanna stopped, looking up at him with her milky eyes, her expression gentle yet probing.

"I cannot see by the standards of men, Pavan, but where my eyes fail, magick guides me," she replied, her words wrapping around him like a comforting embrace.

Pavan blinked, the weight of her words settling over him. "You're blind?" he asked, the realization dawning on him with a tinge of guilt.

Sanna smiled, a soft curve of her lips that spoke of acceptance. "It is the price I paid for the gift of magick. My sight was taken, but in return, I was granted the ability to see beyond the physical realm."

As she bent to prune a rose bush, Pavan watched her with a newfound respect. "You use magick to see."

"Yes. Magick has been generous to me, gifting me with foresight and the ability to see through the eyes of others... including yours," Sanna explained, her voice tinged with the weight of centuries of knowledge. "I saw you in your mother's arms the day you arrived in this world. Like a dream, I was lifted on the wings of a bird, seeing through many eyes the life and hardship you carried with you."

Pavan reached out, touching the stem of the rose bush she tended. The delicate petals creased under his fingers, a stark contrast to the storm brewing within him. "They believed me dead... I never told them the truth."

Sanna snipped a bud, her movements steady and unhurried. "Those who cannot see as we do may never understand. You come from a land of magick, where mountains speak in tongues unknown to many."

Pavan's breath hitched. "You've seen my home?"

"Through your eyes and others like you, I have glimpsed many places." Sanna nodded, her eyes flickering with memories of distant lands. "I have seen tall cities built to the skies, thousands of lights that scatter over the horizon, and so many people who do not see but are blinded to the deepest realms of magick. That is where I have seen those banished from this world, that have bled and died to return. That dark lineage continued, until the day Charles Maison questioned the past, desperate for the future. Now, here you are..."

"You knew my father," Pavan stated, the words heavy with unspoken pain.

Sanna's hand stilled, her gaze lifting to meet his. "He was troubled, consumed by questions I could not answer. In his loneliness, he was drawn to a dark magick, one that took him to a place I could not reach beyond the barriers of blood magick."

Pavan's hand stilled hers on the rose bush, his heart tightening. "He's still in Jorn... but he didn't recognize me."

Sanna's expression darkened, her hand slipping from his grasp. "Magick siphoning is a soul shattering act. To feed off another, power leads to an insatiable hunger—a hunger that devours the soul. It will kill him, if it hasn't already."

Pavan's voice shook as he whispered, "He's done terrible things. He killed Beaumont."

Sanna said nothing, her focus returning to her work, the silence heavy between them. Pavan's mind raced, the anger building within him, hot and uncontrollable.

"Why am I really here?" he demanded, his voice laced with frustration.

Sanna looked up, her milky eyes piercing through his anger. "That is for you to discover, Pavan. Your journey brought you here. When you're ready, you'll understand why."

The hot flash of anger surged through Pavan, his body tensing as he straightened. He scoffed, the sound bitter and sharp.

"This makes you angry," Sanna observed, her voice calm, but Pavan couldn't meet her gaze. "Your destiny will be laid out before you, but it must come to you when you're ready. To know too soon would alter the path that is meant for you."

Pavan closed his eyes, trying to reign in the fury that burned within him. It raged like a wildfire, threatening to consume him. He clenched his fists, nails digging into his palms as he fought to contain it. Slowly, he released his grip, letting the anger flow out of him like a river finding its course.

But as he opened his eyes, he saw the rose bush before him blackened, its vibrant life withering under the weight of his emotions. It crumbled to ash, a victim of his uncontrolled magick. Tears welled in his eyes as the guilt crushed him.

He ran, his feet carrying him through the garden and away from her. The farther he went, the more the anger and grief ebbed, replaced by a deep exhaustion. He stopped abruptly in a field of lavender, the purple blooms swaying gently in the breeze. The scent filled his senses, calming the storm within him.

Pavan reached out, his hand brushing against the soft petals, and for the first time in days, he breathed easily. The garden's embrace soothed his spirit, the peace he found in its depths a balm to his wounded heart.

# CHAPTER

## 14

P AVAN ENTERED THE SMALL dining room with a cautious step, his eyes searching for Sanna, but instead, they landed on the tall elf with a calm demeanor. The elf, dressed in a dark embroidered jacket, radiated a composed authority that immediately unsettled Pavan. The subtle kindness in his expression only deepened Pavan's sense of unease.

"You look well," the elf said, his voice carrying a gentleness that contrasted sharply with the tension in the room.

Pavan hesitated, unsure how to respond. "You are called Mihrk," he finally stated, watching as the elf continued setting out the silverware with a meticulous hand. "Sanna calls you another name, but I have seen your likeness in a Tome of Naems." The single place setting of such fine quality struck Pavan as odd in the bare dining room, cold and stagnant.

"It is a name given to me by the elders of my people in Taudren," Mihrk replied smoothly, his movements deliberate as he retrieved two glasses from the sideboard. "Does my name trouble you, my lord?"

Pavan's stare hardened. "It's not your name that concerns me," he said, his voice edged with suspicion. "It's your kinship."

Mihrk paused, meeting Pavan's gaze with his own steady, violet eyes. "You speak of the daughters of Larissa?"

At the mention of Lilja's family name, a jolt shot through Pavan, tightening his throat as memories of betrayal and loss surged within him. Those violet eyes, so hauntingly like hers, made his heart pound with a storm of anger and confusion.

"I was there when she fled," Mihrk said quietly, his voice carrying the weight of old regrets. "I ran with her, away from the vows and the life she was bound to. I thought I could keep her safe, but the roads were treacherous. Somewhere in the forests beyond Kastrien... I lost her."

Pavan's breath caught, his voice sharp and accusing despite the tremor beneath it. "You helped her escape... and then you let her vanish? She was only twelve years old."

Mihrk's eyes softened, though his gaze did not falter. "I searched until my feet bled, until I could no longer tell one path from another but Lilja was gone. I was given passage aboard a ship bound for Corad." He drew a slow breath, as if steadying himself. "Now she resides in Tauf, with what remains of Ledenjour."

The confirmation hit Pavan like a blow, leaving him feeling both foolish and unmoored. A lump rose in his throat, his emotions twisting into a tangled web of hurt, betrayal, and something far more complicated.

"Come, sit, my lord. We have much to accomplish today," Mihrk urged, pulling out the chair where the place setting awaited.

Pavan's resistance flared up. "I am not your lord, Mihrk. And I am certainly not hungry." His arms crossed over his chest, a physical barrier between him and the elf.

Mihrk's demeanor remained serene. "My lord shall sit, for the food that has been provided."

Pavan rolled his eyes, stubbornly holding his ground. "I'm not playing this game."

"My lord shall sit, for the food that—"

"Alright!" Pavan snapped, his frustration boiling over as he stomped towards the chair. But as he moved to sit, the chair slipped from beneath him, sending him crashing to the floor with a loud thud. Pain shot through him as he cursed loudly, glaring up at Mihrk who stood placidly nearby.

"My lord shall sit, for the food that has been provided," Mihrk repeated, his tone unchanged.

Pavan's anger surged, his fists clenching as he forced himself to his feet. He was furious, yet Mihrk remained unaffected, simply setting the chair upright again. The elf's calmness only fueled Pavan's rage, but with a deep breath, Pavan forced himself to sit with a calm effort, this time without incident.

As Pavan reached for his glass, a sharp slap landed on his hand, stinging his skin and shocking him into silence. He gasped, cradling his hand as he stared wide eyed at Mihrk.

"My lord shall wait to be served," Mihrk said, his voice gentle but firm.

"I am not a child!" Pavan bellowed, his magick stirring beneath his skin, itching to be released.

Ignoring the outburst, Mihrk filled the glass with a red liquid that fizzed lightly, then bowed his head. "My lord shall drink."

Pavan's fury was a storm within him, yet he took the glass with careful hands, his eyes never leaving Mihrk. The elf, as composed as ever, turned away to retrieve a serving dish, revealing a cut of lamb, its center still blood red. The sight made Pavan's stomach twist with nausea.

"My lord shall take small portions," Mihrk instructed, presenting the dish.

Pavan's hand shook, a wave of revulsion rising in his throat. "I cannot eat that," he whispered, the thought of consuming it utterly repulsive.

Mihrk, unbothered by Pavan's distress, responded calmly, "This is your favorite meal after an illness."

"I am in no mood for your games," Pavan snarled, pushing himself from the chair, desperate to escape the twisted scene. But before he could take more than two steps, he was forcefully thrown to the ground, the impact driving the air from his lungs.

"My lord is not well enough to fight," Mihrk declared, his tone steady as he watched Pavan struggle to rise.

"Stop calling me that!" Pavan roared, his frustration spilling over as he lashed out. "I am not your lord! I am Pavan!"

"My lord shall sit, for the food that has been provided," Mihrk repeated, his voice a steady drumbeat in the chaos of Pavan's mind.

Something inside Pavan broke then, the absurdity of the situation driving him to the brink. With a shaky breath, he straightened, his eyes meeting Mihrk's with a mix of defiance and weary resignation. "Very well, I shall play your stupid lord," he spat, his voice cold and drained. "Get out of my sight."

Mihrk did not budge. "My lord is not well. You must sit and eat to gain strength."

"What is happening here, Mihrk?" Pavan demanded, the exhaustion seeping into his bones. "You wish to infuriate me, well here I am, infuriated. You can beat me, bruise me, but I will not yield to this absurdity."

Mihrk's gaze was steady, unyielding. "My lord shall remain in his lessons."

"Lessons?" Pavan echoed, the word striking a chord of dread within him.

"My lord shall remain here in his lessons," Mihrk repeated, his voice firm. "I am trained to fight by the highest ranks of my people. I cannot be swayed by your magick, nor tempted by any force. That is why I was chosen for this task by Sanna."

"You are my instructor… for what purpose?" Pavan's head throbbed, the ache intensifying with every word.

"My lord is to be tested," Mihrk replied, his tone final as he placed a hand on the back of the chair once more. "It will be clear in time. For now, you must sit."

Pavan's resolve faltered as the gravity of the situation bore down on him. With a heavy heart, he sank back into the chair, his mind a whirlwind of questions and doubts. Whatever this test was, it had already begun, and Pavan was ensnared, powerless to resist.

"You have the strength to resist my magick," Pavan observed, his eyes narrowing as Mihrk served him a small portion of the bloodied lamb. "You were also raised in the religion of Taudren."

Mihrk's smile was simple and unwavering. "I was trained since birth to serve the high priests. Like Lilja, I was destined to become a servant for the greater magicks of this realm. But unlike Lilja, my trial was complete by the age of fifteen."

As Pavan watched the elf's methodical movements, placing steamed vegetables onto his plate, adding a small crust of bread, and arranging fruits on a platter, he couldn't help but notice the grace with which Mihrk performed each task. The elf was elegant and slender, but Pavan knew that beneath the narrow cut of his garments lay a man built for power and strength.

His thoughts wandered to the markings of those devoted to the Taudren religion, the lines carved into their skin for every year of service. He had seen those marks on Lilja, faint yet unmistakable, when she had allowed him glimpses of her body. Pavan wondered if Mihrk bore similar scars beneath his clothing.

Mihrk's smirk caught Pavan's wandering gaze, and a blush crept onto Pavan's cheeks.

"How did you come to serve Sanna?" Pavan asked, his tone pointed. "You are a long way from Taudren and your priesthood."

"I was sent to Rhun at the behest of Lahrs, to serve a greater purpose," Mihrk replied calmly. "My journey led me to Sanna's care. Since then, my time in Rhun has been in service to the great family of Enzo."

Pavan scoffed. "To become a slave of a duke?"

"I am my own master, my lord," Mihrk responded, his voice firm. "Just as you are the master of your destiny. But before you can step into the greatness Ehnarea has blessed upon your path, you must learn to be among kings."

Mihrk's words hung in the air, a challenge and an expectation as he stood, watching Pavan with the full plate before him, waiting for him to begin.

A chill ran up Pavan's spine. "I am not meant for greatness," he whispered, more to himself than to Mihrk.

"In good time, my lord."

Pavan moved through the dim corridors, his mind clouded with thoughts he couldn't quite grasp. The pull of the pool was too strong to resist, so when he finally arrived, he didn't hesitate. His fingers moved almost mechanically, stripping away his clothes, leaving them in a careless heap at the water's edge. He stepped into the cold, still water, feeling the icy sting as it closed around his legs, up his torso, until he could go no further. With a sigh, he let himself fall back, floating on the surface, staring up at the mural painted high above him. The artistry was exquisite, the colors and shapes merging into a scene so mesmerizing that it seemed to reach out and pull him into its depths.

His breathing slowed, and the familiar hum of his magick began to swirl around him, mingling with the water, brushing against his skin like a gentle caress. The tension in his body ebbed away, replaced by a calm that was almost foreign to him. As he drifted, the line between wakefulness and dreams blurred, and the world began to shift.

He heard it then, the sound of waves crashing in the distance, a rhythmic pounding that grew louder and louder until he could almost taste the salt in the air. The pool was gone, replaced by the soft sands beneath his feet. Pavan looked out over the endless expanse of ocean, the water glistening under a sky that was both familiar and strange. The tide lapped at his feet, cool and insistent, urging him forward, drawing him deeper into the dreamscape.

She had come to him before, this dark haired girl, a figure who haunted his dreams, and whom he had banished time and time again. But tonight, something was different. He could feel his mind and body reaching for her, a yearning he couldn't suppress. His resolve faltered, and he found himself turning toward the shore, where her voice, soft and soothing, called out to him.

Pavan followed the sound, his steps quickening as he ascended an embankment, his eyes scanning the vast fields of lavender that stretched out before him. But beyond the flowers, the sky shimmered, a curtain of magick hanging between his seaside and something else, something unknown but achingly familiar. It was a doorway, he realized, a portal to the source of the voice that tugged at his heart. Without hesitation, he stepped through.

The scene shifted, and Pavan found himself standing on smooth marble, his bare feet registering the cool, solid surface beneath them. He was dressed in black silk, his form almost a shadow in this place that existed between reality and dreams. The castle around him was grand, sunlight streaming through tall, arched windows, casting long beams that danced on the floor yet there was no one here. He hadn't expected there to be, but the connection he felt was undeniable, that thread of magick pulling him forward.

He moved through the castle, his fingers grazing the stone walls, tracing the curves and dips in the ancient architecture. The magick here was alive, warm and inviting, and it wrapped around him as he ascended a grand staircase. The large doors at the end of a long corridor beckoned him, and with a deep breath, he pushed them open.

The chamber was bathed in sunlight, the air filled with the scent of lavender and the gentle rustling of gossamer curtains that danced in a breeze he couldn't feel. Pavan's breath caught in his throat as his gaze landed on her, the source of the connection.

Her faie form was ethereal, the sunlight casting a golden glow on her long, onyx curls that cascaded down her back. Her skin, warm and olive toned, shimmered beneath the rich burgundy silk of her gown, the fabric wrapping around her in a way that seemed to defy gravity. She turned slowly, and when her eyes, golden and as radiant as the sun, met his, Pavan felt his heart stop.

She was beautiful, achingly so, but it was more than that. Her kindness, her inherent goodness, radiated from her, drawing him in like a moth to a flame. He wanted to stay in this moment forever, to lose himself in her presence, but he knew that this connection, this fragile thread of magick, would not hold for long.

*"Brendolyn,"* he breathed, the name carrying with it a weight that both pained and elated him. To be so drawn to her was a torment, yet he couldn't resist. Her gaze softened as she looked at him, her confusion melting into recognition.

"I am dreaming," she said softly, her voice like a balm to his weary soul as she moved toward him.

Pavan couldn't help but smile, his hand lifting to meet hers as their palms touched. The contact sent a jolt of fire through him, and he looked up, meeting her gaze with a mixture of wonder and fear. "Yes, this is a dream," he confirmed, his voice barely above a whisper. The sound of her voice, the feel of her touch, it was all too real, too intoxicating.

"Pavan," she whispered his name like a prayer, her other hand coming to rest on his cheek, the coolness of her touch grounding him in this surreal moment. Her expression shifted to one of relief, and before he could process what was happening, she had thrown her arms around him, pulling him close, holding him as if she might never let go.

The warmth of her embrace was almost too much to bear. He hesitated, his arms hovering awkwardly before they finally wrapped around her, returning the embrace. For a moment, he allowed himself to surrender to the comfort she offered, to the sense of belonging that had always eluded him.

"Pavan," she whispered again, looking up at him.

His breath was taken, and when he looked down at her, she reached up to caress his cheek, placing a gentle kiss upon his lips. Her lips tasted of warmed spices and honey, something so delicately sweet it made Pavan shiver with delight.

Deepening the kiss, Brendolyn drew him closer, desperate for his touch.

But then he felt the pull, the magick that was drawing him back. Reluctantly, he broke the embrace, holding her at arm's length, his eyes searching hers as he tried to memorize every detail. Those golden eyes, so full of life, pierced through him, making the impending separation all the more painful.

"Do you have to leave so soon?" she asked, her voice tinged with sadness as her brows furrowed.

Pavan didn't want to go, he wanted to stay in this moment, but the magick was insistent, tugging at him, pulling him away. He reached up, his thumb gently brushing her cheek. "I will return soon," he promised, his voice thick with emotion. He leaned in, pressing a tender kiss to her hairline, savoring the feel of her beneath his lips.

Brendolyn nodded, her eyes filled with a longing that mirrored his own. And then, just as quickly as it had begun, the magick snapped him back to reality.

Pavan gasped as he emerged from the water, his body trembling as he stood in the pool, the chill of the night air biting at his bare skin. He was near the edge now, the darkness pressing in around him, his heart unraveling with each breath. The connection, the longing, the desire that had flowed between them was all too much, too intense. He felt raw, exposed, and so terribly wrong.

He dressed quickly, the dampness of his clothes clinging to his skin as he moved through the corridors, his thoughts a tangled mess. He walked until he found himself standing in the doorway of a chamber lit only by the soft glow of candles.

"You cannot sleep either?" Sanna's voice broke through the fog in his mind, and he looked up to see her seated near the fireplace, a book in her hand, the cat curled up in her lap.

Pavan said nothing as he walked toward her, each step heavier than the last. The weight of his magick, the burden of his power, pressed down on him, threatening to crush him. In the dreamscape, he had been light, free from the torment that now consumed him. But here, in the real world, he was drowning. When he reached Sanna, he couldn't hold it in any longer. He fell to his knees before her, tears welling up in his eyes, his hands trembling as he laid them on her lap.

"Take my magick," he pleaded, his voice barely a whisper, thick with desperation. The cat jumped away as Sanna placed her book aside, her milky eyes focused solely on him.

"I cannot," she said gently, her hands closing over his, guiding them into fists. Her refusal was firm, but not unkind.

Pavan broke, the tears he had held back for so long finally spilling over as he bowed his head. "Every moment is agony," he wept, his voice shaking with the force of his emotions. "There is a storm within me, a darkness that I cannot control. It consumes me... I've hurt so many people..." The regret was all too much to bear.

Sanna's grip tightened on his wrists, her voice unwavering as she whispered, "You are strong, Pavan."

But he shook his head, the weight of his despair almost too much to bear. "I don't want this," he admitted, the words cutting deep into his soul. "I just want to be free... free of the pain, the regret... I've spent so many years in silent anguish." His voice faltered, cracking as he fought against the tears. "It was my fault... all of it. I was the key, and I couldn't control it."

Sanna's hands moved to cradle his face, lifting his gaze to hers. "You were just a child," she reminded him, her voice tender.

Pavan sniffled, tears streaming down his cheeks as he whispered, "There is nothing but darkness and pain in the wake of who I am, Sanna. My ancestors' history is dark, and I've followed in their footsteps." His voice vibrated with the weight of his guilt and self-loathing. "This world would be better off without me."

Sanna shook her head, her voice imbued with a gentle strength. "This world is better *because* of you." She wiped away his tears with a delicate touch. "I have watched you grow into a good man."

"I've done so many terrible things," Pavan confessed, his voice fluttering as he faced the harsh reality of his past. "I took Sophie's soul, and the Vohlgrum's in the forest... by my very existence, the lives of those in Eir are reduced to ash. I couldn't save Arienne, whose body blazed in the cathedral. Thad..."

A choked sob tore from his chest, his grief erupting uncontrollably as he clung to Sanna's skirts.

"My will is that of a monster," he rasped, the words laced with unbearable despair.

Sanna stroked his cheek, her gaze filled with warmth and understanding. "You are not a monster, Pavan. You are not the sins of your father, but a victim who has risen from the ashes of the pyre that sought to consume you. Do not let the darkness besiege your heart. Do not let the darkness win."

His voice was barely a whisper as he admitted, "I couldn't save my mother. I couldn't save my family from my father's wrath. He was hitting her that night, and I couldn't stop him. They are all gone, and I am so alone. I don't want to be alone."

Sanna drew him into her embrace, holding him tightly as the dam within him finally broke. His sobs were raw, unguarded, and a release long overdue. Her gentle touch smoothed back the dark hair that now clung to the tears that wet his cheeks.

"You are not alone," she broke the silence with her gentle words. "Nor are you the cause of their fate. It was by your fathers own hands that he has chosen to be consumed by darkness."

"He was here, I can feel it in the walls, Sanna. My father has been the ruin of this world, there is so much blood."

# CHAPTER

## 15

*City of Corad, Realm of Corad. Summer.*

IT HAD BEEN SEVERAL weeks since Pavan had graced her dreams, leaving Brendolyn longing for his presence each night. Yet, each morning she awoke to find her yearning unfulfilled, the dreams a fleeting fracture.

The summer had burst into Corad in a riot of colors and festivals, painting the city in vibrant hues. Still, Brendolyn remained ensconced within the sanctuary of her chambers. From the shade of her balcony, she watched the world dance in the sun's golden embrace yet ventured no further than the cool confines of the library. Her brief forays into the garden were accompanied by Elsa, and even these rare excursions seldom lasted beyond half an hour.

On one particularly sun drenched day, Elsa found Brendolyn ensconced in the library, seated in a sunlit alcove. The princess had a book resting in her lap, but her gaze was fixed dreamily out of the window, her thoughts clearly adrift.

"Gardener Hardon told me the plums are ripe for picking," Elsa remarked cheerfully, hoping to rouse Brendolyn from her reverie.

Brendolyn's eyes remained distant, even as Elsa's hand gently touched her arm. The princess jolted at the contact, the book slipping from her lap, and her cheeks flushing a delicate shade of pink.

"Sorry," Elsa said softly as she settled into the seat beside her.

Brendolyn closed her book with a sigh and looked up at Elsa, offering a half-hearted smile.

"Are you alright?" Elsa asked, her voice tinged with concern. Brendolyn had increased her seclusion and the distant, tearful glances had not gone unnoticed.

In response, Brendolyn extended a hand, passing Elsa an unsealed letter with a familiar, elegant script. Elsa's heart sank as she took the letter, a deep sigh escaping her lips.

"He has written again," Elsa observed, unfolding the letter with a resigned air. It was the third letter from Barrow, and each time, Brendolyn had chosen silence over response.

"*Forgive me, my darling... let me right the wrongs of my conduct when we last met. I cannot live in this world knowing I have wronged you, knowing every moment apart from you brings me closer to despair...*" Elsa stopped reading aloud, looking to Brendolyn, who was absently playing with the ribbon that still clung around her neck.

Elsa scoffed. "He speaks only of his own appeasement. How does he expect you to forgive him... after he struck you?"

Brendolyn took the letter, pointing to a passage at the bottom.

"*I have written to your father, asking for his blessing that I may pursue your hand in marriage.*" Elsa rolled her eyes. "Is he really so stupid? He cannot marry until he is thirty, unless he only wishes to marry Lisetta." There is a long pause. "So, it is true then... now that there is heraldry in Augusta, you will be receiving letters from suitors?"

Sighing, Brendolyn nodded. "*He shall try.*"

"Barrow doesn't stand a chance. Your father will certainly decline him, there are plenty of other suitors that are far better qualified." Elsa sighed, looking over the letter again. The same proclamations of love, the same desperation of returning to Brendolyn's favor.

Brendolyn returned to look out the window, while her fingers gently touched the tattered ribbon around her neck.

"Shall I call for tea, it must be past noon already." Elsa stood, tucking the letter in the front fold of the book between them.

Brendolyn made no response.

Barrow paced the length of the grand chamber, his footsteps echoing off the marble floors like the beating of a frantic heart. His mind churned with dark thoughts, each one more twisted than the last. Where was Pavan? Why hadn't he surfaced? Every shadow seemed to mock him with the possibilities—betrayal, failure, disaster.

His eyes, once sharp and calculating, now glimmered with a wildness that betrayed the paranoia festering within him. He clenched his fists, nails digging into his palms as if the pain could ground him, but it was no use. The more he tried to find reason, the more his thoughts spiraled into chaos.

"Eero," Barrow snapped, turning sharply to face the tall, stoic man who had been watching him with a growing concern. "We must find him. I want every inch of Rhun searched. He cannot have gone far."

Eero hesitated, his brow furrowing. He had served Barrow long enough to recognize the signs of a mind on the brink. "Barrow," he began carefully, "perhaps it would be wise to consult the counsel. They could offer—"

"The counsel?" Barrow interrupted, his voice dripping with contempt. "Those fools have done nothing but hinder us. They lack the vision, the strength to do what is necessary."

"But Barrow," Eero persisted, though his voice softened with the weight of his concern, "they could offer valuable insights, resources that we may not—"

"Enough!" Barrow's voice boomed, silencing him. His eyes narrowed, and for a moment, the madness within them flickered dangerously close to the surface. "I will not be surrounded by cowards and weaklings. They will only sow doubt and undermine our efforts. No, Eero, I need someone I can trust."

"And that is Bannon, I assume?" Eero asked, though he already knew the answer. The name left a bitter taste in his mouth. He had seen the way Bannon's influence had grown, how he whispered poison into Barrow's ear, twisting his mind further from reason.

Barrow's expression softened at the mention of Bannon, a disturbing calm washing over him. "Bannon understands what needs to be done. He is the only one who sees the true path forward."

Eero's heart sank. "But he has persuaded you to remove half the counsel. Men and women who have served this kingdom with loyalty and wisdom. What if—"

"What if they were the ones who were plotting against me all along?" Barrow's voice was low, almost a whisper, as if he were sharing a secret with the shadows. "Bannon has shown me their true colors. They would see me fail, see this kingdom fall. I cannot allow that."

Eero knew there was no reasoning with him in this state, no pulling him back from the brink. The paranoia had taken root, and Bannon had nurtured it, shaping Barrow's fears into weapons of distrust and isolation.

Eero took a deep breath, steadying himself. "As you wish," he said, his voice heavy with resignation. "But you cannot storm Rhun, without breaking the contract and starting a war we have no hopes of succeeding."

"Rhun cannot keep Pavan hidden from me."

"You must not go to war for one man. Think of the people of Jorn, think of those you have already slaughtered in Eir for the sake of this path."

Barrow waved him off, already lost in his own thoughts, his mind a battleground of suspicions and fears. Eero watched him for a moment longer, his heart heavy with the knowledge that the man before him was slipping further away with each passing day, becoming a pawn in a game he barely understood.

As Eero turned to leave, he couldn't shake the feeling that they were all standing on the edge of an abyss, with Barrow being led straight into it by the very man that had taken everything from him.

# CHAPTER

## 16



Y OU KNOW HOW TO fight," Mihrk said, his voice echoing in the long gallery.

The room had been cleared, leaving a wide, open space in the center. Pavan's gaze was fixed on the elf, who stood before him with an air of calm confidence. Mihrk wore a soft, billowy shirt and a dark leather vest over well-tailored trousers that ended just below his knees, exuding a casual yet commanding presence.

"I was taught to fight in Ledenjour," Pavan replied, his tone steady.

"Excellent," Mihrk said with a triumphant smile, extending his arms wide in a gesture of invitation. "Strike me where I stand, my lord."

Pavan's lips twisted into a scowl. "I will not strike you."

"You are afraid that you might hurt me, when I've already made it clear that your magick is no match for—"

"I will not strike a man who has not harmed me and who clearly wishes for me to do so," Pavan interrupted, crossing his arms tightly over his chest. He felt the leather of his jacket constricting around his shoulders, a physical reminder of his restraint. "Do not expect me to yield."

"You are holding your anger," Mihrk said, his voice calm yet probing.

Pavan's jaw tightened, his eyes burning with disdain as he stared into Mihrk's insufferable violet eyes. Despite the elf's seeming innocence, Pavan's resentment toward him was palpable, a lingering pain that seemed unjust but undeniable.

"I am not angry," Pavan lied, his temple throbbing with suppressed emotion.

Mihrk stepped closer, his proximity unnerving. He placed a hand on the flat of Pavan's stomach, causing Pavan to flinch instinctively. When he attempted to step back, Mihrk's hold moved to grip Pavan's hip, rendering him immobile.

"I can feel your anger, Pavan," Mihrk said, his voice a low murmur that sent shivers down Pavan's spine. "Your magick is bottled up with nowhere to go."

"The destruction would flatten this ancient cathedral," Pavan warned, his voice taut with the weight of his power.

Mihrk's smile deepened, a playful glimmer warming his violet eyes. He stepped closer, his hands firmly gripping Pavan's hips, drawing him into an intimate proximity. "Perhaps I shall draw that anger from you," he suggested, his voice low and enticing.

Pavan's throat tightened, his magick swirling ominously within him. "You do not know what you are saying, Mihrk. Do not speak of magick you do not understand," he warned, his hands clenched into tight fists as he struggled to contain his reaction to Mihrk's firm grasp and gentle touch.

"I understand well," Mihrk replied, placing a hand on Pavan's shoulder, his touch both reassuring and unsettling. "Do you think Lilja was the only one capable of withstanding your magick?"

A shuddering gasp escaped Pavan's lips, the weight of Mihrk's words sinking in.

"You cannot ask to bind yourself to me," Pavan breathed, the air around them crackling with a charged energy that mingled with the scent of fresh fern, a clean, vibrant aroma that contrasted with the heat of Mihrk's touch.

"I am unmarked, Pavan," Mihrk whispered, his voice a soothing murmur. "I do not need a bond to quell your magick. All I need is your permission, and my body shall be yours. Your magick may shake the mountains, but it will never break me. Until the day your fate finds its destiny and your markings quiet, I shall be your conduit."

Pavan seized the opportunity to catch Mihrk off guard, delivering a swift strike that sent the elf reeling back. Mihrk's expression was a mix of surprise and delight, his dark hair falling over his face, adding an unexpected touch of mirth to his features. The look in his violet eyes was both a challenge and a promise, sending shivers down Pavan's spine.

"You wish to tame me," Pavan said, his voice edged with a hint of a smile as he assumed a fighting stance, "but you've forgotten to take down your guard."

Mihrk chuckled, regaining his balance with an agile grace. He moved with the fluidity of a dancer, dodging Pavan's thrusts and swipes with ease. Bending his lithe frame into a crouch, he spun and struck with a powerful kick to Pavan's chest. Pavan caught the foot midair, a predatory smile spreading across his face as he twisted Mihrk's leg, sending him crashing to the wooden floor with a resounding thud.

Heavy breaths filled the room, mingling with the intoxicating scent of exertion and sweat. Pavan's adrenaline surged as he lunged forward, his movements driven by a fierce excitement. Mihrk sprang to his feet, ready to engage again. Pavan pressed him, his strikes relentless, forcing Mihrk back until there was barely any room left to maneuver.

"You fight with incredible passion." Mihrk laughed, landing a blow to Pavan's side that made him wince.

Pavan retaliated with a fierce counter, causing Mihrk to stagger, gasp and clutch his own side. "Flattery will not distract me," Pavan growled, narrowly avoiding Mihrk's next punch and delivering a hard uppercut. Mihrk caught his wrist, his gaze steady and intense.

"Your fighting style is precise," Mihrk remarked, his voice a mix of admiration and regret. "Your teacher must have been skilled. But you're letting your magick lag behind. Use it to your advantage."

Seizing the moment of hesitation, Mihrk's leg shot out, kicking Pavan back with such force that he nearly lost his footing. Glaring at the elf, who was now brushing his fallen hair from his face, Pavan felt the room grow stifling. Sweat coated Mihrk's well defined arms, and Pavan's jacket seemed to constrict him further. He longed to tear it off, desperate for freedom as his magick grew tighter.

"Enough," Pavan said, his voice strained, pushingback his damp hair. "I tire of this lesson."

Mihrk approached once more, his presence close and unyielding. This time, his touch was gentler, his hand resting on Pavan's hip with a delicate patience. Pavan swallowed hard, feeling his strength wane. Mihrk, who was keenly aware of this, slipped an arm around the small of Pavan's back, their faces inches apart. Pavan could see flecks of gold in Mihrk's violet eyes, the intensity of their proximity making his pulse race.

"My lord," Mihrk murmured with a knowing smile, his breath warm against Pavan's skin. "You would not tire so easily if you weren't clinging to the magick that festers within."

Pavan shivered, his voice barely a whisper. "It's impossible."

Mihrk's smile widened as he gently traced his fingers along Pavan's cheek. "There is no heart in it, my lord, only duty. Let me bear the burden for you."

His lips grazed Pavan's jaw, trailing along the curve of his neck, savoring the taste of his skin. Pavan couldn't suppress a groan, his hands gripping Mihrk's shoulders as his magick twisted desperately in his gut. He felt a profound sense of vulnerability, caught between the raw need to escape and the seductive lure of Mihrk's touch.

It was a different sensation from being with Lilja, whose magick had clouded his senses like an intoxicating haze. Mihrk's presence was vivid and electrifying, his touch full of passion that beckoned Pavan to surrender. Desperate for release, Pavan allowed his head to fall back, his fingers tangling in Mihrk's dark hair, completely absorbed in the hot kisses that traced his sweaty skin.

Mihrk's hands deftly worked at the front of Pavan's jacket, pushing aside the heavy material to reveal the billowy shirt clinging to his perspiring body. As the jacket fell away, Mihrk eagerly pushed aside the shirt, worshipping Pavan's skin with hot kisses, lost in the intimate embrace. The world outside seemed to vanish, leaving only the heated connection between them.

When Mihrk's firm fingers began to grasp at the laces of Pavan's trousers, his eyes flew open in alarm. "Wait," he said, his voice strained as he gripped Mihrk's wrists. "Perhaps we should bathe first." They both reeked of sweat, but Mihrk merely smiled, pressing a searing kiss to Pavan's mouth.

A fiery longing surged within Pavan, stoked by the blazing desire and magick that simmered in his veins. He tasted the sharp tang of longing on Mihrk's lips, surrendering to the overwhelming desire as Mihrk began to unlace the front of his trousers. The elf's kisses traveled down Pavan's chin, his throat, and he sank to his knees before him in the center of the room.

Pavan's magick roared to be released as Mihrk's lips made contact with the tender skin of his hip. A moan escaped Pavan's lips, his hands gripping Mihrk's shoulders as he reached for the dark fall of Mihrk's hair. The elf's mouth hovered dangerously close to the restraints of Pavan's trousers, his smile a mix of desire and the raw, magnetic force of magick that tingled at the tips of his fingers.

*Let go.*

The whisper echoed in Pavan's ear, a breath of sound that seemed to resonate with the deepest parts of him. He clung to Mihrk's hair as the elf's hot mouth enveloped him, sending waves of satisfaction through his tense body. Each slow, deliberate movement unraveled the tight coils of tension, and the intensity of Pavan's magick grew hotter with every breath. The pounding of his heart and the roaring of his magick became a tempest, a furnace like heat that surged through him.

Pavan gripped Mihrk's shoulders desperately, his entire being quivering with the force of the release. A rush of crashing waves filled his ears, and his magick spilled out, surrendering completely to the overwhelming passion.

As the storm within him began to calm, Pavan's breathing slowed. He felt his body easing back, the intensity fading into a serene afterglow. His grip on Mihrk's shoulders relaxed, and he blinked down at the elf's smiling face with a mix of exhaustion and relief.

Mihrk wiped his mouth with a satisfied smile, stood and straightened the front of Pavan's trousers. The wave of fatigue swept over Pavan, and he stumbled slightly as Mihrk guided him along the corridor to his small, familiar room. The room, a refuge from the chaos, promised comfort and retreat from the storm within.

In the small bed, Pavan found solace. The room was filled with the scent of the sea, a reminder of calm and freedom. As Mihrk carefully removed Pavan's boots and the damp shirt from his back, Pavan's eyes grew heavy. Mihrk's gentle touch smoothed his hair, and the elf's soothing voice offered a final command.

"Sleep," Mihrk murmured, his fingers caressing Pavan's hair before withdrawing.

As Pavan drifted off, he began to dream of the sea. His feet sank into warm, soft sand as he watched waves crash upon the shore. The calming sound of the ocean mingled with the song of a distant voice. At the top of a gentle hill, a figure stood, her onyx hair dancing with the wind. She reached out to him, but his feet remained rooted, unable to move toward her.

He watched her for a long time, her voice flowing through him like a soothing balm. The dreamscape began to blend with the quiet peace of slumber, and Pavan, comforted by the presence of the sea and the hauntingly beautiful figure, drifted further into deep, restorative sleep.

Pavan followed Sanna around the room, which was filled with plants and cages of insects. He carried her basket, keeping it within her reach as she worked. In the quiet moments between their tasks, he found himself reflecting on the time they had spent together in this way. He would help her brew remedies and potions, loading the wagon with the baskets for Mihrk to take back to Rhun.

"You've been calmer these past few weeks," Sanna said, glancing up at him with a soft smile as she placed a pod from a nearby plant into the basket.

Pavan felt his cheeks warm. "I've been reading the books you so graciously gave me."

Silence fell between them as Sanna continued to clip herbs from the potted plants. Her milky white eyes turned toward him, exuding a quiet calm that seemed to see right through him.

"Has Mihrk been helping you more?" she asked knowingly. "Teaching you proper etiquette and how to fight?"

"He has been a great help," Pavan replied, though his voice wavered as he looked away sharply, his heart racing.

"You mustn't feel ashamed of the relief Mihrk has given you in helping to control your magick. There is peace in knowing that he can fulfill his duty to you in a way no one else can."

Pavan fidgeted, the basket swinging slightly in his hands. "What is the purpose of my training? Beyond Mihrk's help with taming my magick. I know there's more to your plan in keeping me here."

"I've seen many futures, Pavan," Sanna began, her voice taking on a somber tone. "Just as I've seen many lives fall and wane in the face of the darkness spreading from the north, beyond the treacherous seas."

"You speak of my father?" Pavan asked, his voice tinged with anxiety.

"I speak of the power that feeds him," she replied, her words sending a chill through him. "There is a great awakening happening, one that could reshape all of Veilore. Your father has walked the path of darkness, becoming a doorway for Venora to truly rise to power."

Pavan paused, stunned. "Venora? The great witch who cursed Jorn centuries ago?"

"She survived the banishment that tore her soul apart. She has returned to the northern lands, and she has placed a powerful monster on the throne of Nyr, one that devours the magick of Ehnarea's children."

"And my father?" Pavan's voice lifted with uncertainty.

Sanna didn't answer immediately, instead she picked another pod from a plant. "Your father chose his path, to be a harbinger of darkness. He seeks the throne of the great kings of old, to bring about a war that would ravage the last free lands of magick. If he succeeds, he could purge every living soul blessed with magick, offering them to the monster. His power is growing... if he takes the blood of the girl, he will become unstoppable."

"Brendolyn?" Pavan asked, his concern deepening.

Sanna's grip on Pavan's hand tightened. "She is not as she seems, Pavan. Her bloodline is ancient, tied to the trees of the Veil. If your father discovers this, he will no longer need to siphon magick. He will awaken within himself the dormant magicks cursed upon your ancestors' lineage."

"You need me to kill Simeon Bannon?"

"No blade can kill him, and your magick is too weak to banish him to another realm," Sanna said, her voice reverent while her gaze drifted to the window where the shimmering ward protecting the cathedral rippled.

Pavan's voice softened to a whisper. "My destiny... I've been linked to Brendolyn from the beginning." The words of Arienne echoed in his mind as he touched the bare wrist where a ribbon once rested. "Sabian isn't her father, is he?"

A heavy silence filled the room as Sanna's milky eyes met his.

"Who is Brendolyn's father?" Pavan demanded, his mind racing. "I've felt her magick, it resonates with something deep inside me that I've never felt for another faie. Her blood is more than simple magick."

Sanna took the basket from Pavan's hands, holding them gently as a soft melody of magick thrummed between them. Pavan wanted to move back but found himself unable to look away from her milky white eyes.

"You are stronger than most, Pavan," she said with a smile, brushing a lock of dark hair out of his eyes. "Perhaps it is right for you to be the one to protect her after all."

"Protect Brendolyn? How can I do that?"

"You will become the strongest you've ever been. With the power you shall inherit, nothing can stop you from protecting the living breath of Eudes."

Pavan scoffed, pulling his hands away and frowning at Sanna. "You expect me to believe she's of the ancient elven line from the heart of the Veil? That's impossible—"

His words caught in his throat as the realization dawned on him. He looked out at the darkening sky beyond the shroud of their protection, then back at Sanna's patient gaze. His heart raced as the pieces fell into place.

"Lahrs is born of the ancient bloodline," he muttered. "That's why he's marrying the Duchess of Entheas, to purify the elven line."

Sanna touched his cheek gently. "Now you understand."

"Lahrs is Brendolyn's true father... he's broken the lineage to create a new magick of faie," Pavan said, feeling something writhe within him. "Hana was Athrun, of the old veilborn bloodline that was destroyed in Augusta."

Sanna nodded. "Together, they've created a new race of magick, stronger than anyone could have imagined. It was forbidden to cross the bloodlines, for fear of creating something too powerful to stop. Now you understand the dire necessity of your protection."

"Has my father discovered her power?" Pavan asked, his voice laced with urgency.

"Not yet," Sanna replied, shaking her head. "But there's little time before he does. Once he learns the truth, there will be no stopping him."

"I can't let any harm come to her... but she's so incredibly foolish. She's just a child."

Sanna chuckled softly. "Yes, Brendolyn is still a child, but she has already seen more of the world's horrors than most. Perhaps this is something you can reflect on in yourself. For you, too, were young when the horrors began on your own path."

Pavan frowned. "If I fail to save her..."

Sanna plucked two buds from the basket, offering one to Pavan. He held it between his fingers, staring at the closed bud, so small and quiet. Sanna held the other in her fingers.

"You are bound to her by the threads of fate, woven together by powers neither of you can see. Apart, your hearts will wither and decay in the darkness that is consuming our world. But together, you will become an unstoppable force."

"You're planning something," Pavan stated plainly. "That's why you are having me in lessons with Mihrk to become a lord. It won't work, Sanna. Lord Bannon shall see through any disguise, he has already felt my magick."

A sad sort of smile formed on Sanna's lips.

As she moved the buds closer together, Pavan watched in awe as the flowers bloomed, their velvety petals unfurling in a swirl of colors. The air filled with a calming, beautiful scent, and tears threatened to spill from his eyes as he watched the blooms pollinate, dancing with magick that swirled between them.

"You shall gain new magick, in time, Pavan. A magick that Simeon has never seen or felt. All this to protect Brendolyn, Pavan. To save the realms from darkness."

# CHAPTER

## 17

NIGHT PRESSED LOW OVER Denorn. Lanterns burned behind smoked glass, their light dull and amber, barely cutting through the chill that clung to the streets. Unlike Jorn's bright shops and city life, Denorn felt like a dull canvas beneath the fall of the cathedral. Ash had long since been washed away by heavy rains formed by the storms brought in from the sea.

Sir Eero reigned in his horse before the Wharmoth, an older inn and tavern that was far too close to the sea cliffs, that smelled of musty rainwater and was favoured by the lesser of those travelling into port. The letter had arrived two nights prior, sealed in unfamiliar wax and carried by a boy who vanished before Eero could ask his name. Now, dressed in unmarked leathers instead of his surcoat, Eero dismounted, handing his horse over to a stable boy.

Warmth and the scent of spiced ale washed over him as he entered through the door while conversation hummed low. He was still shaking the cold from his gloves when he saw Sir Lahrs standing near the large hearth, his silver hair bound neatly at his nape. Gone was the armor, the knight's bearing softened beneath layers of fine elven silk in dusk tones and pale silver thread. At his side stood a tall elven woman of striking presence.

Approaching them in such informality made Eero uneasy. Drawing little attention from the other patrons of the late hour, Eero gently coughed, breaking the quiet conversation Sir Lahrs held with the woman he stood beside. This close, Eero recognised her as the duchess of Tauf.

"Favor find you," Eero said, closing his fist over his heart as he bowed to them both.

"And keep you," Lahrs replied. "Let us take a seat."

It was quick that they procured a booth, tucked away at the back of the inn, hidden beneath a swaying lantern overhead. Eero slid into the bench opposite them, offering a polite smile to the woman beside Lahrs.

Duchess Kristjanna of Tauf was radiant even in Denorn's dim light, her pale hair woven into intricate plaits adorned with tiny shells and river stones that glimmered softly. Her lips curved in greeting, catching the candlelight like frost.

"Is it wise," Eero asked quietly, once a barmaid had set a mug of mead before him, "to meet so openly in Denorn?"

"There is no safer inn," Lahrs said evenly. "Wharmoth is well known to us on our travels."

Eero smiled faintly. "Your letter sounded… urgent."

"You've heard I am to be married."

"I have," Eero said, glancing again at Kristjanna. "My congratulations. Though, I believed the union was to wait until her father's passing. No offense meant."

Kristjanna laughed softly, laying her hand atop Eero's forearm. Rings gleamed on her long fingers, moon bright against his sleeve. "We believed so as well."

"The high elves in Tauf have convened," Lahrs said. "Particularly under pressure from one lord whose influence grows far too quickly in Jorn. With Barrow's succession to the throne, and the year before his coronation, the elves demanded stability—an heir, secured alliances, and visible strength."

Eero frowned. "So the wedding was hastened."

"To anchor the future," Kristjanna said gently. "You grasp matters quickly, Sir Eero."

He flushed faintly and drank.

"As you may also know," Lahrs continued, leaning in, "Sabian is drowning in petitions. Augusta's new heraldry has made it irresistible to those older families vying for a foothold in the royal courts."

"And any acceptance would require a powerful alliance," Eero said.

Lahrs nodded. "There are whispers that the duke of Rhun's son has sent a delegate with his own seal to King Sabian."

"Enzo?" Eero asked sharply. "There is little been said about the older families of Rhun since the War of Thourns."

"So did many," Lahrs said. "But there are still some who uphold the traditions of the ancient ways of the elves and faie in Rhun, and who would find it a benefit to bring Augusta into their hold again."

"Whatever Sabian choses, she will be married."

"She will," Lahrs said quietly. "But not Barrow. Sabian will not allow it."

A chill ran through Eero. He remembered the prince's letters—fevered, reverent, and unhinged with longing.

"Barrow is unraveling," Eero said carefully. "He trusts no one but Lord Bannon. He sees assassins where there are none. I've doubled the guard, but it worsens. Forgive me but, could this have begun before your return to Corad?"

Lahrs's eyes sharpened. "What do you mean?"

Eero hesitated. "He believes he struck Brendolyn. In anger. He's punished himself for it but I wonder if it was real or planted."

"There are many hands that might have guided his mind," Lahrs said darkly.

"But she is cursed," Eero pressed. "Elsa told me herself. Simeon silenced her."

"To ensure she remains so," Lahrs replied. "Brendolyn was present when Beaumont was killed."

Eero glanced around instinctively. The inn was half full, travelers murmuring over dice and drink.

"They cannot hear us," Lahrs said, faintly smiling. "Kristjanna ensures they hear only what they expect."

The duchess inclined her head, amused.

"I wouldn't know," Lahrs said quietly. "Brendolyn won't speak to me or Elsa. There's grief in her. Something festering."

"I've seen faie die of such loss," Eero added.

"That is merely the beginning," Lahrs said. "Many descend into madness. She is dying of a grief no one can mend." He leaned closer. "But there is something you can do."

"I will," Eero said at once.

"When Brendolyn marries, Elsa will be sent to Divna," Lahrs said, displeasure edging his voice. "It was the price Duke Laronn demanded. Once Brendolyn is wed, Elsa loses her protection, and in losing that protection Alaric has the chance to reclaim his hold upon her."

Eero felt the air leave his lungs.

Lahrs's expression was heavy. "I know that you have been closely acquainted with Elsa these past few years. You have come aware of her bond with that man."

"Yes," Eero said, but his heart became grave. "She will not accept my hand, Lahrs."

"I do not expect you to break your Vow. But I beg you consider it for her life, above all else in these darkened times."

Eero stood in the quiet stables of the inn, preparing for his departure to return to Jorn, his breath curling visibly in the crisp morning air. The rhythmic strokes of the brush against his horse's coat brought him fleeting comfort, the gentle rustle of hay beneath his boots grounding him in the present. Yet, his mind churned with unease, the tranquility of the early hour mocking the chaos within. He paused, his hand lingering against the horse's flank, and let his gaze wander over the stillness that enveloped the stable. It was calm—almost too calm—and the silence left him alone with thoughts he wished he could escape.

Fragments of another life gnawed at the edges of his mind, memories that felt like smoke, slipping through his fingers when he reached for them. As a young man, he'd known something different—laughter in grand halls, the sharp tang of steel as he sparred with an older knight, and the weight of a name he'd since forgotten. He had been more than a nameless soldier once, hadn't he? Yet the Field of Thorns had taken it all—his memory, his identity—leaving him with only a title and the emptiness that followed.

His chest tightened as flashes of the past came unbidden. A grand estate. A woman's voice calling his name with warmth. A crest embroidered on deep plum velvet. He clenched the brush, forcing himself back to the moment. Whatever life he'd lived before the battle, it was gone. He had no right to dwell on what might have been.

Eero set aside the brush, turning to retrieve the padding from the low workbench at the furthest end of the stable, but as he stepped through the shadowed archway, a figure emerged from the gloom. The woman stood with striking white hair that caught the dim light, her eerie, milky eyes fixed on him with unsettling clarity.

"Sir Eero," she said, her voice calm and deliberate.

He inclined his head in a respectful bow, though his instincts sharpened with caution. "I am," he replied evenly, standing alone with her in the stables. The woman seemed familiar, though he could not place her.

"You will receive my letter when the time is right," she continued, her words measured, her faint smile enigmatic.

Eero stiffened. There was something unsettling in her gaze, as if she saw through him, past the armor of his composure to the hollow place he carried within. "Do I know you?" he asked, his voice low but steady.

"You will remember," she said cryptically. "For now, know that *he* is with me and cared for."

The words struck Eero like a physical blow, his breath catching in his chest. Something stirred deep within him, recognition, fear, and hope tangled together. "You are Sanna?" he breathed, the name escaping him before he could think to stop it.

She nodded, her eerie appearance both mesmerizing and disquieting against the cold stone of the stables. Without another word, she turned and walked past him, her steps light and unhurried as though she carried no weight in the world.

Eero hesitated only a moment before he rushed after her, his pulse racing. He burst into the outer yard, his eyes darting over the misty chill of the ground blanketed in frost. But she was gone—vanished as though she had never been there at all.

The quiet returned, heavy and oppressive. Eero leaned against the stable door, his chest heaving, and stared out into the early morning light. The name *Sanna* echoed in his mind, pulling at threads of memory he couldn't quite unravel. The calm of the morning seemed cruel now, a mockery of the storm churning within him.

He must return to Jorn with haste.

Lahrs stood with his duchess in the grand hall of Jorn City, the polished marble floors reflecting the flickering light of the chandeliers above. The air was heavy with the scent of incense and the hum of quiet conversations. As they waited, a servant announced Prince Barrow's arrival, and the room fell silent.

Barrow entered, his presence commanding attention despite the underlying tension that clung to him. He approached Lahrs with a faint smile, extending a hand in greeting. "Congratulations on your marriage, Lahrs. The alliance with Tauf strengthens our ties."

Lahrs accepted the prince's hand with a nod. "Thank you, Your Highness. The union is indeed a blessing."

Barrow's expression softened, but a shadow crossed his eyes as he shifted the conversation. "And Brendolyn? How fares she?"

Lahrs hesitated for a moment before speaking. "She has not spoken a word since she left Jorn, Your Highness. She refuses to speak to anyone."

Barrow's brow furrowed in concern, his earlier composure wavering. "That troubles me deeply. Is there anything I can do to help her?"

Lahrs shook his head slowly. "She is grieving, and I fear it is a grief that no one can easily mend. She has isolated herself, retreating into her own sadness."

Barrow's worry deepened, his voice lowering. "I fear for her, Lahrs. The silence... it is unlike her."

Lahrs glanced at his duchess, who offered a reassuring smile before he turned back to Barrow. "She is strong, but this pain runs deep. Time may be the only remedy, but even that may not be enough."

The prince sighed, rubbing a hand over his face. "If there is anything, anything at all that I can do..."

Before Lahrs could respond, the conversation took a darker turn as Barrow's expression hardened. "There is another matter that has weighed heavily on me. Many of the council members have gone missing, some have been found dead."

Lahrs felt a chill run down his spine. "Missing? Dead? What do you believe is happening, Your Highness?"

Barrow's eyes narrowed, a flicker of fear and suspicion crossing his face. "I believe it to be the work of a traitor Pavan. I cannot trust anyone. Lord Bannon has his suspicions, but I fear he may be too eager to find a scapegoat. The disappearances... they are not coincidental."

Lahrs nodded, his mind racing with the implications. "This is grave news indeed, Your Highness. We must tread carefully."

Barrow clenched his fists, the tension in his voice palpable. "I won't let this go unanswered. The traitor will be found, and they will pay for their treachery."

Lahrs placed a hand on the prince's shoulder, offering what comfort he could. "We will find the truth, Barrow. Together, we will uncover who is behind this."

Barrow nodded, though his eyes betrayed the turmoil within him. "I pray we do, Lahrs. For all our sakes."

# CHAPTER

## 18



Y OU ARE WELL, *AMORE*?" Sabian asked, looking up at Brendolyn from behind his vast desk, which dominated the center of the room. His voice was gentle, but the concern in his eyes was unmistakable.

Brendolyn nodded, though her heart felt heavy.

Sabian offered a halfhearted smile, his gaze dropping to the letter in his hands. The names written on the parchment seemed to weigh heavily on him as well. "You are a duchess now, a birthright given to you by your mother's name..." His voice faltered, and Brendolyn swallowed hard, unable to find words in response. "Here are the first of many letters to come."

He stood, extending a hand toward her, holding letters sealed with the ribbons of bannermen from Jorn and even a few provinces of Corad. Each one represented a potential suitor, a future she hadn't yet imagined.

Brendolyn shook her head, a silent refusal.

"You must be married," Sabian said firmly, though his tone was tinged with regret. "I could choose from any of them, *amore*. I could choose whatever man holds the best offer."

She lowered her gaze, tears welling up in her eyes as she tried to swallow the lump in her throat.

Sabian sighed, the sound filled with resignation. "I give it to your hands, *amore...* please, take them."

Slowly, she looked up, meeting her father's gaze. Despite the pain in his eyes, she saw that he was not being cruel—he was trying to do what was best for her, even if it broke his heart.

"I give you the power to decide whom you marry. There are many, but there could be one who might protect your innocence...who might be good to you." Sabian's voice was soft as he placed the letters in her hands. The ribbons fluttered lightly in the breeze coming through the open balcony doors.

Tears streamed down her cheeks as she traced her fingers over the vibrant silks and expensive ribbons. The weight of her new reality pressed heavily on her chest, and she instinctively touched the ribbon around her neck, a silent reminder of what she was losing.

Sabian sighed again, his own heart clearly burdened. "If there were another way... but my hands are tied. The law of Jorn is much different from Corad. You *must* be married."

Brendolyn nodded, feeling a deep sense of resignation.

"Take your time, Brendolyn," Sabian said gently. "You do not need to answer them right away but read them over. Think of what is best for you. I will give my blessing to whomever you choose."

With a final nod, Brendolyn turned to leave, the letters clutched tightly in her hands, as she tried to find the strength to face the future that awaited her.

Brendolyn and Elsa sift through the stack of letters, growing more disheartened with each one. The suitors, all lords and dukes, were much older than Brendolyn—some by nearly twenty years or more. As frustration built, Brendolyn's eyes welled up with tears, and in a moment of anger, she swept the letters off her bed. They scattered across the floor, but one letter landed with a heavier thud that caught her attention.

It was unopened, its seal bearing a plain insignia, not adorned with any of the elaborate ribbons the others had. Curious, Brendolyn tore the seal away and read through the letter. She handed it to Elsa, her expression a mix of surprise and uncertainty.

"Rhun? I thought the duke was really old—oh…" Elsa trailed off as she noticed the title within the letter.

Brendolyn pointed out the detail, with a steady hand.

"His son and last living heir. Loren Enzo. He's closer to your age," Elsa noted, looking up at Brendolyn. She could see the distress in her friend's eyes as Brendolyn fidgeted with the ribbon around her neck.

"You will be married, Bren… if this is who you choose," Elsa said gently.

Brendolyn sat down heavily, her gaze falling on the small portrait that had come with the letter. The young man depicted was far more appealing than the older suitors. He had very light blonde hair, a strong jawline, and soft, fine eyes. Though she knew it was difficult to judge a person by a portrait alone, the likeness was enough to give her a glimmer of hope.

After Elsa retired to her chambers, Brendolyn remained in the library long into the night. She poured over the long lineages of all the great houses of Corad and Jorn, trying to make sense of the choices before her. It was late when Lisetta entered, her presence startling Brendolyn.

"Bren… still abiding by your vow?" Lisetta asked, her tone unusually bright and almost awkward. It wasn't a tone Brendolyn was used to hearing from her elder sister.

Brendolyn nodded silently, offering a shy smile.

Lisetta scanned the table, lifting a few papers as she took in the scene. Brendolyn knew her sister was aware of the new title gifted to her by the late king of Jorn.

"King Beaumont is a generous man… you must have made a true impression on him. I dare say, he liked you very much," Lisetta said, her voice tinged with an emotion Brendolyn couldn't quite place.

There was a long, uncomfortable silence. Brendolyn could almost taste the regret in the air, but she said nothing, her eyes fixed on her sister. Lisetta, usually so composed and elegant, seemed different tonight. Brendolyn noticed the change, and it both shamed and angered her to know the reason.

Lisetta finally broke the silence, her gaze landing on the scattered letters. "They're all so old. Are you really supposed to choose a husband from these ancient fools?"

Brendolyn handed her the letter from Loren Enzo. Lisetta raised an eyebrow, then took up the portrait.

"Well, he's not so bad, I think," Lisetta remarked, handing the portrait back to Brendolyn.

Brendolyn smiled softly as she looked at the portrait again.

"Rhun isn't far from here," Lisetta noted, glancing at the map laid out on the table. There was another pause before she spoke again, this time with a surprising softness. "Forgive me."

Brendolyn was taken aback.

"I haven't been able to bring myself to speak of the past, but I've had time to reflect... and to admire your courage," Lisetta continued. "You were there for me when I needed comfort. You stood up for me then, and you stood your ground with Barrow when he wanted us to remain in Jorn. It was the right decision to come home, and I'm very proud of you, Brendolyn."

Brendolyn's throat tightened at her sister's words. Never before had Lisetta spoken to her with such warmth and sincerity.

Lisetta coughed, awkwardly returning the letter to Brendolyn. "I would consider him, Brendolyn... he has kind eyes." With that, she turned and hurried from the room, leaving Brendolyn to ponder her future.

Brendolyn knew she would have to choose a husband, and the decision weighed heavily on her. She could choose a gentleman, a knight, a duke— they were all there on the table before her. From the furthest shores of Jorn to the very south of Corad, men were vying for her hand, but most wanted only her title. Brendolyn sighed deeply.

Rhun was an unaffiliated land, a realm that had withdrawn from the greater kingdoms after the great war. Yet here, in her hands, was a letter from Rhun's last living heir. Brendolyn read the words again and again, trying to decipher the intentions behind them. There was no mention of Augusta, no reference to her new title. The letter was strangely complimentary to Corad, yet it made no mention of Jorn.

*Rhun would be honored with the addition of such a charming and accomplished daughter of our neighboring realm* the letter read. The words were odd yet pleasing.

Resolute, Brendolyn stood and took the letter to her father, tucking the portrait into her pocket. She found Sabian in his office, where he spent most of his time since returning. His health and color had improved, but his spirit was subdued. As she entered, the warm sunlight streamed through the open balcony doors, a gentle breeze making the room feel less stuffy than usual.

Sabian beckoned her forward with a patient smile, and Brendolyn dutifully extended the letter.

Sabian took it, his smile growing as he read the words. When he looked up at Brendolyn, there was warmth in his eyes.

"Loren Enzo is rumored to be a charming man. I'm glad you didn't consider the brutes who only want your title, my dear. There's a good chance of happiness in Rhun. It was once a great city of Corad, a long time ago," Sabian mused, though Brendolyn could sense a sadness in his voice.

She stepped closer and took her father's hand. He accepted it, his grip firm but careful. He patted the top of her hand and looked up at her with genuine affection, which made Brendolyn beam.

"I'm so proud of you, Brendolyn. Your mother would be, too. Take my blessing with you to Rhun when the time comes. Take with you whatever comforts of home you desire. I'll call for the dressmaker to have you fitted for a wardrobe fit for married life as a duchess, *amore*," Sabian said, releasing her hand. Brendolyn's cheeks warmed from smiling as her father then took up a parchment.

He smirked at her. "Allow me the honor of accepting Rhun's offer at once."

Brendolyn hadn't expected to see a representative from Rhun so soon after her father's letter was sent. Yet here he was, standing in the bright, airy library beside Elsa. The dark-haired elf was dressed in dark gold, his attire fitting the grand surroundings.

"Thank you for your warmest welcome, Princess Brendolyn," the elf said, his voice heavily accented but his common tongue impeccable. He smiled brightly, revealing wide violet eyes that seemed to hold a touch of curiosity and admiration.

"You are welcome in Corad, Sir Mihrk," Elsa replied, her voice tinged with unease as she addressed the newcomer.

Mihrk turned his gaze to Elsa. "Thank you, Lady Elsa. Perhaps during my time in Corad, I can express the admiration my lord holds for you both. Princess Brendolyn, your beauty is indeed remarkable," he said, his eyes lingering on Brendolyn with evident veneration.

A tightness constricted Brendolyn's throat, and she could only manage a strained smile. She cast a look at Elsa, who quickly stepped in to handle the situation.

"Forgive the princess, Sir Mihrk. Her recent vow of silence prevents her from speaking. Perhaps you are familiar with the language of the Silent Sisters?" Elsa offered, hoping to deflect the attention from Brendolyn's discomfort.

Mihrk sighed, a look of sadness passing over his features. "Alas, I am unfamiliar with such a sacred language," he admitted regretfully. He then retrieved a bundle of letters from his pocket and extended them towards Brendolyn. "But I have been given these testaments of promise from Loren himself. He writes with reflection upon the coming season and shares his most treasured thoughts in hopes it eases your heart towards the joining of your houses."

Brendolyn took hold of the letters, her fingers brushing against the fine parchment sealed with gold wax. There was a flutter of anticipation within her, but the ache in her heart deepened as she held them.

"Thank you, Sir Mihrk," Elsa interjected, quickly offering her arm to the man. "Shall we seek company with King Sabian? I am certain he would be glad of your good graces."

Elsa guided Mihrk away from Brendolyn, who was soon overcome by a wave of emotions. Tears streamed down her cheeks as she pressed a hand to her side, clutching the letters tightly. She hurried through the library and out into the gardens where she could breathe a little easier.

Once in the sanctuary of the gardens, Brendolyn allowed the tears to subside before daring to open the first letter. She carefully unsealed the gold wax and unfolded the parchment. Her eyes scanned the neat handwriting as she read.

*Dearest Brendolyn...*

*As I pen these words, my heart feels the distance between us like a palpable thread, weaving through the realms to reach you. Each stroke of my quill is imbued with a longing to bridge the space that separates our worlds and to draw us closer.*

*The news of our impending union fills me with a profound joy that I can scarcely contain. Your father's letter was a beacon of hope, illuminating the path before us with promise and anticipation. The prospect of joining our lives is a source of great excitement, and I am honored beyond words to have the opportunity to call you my own.*

*Though we have yet to meet, I have been enchanted by the tales of your grace and the light you bring to those around you. They speak of a spirit as luminous as the dawn, and I find myself eagerly awaiting the moment when I can behold this radiant presence in person. It is my sincere wish to make you as happy as you have made me with the thought of our future together.*

*In Rhun, we cherish the traditions of old, yet my greatest hope is that our bond will create a new chapter filled with love and understanding. I am devoted to making our union one of deep affection and mutual respect, and I am eager to discover the many facets of your heart and soul.*

*If you have any questions or if there are dreams you wish to share, know that my heart is open to you. I am filled with anticipation for the day when we can begin this beautiful journey together, hand in hand, as partners in both life and love.*

*Until that moment arrives, please carry with you my deepest admiration and the sweetest of affections. I await with bated breath the day when our paths will finally merge, and our shared story will begin.*

*With all my heart,*

*Loren Enzo*

# CHAPTER

## 19



*Jorn Castle, Realm of Jorn.*

THE CHAMBER IN JORN was silent, its walls dark stone and adorned with faded tapestries depicting the triumphs of Barrow's lineage. A single iron chandelier hung above the long oak table, its candles casting flickering light across the polished surface and the faces of the men seated around it. The room smelled faintly of old wood and smoke from the hearth, where a low fire crackled, unable to dispel the chill that hung in the air.

Barrow sat at the head of the table, his broad shoulders hunched forward, his hands clasped tightly before him. His eyes were shadowed by lack of sleep, and the lines etched across his face seemed deeper than usual. Across from him, Lord Bannon leaned back in his chair with a relaxed posture that contrasted sharply with the tension in the room. Simeon's thin lips curved into a faint, confident smile, his eyes glinting with an unsettling mix of ambition and amusement.

"It's the only path forward, Barrow," Simeon said, his voice smooth as silk. "Entheas is where he's fled. If you send men now, you might catch him before he vanishes beyond our reach entirely."

Barrow's jaw tightened, and his knuckles whitened as he gripped the edge of the table. "No." The word was firm, unyielding. "You're too quick to assume. Pavan would not leave this realm. He wouldn't dare."

Simeon's smile widened fractionally, but his tone remained patient. "You give him too much credit. Desperation makes men do strange things. If he feels there's no place left for him here, why wouldn't he run?"

"Because he's no coward," Barrow snapped, his voice echoing off the stone walls. "Whatever else Pavan might be, he's not the sort to turn his back on this realm. He's a thorn in my side, but he's a loyal thorn."

Simeon's expression cooled, and he leaned forward, placing his elbows on the table and steepling his fingers. "You're letting your personal grievances cloud your judgment. I've given you evidence—reports from the northern border, sightings of a man matching his description, and the disappearance of several faie near Entheas. All signs point to him seeking refuge there."

Barrow's eyes narrowed, and he tapped his fingers against the table, a steady, deliberate rhythm. "And yet, none of it feels right. No, there's something we're missing. Something we haven't considered."

The faintest flicker of irritation crossed Simeon's face before he masked it with a placid smile. "Then enlighten me, Barrow. What grand truth do you think we're overlooking?"

Barrow's gaze bore into Simeon, his voice low and deliberate. "Pavan's movements have always had purpose. He doesn't act without a plan, even when it seems chaotic. If he's disappeared, it's because he's preparing for something. He's not running, he must be biding his time."

Simeon's fingers drummed against the table, a measured counterpoint to Barrow's conviction. "Even if you're right, and he's lurking somewhere within Jorn, waiting serves no one. Entheas is a risk we cannot ignore. If he's not there, our presence will still serve as a deterrent to anyone who might think to harbor him."

"And what would that accomplish?" Barrow shot back, his voice rising. "You'd send men into a foreign land, strain our resources, and provoke unnecessary hostilities with our recent allies. No, Simeon. I won't gamble the strength of Jorn on your whims."

The air between them crackled with tension, and for a moment, neither man spoke. The fire in the hearth snapped, sending a shower of sparks up the chimney.

Simeon's smile faded entirely, replaced by a steely determination. "You're making a mistake. Hesitation will cost us more than decisive action ever could. When Pavan resurfaces, and he will, it might be too late to stop him."

Barrow stood abruptly, the legs of his chair scraping against the stone floor. He loomed over the table, his voice a growl. "Enough. I will not send men into Entheas. Not now, not on your word alone. You've given me nothing but speculation, Simeon, and I won't risk my realm on shadows."

Simeon rose more slowly, smoothing his tunic as he did. His eyes gleamed with an unsettling calm, and he inclined his head slightly. "As you wish, my king. But remember this moment when the consequences of inaction come to your doorstep."

Barrow watched him leave, his jaw clenched tight. The heavy door thudded shut behind Bannon, and the silence that followed felt oppressively heavy. Barrow's hands curled into fists at his sides as he stared into the fire, his thoughts a storm of doubt and determination.

"There's something we're missing," he murmured to himself, his voice barely audible over the crackle of the flames. "And I'll find it, with or without you."

A knock broke through his turmoil. Leuthere entered, his expression grim as he gestured to the man behind him. The messenger was gaunt and pale, his hands unsteady as he clutched a sealed letter. He stepped forward hesitantly, bowing low before Barrow.

"My king," the messenger stammered, his voice barely above a whisper. "This... this came for you."

Barrow took the letter, breaking the wax seal with a sharp motion. His eyes scanned the parchment quickly, his expression hardening with each word.

*Barrow*

*Upon the third sunrise this day hence, I shall stand upon the Field of Thourns. Come out to meet me and end this festering wound. Best me, my life is forfeit in your hands in recompense upon the kingdom I have slain. Fall under my hand and my life is no longer in debt, I walk free.*

*Do not forget the honor of these realms.*

*Pavan of Eir*

Without looking up, he barked, "Bring me Eero. At once."

Leuthere nodded, retreating from the room as the messenger stood frozen in place, uncertain of whether to stay or leave. Barrow's grip on the letter tightened, the edges crumpling beneath his fingers. The flames in the hearth seemed to burn brighter, casting long shadows across the room as a grim resolve settled over him.

Snow falls gently over the Field of Thourns, blanketing the landscape in a serene layer of frost. The air is crisp and cold, the kind that stings the lungs and carries whispers of the past.

There was caution in the men who camped just beyond the river's edge, barely within the realm of Rhun. They sat in stone silence, fearful of the wards that protected this land with formidable magick. Eero had reassured them, as they came with peaceful intent, that no harm would come to them.

"We carry a dozen swords among us, and twice as many in daggers," came the hushed trepidation of one of Eero's men that followed under his name.

"Have heart in my Vows, Dehrek," Eero had replied.

Eero stood at the edge of the field, his breath forming clouds in the chill as he surveyed the emptiness before him. The memories of the great war, a terror that still haunted him, lingered like shadows at the edge of his consciousness.

"Eero." Barrow's voice broke the silence as he stepped up from the singular path of footprints up the embankment. "There you are."

"This land is unpredictable," Eero stated calmly beneath his breath. "There is no movement in the furthest line of trees."

"Do you believe he will show himself?" Barrow's voice was laced with frustration and fatigue. "It has been months. Winter has come early, and I cannot imagine he has survived this long in the forests alone."

Eero turned to look at the prince, noting the pallor of his skin and the trembling in his hands. Barrow looked so worn and weary, stirring a deep sense of urgency in Eero. He knew that the arrival of Pavan was inevitable, but the real question was whether Barrow could prevail in battle against a man Eero knew to have trained in combat.

"Let me stand in your stead," Eero said suddenly, his voice firm.

Barrow's eyes narrowed with hurt. "You think me weak?"

Eero's gaze softened, but his resolve remained unshaken. "You are not weak, but this man is trained in the wilds of Entheas, in the battlement of Eir. I am your friend, Barrow and as your friend, please allow me to speak freely." He waited for Barrow's reluctant nod before continuing. "Your skills are many, but we both know that your prowess with a sword is not as refined. As your sworn knight, it is my duty to protect you, and according to the rules of engagement, you have the right to a placeholder. Let me fight in your place. I will do my duty to protect you and your crown."

There was a long, tense silence as Barrow processed Eero's offer. The weight of his responsibility and the enormity of the situation pressed heavily upon him. Finally, Barrow shook his head, his voice tinged with a mixture of pride and frustration. "I cannot allow you to do this, not when honor demands that I face him myself."

Eero sighed, his breath mingling with the falling snow. "We are no longer in Jorn, Barrow. This realm is not forgiving to those who spill blood on their soil."

"Superstition, magick." Barrow scoffed. "You more than most should understand the tinge of madness that lingers here. Duke Aerric has not been in his right mind since the second battle of Thourns. They have whispered of his wards as nothing but stories to scare children."

Eero frowned and drew his cloak closer around his shoulders to starve out the cold that crept into his bones, looking out into the distance as if a whisper danced upon the wind. He knew the stories, as many in Jorn did.

"Magick is a mystery in this realm, and we must make our next move in caution. We know Pavan has hidden himself in this land, under the guise of his magick. If he has planned his next move, if you are not cautious it will be the downfall of your kingdom."

Barrow's eyes narrowed. "You believe this is his plot? To conquer Jorn?"

Eero nodded solemnly. "I believe that if you do not return to Jorn, darkness will cast a shadow. There is honor in dying my friend, my king. But there is greater honor in ensuring that the realm you protect does not fall into ruin."

Barrow's expression was one of deep contemplation, and after a moment, he finally nodded, his decision made. "Very well. If it is the only way to secure our future, then I accept your offer."

Eero bowed his head, a sense of duty and resolve filling him. "Thank you, Barrow. I will not fail you."

As Barrow turned to walk away, Eero stood alone once more on the frost-covered field, the weight of his decision and the chill of the winter air mixing with the resolve in his heart. The battle to come would be fierce, but Eero was prepared to face it with honor, standing in the place of his friend to protect the future of their realm.

They sat on horseback, in the morning they were meant to meet Pavan, but there was no one. Behind them stood Eero's guards, a group of twelve men. Barrow looked back at them as they shifted. Barrow looked to Eero.

"Where is he?" he hissed.

"It is not quite noon, Barrow," Eero whispered in return.

His breath was visible before his lips. As the soft flourish of snow fell about them, blanketing them all, Eero sighed. Ahead of them from the snow fall emerged Pavan. Tall and dark haired as he was before. Strong and dressed warm, he came alone.

Barrow dismounted and Eero followed after him.

Together they walked towards the approaching man. Standing ten feet away they stopped. Eero looked at Pavan, who looked at them both, his eyes as white as milk.

"As decreed by the laws of combat, I shall take the place of Barrow upon the field."

Pavan said nothing, looking from Barrow to Eero, then he nodded. Eero looked him over, dressed in his thick furs, his burgundy tunic neatly pressed as well as his breeches brushed and boots shined.

"Do you have any final words before your demise?" Barrow seethed, his anger towards the man before him greater than ever.

Pavan's eyes lowered, but he said nothing.

"Very well then. Proceed," Barrow whispered to Eero, turning on his heel and walking back to the saddle of his horse. Climbing up with some struggle, he managed to mount, pulling at the reigns as the horse side stepped, glaring hard before cantering away, returning to the shielded guard of Eero's knights.

Eero looked at the prince briefly before turning to Pavan, regret written on his face.

"You are a fool..." he muttered and then pulled his sword from the hilt as he looked at Pavan, who stood exactly as he was. "I do not wish to kill you, Pavan... you are a good man, and I know you are innocent."

Those words made the man turn his head and unlatch the clasp of his fur cloak, tossing it aside, exposing himself freely to the cold. Eero saw the greatsword upon his back and the blade concealed beneath the fur cloak.

Eero sighed. "Why Pavan? One of us must die... why let this be our path?"

Before him Pavan pulled the sword from behind his back, holding it within his grasp as he looked Eero over with his milky eyes.

"To be free." Pavan's voice resonated and the deepness rang within Eero's head, haunting him.

Pavan swung, his hands skillfully wielding the blade as it caught on Eero's sword, who blocked it with ease. Pavan stood back, circling around to the right, his back now to the forest some yards away, his body flexing as he gripped the large sword.

"You fight well." Pavan commented.

Eero breathed heavily. "I had an excellent teacher."

They danced, equally matched as they swung and parried. Blocked and swung again. Back and forth like a choreographed dance in the silence of the snow. Metal clanging and the whines of horses were the only noise to break the silence. Finally, Pavan stepped away, circling again around where Eero stood, catching his breath.

"He must have been a great swordsman. Do you remember it, the training yard of Jorn?"

Unbelieving, Eero watched as Pavan stood, unhindered by the exertion. Eero winced and dug his foot into the ground beneath him. Snow crunched beneath his feet and as Eero swung again, Pavan stepped aside. The blade fell and landed hard, cutting into the dirt. Recovering quickly Eero thrust, but the blade of his sword ran along the broadsword.

"I did not train in Jorn..."

Eero stumbled around, taking a moment to make his breath slow.

"Where was it then, how could it have been? A sworn Knight of Jorn, protector of the new king," Pavan breathed, his voice dancing in the air.

Eero gripped hard at the handle of his sword. "Do not play tricks on my mind. I am on your side, Pavan. We can stop this, together we can return to Jorn and set things to right."

Swinging his sword, Pavan swung, but Eero blocked him, returning to the dance of strength.

"You are not a fool, Eero," Pavan replied.

"Please, I cannot kill an innocent man," Eero begged, feeling the strength in his arms begin to fade.

"Your honor to the Brotherhood suits you." Pavan nodded, bowing his head.

"It was not the Brotherhood that taught me honor," he grunted and then heaved, swinging his sword once again, but it was blocked with a singular blow. Eero winced as his mind began to ache. "My honor..."

He would die on this very field. A shift of pain echoed in his mind, returning to this place of quiet. So long ago, he remembered the stench of blood as he held the small hand. Eero could not remember who it was. Only the memories of loss clouded him, pulling at his heart. Anger simmered beneath the surface, infused with the magick he fought to suppress. The weight of agony coiled in his gut as he knelt before the lifeless body.

His battle cry shattered the icy stillness and Eero charged forward with ferocity, his sword arcing upward in a powerful strike. But Pavan moved like a shadow, his blade rising to meet the attack in a flawless, fluid block.

Steel clashed, the sound reverberating like a bell of war.

Eero's eyes widened in disbelief as Pavan released his sword mid-block, letting it fall into the snow with a dull thud. His palm opened as if in surrender, yet the defiance in his stance remained unbroken. Fueled by instinct and confusion, Eero lunged. His sword sliced through the air, the tip grazing the thick fabric of Pavan's jacket just below his left breast. The sound of fabric tearing was almost imperceptible beneath the howl of the wind.

But then, Eero faltered. His breath hitched, and his hands trembled as he stared into Pavan's eyes brimming with unyielding resolve. Eero shook his head, confusion bleary in his mind.

"Do it," Pavan said, his voice steady, commanding.

"I... I can't," Eero rasped, shaking his head as his grip on the hilt slackened. His fingers clenched and unclenched, betraying his inner disorder. His knuckles whitened as he gripped the sword tighter, the weight of his indecision crushing him. "I can't," he repeated, his voice breaking.

Around them, the wind whipped, picking up snow in a deluge of icy shards that sliced and burned Eero's skin. Pavan's expression softened, yet his magick surged to life, a silent command that rippled through the air.

Eero gasped as his hands betrayed him, moving of their own accord. The magick twisted around his arms like invisible chains, dragging the sword forward, its tip aimed at Pavan's chest.

"No... no, no!" Eero cried, his voice cracking with desperation. But the magick forced him onward and Pavan's clenched fist drew the blade closer.

The sword pierced flesh, the sensation of resistance sharp and sickening. A choked gasp escaped Pavan's lips as the steel plunged through his chest, driving deep until the hilt rested against his padded jacket.

All at once the wind stopped.

For a moment, the world stood still. Eero's hands remained on the hilt, inches from Pavan's body. His own breath came in ragged gasps as he locked eyes with Pavan. The milky gaze, once resolute, now glistened with unshed tears.

Pavan exhaled a shuddering sigh, blood pooling at the corners of his lips. His knees buckled, and he staggered backward, the blade sliding free with a grotesque sound. Blood splattered the pristine snow, staining it crimson as Pavan collapsed, his body crumpling into the cold, unforgiving ground.

Dropping to his knees beside him, panic overtook Eero's senses. His hands pressed against the wound, warm blood seeping between his fingers. A single tear escaped Eero's eye, freezing on his cheek as he choked back a sob. He knew the magick to heal, it was within his grasp, but Pavan's bloodied hand shot up, gripping his arm with surprising strength, and drew him closer.

"No," Pavan rasped, his voice barely audible over the wind.

Agony twisted in Eero's gut as Pavan's hand reached for his face, his fingers brushing against Eero's cheek in a final act of connection.

Then a voice rang out, soft and familiar, and it froze Eero's blood.

"Eero," it whispered, a sound so achingly familiar it stole the air from his lungs.

He looked up, and his heart lurched.

Sanna lay before him, her own milky white eyes glistening with tears much like Pavan's had. Her cropped white hair framed her serene, heart wrenchingly familiar features. She smiled through the blood that trickled from her lips, her voice wrought with emotion. Eero's hands pressed against her chest, crimson seeping through his fingers.

"Don't..." she begged, her voice fragile as snowflakes.

Eero's face twisted in confusion, his emotions surging and overtaking him as he looked down at her. Her hand rested warm against his cheek, a slight tremor but deliberate in its touch. He inhaled sharply, his chest tightening as memories long buried flooded back, drowning him in their weight and clarity. Everything he never knew he had lost came rushing forward, unrelenting and vivid.

Now, kneeling over her broken form, the memories consumed him.

Tears fell along his face as he choked out, "I remember you."

"By your hands, I go to the Veil, Eero," she murmured, her voice frail yet unwavering. "I am glad it was you to send me to the arms of my goddess."

"Thus I am unmade and remade in her light..." Eero wept, as blood poured heavier over his hands that pressed into the wound of Sanna's chest. "Light of her hand, soft as the flame, come now and call thy child by name. Close weary eyes, hush every cry, the stars are waiting beyond the sky. Breathe now no more, drift on the stream, into her light, into her dream. Where no more pain and no more fear, Ehnarea waits to draw thee near. Go, gentle soul, the veil is thin, the fire shall fold thee safe within. And those who stay shall sing thy grace, till we too walk the star lit place..."

Sanna's breath stilled, and her hand slipped from his cheek. Eero knelt frozen, staring at her serene expression. His chest heaved as he threw his head back, tears falling freely.

The ground beneath him began to tremble, a low rumble growing into a quake. The trees of the forest writhed wildly, their branches groaning as if alive.

Eero stumbled to his feet, stepping back as something massive emerged from the shadows. A Vohlgrum, a beast of legend, stepped into the clearing, its enormous frame radiating raw power. Its eyes glinted like molten gold as it moved with deliberate purpose toward the body. Eero's heart pounded, and he instinctively raised a hand, signaling his men to halt.

Behind him, Barrow approached on horseback, his face pale with unease. "What is it doing?" Barrow demanded, his voice tight.

Eero spared him a glance before turning back to the beast. "The Vohlgrum has claimed the body," he said quietly, his tone reverent.

Barrow scowled in confusion.

Eero stepped back further, his voice firm. "We cannot harm it. To kill a creature on these lands is forbidden." He cast one last look at the Vohlgrum, which now stood sentinel over Sanna's body, shielding it from view.

Barrow's jaw tightened, but he gave a curt nod. "Return to camp!" he barked at the soldiers.

The men began their retreat, and Barrow muttered, "We'll leave it for the night. Come morning, we'll claim what remains."

He was shivering in sleep. Eero tossed and turned as memories flooded his dreams. Dark shadows encroached upon the young boy in the cold vacant corridors of the large castle which smelled of sea brine and old musty tapestry. Memories danced in unison as Eero sat beside his brothers, his father who was seated on a large oaken throne with a golden circlet upon his head.

Memories flushed through him, awakening the overwhelm of emotions that swam violently through him. Memories of ash falling heavily from the sky, the stench of blood burning through his nostrils as he walked the length of stone corridors amongst the fallen. Blood soaked linen draped over twine to shield the sight, hearing the endless screams of death consume him. Pulling him deeper into memory, into his past, until he heard the agonised wails of a woman.

Eero stood before his mother's bed, watching her helplessly as she fought against the clamour of midwives and healers that chanted around her. Eero watched helplessly as his mother bled out, while the cacophony of death rang out through the castle beyond the shut doors, seeing the swaddled thing wrapped in his mother's arms, unmoving.

Waking in a sweat within his tent to the darkness, Eero sat up, a caress of wind soothing his clammy skin. At once, he stood to dress in haste, pulling on his woolen jacket and stepping out into the cold night. Fresh snow covered the ground and the sky above was clear. There was no ash, no stench of war and death upon the air.

Stars shone down upon him as Eero took a deep breath and as the rest of the camp slept he walked in silence, unnoticed, to the fields where the body remained.

As he approached, his heart became heavy seeing Sanna laying there, her body untouched by snow or frost. Nearby was the Vohlgrum, standing on strong legs, watching him approach.

Eero licked his lips. "Let me take her to Pavan," he said with more authority.

The beast tilted its head looking at Eero.

"You know Pavan?" he asked and the creature huffed, clacking its jaw. Eero approached slowly. "Can you show me where he is?"

Retrieving the furs that she had worn before, Eero lifted her body from the snow to lay her in the fur cloak. She was lighter than he imagined as he took her body in his arms, cradling her to his chest as he carried her.

Turning to look at the Vohlgrum who watched him, he said, "I am ready." Without more prompt, the Vohlgrum walked, its large paws crunching into the snow.

Dutifully Eero followed, one step after another, ignoring as his arms became tired and his legs began to shake as they walked miles. They walked and walked in silence, until they reached the field of lavender.

Here is where the Vohlgrum stopped.

Eero remembered this field clearly in his mind. He stepped forward, walking between the purple bushes, untouched by the frost or snow. As he made his way, his heart grew heavier. He felt a deeper chill as he neared, his throat began to tighten, bringing Sanna's lifeless body closer to his chest as he stepped through the barrier of the magick housed over the cathedral. Looking up at the pristine structure before him, the place he remembered stood as it always has been.

Eero pushed forward, approaching the doors that lay open, as if waiting for him. It was dark and silent inside. Empty, lifeless. Eero walked the length of the nave, coming to stop at the stone slab jutting out at the crossing. It was here that Eero placed her down, arranging the furs about her body and then placing her arms gently at her sides. As he looked at her, his tears began to fall.

"You go where I cannot see you." Eero arranged her hair, tucking them away. "*May favor find thee, until we meet again.*"

The pain came suddenly, crippling and raw. It twisted deep in Eero's gut, and he dropped to his knees, breath stolen from his lungs. He crumpled onto the cold stone, a quiet groan escaping as he folded in on himself.

"Eero."

A voice broke through the barrage of grief and he lifted his head sharply.

Pavan stood in the open doorway, tall and shadowed by torchlight. His green eyes met Eero's, heavy with despair. The sight of him twisted something deeper inside Eero, a tightening in his throat, his ribs, his heart.

"I remember her…" Eero rasped. "Before Jorn. Before all of it."

Pavan said nothing. Slowly approaching from the darkened corner of the chapel, he waited.

"How could she let me do it," Eero went on, and the guilt that poured from him was suffocating. "I was meant to strike the final blow, but I… I couldn't." He blinked rapidly, as if trying to push the memory away, but it came back again. Sanna's face. The weight of his sword. Her hand guiding it. "She pulled the blade onto herself. I didn't know…"

A hand rests on his shoulder and he looked up into Pavan's eyes. The grief there matched his own but there was no judgment, only understanding.

"It is as Sanna wanted," Pavan murmured as he drew his hand back. "By her planning she wrote to Barrow in my name, called him to these lands knowing you would be the one to take Barrow's place. She had seen a hundred times this moment, when by your hands she was released from this world."

Eero could not say anything, only looked upon the peaceful face.

"I can see her soul across the veil already," he whispered.

Pavan reached into his coat and pulled out a folded letter. The parchment was worn at the edges from how often he'd held it. "She left this with me. It's addressed to you."

Taking the letter in hand, Eero could not dare to open it, his calloused fingers brushed over the elegance script.

"You are the last of your house, Eero," he said softly. "I have seen the memories she took from you, before all this. It was not cruelty…"

Eero closed his eyes, barely breathing.

"She did it to protect your heart," Pavan continued. "To give you the strength to keep your vow to Beaumont. You were never meant to carry the weight of your past. She chose to carry it for you."

Eero's breath hitched. "And what am I now?" he asked bitterly. "Loren Enzo is now to take my father's house, he died of his madness in the end, taken to the Veil to face his choices at the Tree. I cannot go back, Pavan. I cannot abandon Barrow to the will of Bannon, you know I cannot."

"I understand," Pavan said, voice steady. "She made the right preparations. Another now bears your name, some already speak it without question. He'll arrive within the week, and by my own hand, I'll see him welcomed to court in your place."

Eero gave a slow nod, then extended his hand, returning the folded letter to Pavan. "Burn it."

Pavan hesitated. "She wrote her final words for you."

"I know her words," Eero said quietly, shaking his head. "But there must be no trace left of that name, *my* name. You understand that, Pavan. I remember my vow to Beaumont. I remember what was asked of me. Take it. Read it if you must. But *burn* it."

Pavan held the letter gently, like it might vanish on its own.

"She saw the best of you, Eero," he said after a moment. "You are a good man. Stay with Barrow. He will need your loyalty more than he knows."

Eero's gaze dropped to Sanna's still body, and when he spoke, his voice was a shadow. "You'll need to take the memory too, won't you?"

A silence settled between them, close and heavy.

Pavan stepped nearer. "It will be altered, yes."

Eero's breath wavered. "But this moment—*this one*—you'll take it from me. Lord Bannon will demand it, won't he?"

Pavan met his eyes, grief flashing behind his calm expression. He lifted a hand and gently touched Eero's temple. "I'll make it as painless as I can."

Tears slid down Eero's cheeks. He swallowed hard, voice cracking.

"Make it hurt, Pavan... so I know it was real."

# CHAPTER

## 20

Eero emerged from the forest just as dawn crested the horizon, gold pouring like molten glass through the canopy. The light touched his face, but it did nothing to thaw the cold sinking into his bones. His steps were slow, uneven. His sword arm hung stiff at his side, his fingers still curled slightly, as if they refused to forget the weight of a blade.

Behind him the trees whispered as he passed, a mournful sigh carried in the wind, but somewhere deep in the wood, something shifted. He could feel it.

As the encampment came into view, the soft clang of metal, murmurs of waking men, and the crackle of fire met his ears. But they sounded distant. Faint. Unimportant.

He paused at the edge of the camp and a hand drifted instinctively to his belt, but his sword had been left behind. The memory of blood—Pavan's blood plagued his mind.

"Where have you been?" Barrow's voice snapped him back. He looked exhausted yet distrust flickered in his eyes.

Eero opened his mouth, but the truth stuck in his throat.

*I killed him.* He remembered it. The feel of steel sliding in, Pavan's body falling, his hair splayed across the stones, stained red. The way those bright green eyes dulled into shadow.

"I..." Eero hesitated, brow furrowing. The words tangled and warped as soon as he tried to speak them aloud. His mind was full of holes and ragged edges that didn't connect.

"The body is gone," he said at last, voice low and hoarse. "I followed the creature's trail, but it vanished. There's nothing left. No blood. No sign. As if it was never there at all."

Barrow frowned, watching him closely, but said nothing for a long moment. Then, slowly, he reached out and placed a heavy hand on Eero's shoulder.

"You look like a ghost," he murmured. "Come. Let us return home."

Eero nodded numbly, but every step felt foreign, as if his body no longer belonged to him and the warmth of Barrow's touch barely registered.

He couldn't stop seeing it. Pavan's face. His own hands slick with blood.

As they walked, the camp came to life around them, men breaking down tents, packing saddlebags, preparing for whatever came next. But Eero heard none of it. He didn't hear the wind hiss in his ears like breath and as he glanced once over his shoulder, the forest stood silent.

No whispers of magick reached him.

The chamber was lit dimly by a few dying sconces, their light dancing weakly against stone walls that drank more heat than they gave. The cold of evening had seeped into the floor, curling up through boots and bones, and Simeon Bannon felt it in his joints. Outside, snow was falling again, muting the return of the knights as they crossed the gates of Jorn. But inside the tower, the cold was not from winter, it was from something else.

Leuthere stepped forward from the shadows of the door and gave a short nod. "My lord. He's here."

Eero was ushered in without ceremony. His cloak was wet from snow and his short, cropped hair shimmered with droplets. His face bore no fear, only a quiet tension, as if he knew the chill in the room was not from the stones alone.

Simeon stood from his place near the hearth, his dark eyes narrowing.

"Where were your protections?" His voice cracked the silence, stern and sudden. "What kind of fool ventures out without the kings guard, knowing the threat to Barrow in those lands?"

Eero didn't flinch. "I made my choice."

Simeon's lip curled. "A poor one."

Silence bloomed between them, heavy and cold.

"Then show me," Simeon demanded. "I want to see the death of that traitor."

Eero's jaw tightened. "I am not one of your knights, Lord Bannon."

But he did not resist as Simeon drew closer, extending a hand. Magick crackled faintly in the air, and Simeon's eyes glowed dim with power. His fingers pressed against Eero's temple, and the chamber disappeared.

He plunged into the memory like breaking through ice.

Crisp snow. Silence. The distant echo of voices. Eero stood over a fallen man, his sword drawn, breath heavy. The scent of death clung to the wind like rot beneath frost. Bannon could feel it. Taste it.

A flash as steel met steel. Pavan was there. The dark haired man struck with fury but no form. Simeon felt the weight of Eero's sword as if it were in his own hands, guiding it, parrying, striking, until finally... a lunge.

Steel sank into flesh.

Pavan fell, gasping, blood blooming dark across white snow. But it did not end there—Eero was above him, knee pressed into the bloodied chest, hands tightening around his throat. The traitor's mouth opened, blood trickling out, but the scream never came. The sound of a neck breaking cracked through the memory like dry branches underfoot.

Staggering back Simeon took in a sharp intake of breath, the memory breaking like glass. He stumbled and let out a low, delighted laugh. The sound echoed, unhinged.

"Just a faie," he murmured, smiling, "with trickery in his heart."

Eero's expression was hollow, stunned still by the weight of what Simeon had pulled from his mind. "There was no body," he whispered. "The lands of Rhun swallowed him."

Simeon's smile faded. He felt the drain now, the dull ache behind his eyes as the magick siphoned from him by the depth of Eero's memory. That place, that moment, had cost him more than he'd expected.

"Let the land take him, he is now nothing but a thought," Simeon said. A sudden hardness overtook him, cutting through the lingering amusement. "Your services are no longer required in Jorn, Sir Eero."

Stillness.

Eero raised his gaze. "I am not one of your men to dismiss, Lord Bannon. No one has that power."

"Your loyalty to Beaumont is unshaken, even in his death. A blind faith in a long rotten corpse." Simeon's nostrils flared. "All men have fallen under my command."

Eero reached to his sleeve and rolled it back. Pale skin was revealed, marred by a raised mark of an almond eye, encircled by flame, with radial lines extending like the spokes of a compass and three teardrops curved beneath.

Under Simeon's gaze, the markings shimmered, ignited by unseen magick, glowing softly in hues of gold and white—the Vow of Light, ancient magick bound to the Aenarii.

Simeon's eyes darkened and he took a step back.

"You are full of secrets, Sir Eero."

Eero's voice was steady, though faint with the toll of memory. "I have never hidden my intentions. I gave my blood oath to protect Barrow since my service to Beaumont began nearly twenty years ago. No command in this Realm shall break that Vow, not even the hand of the king."

A silence passed between them.

"*Thus I am unmade and remade in her light.*"

It was not defiance, but a truth, spoken like scripture. And in that moment, Simeon saw not a knight or a soldier, but a man built from something older than his schemes. And something he could not control.

Simeon turned away, jaw clenched, and fury ignited behind his eyes.

# CHAPTER

## 21

T HE WINDS THAT CAME from the east that morning carried a bitter stillness, as though the world itself had paused to listen. In the grandeur of his chamber, King Sabian sat beneath a canopy of stained glass, its colored light dulled by the overcast skies. In his hands, a parchment sealed with the crest of Jorn lay opened, its black ink already smudged by the sweat of his palms.

King Sabian read the words again.

*"Pavan of Eir, known traitor to the thrones of both Jorn and Corad, was found wandering beyond the hills of Rhun. He was struck down by my knight, Sir Eero, for his crimes, and is no longer a threat to any realm. His body, consumed by the lands, is unrecoverable. May peace return in his absence. May our banners unite in the coming years."*

It was signed in Barrow's own hand.

Sabian exhaled, his breath catching midway, collapsing into a sigh that echoed into something deeper. He let the letter fall into his lap and closed his eyes. Tears came slowly at first, slipping down his cheeks like melting frost.

Beaumont.

He pressed a hand to his lips as the name rippled through him. His dearest companion. His light in the years of shadow. Gone, stolen by the blade of a boy he had once welcomed into his heart. Pavan, the man of Eir who saved him from death's own treacherous sting.

Sabian hunched forward in his chair, his crown casting a thin shadow across the marble floor. His grief was not loud. It was a tide, low and relentless, filling the hollow places of his chest until he could no longer sit upright. His knuckles whitened as he clutched the armrests, and his tears fell freely.

Far below the tower, within the silk marbled shine of her chambers, Lisetta was swallowed by her grief.

The fire in her hearth had long burned down to glowing embers, and the scent of chamomile did nothing to soothe the shaking of her shoulders. She lay curled among pillows, her face buried in silk as her sobs came in ragged gasps. Clara, her lady-in-waiting, sat at the edge of the bed, gently brushing her hand across Lisetta's hair, whispering soft comforts that barely met the ears of the grieving princess.

But Lisetta's tears were not for Pavan.

They were for herself. For the fear she had carried like poison in her chest since the night she saw his eyes darkened with rage. For the hand that had reached for her throat, covering her mouth to silence her as he took her purity. For the scars left behind on her skin.

"It's over," Clara murmured. "It's truly over now."

Lisetta sobbed harder. Not from sorrow but from release.

For the first time in weeks, she allowed her eyes to close without dread of what might come in dreams. The letter had brought peace to her nights, knowing the man had paid for his crimes.

In the still gardens of Corad, Brendolyn sat on a cold stone bench, the letter open in her lap. Elsa sat beside her, silent as the statues around them.

Birdsong had kept their song in spite of her grief that overtook her body and above them the skies remained bright. Brendolyn did not move. After receiving the letter without ceremony from her father that morning, he pressed her hand, as if to signal an end to a long standing nightmare. She had expected news of another kind, not the words unmistakably Barrow's, the words were blunt, cruelty written.

*Pavan is dead.* Pavan. Executed like a beast.

Elsa dared not speak for there was nothing she could say. Her hand hovered near Brendolyn's, but she did not touch her. This was a silence that could not be interrupted.

Brendolyn stared blankly ahead, the garden blurring before her.

He had promised to return to her dreams, but the nights remained in silence. Remembering the night that Beaumont had been killed, knowing the truth behind her eyes whenever she closed them. Seeing Simeon Bannon take the life of King Beaumont, who poisoned the mind of Barrow.

A single tear, hot and cruel, spilled down her cheek and fell onto the letter. The ink smeared, bleeding like a wound but Brendolyn did not wipe it away.

She sat in the garden with her grief unfurling like frost across her bones.

# TURN

S ILENCE CLUNG TO THE chamber like mist, Pavan was alone with Sanna's body. She lay still upon the stone platform, her face peaceful, her hands folded over her chest where the gaping wound of the broadsword split the fibers of her bloodied padded doublet. A final hush blanketed the room as he placed the candles around the platform, at the points of the lines he had drawn out in chalk, following the instructions he had been given.

Pavan should have stopped her. When she walked from the cathedral in his clothes, her steps steady, her gaze distant. *Do not be afraid for me*, she had whispered, cupping his face with fingers that radiated with fading warmth. *I go in search of my destiny, as I leave you in search of yours.* Pavan had watched from the shadows, saying nothing. How could he? It had to be her choice.

Turning his wrist with intent, magick sparked from Pavan's fingertips, lighting the candles in one single flame. Wax hissed and purple flames danced from each exposed wick, illuminating the cool low light of the room. He stood at her left, drawing a breath so deep it scraped his throat raw.

Then he began to speak with words that were old, passed to him by the written tomes given to him by Sanna. He chanted them, voice steady at first, then stronger, until the very air seemed to vibrate with each syllable.

The candles' purple flames flickered as shadows writhed, and Pavan felt it, that ripple of magick, coiling up through the soles of his feet, climbing the length of his legs and arms, wrapping around his heart.

His breath hitched. Outstretching his hands, runes began to etch themselves across his skin, glowing faintly beneath the surface like veins of molten gold. Unlike the markings he had seen before, Sanna's magick was awakening from beneath her skin, a warm glow that began to pull from the glassy skin.

A rush of warmth, a pull like gravity reversing. Sanna's magick, her lifeblood, poured from her into him, threading into his marrow, his soul. It was like being set aflame from the inside. He gasped, unable to pull away as tears streamed down his cheeks.

Ancient magick surged through him like a tidal wave of pure, agonizing waves. Every nerve sang. Every bone ached as her power filled him, pressed outward, and then burst, spiraling around the room in a ring of blinding light. His hair, once dark, fell about his shoulders in a shocking wave of white, an unearthly cascade glowing softly in the dawn light. His eyes flared open, brighter than emerald fire, vivid green flames blazing with newfound power.

He screamed. The sound echoing and broken, scattering the crows perched on the high spires outside. Then silence fell, heavy and complete.

Pavan dropped to his knees, breath ragged, and his hands shook while his vision swam with color and light. He blinked, slowly regaining his senses as the magick settled, coiled deep inside him like a sleeping dragon. The sun had risen.

Brilliant light poured through the stained glass, casting the chamber in a kaleidoscope of gold, crimson, and violet. He turned his head toward the platform.

Empty. Sanna's body was gone. Only her fur cloak remained, draped like a fallen banner across the stone. Lightheaded, Pavan tried to shift, to stand to his feet, but there was resistance, his body growing stiff. Unable to move, Pavan felt himself falling, his head colliding with the marble as the room fell into darkness.

It was the rush of the tide that first alerted Pavan awake. Slowly opening his eyes, he knew he was dreaming. Blinking in the light of the unmoving sun, Pavan shifted to sit, sand soft as silk beneath his palm. A familiar face of longing shifted within him, knowing he had been here before, had felt the sand beneath his fingertips.

"Pavan." He heard the voice in the wind making him tremble.

Scrambling to his feet, Pavan longed to hear the voice again, and followed it up the bank of sand drifts and grass. A rush of sweet wind guided him down the sloped hill of green, towards the doorway that lay beyond.

A rush filled him and he gasped as he stepped through, now standing in the barest of rooms made of shimmering marble floors. Along the furthest wall was open space, covered by gossamer curtains that fluttered in a breeze that perfumed the air with lavender.

"I know you are here." Pavan looked around the room, to the large bed of white silk, draped with opalescent shards of glass that hung from the ceiling, catching the light of the rising sun through the open windows, casting a shimmering dance across the room.

"It is forbidden to cross the threshold." His voice was a soothing balm.

"I thought I had lost you forever." Pavan stepped further into the room, searching with desperation. "Please, Thad, show yourself."

He waited, his heart racing in his chest, the magick was pulsing around him, amplifying the desire he felt, eagerly awaiting the first glance. He could feel Thad's presence, but he was hidden from his sight in the shimmering light of the room.

Pavan shivered. "I cannot lose you again."

"I am gone, Pavan." Thad's voice was certain. "I remain only in your memory."

Turning where he stood, Pavan saw the figure walking towards him, dressed in white linen, copper hair lying about his shoulders like a copper flame. Pavan nearly fell to his knees at the ethereal beauty of the man he had lost.

"You are here." Pavan waited as Thad's form walked slowly towards him.

Standing a foot away, Thad's blazing orange eyes looked deep into his own, causing pain to bloom in the pit of his stomach. Tears began to well as the warmth of the room, and the sun began to dwindle. Sadness creeped into his heart as he reached Thad, touching the smooth curve of his jaw and the slender dip of his neck.

"I am dead, Pavan." Thad's voice lamented.

Pavan shook, tears blurring his vision as he tightened his hold on Thad, cupping his face between his hands, looking deeply into the familiar face.

"What life is there in this, should I lose you, Thad?" he begged, unable to stop his grief from shadowing the room in a chill. "You are here. I can touch you and feel you with me. Don't say you are gone, not now."

"There will always be a part of me that remains with you. That door shall be shut away and fall to the wayside of your mind. But my time by your side has come to an end, as should your grief for my death," Thad whispered.

A single tear rolled along Pavan's cheek. "My existence is a curse, that I shall be kept from death's door, that I may join you in the Veil. I curse my immortal magick that barres my blade from piercing my heart..."

"Think not of your demise, Pavan." Thad gripped Pavan's collar with such fierceness that it made him flinch. "Your destiny is yet complete. Do not think of what could have been and think instead of what is to come. It is to Brendolyn your eyes should look. Love her, Pavan. Choose her. In all of this, you must keep her safe from the darkness that comes next."

Leaning in, Pavan brushed his lips along the curve of Thad's chin, reaching for his mouth but a sharp stutter caught in his chest. A jolt stole the breath from his lungs and pain crept upward from the soles of his feet, burrowing into his bones. Cold tendrils slid through his veins like rising ice, climbing higher and higher until each breath tightened into a gasp.

"Pavan, lie down." Thad's voice came muffled, distorted by the sudden haze clouding Pavan's vision.

He blinked hard, gulping against the tightness in his throat, and the piercing ring which filled his ears. His knees buckled, but strong hands closed around his arms, keeping him upright.

"You're going into shock."

Light burst behind his eyelids. He winced and thrashed his head as the world fractured bright panels of fluorescent white streaking overhead. The sharp scent of sterilization stung his nose while fabric rustled and hands moved, distant yet everywhere at once.

Pavan forced his eyes open watching as Thad leaned over him, blurred and wavering, pushing the gurney at his side. His copper hair fell in short, disheveled strands over his brow but something was wrong. Panic surged and Pavan struggled to move.

"Room one," a deep voice ordered from the right. A tall figure in a lab coat kept pace beside the gurney, his bronzed skin washed to an ashen hue under the fluorescent glare.

Pavan tried to lift his hands, but leather straps bit into his wrists, holding him flat against the rattling frame.

"Hold still," Thad warned, low and sharp, as they hurried down the corridor. "If you fight, they'll sedate you again."

He winced, forcing his eyes open even as the world tilted. Something inside him was pulling awake, dragging him upward and downward all at once. The lights overhead streaked past in blinding white lines, and his body alternated between weightlessness and crushing heaviness. Nurses flanked the bed, avoiding his gaze as they wheeled him into a room crowded with machines.

"I'm not crazy," Pavan whimpered, breath catching on the harsh sting of bleach. "It was real. It was all real…"

Thad didn't answer. He swung his stethoscope from around his neck, fitting the earpieces in place, and pressed the cold diaphragm to Pavan's heaving chest. Pavan bucked against the restraints, desperate to get away from the tightening, choking feeling but he couldn't move.

"Pulse is spiking," Thad snapped to someone out of view. "He's in shock. Medicate him now or we lose him."

"No—" Pavan twisted as a nurse stepped forward, a syringe glinting in her hand. She seized his forearm, fingers digging into the thick muscle to hold him still. He couldn't stop the sharp prick, or the hot bloom that followed as the IV catheter slid into place.

"Get him stable, Doctor," the deep voice barked again.

The lights flickered and Pavan's throat clenched.

He craned his neck toward the looming figure in the white coat checking the bag above his head. Numbness crawled up his arms, prickling across his skin as he blinked up at Beaumont.

"We've already given him the maximum dose," Thad said, frustration tightening every word. "I don't know if we can stop what happens next."

The room stuttered with flickering shadows. Pavan's body slackened, but his mind stayed painfully awake. He lifted his head, vision swimming, and stared down the long hall stretching beyond his feet. One by one, the lights at the far end snuffed out as darkness swallowing bulb after bulb, creeping steadily toward him.

Cold dread spilled through him. He swallowed hard against the copper taste rising in his mouth, unable to stop the thin streams of blood sliding from his nose, his eyes, and the corners of his lips. He gagged as the cold overtook him.

A shape materialized at the foot of the bed, clothed in black, their hair trailing smoke with eyes red as fresh blood. Pavan trembled—he was looking at himself. A placid smile curved across the mirrored lips.

"I'm pushing another dose," Beaumont's voice said, muffled and distant, drowned out beneath the thunder of Pavan's heartbeat.

But all Pavan could see was his own face leaning over him, watching calmly as he choked on his own blood, whispers of agony fluttering through him.

# CHAPTER

## 22

*City of Jorn, Realm of Jorn. 2005.*

B RENDOLYN STEPPED DOWN FROM the carriage and the air of Jorn struck her at once, a colder wind than she remembered, tinged with sea salt and the faint perfume of blooming trees. Spring had arrived in the north, but it clung to the last edge of winter still, and a gray mist covered the distant hills like a memory not yet faded.

She had sworn to herself she would never return.

And yet, here she was, standing once more before the towering gates of Jorn's castle, its spires rising into the clouded sky. The very air carried a tension she could feel in her chest, tight and unyielding.

The invitation had come at the turn of the season, sealed with the dark wax of King Barrow's new reign, a letter that spoke of peace and festivity, of a coronation to be honored, and of the kingdoms now bound in safety. King Sabian had read it aloud in the comfort of their dinner hall, his voice resolute.

"You will go," he had said, though gently. "The realm will expect it, *amore*. According to the titles of Augusta, beneath the banners you shall sit within Jorn."

"She cannot go back there, Father," Lisetta protested on her behalf but their father would not relent. "Not without security."

"It is beyond my power, there are rules to be followed. There is some comfort, *amore*, that you shall be introduced to Loren Enzo." A deep sigh befell the king. "You shall take your leave of us and find your home in Rhun after the Spring."

Brendolyn had tried to protest, but her father's eyes, tired yet unwavering, left little room for argument. The wedding was set for the summer solstice, less than three months away. It would be the first time she would see his face beyond the miniature portrait enclosed in his letter. And so, with her heart brimming with doubts and questions, she agreed. To satisfy the unease of Lisetta, both Brendolyn and Elsa were accompanied on the long arduous travels with a knight she herself hand picked.

"Take care of them, Vasco," Lisetta had instructed the tall man with dark hair and massive arms that filled out his black tunic.

"As I vow." Vasco had nodded with a closed fist over his heart.

Now, as the grand doors of the castle creaked open before her, Brendolyn hesitated. Her heart fluttered like a trapped bird in her chest. Every torch lit corridor of this place whispered of old fears and faded joys, and though her chin was high, her soul shuddered remembering the last visit to this Realm.

Elsa stood beside her, calm and attentive, wrapped in a cloak of forest green. She reached for Brendolyn's hand and squeezed it softly, her smile small but steady in a silent gesture of comfort that said *I know, even if you cannot say it.*

Brendolyn met her gaze, grateful.

They stepped into the castle together, the heels of their boots echoing against the marble floors. Behind them was the tall presence of Vasco, who walked just a few paces behind them. Gold banners hung from vaulted ceilings, threaded with crimson and newly embroidered for the celebrations. Servants and courtiers passed with subtle bows, their eyes trailing curiously in their direction.

"You are welcomed into Jorn, Lady Brendolyn." His voice was slick and oily, which made the hairs on Brendolyn's neck stand up. She turned slightly as the formidable knight stood before them.

While Elsa grasped Brendolyn's arm tighter, Brendolyn, herself, held her chin higher, bowing slightly in acknowledgement to the man who leered at them. Breaking free of her connection from Elsa, she formed the words with her hands.

Elsa had no choice but to say, "Many blessings, Sir Leuthere."

"Your time of grieving has ended, Lady Brendolyn yet you persist upon allowing others to speak on your behalf?" A frown was visible on his tightly sun tanned skin but there was something unsettling in the dark set eyes, a hateful loathing that knew too much.

Swallowing thickly, Brendolyn felt trapped. Quickly signing again, she hoped Elsa would catch it in time.

"There is no end to grief when the one you mourn was taken from this realm to the Veil before his time. Nor is it within my power to cast aside the vow I made, while the death of a beloved king remains an unrighted wrong, wrought by the hand of a traitor."

A slow smile crept across the knight's lips as he stepped forward, his movement light yet deliberate, a quiet gesture meant to intimidate. But before he could advance further, there came a sudden blur of motion behind where Brendolyn stood as still as a statue in fear of the formidable man. Vasco's arm rose, and his massive hand struck Leuthere's chest, halting him in place.

Leuthere's eyes hardened and his sneer twisted into something uglier, his lip curling. "You dare lay a hand upon the captain of the guard?" he spat. "I could have your hands taken for such insolence."

Vasco did not flinch. His voice was steady and unyielding. "I am a Knight of the Brotherhood. My vow stands in guardianship of Lady Brendolyn until she enters Rhun. While I draw breath, you will keep your distance."

For a heartbeat, something cold flashed in Leuthere's gaze, then he stepped back, his expression shuttered, and his voice stripped of warmth. "As you say."

"We grow tired," Elsa stated without prompting. "It was a long journey from Denorn Harbour to the castle. We take our leave of you Sir Leuthere and hope to not see you this evening."

Before the knight could respond, Elsa looped her arm in Brendolyn's, taking her away towards the grand staircase, being followed closely by Vasco as they ascended the stairs. Rounding the curve, she dared glanced back, seeing Leuthere watching her. His cold eyes never left her as she went.

The chamber was cold when the door opened. Not merely cold but touched by something dark. Leuthere stepped across the threshold, and the torches along the walls flickered as though they sensed him. The heavy doors groaned shut behind him, sealing the silence within.

At the heart of the chamber, fire roared in a great iron hearth. Yet even its flames seemed reluctant to burn brightly in the presence of Simeon Bannon.

He sat slumped upon a carved chair of blackened oak, his head bowed and his fingers resting lightly upon the armrest as though he were listening to something no other could hear. When Leuthere entered, the air shifted and Bannon stirred.

Slowly, he lifted his gaze. The firelight caught his eyes, revealing two deep ashy stone eyes rimmed by red, telling something vast and unseen that moved behind them in the lowest light of the room.

"You come bearing tidings," Bannon said. His voice was low, but it carried through the chamber without effort. "Else you know not to disturb my hours of rest."

Leuthere inclined his head. "Lady Brendolyn has arrived in Jorn."

Bannon's expression did not change. "She was summoned. It is only natural her arrival would come so soon before the pending ceremony."

"Yes," Leuthere said. "It is not the lady who causes disturbance."

A faint flicker passed through the flames and Bannon's fingers tightened. "Speak plainly."

"A Knight of the Brotherhood walks beside her," Leuthere said. "Vasco, they call him. He was not known to be in Corad, nor sworn to the royal family. My accounts of the Brotherhood are steeped in the roots of their traditions. They have not extended themselves beyond the Isles of Nihtar for generations."

The name did not echo, yet the air itself seemed to recoil. For a long moment, Bannon did not move. When he rose at last, the shadows in the chamber lengthened unnaturally, stretching toward him as though drawn by unseen threads.

"The Brotherhood do not bind themselves lightly to royal blood," Bannon said softly. "Sabian must be more paranoid than I anticipated."

"Sabian sends his daughter to Rhun," Leuthere said. "He has become mad with superstition. Even the borders of Corad are closing. We have seen a sharp decline in trade with the southern realm since the death of Beaumont."

Bannon stepped closer to the fire. "Older magick," he murmured as the flames bent toward him. "He is bound to his vow but not further than the reach of her impending marriage to the duke of Rhun. Beyond those borders she will be out of my reach."

He lifted one hand, and the air before him rippled like disturbed water. Within the shimmer, faint images formed of a crown of gold upon the brow of a young king and a throne veiled in shadow. Leuthere gazed in awe as the magick thickened the air, a suffocating heat blazing around them like a furnace.

"The coronation draws near," Bannon said, his voice a rasping breath. "Barrow stands at the threshold of his becoming but his spirit is still malleable. His dreams... receptive. We cannot lose control of what we have gained."

Leuthere watched the vision in silence.

"With a word," Bannon continued, "I calm his doubts. With a whisper, I guide his future. In claiming the life of that faie trickster, he is now desperate to have Brendolyn as his prize." He closed his hand, and the vision shattered into ash.

"You plan to break the engagement between Loren Enzo and Brendolyn?"

Bannon reached into the fire, scooping up a wisp of flame, letting it dance upon his long pale fingers. "It shall be as it falls. When the time comes, Barrow shall have the power to extract his new bride from her secluded prison in Rhun."

"War?" Leuthere need not ponder the meaning behind Bannon's surmising.

"A necessary faction to bring the Realms to their knees." Bannon closed his fist, snuffing out the wisp of fire. Turning to face Leuthere with a fierce roughness, he said, "If we take Rhun, then we can claim those that were once her allies."

"The Brotherhood remains a threat to your plans?"

"A vow bound knight within Jorn," he said. "So close to the coronation... shall unravel the tapestry of the legend we have woven."

Leuthere's voice was quiet. "You wish him removed."

Bannon's gaze sharpened. "Yes," he said, then, after a pause, "But not yet."

Leuthere frowned slightly.

"To strike now would awaken forces better left sleeping," Bannon said. "If Brotherhood blood were spilled in these halls, their order would feel it. They are not a force we can go up against."

He turned back to Leuthere, and for the first time, something like anticipation glimmered in his eyes. "Patience," Bannon said. "Our plan remains unchanged, but should the time arise, then I shall return to his disposal, when it is less noticeable by those who would suspect our plans."

A slow, terrible smile curved his lips.

"For even magick older than crowns and kingdoms," he whispered, "was shaped by hands that could err. Travel to Denorn, Leuthere... await my call."

# CHAPTER
## 23

B RENDOLYN STOOD BEFORE THE tall mirror, her gown of pale rose threaded with gold shimmering faintly in the candlelight. The fabric was soft against her skin, embroidered with delicate sigils of Corad's lineage, subtle to the untrained eye, but unmistakable to those who knew the language of legacy. Elsa moved quietly behind her, fastening the last of Brendolyn's curls with nimble, careful fingers.

"You look beautiful," Elsa whispered, tucking in the final hairpin.

Brendolyn met her friend's gaze in the glass and gave the smallest nod.

"Are you nervous?" Elsa asked gently, her voice hushed like the hush before snowfall.

Brendolyn nodded again.

Elsa's lips pressed together in a faint smile of reassurance. She said no more as words were unnecessary. Whatever happened tonight, she would remain at Brendolyn's side in spirit, even if the rules of the station forbade her presence in the halls.

A soft knock at the chamber door interrupted them. Vasco waited there, tall and resolute, clad in the dark livery of the Brotherhood, his armor polished to a muted gleam.

"It is time," he said, his voice quiet but firm.

Brendolyn inhaled sharply, her pulse quickening. She knew the rules—no companion of her choosing could attend her in the great hall now that she was a lady and not a princess. Elsa's hand lingered on hers for a brief moment, a final tether, before she stepped back.

"I'll be here when you return," she murmured.

Brendolyn's fingers brushed hers once more, then released, letting go of both her fear and her comfort. Vasco extended an arm, and she placed her hand in his. Together, they left the room.

The castle stirred around them as they walked the echoing stone halls. The distant murmur of preparation for the banquet grew louder with each step. At the top of the grand staircase, Brendolyn paused, catching her breath. There, on the second landing, stood King Barrow.

He wore blue and silver, the circlet resting easily upon his brow, though his posture betrayed tension. When his eyes met hers, the chill within them thawed slightly in surprise. For a breathless moment, the world narrowed, her heart thudding so loudly she feared the sound might reach him.

Vasco's grip was steady at her side, drawing her back to the stairs. Together, they descended, moving with measured grace. Barrow gave a short bow, his gaze fixed on her. Brendolyn said nothing, her expression composed. Vasco guided her forward with quiet assurance, leaving the young king at the landing as they entered the firelit splendor of the great hall.

Candles shimmered in floating chandeliers overhead, their flames dancing in time with the music rising from the minstrels' alcove. Tapestries of silver and crimson draped the stone walls and tables were laden with delicacies from both Jorn and Entheas, proof of the uneasy peace brokered with wine and gilded plates.

As Brendolyn stepped into the hall, warmth rose in her cheeks. Eyes followed her, some recognizing the former princess of Corad, others curious, judging, admiring. She held her gaze steady, until it faltered.

Across the room stood Lahrs. He was draped in the ceremonial silks of his people in Entheas of layers of white, silver, and lavender. His long white hair fell freely, braided elegantly away from his face in the traditional style of noblemen. Beside him, Kristjanna shone like starlight, her gown catching the chandeliers, glittering with gold as she moved.

His smile was soft and familiar, touched by genuine warmth. Brendolyn did not hesitate. Foregoing formality, she stepped forward, letting herself relax into the presence of the man she had not seen in so long. Vasco's hand remained lightly on her elbow, guiding her with quiet assurance, yet allowing her the space to move freely and approach Lahrs and Kristjanna, who smiled warmly at their approach.

Brendolyn threw her arms around his middle.

"I had hoped the days of our separation had not changed you," he said with a grin, his voice low but full of warmth as he stepped back just enough to let her composure return. Brendolyn smiled.

Lahrs's eyes narrowed slightly as they took in the knight at her side. Recognition flickered in his gaze, subtle but undeniable. The presence of a Knight of the Brotherhood was no small thing; the weight of that station had consequences even here in the glittering hall. His brow knit, a mixture of concern and quiet awe crossing his features, though he said nothing aloud.

Vasco gave a slight, knowing nod to Lahrs, acknowledging the silent understanding between them before returning his attention fully to Brendolyn.

"You are well, Bren?" he asked, to which Brendolyn gave a gentle nod. "That is good to hear. I wished to have visited you sooner, but trades from Entheas prevented my travel into Corad."

Brendolyn felt like she wanted to cry. She wanted to wrap her arms around Lahrs again and beg him not to leave her side.

"Your letters have given her great comfort," Vasco said from her side. "She and Lady Elsa read them nightly."

"Oh, my dear, they are calling for the dances," Kristjanna whispered.

The spell broke and Brendolyn's cheeks warmed with sudden anxiety. Vasco offered his arm, and she took it, letting him guide her toward the seating near the outer edge, sitting at one of the long tables covered with a linen cloth.

The music shifted into a waltz. Lords and ladies flowed onto the floor, gowns like petals caught in a breeze, the hall blooming with movement and color. Brendolyn sat nervously watching the scene unfolding before her, Vasco was seated so near to her, it was unmistakable why his presence was necessary. Yet he did not watch the dancers, his eyes scanned the outer edges looking for harm or threat.

A figure across the hall caught her attention. He was tall, broad shouldered, and dressed in a gold trimmed tunic, white blond hair falling to his shoulders. His noble features held calm and keen intelligence, and yet there was an ease to his manner that made him approachable. He kept his gaze fixed on Brendolyn, intrigued and gentle, causing her heart to skip.

"That's him," Vasco murmured quietly, a hint of a smirk in his tone as he noted her reaction. "Loren Enzo."

The man approached, bowing with one hand pressed lightly to his chest. Vasco held up a hand, pausing the momentum of steps so there was a distance between them. Leaning forward slightly to eye the man with a cautious gaze, Brendolyn felt the power between them, a long arduous silence as Vasco determined the threat. Without finding one, Vasco leant back, motioning Loren Enzo to speak.

"Forgive me for my forwardness," he said with a charm that made Brendolyn's pulse flutter. "But I thought it rude to let the music pass us by when I might spend it in better company. I am Loren Enzo." He looked directly at her, eyes a radiant green. "Would you honor me with this dance, Lady Brendolyn?"

Vasco's hand lingered near hers, a quiet shield. He gave the faintest nod, an unspoken assurance, and Brendolyn drew a deep breath, lifting her chin. Her gaze met Loren's and she stepped forward.

They moved onto the dance floor, and in a single, effortless motion, Loren drew her into his arms. The music seemed to embrace them first, swirling around their feet as though it had been waiting for this precise moment. Brendolyn let herself be carried by the rhythm before her mind could catch up, each step and turn melting seamlessly into the next.

He held her close, but with respect, his palm resting just above her waist, fingers entwined with hers. Her heart leapt and scattered at once, a riot of sensation she could not name. Words hovered on her lips, eager to form, yet none came. Her throat tightened shut with painful burning.

Loren's gaze softened as he noticed her silence. "We do not need to speak," he murmured, his voice a low caress. "Let us simply enjoy the moment. Feel the music... let it carry us."

Brendolyn exhaled, letting the tension slip from her shoulders. The music and Loren's skill guided her, her movements becoming instinctive, elegant, alive. Around them, the dancers twirled in a living tapestry of silk and light, but in this circle of one, the world narrowed to the press of his hand, the warmth of his presence, and the sway of the melody beneath their feet.

Brendolyn smiled and nodded.

For the first time in months, Brendolyn let herself breathe. There was no expectation as she let herself be guided over the floor, surrounded by the courtiers of Jorn in a wave of colors, and in Loren's hands, a great calm overcame her.

Barrow stood near the edge of the great hall, his goblet untouched in his hand, the wine within rippling faintly with each pulse of his clenched grip. The music swelled through the vaulted chamber, sweeping nobles across the polished floor in elegant arcs of silk and color but his eyes tracked only one figure—Brendolyn.

She danced in the arms of a tall man with white hair that shimmered beneath the chandeliers like silver thread. The stranger moved with practiced grace, confident and fluid, and Brendolyn looked serene, happy. His frown deepened when she smiled.

Not the polite, courtly smile she offered to diplomats and dutiful lords. No, this was different. Softer. Real. It struck Barrow like a blade between the ribs. His chest tightened and he swallowed hard, trying to ease the bitter tang rising at the back of his throat.

"Who is that man?" he asked, his voice sharp, low.

Sir Eero stood beside him, silent until now, his arms folded loosely across his chest. He followed Barrow's gaze, examining the dancer with a brief nod of recognition.

"Loren Enzo."

Barrow's lip curled and then he scoffed. "The duke's son? I never thought I'd see that man show his face in Jorn."

"He accepted your invitation," Eero said casually, though there was caution beneath his tone. "It was sent to every bannerman within the Three Realms. And Loren is no recluse. In fact, he is highly regarded in Rhun since his father's death. He took over the Castle of Caerh with speed in uplifting those in that secluded city. They expect him to be married soon."

Barrow's jaw ticked. "It is a danger that the realm should flourish under no banner." Turning to Eero with narrowed eyes, he said, "What lesser daughter is set to be his wife?"

Eero held the prince's gaze, a flicker of warning in his eyes. "Brendolyn. They whisper of their union to be held before the summer solstice."

The words struck like a blow to the skull and the hall swam slightly around Barrow. He blinked, once, twice, as though he hadn't heard properly. His fingers tightened around the goblet until the stem threatened to snap.

"She... she agreed to this?" he asked, his voice low but thick with venom.

"It was her choice," Eero replied, steady but careful. "As I understand it, since being given the namesake of Augusta by your father, she has received dozens of proposals, and by the laws of Jorn she must be married within the year. Loren Enzo is rumoured to have no use of her titles in Augusta but seeks to alliance himself with Corad again after the madness took his father."

Barrow scoffed bitterly, turning his eyes back to the dancing pair. Loren twirled her expertly, their movement seamless while Brendolyn laughed quietly, her expression brightened by candlelight.

"She still does not speak," Barrow hissed under his breath. "She vowed silence, did she not? You told me she loved me. That she mourned for me. If that were true, if she truly loved me, she would not run so quickly into the arms of another."

Eero's jaw tightened visibly. He glanced around the hall, Barrow's voice had risen loud enough that a few curious glances were turning their way.

The knight stepped slightly closer, lowering his voice. "This is not the time for this, Barrow. The feast is about to begin. Emotions will not serve you here."

But Barrow heard none of it. His eyes were still on Brendolyn, his breath shallow with fury and disbelief. He felt as though the floor beneath him were shifting, like ice was cracking under his feet. Everything that had once tethered him, her memory, her silence, the unspoken hope that she waited, had begun to collapse. A deep rooted need surfaced and crawled over his skin. Eating away at his heart, thoughts of the words given to him by the lips of the faie who stole to his bed.

*She is yours*, the voice whispered, festering in his heart. *You must make her yours.*

Without another word, he turned away from Eero and glared across the hall, watching as servants began carrying in silver trays of steaming meats and spiced vegetables. Musicians shifted to quieter melodies as courtiers drifted toward their tables.

Jealousy clawing deeper into his heart.

The heat of the hall clung to Brendolyn's skin as she stepped into the open air of the balcony, her hand resting in Loren Enzo's arm. The moon hung low above the seclusion of the castle, silver light spilling across the marble floor in long, dreamy trails. A cool breeze kissed her flushed cheeks, welcome after the whirl of dance and music inside.

She let out a breath, only now aware of how tightly she'd been holding it.

Loren released her hand gently, turning to face her. His face was bathed in moonlight, sharp angles softened by the night. He was more striking than his portrait had suggested. His hair, fell neatly to his shoulders, and in his eyes, emerald green and alight with depth, Brendolyn caught the unmistakable glimmer of something familiar within them.

She smiled, then hesitated.

That smile faltered the moment she truly looked into his gaze. Something within her twisted, a sudden tightness in her chest as if caught between longing and guilt. She lowered her eyes quickly, studying her hands as though they might hide her heart.

Loren tilted his head, his voice deep but gentle. "Are you unwell?"

She shook her head but still, she could not lift her gaze to meet his.

A pause passed between them, heavy with unspoken things. Then his voice again, measured and understanding. "You can still change your mind, Brendolyn. We do not have to marry... not if your heart lies elsewhere."

Her breath caught.

Almost involuntarily, her eyes flicked to the balcony door, and the shadows beyond it, the muffled echo of music and laughter. Somewhere in that great hall, she had felt Barrow's gaze. Had known, without turning, that he had seen her dancing.

"He is a great man," Loren said softly. "Your young king."

Brendolyn froze.

Slowly, she turned her face up to his, unsure what she expected. Loren did not smile, but neither did he look away. He searched her eyes with something deeper than judgment.

"I know you cannot speak," he continued, "but permit me to speak freely. You may stop me at any time."

She hesitated, then nodded once.

Loren exhaled as if that alone gave him courage. He leaned lightly against the carved marble rail, his stance more open, less formal.

"You loved him. I see it plainly now. You are not merely familiar with Barrow. But you are tied to him in ways that linger. That cannot be easily unknotted."

Brendolyn blinked, her chest heaving as a flutter of anxiety danced through her but gave no gesture to stop him.

"He loved you once," Loren said. "I'd wager he still does by what I have seen. The way he looked at you, how still he became when you danced. There was pain in his eyes and jealousy in his heart."

That last word struck her with uncertainty.

Loren stepped closer. "I will marry you, Bren, with no hesitation. But if there is even a flicker of doubt, if your heart still belongs to him… say so. One nod, and I will release you from this engagement. I will walk away. No scandal. No bitterness. You will be his." He took her hand then, his palms warm against her fingers.

Brendolyn's heart ached. She looked up at him, *truly* looked at him. There was something noble in his bearing, but also something profoundly sad. A man who offered understanding over pride. His offer shook her as she hadn't expected it. Not from a man she'd only just met. Her throat tightened and her lips parted to speak, but pain clutched deep in her chest and no sound escaped.

A tear slipped from her eye and traced a slow path down her cheek.

Loren dropped her hand, stepping back. His expression shifted and she could barely discern with the strained magick that was nearly torn from her. Was it embarrassment? Regret?

"Forgive me," he said, his voice quieter now. "I shall return to Rhun promptly. There is no shame in choosing love."

He turned to go and panic surged in her chest. She reached out and grasped his arm, her touch urgent and trembling. Loren stopped and glanced back at her. Brendolyn grimaced, willing the words to rise in her throat, just one. *Please. Anything.* But nothing came.

Only silence, and the bright sting of emotion as she squeezed his sleeve tightly.

Loren's expression softened. "I understand you want to keep the engagement intact?"

She nodded, desperately trying to hold her tears back. There was no dramatic proclamation. No sweeping confession. Only a soft smile from Loren as he brought her hand to his lips and kissed her knuckles with reverence.

"Shall I take you back inside, Brendolyn? You have grown cold."

She hardly noticed the chill, or the shivering in her body. She shook her head.

Loren Enzo laughed, a soft breathy sound. "If I do not return you soon, your guardian shall end me and then there shall be no need for a wedding."

Her laugh was freeing, it did not cause any pain to allow herself to laugh. In doing so, there was brightness in his green eyes that reminded her of the past, of so many things that caused her pain, but it felt good to laugh again.

"I shall endeavour to earn that sound again." Loren smiled and tucked her hand under his arm. Guiding them towards the archway of the castle he lead them into the throng of the courtiers, where hardly anyone noticed their entrance.

They took a long walk around the outer edge of the grand hall, allowing Loren to just walk arm in arm with Brendolyn. Drawing the quick glances of passing ladies and notable men, they began to whisper about them, but it was Loren's name they spoke of, whispering about his wealth, and his mysterious life in Rhun. Brendolyn felt troubled by the glances, as Loren paid them no mind. She felt at ease in his company, but she was growing tired.

"I believe there is your guardian." Loren walked them forward, guiding her in the direction of Vasco who stood at the far wall, closest to the grand doorways that lead out of the great hall. His eyes had followed them, watching them as they took their turn about the room.

"They shall be calling for the feast within the hour," Vasco stated.

"I believe Lady Brendolyn grows tired and would request a dinner tray brought to her rooms instead." Loren smiled politely, patting her on the hand. "And good company with Lady Elsa."

Bowing, Vasco agreed, holding his arm out for Brendolyn to take, for a moment she hesitated, then reluctantly took hold of the knights padded armour that was colder than the tunic Loren wore. There was more muscle beneath the graves, and a stark difference in how he held her.

Brendolyn followed Vasco, allowing him to escort her from the great hall; she stole a quick glance back towards the duke, watching him disappear into the swirling colours of courtiers.

Once in the comfort of the apartment, she explained to Elsa what had happened between herself and the duke, while Elsa helped unpin Brendolyn's hair.

"Are you alright," Elsa whispered, wrapping her arms around her friend's shoulders.

Brendolyn wiped away her tears, raising her hands. *"Loren is an honorable man. He offered to release me, if I still loved another."*

"That is thoughtful."

*"I could not go back on my promise to Loren... is that wrong, Elsa?"*

She squeezed her tighter, resuming to unpin Brendolyn's hair and brush out the tangles. "Your choice is admirable, Brendolyn. You will be well guarded in Rhun. They have wards of magick that protect their lands, much as they do in Tauf. Lahrs told us it was so. There is little chance of Lord Bannon reaching you there."

Standing in silence, Brendolyn began to untie the bodice of her silk gown, loathing the tightness that engulfed her. Elsa took the gown, laying it gently over the bed to be put away after being wrapped in paper. She paused, looking back towards Brendolyn.

"Shall I seek dinner to be brought up? I know Audry to be near this wing."

Slowly, Brendolyn nodded, watching as Elsa hastened from the apartment, leaving her in silence. The quiet was unbearable.

There, in the solitude of her room, she sat at her window, staring into the darkened courtyard far below. Her thoughts swirled like leaves caught in a storm.

Barrow.

The young prince who had once looked at her as if she held the stars within her eyes, was now a king who was colder, closed off, and wounded by choices that had torn their paths apart. Since the death of King Beaumont, he had become someone else, someone Brendolyn could no longer reach.

Then there was Pavan.

The gentle soul, now lost to death and shadow. Her heart mourned him daily, aching for the light he had once carried. His kindness, his magick. She had loved him too, differently, deeply. And she still felt his absence like a wound that would never close.

But now there was Loren. A young duke given to the realm of Rhun.

A land cloaked in mystery and legend, a place she had only read of in books and whispered stories. He was kind. Steady. Beautiful in his own way. But she did not know what awaited her beyond Rhun's borders. Would he remain gentle once they crossed into his kingdom? Would the man who stood beneath the moon remain when the torches burned low?

Brendolyn curled her knees to her chest.

She had chosen but her heart did not yet know what it meant to live with that choice.

Loren Enzo left Brendolyn long before the music faded from the hall, watching her disappear into the depths of the castle in the company of Vasco. A man he had learned was trustworthy. But there was a shift within him, a dark pull as he watched her leave, a gutted ache in her absence.

He did not remain in the gilded great hall where laughter bounced from every archway, still drifting through open doors. Instead, he slipped into the servants' stairwell, a way he knew well, where the stone walls pressed close. His footsteps echoed softly as he descended, each step heavier than the last. Halfway down, the weight inside his chest became unbearable.

It came without warning, a sudden wave of despair so sharp it stole the breath from his lungs. A knowing deep hollowness that became unbearable. Loren stopped, gripping the cold railing as his vision blurred. The silence of the stairwell closed around him, vast and absolute. Most of the servants had already withdrawn to their quarters. The castle, after hours of revelry from the lives of the wealthy above him, had begun to sleep. Unable to prevent himself from the overwhelming surge erupting from the depths.

The first tear fell, then another. He bowed his head, shoulders trembling as grief clawed its way through him. A kindling of magick began to flicker to life and the stone beneath his hands began to frost. Thin veins of ice crept outward across the steps, blooming like pale flowers. The air around him cooled as magick stirred, drawn from the storm in his heart and guilt tightened its grip.

He had taken Brendolyn from Barrow. He had seen the truth in her eyes. Her heart belonged to the prince, not to him and the knowledge burned through Loren like fire beneath ice.

A sudden gasp shattered the silence and Loren turned sharply.

Around the corner stood a maid, her arms full of bundled linens, and her eyes wide with shock at Loren's figure in the darkness. One of the cloth bundles had slipped from her grasp and fallen to the floor. He rose at once and crossed the corridor.

"I did not mean to frighten you," he said gently.

The maid blinked, startled, then shook her head. "It is I who should apologize, my lord."

He knelt to gather the fallen linens and handed them back to her. Up close, he recognized her—Audry. He had seen her before in the outer halls, quiet and diligent, rarely speaking above a whisper.

"Is it not late for the laundress?" Loren asked, a faint smile touching his lips.

Audry returned the smile, shy but sincere. "I prefer the night, the laundry house is quiet then. It is the only place in the castle where one can breathe."

Loren glanced at the thin ice spreading across the floor and felt a flicker of shame for being the cause. "Allow me to walk with you. The stone can be treacherous in this cold."

She hesitated, then nodded.

They walked side by side through the dim corridors. Their footsteps were soft and their shadows long against the walls. Torches flickered as they passed, casting warm gold over pale stone.

After a moment, Audry spoke. "Forgive me, my lord, but why are you in the servants' stairwell? You could be in better company tonight."

Loren's gaze lowered briefly. "I have never cared for crowds," he admitted. "I was secluded for many years. The noise of court and celebration still unsettles me."

Audry considered this in silence.

The laundry house waited at the far edge of the castle, where the walls were thick and the air heavy with steam. Inside, vast troughs of boiling water sent clouds of vapor toward the ceiling and lines of linen hung from beams overhead, swaying gently in the warm currents of air.

Audry set her bundles down and began her work.

She lowered the linens into a great basin of steaming water, her sleeves rolled to her elbows. She lifted the cloth and carried it to a second basin of cold water, guiding it through a tilted tray that pressed the moisture free. Each movement was practiced and steady while Loren watched quietly.

"You must think us foolish," Audry said lightly as she worked. "All this effort for cloth that will be stained again before dawn."

"Not foolish," Loren replied. "Necessary."

She smiled at that and continued.

After a while, he spoke again. "There is tension among the courtiers tonight."

Audry did not look at him. "There always is."

"They speak of the traitor," Loren said. "Of Pavan. And yet the unease remains. Barrow is not yet king."

Audry's hands slowed and the warmth in her expression faded as a shadow crossed her face, hardening the soft beautiful lines of her face.

"I did not mean to offend you," Loren said softly. "There is no shame in being affected by the death of the King Slayer."

Her head lifted sharply, offense flashed in her eyes, bright and sudden.

Loren straightened, drawn by the intensity of her reaction. "Do you believe him guilty?" he asked quietly.

Audry hesitated, then looked away as her fingers clenched the damp linen.

"There are truths the court refuses to see," she said. "Lord Bannon and his knight, Leuthere, have done things in these halls that no one dares to name. Maids beaten. Girls silenced. Lesser ladies were treated as though they were nothing. And Lord Bannon turns his gaze away, because to him servants are beneath notice."

Her voice grew stronger, rattled with anger.

Loren felt heat surge through his veins and he stepped closer without realizing it.

The air around him cooled as a creeping of ice began to chill the air. Audry noticed and her anger softened, replaced by something more fragile. She studied his face as though searching for something she could not quite grasp. They stood so near each other, it made Loren feel an ache of danger.

"Your eyes remind me of someone. When I try to hold the memory, it slips away." She laughed softly, uncertain. "It is strange," she murmured, lifting her hand to his chest. "You remind me of him. The traitor…"

Loren's lips curved in a faint smile. "Pavan is dead."

Audry nodded. "So they whisper. But there are a great number of things left unspoken that trouble me, my lord."

"What things?" Loren asked.

"There was no pyre," she said as her fingers brushed his hair. For a moment, she seemed lost in his gaze. "No ceremony to release his soul."

Loren's expression hardened slightly. "What ceremony is given to traitors?"

Audry's eyes flashed and in a sudden surge of emotion, she rose onto her toes and pressed her lips to his.

Fire coiled through Loren's body as magick stirred, sharp and dangerous, rising from a depth he struggled to control. Desperation burned through him like hunger and for a heartbeat, he clung to her, the world narrowing to warmth and breath and feeling. Her mouth was inviting him in, her gentle hands raking through his hair in the damp warm air, then he tore himself away.

He stumbled backward into a pile of folded linens, his breathing hard as he pushed the magick at bay, quelling the hunger. The air around him pulsed but Audry stared at him, her face flushed, and her eyes wide.

"You are a *fool*," she whispered. "To come here is foolishness. I have seen your magick before."

Loren straightened slowly, forcing his body into stillness, forcing the magick into silence. "You are mistaken," he said, his voice low and strained. "This was a mistake. We speak no more of it, please."

Audry's gaze dropped.

"Keep your secrets, Loren Enzo," she said quietly. "Carry them back to that realm so shrouded in mystery. Take your new wife with you. Forget those of us who live beneath the weight of dark magick."

# CHAPTER
## 24

Late in the evening hour, a few days after her interaction at the last feast, Brendolyn sat alone in the library when a familiar knight stood before her. She prickled, averting her eyes but to her dismay, Sir Eero sat in the chair opposite her. She kept her eyes upon her book, but none of the words registered in her mind as the knight she wanted to hate sat near her.

"I know I have no right to speak with you, but I...."

Brendolyn looked up to the knight as he spoke, but Eero's words fell away.

"Forgive me." His words were barely over a whisper.

Brendolyn was shocked but shielded her expressions from showing it. The man changed from the head strong, sure of himself man to the pained and broken man before her now.

She could see now the dark circles under his tired eyes and the wrinkles set in the corner of his eye and creased his brow. When did the young knight become so old? Brendolyn pitied him. She pitied the duty he found himself in, knowing the innocence of the man he was meant to slaughter.

He had succeeded. He had killed Pavan with his own hand and Brendolyn could see the man was now haunted by that ghost. Now his words registered with her—he was asking to be forgiven, he was asking *her* to forgive him. Was it even her right? Their eyes met yet she could say nothing.

He spoke then. "You cannot speak. They have told me you have taken a vow of silence, to honor King Beaumont." His mention made her sit back straighter and he shifted uncomfortably. He knew the truth, he knew everything. "What happened in the fields of Thourns, what I needed to do to ensure…" He pressed his lips together in a firm line, trying desperately to find the right words.

Brendolyn felt her stomach knot, seeing now as hidden tears began to fall down his cheeks. At once he stood. "I should not have come to you, it is improper."

She reached for him but he turned from her too quickly and strode away. Brendolyn listened to his foot fall on the stone as he retreated from the library, leaving Brendolyn alone once more, but now she could not read. She could not think save for the racing thoughts in her mind and she tossed the book aside.

The sound of it striking the table was soft, yet it felt loud in her chest. The words she had been reading still clung to her mind, heavy and suffocating, but she could no longer bear them. She needed air. She needed distance. She needed to be somewhere her thoughts could not reach her so easily.

The promises she had made to Vasco to remain in the library dissolved like mist. The pleasant voices, the careful conversations, the polite smiles that hid sharper whispers behind them all became unbearable and the room felt smaller with every breath she took.

She rose suddenly and left.

Her steps were quick, almost reckless, as she moved through the familiar corridors. She took the route she knew by heart, past tall shelves and silent alcoves, through narrow back passages rarely used by courtiers. The world beyond the library shifted as she went, from warm lamplight to shadow, from quiet refinement to the low murmur of kitchens where servants moved like ghosts in the late hour.

She slipped past them without being seen.

The doors at the back of the castle yielded with a faint creak, and she stepped into the evening. Suddenly met by wet cool mist, carrying the scent of rain and crushed leaves. Gasping, Brendolyn drew in breath after breath as though she had been drowning and only now broke the surface. Her skin prickled, as her heart began to race. The tears came without warning, spilling down her cheeks faster than she could stop them.

She did not slow.

Her feet carried her through the hedge rows and winding garden paths, guided by memory rather than sight. She knew this place too well, had sought it out too many times in moments she could not name. Lanterns glowed faintly in the distance, their light blurred by mist, but she turned away from them, deeper into shadow.

Soon she reached the hidden clearing.

Here, the trees grew close together, their branches weaving overhead like interlaced fingers. The wind moved through them in a quiet rhythm, bending leaves and limbs in a slow, graceful dance. It touched her face gently, brushing away the heat of her tears.

She stopped at last. Her shoulders tensed, then stilled. Her breathing, once ragged, began to soften. Each breath came slower than the last, until the ache in her chest loosened its grip. The cold wind kissed her skin and she closed her eyes to the sensation.

Prickles of chill traced her arms and neck, rising like invisible fingers along her skin. The mist drifted through her hair, tangling strands around her face, lifting them and letting them fall again. For a moment, she felt as though the night itself were holding her.

Her thoughts, once loud and relentless, began to quiet.

The weight of the hall, the eyes that watched her, the expectations that pressed against her ribs all faded into distance. Here, there were no titles, no whispers, no careful rules. There was only the sound of leaves, the damp scent of soil, and the steady beat of her heart slowly finding its rhythm again. The wind shifted again.

At first, Brendolyn thought it was only the branches moving above her, the leaves whispering secrets to one another. Then she felt something else, a change in the air that did not belong to the night alone.

Footsteps on gravel were soft, careful, almost hesitant. She did not turn at once. Part of her feared that if she looked back, the fragile calm she had found would shatter.

"Lady Brendolyn."

Vasco's voice reached her through the mist. It was low and steady, yet there was something gentler beneath it than she had ever heard before.

She opened her eyes slowly and turned. Of course he would have been watching, would have followed her wherever she went.

He stood at the edge of the clearing, his dark cloak damp with mist, the silver of his armour muted by shadow. The lantern he carried cast a small circle of light around him, its glow dancing as the wind brushed past. Beyond that fragile halo, the garden dissolved into darkness, and for a moment, he did not move.

"I feared I had lost you," he said quietly. "You have gone so far, Lady Brendolyn."

Brendolyn shook her head and her throat burned with desperation to speak, wishing to shout to the stars beyond the mists of her grief. Her cheeks were still wet with tears, her lashes heavy with moisture. She felt suddenly exposed beneath his gaze, as though he could see every thought she had tried to bury.

Vasco took a step forward. Then another.

The lantern light followed him, spilling across the grass, the roots of the trees, and the pale petals scattered across the ground. When he reached her, he stopped a few paces away, leaving space between them that felt deliberate and almost reverent.

"You should not be alone in the gardens at this hour," he said. Extending a hand, Brendolyn gently took it, his fingers warm in her own. "Come, let us seek company with Elsa."

Barrow found solitude in the portrait hall. As the evening progressed and the misty rains transformed into a healthy downpour beyond the large glass windows, he looked into the scenes of the history of Jorn to get away from the tirade of preparations for the coronation. His mind was altered by the events of recent years, the scenes he once cherished now held a veil of sadness and recent coldness. Remembering the moments, he shared a smile with Brendolyn as she listened in rapt attention to each detail of every painting and guilt plagued him.

Barrow hated the man who now lay dead and rotting, feasted upon by the crows and beasts. He was glad the man who caused so much hurt was gone, Barrow was giddy with the bloodshed. But the man had done his worst, he had succeeded in taking everything from him. His father was taken... and his love. Now a sweltering pang kindled deep in Barrow's gut and jealousy plagued him.

Brendolyn was his, only *he* could ever love her the way he did. No other man could ever comprehend how precious the faie girl was.

Barrow turned suddenly, startled by the steps that fell on stone flooring. Believing it first to be Sir Eero, Barrow began to call out but halted suddenly as the very same man with white hair appeared. He stopped and looked over Barrow cautiously.

"Pardon me, Your Majesty... I had not realized there would be anyone in the portrait gallery. Everyone seemed preoccupied with preparation."

The man bowed, beginning to turn but Barrow breathed out, letting his jealousy cool.

"Stay," he blurted, and the other man stopped. They faced each other again but Barrow was awkward and unsure of what to say.

"Thank you." Loren Enzo ventured, timidly turning to examine the first painting. "Remarkable." His gaze scanned the colors that blotched the painting before him, making up the many features of a scale of a nursery. Standing within the depth of the room was a woman in blue, a small bundle in her arms as a small boy stood beside her.

Barrow had always skipped over this portrait of a great-great aunt as it reminded him terribly of his mother.

"Lady Daneah of Augusta. She died not long after this portrait was painted." Barrow felt heat flood his cheeks. Why would he tell this man that?

"The little boy is Prince Barendan, I believe." Loren Enzo took a sidelong glance at Barrow beside him.

Barrow clenched his jaw. "Yes. You know your Jorn history well, sir."

The duke turned to him, a placid smile on his lips, and Barrow felt heat rise again to the sides of his neck under the man's gaze.

"I have read an awful lot over the years. Being shut in made me bookish. I should be ashamed, but for me, the wonders of a page cannot be compared to anything else."

*What a queer thing to say*, Barrow thought, looking at the white haired man. He was serious and Barrow felt eased slightly.

"Brendolyn admires poetry." Barrow watched in horror as the duke's eyebrows rose. His own tongue betrayed him to speak in such a way. Barrow wished to run away, but the duke stood between him and the door. Aghast, he found himself speaking again. "She loves a good book. I have read to her many times over the years. Her favorite is ..." He stopped.

Barrow's cheeks began to heat as his throat clenched around his words. Daring to look up at Loren Enzo, he had an expression that Barrow couldn't quite read. Not annoyed, or sneering, but patience.

"It embarrasses you to speak with me about Brendolyn?" His words so plain and straightforward made Barrow's head spin. Loren Enzo was kind in his tone, so it was a simple observation rather than a snide remark.

"It is awkward, sir. You shall be married to her, while I rot in my own stupidity for not acting when I should have." Barrow felt the tightening in his chest easing. This man was not a bad man, he was highly thought of by many from his court. His people of Rhun were not destitute. Barrow knew that Brendolyn would be safe and possibly happy in this man's company. But it hurt no less to admit his jealousy and it pained his heart to let her go.

"She will want for nothing. She will be safe." Loren's words were life fuel to the fire in his chest.

Barrow locked eyes with him then. "Will you make her happy?"

A quirk of a brow came from the white haired man. "She will be as pleased as she wishes from me. With every endeavor I seek to please her shall remain at her fingertips... whatever breath she holds will be enough to satisfy me to never stop pleasing her until the moment my life is forfeit. No candle shall burn out for her, nor shall her plate run without food to sate her. If I do displease my lady, I shall cut off the offending appendage and feed it to my hounds. Shall my tongue speak ever ill of her I shall cut it out myself. If my eyes look on anything but her with pleasure I shall gauge them out and render me blind. But, if it pleases her to never speak a word in my ear nor look upon me for a moment, if I am banished from her sights as long as our days are numbered, so long as it pleases her I shall live in a hovel and do it gladly, knowing that it pleases her."

Barrow felt jealousy return deep within his gut. Barrow hated the man, suddenly aware of his perfect posture and his perfect complexion. He spoke with too much civility. Barrow regarded the memory of watching him dine the previous night and how evenly placed and practiced his meal had been received. How he spoke and delighted the lord and ladies who sat around him.

"Perhaps you are right." Barrow's jaw was clenched too tight.

"I should return to my chambers, it is near time to be received into the banquet hall." Loren Enzo bowed, turning away as quickly as he had arrived, leaving Barrow to stand in the portrait hall.

Brendolyn was dressed in a newly fitted gown. Having learned sometime after telling her father which suitor she chose, Brendolyn endeavored to read about Loren. He was skilled in so many things, and he particularly loved to dance. Brendolyn sought a letter to Lahrs, asking what the favorite color of the house of Enzo was and received the reply of the house colors, but that Loren Enzo was always rumored to prefer the color gold.

She suddenly felt ridiculous, standing looking at herself in the gold silk gown, embroidered in shimmering gold threads. Her hair was let down, as she did in her youth, having Elsa plait tiny strands of golden string into the curls, pulling them back to expose her pointed ears. Her father, if he was here, would surely ridicule her, explicitly ordering her to hide her heritage but Brendolyn no longer needed to hide who she was. They would look, they would talk, but she did not care.

Brendolyn turned, seeing her hair reach beyond the line of her elbows, nearly to her fingertips. Brendolyn let her eyes travel the length of herself, returning to rest upon the bare neck and collar bone. She felt naked, without the ribbon, but she knew it was safe, secured around her wrist that was covered by the well fitted sleeve.

"They have just announced the start, Bren." Elsa appeared, dressed in her nightshift and dressing gown.

Brendolyn turned, looking down cast.

"I wish to be coming with you, as well…" Elsa kissed Brendolyn's cheek. "Tonight is by invitation only, and I was not invited."

Brendolyn stepped from the apartments where she had always been housed, the familiar doors closing softly behind her. Vasco walked at her side, his presence steady and unhurried, as though the castle itself bent slightly to his stride. Together they descended the worn stone stairs, their footsteps echoing through the quiet corridor lit by candlelight.

She paused midway, drawing in a breath that felt too shallow for her chest. Her stomach fluttered like a trapped bird. Her palms were damp, fingers curling into the fabric of her gown as she tried to gather herself. Vasco did not speak, but she felt his glance upon her in a silent watchful calm.

Ahead, the doors to the great hall stood wide open. The herald waited there, his staff gleaming faintly in the light. Brendolyn inclined into a delicate curtsy, and Vasco dipped his head in courtesy before they passed beyond the threshold together.

The great hall opened before them in a blaze of sound and color. Lords and ladies, only the most honored guests of the crown, stood in elegant clusters, their voices weaving with the music that drifted from unseen minstrels. Greens and sapphires, deep reds and warm browns shimmered beneath the chandeliers. For a heartbeat, Brendolyn felt painfully out of place, foolish even, as her own gown in spun gold caught every flicker of flame. One by one, eyes turned toward them.

She felt the whispers before she heard them. Each step forward seemed heavier than the last, the air pressing against her ribs. The pit of her stomach dropped, and anxiety coiled tighter with every gaze that lingered too long. Vasco's stride never faltered, yet she sensed the subtle shift of him closer to her, as though he could shield her from the weight of the hall simply by walking beside her.

Tears burned at the corners of her eyes. She wanted to flee from the hall, from the eyes, from the memories that clung to these walls. Her breath came unevenly, but she forced herself onward and then she looked ahead.

From the raised platform at the head of the hall, the prince's gaze found her. His eyes were fixed upon her, wide and unblinking. He stood tall and regal in sapphire and silver, every inch the heir to the crown, yet something in his expression unsettled her more than the whispers ever could. His golden hair had grown longer, brushing the breadth of his shoulders, and catching the light like molten metal.

Brendolyn slowed, her breath slipping from her as though the world had tilted beneath her feet and beside her, Vasco walked, his presence the only thing keeping her from shattering entirely.

Standing to the right, she saw him—tall, confident, and a welcomed sight. She blushed, seeing his tunic of gold, his hair brushing his shoulders. Brendolyn walked to him directly, ignoring the whispers of impropriety as she took his arm. Smiling up at Loren Enzo, he smiled back at her, if only a little bit.

Music struck up, beginning the king's waltz. She stood at Loren's side watching the many couples begin to dance, the traditional line dances, regal and done for every turn.

Loren leaned closer to her. "You certainly make an excellent entrance."

Brendolyn smirked, earning another smile from him.

"Shall we cause more of a scene? I am in a playful mood to rattle this realm." His look of mischief and the smile he flashed her, made Brendolyn's heart flutter.

She nodded.

He led her to the floor, as if to join the lines of lords and ladies dancing, but as he turned, bringing himself to stand directly in front of her, his hand firmly in hers, his other hand placed just at the dip below her arm, his fingertips grazing the bare skin of her upper back, Brendolyn felt her cheeks grow hot, looking up into his sinful green eyes.

"A true waltz is perfected by the magnificence of one's partner. And you are *magnificent*, Bren," he said.

As the music picked up, so did Loren, who began his waltz, guiding her through unseen steps, in a dance never before witnessed in the king's court.

She gasped as the movement thrilled her, being guided around the room, her feet light and lively. Brendolyn was surprised as Loren's large hands, both directly on her waist, lifted her from the ground and as he turned, she felt like she was flying. Being in the air for only a minute, he righted her again, and without missing the tempo of the music, returned to the steps only he seemed to have perfected.

She was exhilarated, her hair dancing behind her as they circled the room. Repeating the steps and being lifted into the air, she had not realized the other dancers had stopped. She could not see the prince, nor his jealous gaze upon them whenever Brendolyn smiled.

Brendolyn could only look at Loren. She felt safe, she felt happy. If only for this one moment, Brendolyn was perfectly content.

The music ended, and there was sudden applause. Loren bowed to Brendolyn, offering her his arm. She took it, breathing heavily as they walked from the dance floor, hearing the band strike up again, as the courtiers began their next dance.

He led her to the less crowded area of the great hall, near a heavily draped window which overlooked the gardens. Glancing down at her with slightly flushed cheeks and a dazzling smile, Loren lifted Brendolyn's hand, placing a gentle kiss at the base of her palm, near her wrist.

It was the only dance she danced that night, before she was swept away from him by Duchess Kristjana. The beautiful elf took her arm in hers, guiding her around the room, engaging in conversation with courtier after courtier, leaving Brendolyn to marvel at her beauty and grace.

At last, they were alone and Brendolyn sipped the drink she had been offered. Seated on the chairs on the outer edge of the hall, she watching the dancers, when Kristjana addressed her directly.

"You and your duke have been quite the objects of talk this evening. I did not think it could be possible to outshine the young king at his own party." Her voice danced, giving Brendolyn chills.

Brendolyn smiled.

"Oh dear, Lahrs seems to be in lively conversation with the Lord of Arms, I need to rescue him, but I shall return in just a moment." Kristjana squeezed Brendolyn's hands affectionately before she stood and sauntered away through the crowd.

Brendolyn set her drink aside with careful fingers, as though the crystal might shatter beneath her touch. The night had grown long, and weariness pressed upon her eyelids like a quiet weight. These gatherings were meant to endure until dawn, full of laughter and music and endless conversation, yet she felt herself slipping further from their brightness with every passing hour. All she wanted was silence, darkness, and the safety of sleep.

She rose slowly from her seat.

Her gaze moved across the great hall, over the heads of courtiers and lords and ladies, searching for familiar faces. She looked for the duchess, for Lahrs, for any presence that might anchor her to the moment, but she found none. The hall had become a sea of color and motion, strangers wrapped in silks and jewels, voices blending into a single, overwhelming sound. She turned her head again, this time seeking Vasco among the crowd, but he was nowhere to be seen. His absence struck her more sharply than she expected, as though a steady light had been quietly extinguished.

For a moment, she felt very small.

Then, at the edge of her vision, something shifted—a figure in dark clothing stood apart from the revelry, half swallowed by shadow. Her breath caught, imagining Lord Bannon in the corner of her eye and fear rose in her chest, sudden and unbidden. She turned her head fully, searching the place where she had seen him, but there was nothing there, only laughter, bright gowns, and indifferent faces.

Brendolyn's heart began to race and her throat tightened, as though unseen hands were closing around it. Heat crept along her skin, and the hall felt too close, too crowded, too alive. The music that had once seemed beautiful now pressed against her ears like a storm. She felt trapped inside a world that no longer made sense to her.

Without thinking, she turned on her heel.

She moved quickly through the crowd, past voices that did not call her name and past hands that brushed her sleeves without noticing her distress. The nearest open door offered escape, and she slipped through it as though crossing a threshold between two worlds. The corridor beyond was quieter, cooler, and with every step she took, the music behind her faded into something distant and unreal.

Her breaths came unevenly as she walked, each one an effort to reclaim control of herself. At last, she could go no farther.

Brendolyn stopped beside the stone wall and leaned against it, her hands trembling slightly as she pressed them to the cool surface. The silence wrapped around her like a fragile shield. In that moment, surrounded by emptiness and echoing corridors, she realized how alone she felt, and how deeply she had hoped to find Vasco come along the corridor looking for her.

*Breathe*, she told herself.

"Bren." Barrow's voice made her jump.

She turned, watching him looking at her. He was handsome and it made her stomach turn. His now kind face mocked her as she remembered the anger in his eyes as he struck her. Brendolyn clenched her hands into fists, stopping herself from touching the cheek that clashed with Barrow's hand.

"Will you not speak to me?" He has moved closer to her.

She felt a chill as his hand touched her sleeve. Trailing up the line to her shoulder, his fingertips grazing the bare flesh of her neck, Brendolyn shuddered, unable to look up at him. Barrow smelled of heavy wine.

"I have thought of no one but you..." he whispered, leaning into her and Brendolyn shuddered. "If I can hear your voice just once. To touch your lips." Barrow's hand moved up, caressing her jaw. A thumb gliding along to touch the curve of her lip.

Brendolyn let a shaken breath escape her and looked up to meet his blue eyes. He was so close, she could feel his body pressed to her bodice, the other hand curled around her middle, holding her to him. Revulsion for him caught Brendolyn off guard, unable to stand being touched by him any longer. She shook her head and pushed him back with her hand.

"Just one last kiss, my darling." He leaned against her, his mouth pressed to the line of her jaw, his hand at the curve of her neck. Brendolyn shut her eyes and turned her face away as her throat was set afire. She wanted to cry out, but she was afraid.

Brendolyn's palms pressed firmly against Barrow's chest, but he did not move. His breath was hot against her skin, and his lips brushed the hollow of her neck, desperate, and unrelenting. The arm around her waist tightened, holding her there, like a prisoner in his grasp. Her back struck against cold stone.

Her heart pounded wildly in her chest.

She pushed harder, her hands splayed wide against him, but the man was immovable, lost in whatever desire gripped him. His mouth found her jawline, grazing the line of her chin, seeking her lips as if they could save him.

*No.* Her hands shook with effort as she fought against him, but her body had little strength, her silence rendering her powerless in a way that terrified her.

Then suddenly, a crash of force and motion.

Barrow's body was ripped away from her with violent speed, the air displaced in a breathless gust. Brendolyn stumbled backward, gasping as the world tilted and a deep thud cracked against the stone wall beside her. Turning in a hurry, she expected to find Vasco standing there but instead, Loren Enzo held Barrow by the throat, lifting him above the stone floor.

Barrow's boots scraped against the wall, his toes barely touching the ground as the duke of Rhun pinned him high, one fist tangled in the front of his tunic, the other pressing hard against the king's throat. The fury that radiated off Loren was cold.

Loren's eyes blazed with quiet rage as he held Barrow inches from his face. "Do you fancy yourself entitled to her affection? Is that what this was?" His voice dropped to a growl. "You mistake love for possession. You mistake silence for consent."

Gasping, Barrow's lungs strained as he clawed at Loren's arm like a drowning man grasping at endless water. One hand struck out at Loren's shoulder, but it was like hitting a stone for Loren didn't flinch.

"Unhand me," Barrow spat, voice tight with fury and breathlessness.

Loren's face moved close, his voice low and feral, scraped raw from the furnace of his chest. "You dare command me, when you cannot keep your filthy hands off another man's wife?"

Barrow thrashed, his heels scraping against the wall as he kicked for purchase, but Loren held him like a creature caught mid lunge.

"I am the king!" Barrow hissed. "This is my kingdom!"

"You are not *my* king," Loren growled, shoving him back against the stone with a thundering crack. The torches lining the corridor guttered in their sconces. Brendolyn felt it like a pressure in the air, Loren's fury, quiet and dark as a storm still building. But behind it pulsed something deeper, a magick that was unforgiving.

Barrow recoiled at the force, but his tongue remained venomous.

"She is not your wife," he rasped through the tightening of his throat. "Not yet. And she may never be. Not until the sovereign ruler of her namesake in Augusta signs her contract." His words dripped with bitter triumph, his fear now warped by petty power.

Loren's jaw flexed. Still, he said nothing.

Barrow laughed, bitter and cruel, licking at the edges of madness. "You cannot marry her. Not until I say so."

Loren's grip loosened and Barrow fell, stumbling to catch himself against the wall. His hand raked through his golden hair as he lifted his chin, trying to reclaim the air of a man in control, but when Loren stepped forward again, he flinched.

Brendolyn's hand intercepted Loren's raised arm, soft fingers wrapping around his wrist and pressing it against her chest. Her eyes shimmered, not with fear, but with silent command. Her presence alone stilled him.

Loren's fury faded like mist on a breath and he turned to her, his fingers reaching for hers as if she were the only solid thing in a world that had tilted. Behind them, Barrow straightened himself, bruised pride twisting his face.

Brendolyn did not flinch, she turned away, tightening her grip on Loren's hand and pulling him with her swiftly and deliberately away from the young king's shadow. Loren followed without hesitation. They moved through the corridors, deeper into the castle's quiet, until they reached a shadowed alcove beneath the carved visage of a stone goddess whose eyes wept streams of ivy.

There, Brendolyn faltered. Her hands rose to her face, her breath coming fast and uneven. The tears came freely now, burning as they fell. She bent slightly, one hand clutching at her side. The pain lanced through her ribs in rage and grief colliding like storms inside her.

Her hands balled into fists so tight the nails bit into her palms, drawing crescent moons of red and her throat seared with the force of the scream she could not release.

"Brendolyn," came Loren's voice, softer than the fluttering of the breeze.

He didn't touch her, only waited, steady and quiet, always watching her. She wiped at her tears with shaking hands, forcing the sobs back, and trying to wear her composure like armor. But it broke the moment she stepped into him, wrapping her arms around his waist, pressing herself against him.

"You are safe," he whispered into her hair.

And she wept into his tunic, her breath stuttering against his chest. Loren held her, his chin resting atop her head, one hand smoothing down her back. He didn't rush her, nor asked for anything. He only held her until her sobs began to soften into breaths. Finally, she drew back and looked up at him.

His green eyes searched hers, aglow in the torchlight. A gentle and steady force in the darkened corridor and something else that was so close to her now, but Brendolyn could not quite put words to the feeling.

"Shall I walk you back to the hall?" he asked, reaching up to brush a tear from her cheek with the back of his fingers. "Vasco shall be wondering where you are."

Brendolyn hesitated.

She should return. Let the music and laughter bury what had happened in the shadows. But the memory of Barrow's hands, rough, uninvited, lingered on her skin like a stain. She wanted it gone, wanting to remember what goodness felt like.

Reaching up, she brushed her fingers through Loren's white hair. It was soft, like silk. Her other hand found his cheek, thumb resting against the line of his jaw. When she rose onto her toes, her lips met his in a kiss that was brief.

Loren inhaled, eyes wide as she pulled back only a little, but he kissed her back, his mouth desperately hot against her. Loren's hands came to rest upon her waist, kissing her with such passion she had begun to lose her breath. Holding her firmly against him, she clung to him delving deeper against the pull he held over her.

A spell too quickly broken when a sharp cough sounded abruptly behind them.

She broke away to glance over Loren's arm to see Vasco standing there, his large arms folded over his chest and a quizzical glance eyeing them.

"Duchess Kristjana was concerned when she saw you leave suddenly, Lord Enzo," he admitted, trying to hide his amusement when Loren turned his head away. "Perhaps her concern was misplaced in believing there was danger."

Brendolyn's cheek felt flush.

"There is no danger, Sir Vasco," Loren answered. "It was foolish to wander too far."

"The danger remains in unwanted eyes, your realm would not take too kindly to an interruption to this union." There was deliberacy in what the knight said, drawing closer with a warning in his eyes.

Taking Brendolyn by the arm, Vasco forced a separation from Loren that spoke of the dangers in the actions of their intimacy alone together.

"Blessed night, Sir Vasco." Loren bowed solemnly, his features suddenly aloof and cold. His eyes glanced down at Brendolyn politely. "Forgive my action's Brendolyn. Goodnight." Without a second glance, he turned on his heel, disappearing in the corridor.

Being guided by Vasco back in the direction they came, they head towards the stairs leading to her rooms. She glanced quizzingly up at him. When he noted her glance, he sighed heavily.

"I had the good fortune of happening upon King Barrow in the corridor as I had come in search of Loren's distress." His tone gave Brendolyn a chill as they stopped before the bottom step. "I am not ignorant of your past, Brendolyn. I have had a letter from Duke Lahrs not long after taking charge of receiving you into Jorn. But I do not take lightly the connection of your past, what this meant for you to come here, but I heed you a warning to not stir the balance of the young king's mind."

Brendolyn gulped, her heart racing in her chest.

"Barrow wishes to stop your marriage to Loren," Vasco continued on in a soft, even tone. "He would go to any lengths, Brendolyn. He would start a war with Bannon's aide to have you…"

Pain burst behind her eyes and tears sprung in the fear that radiated through her bones. Vasco spoke no more, patting her hand before guiding them further up the steps and steering them into the cold corridors in search of the seclusion of her chambers.

# CHAPTER
## 25

THE BELLS OF JORN tolled in slow, somber rhythm as the final hour approached.

Sunlight, thin and strained through the overcast sky, filtered through the stained glass of the great hall, bathing the marble floor in fractured hues of crimson, violet, and blue. The air in the great hall was cold despite the crowd that gathered. Nobles, dignitaries, and lords of the realm of Jorn stood assembled in their finest attire, their eyes fixed on the stone steps of the dais beneath the hung banners where the ceremony would begin.

Barrow stood still as stone, robed in ceremonial garments of red that ran over his body like a river of blood. His golden hair had been combed back set beneath the circlet where the crown would be set. Such was the law of Jorn when a sovereign heir might rule in mourning for the first year, but only if the people, through their lords, still willed it a year hence, could he take up the seat of his forefathers. It had not been the full twelve months when Lord Bannon had begun to receive letters from the lords of the realm in commission to enstate the throne sooner and he could not refuse.

After the death of Pavan, the King Slayer, it was all but final. Barrow was to be named the rightful king, every bannerman throughout the Realm of Jorn, into the reaches of Entheas came to witness the dawning of this new age.

Now the silence of that waiting shattered as Bannon stepped forward, flanked by six ceremonial guards, each in bronze armor. Barrow felt the pangs of something, knowing

Amadeus Astor was dead at the hands of those that followed Pavan. Now it fell to the Hand of the King to perfect that honor. Upon a velvet cushion rested the crown and Barrow's jaw tightened, his eyes locked on the artifact that had once belonged to his father, and his father's father.

"All hail His Majesty, King Barrow of Jorn," Lord Bannon proclaimed, his voice carrying across the stone chamber with calculated strength.

Applause followed like a rolling tide. Barrow forced a breath into his lungs, lifting his chin as he turned to face his kingdom for the first time as sovereign. He descended the dais in a slow procession, his heavy ceremonial cape dragging behind him like a curtain of blood-red velvet.

Among the faces lining the path, his gaze caught on a pair that stole the air from his chest. Brendolyn stood to the right, standing so near to the duke of Rhun who held himself with quiet pride, his pale hair brushed back neatly, and his expression unreadable. The sight of them together burned behind Barrow's eyes like a brand. Just behind them stood Sir Eero, his posture dutiful beside Princess Fiona, Barrow's sister. She wore a delicate veil of gossamer lace, but her smile was visible beneath it, a soft, almost bittersweet expression that offered no comfort.

The ceremonial march continued, and Lord Bannon's voice once again rose above the crowd, declaring Barrow's titles to the people of Jorn. The moment stretched, then concluded with a flourish as Simeon's announcement echoed against the vaulted ceilings.

Walking the full length of the hall with measured pace, Barrow never broke his posture until he passed the final arch and vanished from view. Behind closed doors, he removed the weighty cape from his shoulders and returned the royal scepter to the waiting councilors, his hands shaking slightly as he released it.

He lingered in the quiet that followed, his breath uneven. The coronation had ended, but the dread remained. Withdrawing to the privacy of his personal chambers, the door closed behind him like a final drumbeat. The fire had burned low in the hearth, casting flickering shadows across the room's aged stone walls. He had barely poured himself a glass of wine when the door creaked open again and Simeon stepped inside, his hands clasped behind his back, a thin smile cutting across his pale face.

"You bore it well," Simeon said, his voice smooth. "Duty weighs heavily on all great men. But you carried it like a king should."

Barrow frowned. "I have no use for such trivial celebrations. I have been king for this last year." He leaned forward, snatching the metal from his brow to toss it aside, it clamored loudly.

"Of course." Simeon bowed, but his keen eye looked adrift.

"Speak," Barrow hissed. "There is something on your mind."

"There is news of a disturbing kind." Simeon sounded more disturbed than he looked, and it gave Barrow a needle of unease. "Sir Vasco has abandoned his post, and with the coming depart of Duke Enzo, there has been a request of leave of the head of your guard."

Grinding his teeth, Barrow wished not to think of the white haired man as he could still feel the hand upon his throat. Barrow gulped but could not speak.

"Sir Eero has been called upon to take charge of Lady Brendolyn's departure, for her company shall be a solitary one."

Barrow twitched, his glance flickering towards the lord who stood so solidly before him. "Solitary?"

"Of course." Simeon smiled, his teeth a wide grin that showed far too many teeth. "Lady Elsa shall be taken to Divna before the week is out, the sisters have sent a carriage to collect her for her charge."

"I thought Sabian had requested a retraction at the end of service, to keep Elsa with Brendolyn in Rhun..." He felt sick.

"A new declaration set in motion the removal of service by Jorn law."

Unease settled within him and Barrow was awash with guilt as he watched Bannon approach the desk and set down a small glass vial. The liquid inside was a pale amber, catching the light like honeyed sap. He sneered down at it.

"A tonic. For the nerves," Simeon offered. "Nothing more."

Barrow eyed it briefly before snatching it up and uncorking it. The scent was sharp and bitter. He drank it down in one gulp, grimacing as it coated his tongue and throat. With a hiss between his teeth, he raked a hand through his hair, pushing the golden strands from his damp forehead.

"Who signed such a proclamation?"

Simeon watched him quietly. "You did, my king."

Night had fallen thick over the kingdom, draping the hills in a velvet darkness pierced only by the silver glint of a waning moon. The roads were empty save for the soft clatter of hooves and the quiet turning of wheels. No torchlight marked the carriage's path, only shadow, rolling like smoke down the winding path toward Denorn.

Inside, Lord Bannon sat in silence, the rhythmic motion of the carriage doing nothing to stop the storm beneath his composed exterior. The empty glass vial rested in the folds of his gloved hand, his thumb brushing the curved rim again and again, as though he could summon meaning from its absence.

He had pocketed it with care the moment Barrow turned his back on him in the great hall of Jorn. So easily dismissed. So blindly trusting. Now, Simeon left the palace under cover of night, not out of exile or shame, but strategy. He needed distance. Solitude. A return to Denorn where no royal watchful eye could pry into his workings.

The carriage passed under the rusted gates of the estate without halt. The guards knew better than to question his comings and goings. The manor itself rose like a monument of shadow against the stars, its towers swallowed in ivy and its stone blackened by centuries. No lanterns were lit at the door. Only the cold breath of night awaited him.

Simeon stepped down from the carriage, his cloak catching the wind like wings. Inside, the house was silent save for the crackling of a low fire left burning in the hearth, casting long, broken shadows across the grand foyer. He moved through the halls like a phantom returned to his crypt, his boots soundless on the ancient rugs.

At the top of the north wing stair, he came to his study.

He swept his hand slowly across the surface of his desk, fingers brushing over aged scrolls, bound grimoires, and half-finished correspondence. His office was a quiet sanctuary of intellect and strategy, but it was hollow now, emptied of the raw, intoxicating magick that once surged through his blood like wildfire.

That connection, the voice that had once whispered to him in shadowed dreams, had grown faint in recent months. Still, power would return. It always did.

A sharp clack against the window snapped his attention outward. Simeon turned, his brow raised. A misshapen silhouette shifted against the fading light, feathers warped and mottled, a creature more than bird. Its talons scraped against the stone as it tilted its head, one eye gleaming like wet coal.

He unlatched the window and the thing hopped in without hesitation, ruffling its filthy plumage. It hobbled upon the tops of the desk, before making a wretched noise, its body shivering and convulsing before crumpling in a misshapen heap as if the very fibers of its being ripped apart, revealing a tarnished leather tubing within. Simeon took it without hesitation. Ignoring the smear of blood on his fingertips, he retrieved the scroll of parchment. The paper was brittle and damp, the ink a deep rust red.

The language was old and a slow grin stretched his mouth, showing teeth.

*My magick strengthens as the moon waxes and wanes. Upon the King's thirtieth birthday, we shall join again to claim what is rightfully ours. Patience now, Simeon. Patience.*

Simeon turned toward the candle burning low beside his desk. With a flick of his fingers, he held the parchment above the flame. But instead of orange, it ignited in black that consumed the note in a sudden, silent blaze. Ash drifted to the floor, vanishing before it touched the stone.

Tired, Simeon struggled to stand, making it to the high backed chair near the cold hearth. He could light it, to warm his aching bones, but the waste in magick alluded him. Instead, he wrapped his cloak tighter around his body, blinking against the coming exhaustion.

A knock came then. Simeon flicked his wrist, hissing as the door swung open, letting in the captain who dragged a familiar man who grappled and cursed under the harsh grip.

Alaric.

"Found him in the scullery stealing food."

Forced to his knees at the center of the room, his tunic had been stripped away by the swift cut of Leuthere's dagger. Alaric's frame bore evidence of a cruelly carved curse. Long, narrow ridges carved across his chest, some still pink and taut, others already faded into cruel white. One trailed up toward his neck, barely missing the line of his jaw.

Simeon leaned forward in his chair, fingers steepled, and his eyes gleaming in the stray light that filtered in through the windows.

"A faie did this to you," he said, his voice smooth as velvet and twice as dark.

Alaric's fists clenched over his knees, but he said nothing.

Leuthere's lips curled. "And not just any faie."

Simeon's smile thinned. "*Thaddeus Brousevier.*"

A flicker of emotion passed across Alaric's face.

Simeon rose slowly from his chair, moving toward the boy like a shadow with weight. He knelt down to trace his fingers over the dull jagged scars of ancient runes made in haste. "How did it happen?"

"He disguised himself as a whore, gave me a potion." Alaric gulped, his revulsion thick in the air. "He fucked me, giving me this scar..."

Simeon gripped hard at Alaric's hair, pulling from the root and making him hiss. Leaning so close to his face to look into the eyes, he realized the magick was fading. Trailing his fingers down the sweating temples, Simeon wrapped his fingers around the delicate throat before him.

"It is not a scar, but a warning." Pressing his thumb into the angry red skin caused Alaric to scream. He drew back after the force of the unfinished magick kicked back, unwilling to yield to Simeon's touch. "A pitiful rebuke to ward off the use of any enchantment... you will rejoice in knowing Thaddeus is dead."

Alaric looked up sharply.

Simeon tilted his head. "Faie bleed like men. Eventually, they break like them too. His name will rot beneath the ashen and fallen stone of the Chapel of Light, forgotten. But your rebuke shall endure beyond that death, he ensured to that end."

Leuthere crossed the room then, circling Alaric like a carrion bird. "There is victory in every wound, Alaric. And yours? A testament to survival. But now, you'll need to serve it with purpose."

Simeon turned his back, facing the fire. His voice, however, remained steady and commanding. "Lady Elsa shall not remain at the princess's side. We've pulled the root clean from the soil."

Alaric's brow furrowed. "She wouldn't go willingly."

"She didn't," Leuthere replied. "But by the new enstated lands of Augusta returned to that bitch the king is keen on, it remains that she must be married and married she is to be to the Duke of Rhun. A land of traditions, where only those of Rhun remain in service. No Corad blood shall serve under the Rhun banner, in turn Lady Elsa shall be sent away. To Divna."

"Divna is unguarded, they rely upon duty and Vows." Alaric's voice was hoarse. "It would be easy to retrieve her."

Simeon turned then, meeting his eyes. "She is not your concern, not yet. Your payment in sparing your life shall be in blood."

Alaric's face drained of color, his throat bobbing up and down in fear.

Leuthere stood behind Alaric, his large hand resting on the dips of his shoulders, dangerously close to the bend of his throat. Fear began to blossom anew, lingering in the air to permeate it with delicious victory. Simeon smiled, watching as Leuthere pressed his fingers into the soft flesh of Alaric's throat, choking him. Alaric began to garble, grasping at the arms that were immoveable, his body thrashing in the chair.

"He won't kill you, not yet." Simeon smiled again. Leaning down to look Alaric in the face that was now turning purple, his eyes bulged desperately, pleading as pools of saliva dribbled from his mouth. "I will arrange passage for you to Divna, if you agree to one small act of service. Your blood payment."

Desperation clawed at the man, nodding and shaking, until at last Leuthere released him. Alaric heaved forward to clutch at his throat, desperate for air.

"Come with me," Simeon commanded, sweeping back.

They descended the steps, delving deeper and deeper into the belly of his vast estate, knowing Leuthere managed to hoist Alaric along, they came to the cellars. Taking down a lantern from its hook, Simeon unlatched a large oak door, stepping into the near blackness, the stream of light illuminating the dirty, damp chamber with cobbled stone beneath them that sloped slightly to the center.

At the center of the room knelt a man stripped of all clothes, arms outstretched, chained to two thick pillars of stone slabs. Sir Vasco looked less than a man, bloodied and bruised, his skin broken from the whip Leuthere enjoyed using to flog his captives.

"I come with your salvation," Simeon spoke into the darkness. Behind him, Leuthere pushed Alaric who stumbled forward, a blade thrown down at his feet.

"It is a sin," Alaric hissed, seeing the markings of the Aenarii upon the man's flesh, knowing the significance.

"You will spill *all* his blood, or it shall be *your* blood as payment."

Alaric flinched, resisting, but soon his hand took hold of the daggers hilt. Simeon's mouth curved around a smile, watching with blood thirsty eyes as Alaric struggled to his feet.

# CHAPTER

## 26

T HE GARDENS OF JORN shimmered in the golden hush of early evening, bathed in the soft glow of spring's awakening. The air was sweet with the scent of new blossoms and ivy climbed in elegant spirals around the carved stone archways. Somewhere nearby, a fountain murmured, its gentle splashing a quiet harmony to the distant sounds of noble laughter and subdued conversation.

At the garden's heart, Brendolyn walked the gravel path beneath a canopy of ivy, Princess Fiona at her side. A few paces ahead strolled Duchess Kristjana and Lahrs, while Sir Eero lingered behind, ever watchful. Her eyes scanned the gardens, watchful for the approach of Vasco, who had not attended her in some time.

It had been suggested that they walk the grounds, a proposal Brendolyn had been unable to refuse. Though she had once been formally introduced to Princess Fiona, this marked the first time they spoke without the buffer of the princess's usual entourage.

Fiona's voice was careful, threaded with warmth and admiration. "I've heard much about you," she said gently. "From the court... and from my brother."

Brendolyn's smile faltered, barely, but she quickly recovered, her composure held in place. She dipped her head, offering a delicate smile, though her throat felt tight and no reply came.

"I understand you've taken a vow of silence," Fiona added, more softly now.

Brendolyn slowed her steps, nodding once.

"I mean no offense," Fiona said quickly, her voice tinged with regret. She reached out, brushing her fingers lightly over Brendolyn's sleeve. They were nearly the same height, yet there was an effortless elegance in Fiona's bearing, poised and luminous in a way Brendolyn couldn't help but admire.

Farther up the path, Duchess Kristjana and Lahrs turned back to glance at them.

"Is everything alright?" the duchess called.

"All is well," Fiona replied. She turned her emerald eyes back toward Brendolyn with a glimmer of mischief. Glancing sidelong at Sir Eero who stood stiffly a few steps away, politely avoiding their gaze, she called out, "Trying to be coy, Sir Eero? I see you there."

The knight bowed slightly. "Ever at your command, princess."

"*Princess*," Fiona repeated with mock severity, looping her arm through Brendolyn's as they walked. "Do you hear him, Brendolyn? Always claiming to serve me yet constantly giving orders. I walked the gardens forty times yesterday and simply wished for a ride into the countryside, but did he allow it?" She threw a teasing glance over her shoulder and stuck out her tongue. "He did not."

Brendolyn glanced back as well, noting the faintest twitch at the corner of Sir Eero's mouth, a smile so quick and fleeting, and yet full of meaning. There was more behind his silence than he ever allowed himself to say.

"I've spent years in his constant company," Fiona went on, sighing dramatically, "and he refuses to share anything about his family. I don't even know where he grew up."

"Nihtar."

The word came like a bell toll, halting Brendolyn mid step. Her eyes lifted, startled, to the source of the voice. Standing beside Lahrs and Duchess Kristjana was Loren Enzo. Brendolyn hadn't noticed when the young duke of Rhun had joined them, but the sound of his voice sent a shiver racing up her spine. Fiona gasped beside her.

"Nihtar? The Brotherhood?" she echoed, turning quickly from Brendolyn to face Eero, stepping closer to him now. "How do you know that?"

Loren answered before Eero could. "I trained in Nihtar, when I was young. We are... acquainted."

There was something strange in Loren's face, an unease Brendolyn had never seen in him before. His eyes snapped to hers with an intensity that stole the air from her lungs.

"I believe I bested you in hand-to-hand," Eero said, voice low and even.

Loren crossed his arms over his chest, recovering with a faint smile. "But how skilled are you with a bow?"

"I'd enjoy a demonstration," Fiona said brightly, sliding her arm back through Brendolyn's and pressing closer. "We should commission a duel, Sir Eero against Duke Enzo in the ring."

"That would be treason," Lahrs remarked dryly, though a smile tugged at his lips. "Striking the Hand of the King is as good as striking the king himself."

"I am no Hand," Eero replied flatly.

A silence followed, stiff and cold.

"I was never granted such an honor," he continued. "I remain captain of the royal guard. And in that, it is my duty to protect the royal family, as I have done since the war."

Duchess Kristjana quickly stepped in to shift the mood. "The sun grows hot out here. Perhaps we should bring the girls inside for tea?"

Sir Eero bowed in quiet assent. Brendolyn felt herself being guided by Fiona's gentle pull, her steps sluggish, and her mind unwilling.

"I might request a word with you, Sir Lahrs," Loren said suddenly, tearing his gaze from Brendolyn to meet her old companion's eyes.

She wanted to stay. Wanted to hear what they might say, what truths lay buried beneath their civility. But Fiona was already leading her away, and the hush of the garden closed behind her like a door.

They had walked just far enough to be out of view, tucked between high hedges where the lantern light flickered soft and gold. The garden sounds had faded into a low hum behind them.

Lahrs stood with his hands behind his back, posture composed but eyes watchful. He regarded Loren Enzo with the same measured scrutiny he had shown many a noble, but there was something more curious in his expression now an unspoken wondering, a subtle pull between suspicion and hope.

Loren took a breath. "I would ask your blessing to marry Brendolyn."

Lahrs's mouth opened slightly, then closed. His head tilted, almost imperceptibly, as though Loren had spoken in a language he hadn't expected to hear. His composure did not falter, but the slight narrowing of his eyes betrayed a rare ripple beneath the surface.

"I have not the power to give that consent," he said quietly.

"I ask it of her father," Loren said, his tone sincere, unmoving. "Her *true* father."

Lahrs looked away, just briefly, a flicker of something wounded and quiet crossing his face. "I cannot claim her." He masked it quickly, but not quickly enough.

"Your blessing." Loren stepped closer, reaching out slowly to take hold of Lahrs' wrist as he lowered his voice. "*Elhaara tal'duain.*"

"You draw great risk coming here," Lahrs said softly.

"I vow to protect her, Lahrs. You know better than anyone what I am." Loren's voice was low, unlike the Loren he had perceived before. "What I am capable of…"

"Can you protect her from herself, when the very light of her eyes has dimmed?"

"By the very blood in my veins." Loren nodded.

"Sir Vasco has vanished." Lahrs grew serious, stepping closer. "Only you know how a man bound by vows of the Aenarii could leave her side."

The light filtered dimly through the glass. Brendolyn sat at the small table, where they quietly took tea together.

Fiona was the first to speak. "Have you considered whom you might choose for your ladies' maids once you're settled in Rhun?"

Brendolyn's head turned, eyes narrowing with faint confusion.

Fiona's smile was tight, sympathetic in a way that made Brendolyn's stomach twist. "Adjustments must be made, you see. There are... expectations. Customs."

"Fiona," Sir Eero warned, standing near to them. His voice was abrupt and the usage of the princesses name so informally took Brendolyn aback, but his tone shifted something in Fiona, her fair cheeks blushed, averting her gaze.

"We had hoped Lahrs would be here, to soften the blow, Brendolyn," Sir Eero said with the finality of stone. "Elsa was taken this morning by carriage to Denorn, where she shall board a ship and sail to Divna."

Brendolyn's breath caught. There was a slow movement at her side, as Duchess Kristjana, who had been stunned silent by the princess's former expression allowed her at last to hasten to Brendolyn's side.

"Duke Laronn's agreement with Lahrs all those years ago allowed Elsa to remain in Corad as your lady in waiting until your day of marriage." Duchess Kristjana smoothed some of Brendolyn's hair, rubbing her hand gently. "We wished it was different, my darling, but we cannot change what has passed. Nor what is expected of your joining with the house of Enzo."

Brendolyn tried to contain her tears, but they slipped free, scorching paths of torment along her cheeks, unable to look at any of them.

"Only those of Rhun might be in your inner circle as is the tradition of that great hidden realm."

Unable to cry, her throat burned with agony, pulling her hands free, she stood abruptly. Fiona called after her, but she could see out of the corner of her eye as Eero held her back. Brendolyn was glad of it, she didn't want to be followed or talked to.

Brendolyn's fingers curled into fists as she ran, knuckles white and shaking. She hated Loren Enzo, with his delicate words and polished smiles. She hated the walls of Jorn and the eyes that followed her. She hated the cold that had crept into everything since she arrived. She hated them all.

# CHAPTER

## 27

EAGER TO BE FREE of Jorn Castle, but not eager to travel into a strange land to accept foreign customs, Brendolyn found herself sitting upon the bench in the shadowed chapel deep within the castle, with only the light of a singular slit of stone where natural sunlight emerged, it was in this quiet sanctuary she was able to find solitude.

Not many visited the chapel, and those who entered whispered soft prayers.

Brendolyn stiffened, her head bowed, but the shift of fabric beside her as someone sat upon the bench. He was quiet, she glanced at the soft leather of his boots that had been brushed. Slowly raising her eyes to take in the travel breeches of dark wool, the hands that were locked together in his lap, finally, she looked up at the emerald eyes of the man she would soon call husband. He wasn't looking at her, but at the statue of the goddess that stood at the head of the room, where hundreds of candles burned at her feet.

"I don't believe I have ever visited this part of the castle," Loren spoke in hushed tones, but in the quiet of the room it felt loud. "It is a beautiful chapel."

Brendolyn said nothing, her gaze quickly averted, looking at the statue when his emerald eyes shifted her way. He leaned forward, bowing his head to let the fall of his silver white hair cascade down, obscuring his features.

"I heard your friend was sent away." He sounded almost sad.

Unable to give him the satisfaction of promising the best servants in Rhun, Brendolyn kept her eyes averted, attempting to remain strong but the pain in her heart was nearly unbearable. The ache was deep, undeniable, as a single tear began to fall along her cheek.

"Bren," he whispered her name.

She swallowed, counting the candles, keeping her mind off of Loren but his hand was gentle, taking hers in his own. Bringing it to his lips, she scoffed, trying to turn her eyes away.

"Bren." His words were more stern, reaching his other hand up to wipe away the tear in her eyes. "I have sent Mihrk to inquire with Duke Laronn, to retract this contract that keeps you apart from Elsa."

Brendolyn gulped. *Do not make promises you cannot keep*, her mind screamed, willing the man to leave her be in her misery.

"Bren," he whispered again, pleading.

Finally she looked, turning her eyes towards him.

"Give me time to prove myself to you, Brendolyn. I give you my oath of protection, as well as my oath of whatever may bring you happiness, it shall be done." He paused, looking her over so intently it made her blush. He opened his mouth to speak and in the solitude of the chapel he leaned close, Brendolyn's heartbeat quickened.

She would be his within a few months, and thus Brendolyn had read more about the customs of Rhun. Reading into their wedding ceremonies and their laws, trying to familiarize herself with the lengths the small realm had gone to in order to separate themselves from the rule of Corad. She knew it was forbidden to be within the same room as a man who was not your husband, but here they sat.

"We must find you a voice," Loren breathed, more to himself than to her. "I understand you know languages of this realm?"

Slowly, Brendolyn nodded, raising her hands to speak, the words were slow to form on her fingers, he watched mesmerized. "*I have no voice, Loren. I speak and yet you do not understand the depths of my pain. Please, do not let me to wither away into nothing.*"

"A silent language." Loren mimicked a few of the hand movements, almost perfectly. Speak. Pain. Wither. "I shall find myself a tutor. While I search, would you teach me?"

Reaching out a hand, Brendolyn touched his chest, just above his heart making the movement with her hand in a slow deliberate way as she had done before. "*Loren.*"

He did the same. "Loren."

"Princess Brendolyn." Entering the chapel, Sir Eero emerged. "The carriages have been called." He stopped short when he saw them sitting there.

Brendolyn blushed, lowered her hand, and stood.

"I expect it is time for your departure," Loren sighed, giving a nod as he also stood, towering over her. "We shall meet each other again, in Rhun."

It was strange to be within the carriage ride south, seeing the road that stretched out before her through the lands she had never seen, nor imagined she would ever see in her lifetime. Across from her, on the bench sat Sir Eero, dressed in a black doublet, his expression grave as he lent back, his eyes casting mournfully out the window, at the vast lands beyond the small windowpane.

It was curious to Brendolyn that Sir Eero had volunteered to travel south with Brendolyn into Rhun, taking it upon himself to be certain of her safe journey, while Loren Enzo remained in Jorn. There were things the young duke needed attending to while in the great city before returning to Rhun.

Brendolyn was used to the silence but sitting in such confined space with Eero she felt the pull to speak with him. She glanced his way whenever he shifted in his seat, but the knight refused to look at her.

"*You are infuriating.*" She motioned with her hands, exasperated by his coldness.

He glanced at her, but kept his silence, turning his eyes again to the other window, his movements intolerably slow.

"*Boring, hardheaded man. You make me angry...*" Her movements were fast, but she felt the need to shout at him.

Drawing his eyes towards her, there was a playful smile at the corner of his mouth. Shifting, he jostled in his seat when the carriage moved jarringly around them but his eyes remained on her, giving her his undivided attention.

Brendolyn went on. "*You have no right to be near me after what you have done to Pavan. I trusted you and you broke that trust.*"

"Brendolyn…" he began, but she refused to let him speak over her.

"*I am not finished.*" she clapped her hand hard. "*You may not understand what I say to you, but you will listen. Too long I have gone unheard, too long have I remained in silence when I wish to shout my intolerance of your selfish black hearted deeds. You took him from me! You have taken Pavan from this world and I shall never forgive you for it!*"

Exerted, she breathed heavier as her emotions grappled within her, desperate to emerge. Gasping for breath, Brendolyn leaned back, glaring at the knight who had sat in silence as she vigorously spoke with her hands. Her hands now red and aching. Vigorously wiping at the few errant tears that slipped free over her cheek, she let the sway of the carriage rock her from side to side.

"Bren…" His voice was gentle. "You have every right to scold me. It is necessary for what I have done in your eyes."

Her chin wobbled, glaring at the knight.

"You have every right to be angry and are correct in scolding me. I am a black heart who deserves your loathing for taking the life of an innocent man." Eero shifted, his body language visibly uncomfortable, leaning on his leg to draw slightly closer to her, but no further. "I do not deserve your forgiveness, but perhaps in time you will understand what I had done, and why it was necessary."

Brendolyn crossed her arms, tightening her jaw.

Sir Eero sighed. "No more reprimands. You have spoken plainly to me, I have minimal mastery of the language of the Silent Sisters, but your diction is perfectly understood."

Her arms loosened, furrowing her eyebrows, slacking in her hold enough to slowly move her hands to form the words. "*You understand me?*"

"I was trained in Nihtar with the Brotherhood, in that training we were giving formal instruction on all the languages… I furthered my knowledge when I took the Vow of Light when I was in my youth." Eero glanced at his hands, rubbing them together. "It is not common knowledge that I hold that kind of magick, nor of my elven heritage."

"*You have kept your birth hidden?*"

"Beaumont knew of my truth. He vouched for me when I was injured in the Battle of Tears, the last battle before the end of the war. I owed him my life, and my services. He knew the vow I took." Eero laughed bitterly, then his eyes glanced out to the fields beyond the window. "My vows extended to Barrow. He was so young when I met him, such a kind boy…"

Her heart fluttered, watching the man before her visibly crumple, and as tears began to well in the sad grey eyes, she felt ashamed for her hatred. She listened to the brokenness in the man before her.

"I know of his evils, Bren," Sir Eero said on a breathless whisper, looking at her again. "I know of what Simeon Bannon has done, and the hold he has upon Barrow's heart. It cannot be undone, not by magick any of us hold."

Terror flickered within her, fluttering in her chest as the carriage rolled further into the realm of Rhun. With Pavan dead, and the threat of the magick Simeon Bannon held, what was to stop him from taking over the realms. A new set of fears overwhelmed her, her throat tightening as the pain of the curse tightened its hold.

"You can trust Loren Enzo."

Brendolyn scoffed, her hands moving quickly. "*He has made it difficult to trust him.*"

Eero laughed. "He has shown great promise, Brendolyn. What is your reservation in finding comfort in his company? You looked content in the chapel."

"*He made empty promises.*"

"You doubt he will keep his word? What else has he done that had caused you such disfavor? He is not a prince, but he rules this realm and his people love him dearly."

Brendolyn frowned. "*I never loved Barrow because he was a prince, it would not make a difference if my husband was not one either.*"

"Love." Sir Eero's smile fell and he shook his head. "I understand your reservations. You gave your heart so freely and in that yielding of your heart you were broken. I will not advise that you not shield your heart, but you must know the security of being with Loren Enzo. He shall protect you from Simeon Bannon."

Sitting across from the princess, Eero could see the hurt on the young face. Brendolyn was quiet after the beginning of their journey.

The carriage rocked from side to side with the sway of the road, while outside the window began to shift from the tall birch woods to the dense, thick evergreen forests of the wildlands at the edge of Rhun. He knew the forests well, having spent so many years of his youth hunting in these lands. A deep ache bloomed within his chest, growing as they passed through the shift of trees, beyond the watchtowers where those that watched over the lands kept the wards active.

It was dangerous to return, Eero understood, his thoughts drifting further towards his past as they drew closer to the great city of Rhun, protected behind the thick stone walls. Now the princess would be introduced to the old customs of the court. Ancient rituals of archaic elven make, prayer in the morning hours before the sun rises, and a land bound by blood magick.

Beyond the shade of the window, as they began to round the bend towards the great iron gates, Eero peered out the window with a souring taste to see a purple banner fluttering in the breeze amidst a canvas tent just outside the great stone walls.

"*What is the matter?*" Brendolyn's hands moved with quickness, but from her spot upon the bench she could not see what approached.

"There is a crossroad," he sighed heavily, feeling the carriage begin to slow in speed as they approached. "In the custom of the old ways, there is an exchange that must happen. A ceremony of renunciation and reception into Rhun. In the time before the war, a bride would be dressed in a white veil and gown, paraded out into the streets of Rhun city by a host of bearers, so the people may throw down white pedals to bring with them the new beginning..."

Brendolyn was frightened, looking out as they drew closer to the coming entourage.

Eero lurched forward as the carriage rocked to a stop. "There has yet to be a marriage outside the rule of this realm, Brendolyn. Since the war drove the mad duke to close these lands, none but those who are welcome have admittance beyond the walls."

Before she could answer the carriage door was unlatched, opening to let in a drifting sea chill. A sharp tang of the sea welcomed them and Eero stepped out first. His eyes narrowed at the line of men dressed in familiar leathers, their cloaks of deep violet. All eyes watched as he helped Brendolyn from the carriage and he could feel her fingers shivering in the cold breeze.

"Welcome to the Duchess of Augusta," A tall general stepped forward, his voice heavily accented, wearing a golden circlet around his neck to show his rank. He bowed, pressing a closed fist to his chest.

Brendolyn tightened her hand in Eero's refusing to let him go.

Eero bowed. "I am Sir Eero Stoian of Jorn, escort of the duchess. We have travelled a long distance and her highness wishes to advance to Castle Caerh for rest before beginning the Rite of the Veil."

"Your Rhúnael is near perfect, Sir Eero, but I cannot allow a *veshari* to pass beyond our gates without proper purification." The man bowed slightly, his voice an even tone and diction. "So is our way."

Eero bowed out of habit, but his hand was being pulled, feeling the magick beneath his fingertips growing tighter as he felt Brendolyn's anxiety grow. Stepping forward, at the beckoning of the man, Eero led them towards the tent. The wind whipped mercilessly over the downs of the grassy nulls from the sea that lay to the east.

Entering the warmth, they were greeted by the smell of lavender incense and oil. It was a simple tent, furs lined beneath their feet, and silk hung from the poles to further shield from the wind that rustled the outer canvas. A single curved lamp hung above their head to illuminate the small space.

"Favor find you," a soft melodic voice said and an older woman with soft brown hair stepped closer. "I am Lady Venhi, head of the household of Castle Caehr under the rule of Duke Loren Enzo."

Brendolyn stepped back, dropping Eero's hand to put him between them.

"Favor find you, Lady Venhi, I am Eero Stoian of Jorn and this..." He shifted his weight slightly, to make Brendolyn visible.

"Yes, I am aware of who you are, Sir Eero, and I understand you are of the Brotherhood." Lady Venhi was well spoken, maneuvering across the soft furs to the far side of the tent where she drew back a thick drape of canvas.

The gown waited on a tall wooden mannequin. At first glance it looked almost unreal. The muslin silk fell in long, fluid layers that pooled around the base like gathered moonlight. Each panel was feather light yet edged with delicate silver bells. They were so small that it could be believed they might have been shaped from droplets of metal. When the lanterns stirred the air, the bells gave the faintest chiming hum. Tiny shards of polished glass were stitched among them in curving patterns, catching every flicker of light and scattering it across the walls of the tent in bright glints.

Lady Venhi stepped close and lifted one of the panels with practiced reverence.

"This gown belonged to the first duchess who ever took Rhun's rites," she said. "And to every duchess after her, each added her own needlework, her own blessing, her own memory. These bells are meant to call the attention of the ancestors. The glass is placed to reflect any ill spirit that may try to follow you."

Brendolyn moved nearer, her reservation fascinated by the magnificent gown before them. The mannequin stood taller than her petite frame, carved with the long, elegant shape common to the women of Rhun. Sir Eero watched in silence but his eyes did not leave the garment. Recognition fluttered in his chest when Brendolyn's fingertips trailed along the stitchwork along the bodice.

Lady Venhi lowered the silk and turned toward Brendolyn.

"When you put this on, you will step into Rhun as one of us. You will set aside the clothes you brought from Corad and the colors that mark you as a *veshari*. Those things belong to the life you walked before today. Here, you take on our customs, our rites, and our history. Nothing from your old wardrobe goes forward with you. Only what Rhun gives."

Eero kept his gaze on the ground when Lady Venhi gently asked Brendolyn to remove her gown. He turned away at once, giving her as much privacy as the small tent could offer. He listened instead to the rustle of silk and the soft clink of the tiny bells as the old garment was lifted from the mannequin and prepared for her.

Behind him, Lady Venhi's voice remained steady.

"Duke Loren Enzo sent word this morning. The decree is clear. None may enter the gates of Rhun but the chosen bride. She walks the Rite alone."

Eero felt the words settle like cold iron across his spine and his jaw tightened. He had known there would be restrictions—Rhun guarded its customs with ancient severity. Still, hearing the truth spoken aloud made each breath feel heavier. Brendolyn would cross those gates without him. Whatever waited on the other side, she would face it in the company of strangers, wrapped in traditions she barely understood.

He closed his eyes for a long moment and when he turned back, Brendolyn stood in the gown.

The muslin silk draped around her as if it had been woven for her alone. The pieces of mirrored glass cast pale glimmers across her skin. The headdress rested snugly over the crown of her long dark hair, anchoring the white veil that Lady Venhi would soon place over her face. For a moment Eero could only look at her, rooted where he stood.

"Thank you, Lady Venhi," he managed, though his voice felt distant in his own ears.

He stepped toward Brendolyn and reached for her hands. Her fingers were cold, fragile in his grasp, yet still steady. "I cannot go with you," he told her quietly. "Once you pass through those gates, the road ahead is yours alone. When you leave on horseback, I will walk beside you for only a little while. After that, Rhun must take you in without me."

Brendolyn lifted her hands and signed with quick, stuttered movements. *"It is too soon, I cannot say goodbye now."*

Eero nodded, feeling an ache rise in his chest. He did not know how he would release her hand when the moment came.

Lady Venhi ushered them toward the outer doors. The wind was waiting, sharp and restless along the hillside. The sky above the great gates churned with pale gray clouds that swept low enough to brush the peaks. A white horse stood bridled and ready, its mane tossing with every flick of its head.

Eero guided Brendolyn to the animal's side while the bells on her gown chimed with every step. He placed his palms at her waist and lifted her upward. She settled onto the saddle with a soft exhale, gathering the fabric so it would not drag. The veil hung loose for now, stirring against her cheek in the wind.

He took her hand again as the guards of Rhun approached. Their leather breastplates creaked with each stride, their expressions carved from stone. Together, Eero and Brendolyn walked forward, the white horse pacing between them as the grand gates loomed higher and higher.

The threshold waited and when they reached it, a tall man stepped into Eero's path, but his arm barred the way with practiced finality.

"Only the bride."

Brendolyn's fingers tightened in Eero's for a heartbeat. A single breath. A last pause between two lives. He looked up into her golden eyes and everything he wanted to say crowded his throat, trapped behind the knowledge that he could not follow her.

Her fingers slipped from his grip and a moment later, the white horse stepped forward and carried her into Rhun.

# CHAPTER

## 28



*Castle Caerh, Rhun*

THE GATES OF RHUN closed behind her with a deep, echoing thud that seemed to settle in her bones. Brendolyn kept her hands tight around the reins as the horse stepped forward. Lady Venhi walked beside her, one hand resting lightly on the horse's flank for guidance.

"Lower your veil now," Lady Venhi instructed in common, her voice soft but firm.

Brendolyn let the sheer white cloth fall over her face and the world dimmed to a pale haze. Only shapes and light remained, muffled and distant, as though she were drifting through a dream she could not quite hold on to.

They entered the city streets.

The sound hit her first—hundreds of voices hushed together, a collective breath held in anticipation. Through the veil she saw the blurred outlines of villagers lining both sides of the road. Each person held a bloom of white in their hands. Some clutched them to their chests. Others held them aloft.

When her horse stepped into the center of the path, the villagers began tossing the flowers forward. Pale petals scattered across the stones in soft flurries. They fell in front of her, around her, brushing against the gown's silver bells. The scent of them rose up through the veil, fresh and sweet.

Rhun had been waiting for her.

The road bent gently through the town. Stone shops rose on either side, weather worn and moss veined, their windows glowing with lanternlight. The wind carried the scent of the sea, and distant gulls cried overhead. Every face she passed watched her with open curiosity, reverence, or quiet uncertainty. The bells along her gown chimed with every shift of the horse's stride, a constant whisper that marked her as the foreign bride entering their ancient rites.

Ahead, beyond the rooftops, she saw the dark silhouette of Caerh.

The castle rose like the spine of a mountain, its spires tapering into the gray sky. Ocean rains had darkened the stone, giving it a mottled, ancient sheen. It looked both proud and tired, as though carved from the bones of time itself. Brendolyn's breath caught beneath the veil. Each moment carried her closer to it, closer to the future she had chosen, closer to the life she was expected to take on.

Her nerves churned, tightening in her stomach.

The castle gates opened with a rattling groan of iron, swallowing the sound of the city behind her. She followed Lady Venhi down a long lane framed by towering trees whose branches swayed in the wind. Their elongated shadows stretched across her path like fingers reaching toward her.

At the front steps, the horse stopped. A butler in dark livery waited at the base of the stairs, his posture was impeccable, though his expression betrayed a flicker of surprise when he saw her. He reached up carefully, steadying her arms as she dismounted. Her feet touched the stone, colder than she expected, and the bells sang faintly as she adjusted her gown.

The butler led her through the grand doors into the wide stone foyer.

The air inside was colder still. A draft whispered along the floor, stirring the hem of her gown. The high ceiling arched like the ribs of some ancient beast, and the walls glistened faintly with moisture from the sea winds.

Nearly fifty attendants stood assembled—maids in gray linen, footmen in deep green, stewards with ivory cords, all arranged in tidy ranks. Their eyes lifted to her the moment she entered and Brendolyn felt the weight of their expectation settle on her shoulders, heavier than the headdress.

Lady Venhi stepped behind her and Brendolyn felt cool fingers at the crown of her head as the headdress was unfastened. The veil slid away, leaving her face exposed to the cold air while the attendants bowed in unison.

Brendolyn stood very still, fighting the urge to reach for Eero's steady presence but he was far beyond the gates now and could not come to her. She was alone in a castle of strangers, wrapped in the hopes of a land that did not yet know her.

Lady Venhi guided her out of the foyer, her footsteps echoing softly across the stone. The attendants dispersed behind them, slipping into the shadows of the castle like ghosts returning to their posts. Brendolyn followed in silence, her gown brushing lightly against the cold floor, the silver bells giving a faint whisper with each careful step.

The corridors of Caerh were dim. Torches flickered along the walls, their flames small and subdued, unable to fully chase away the chill. The stone breathed cold air, carrying faint hints of seawater and old dust. Brendolyn drew her arms closer to her body as they moved deeper into the castle.

"Caerh was carved from the cliffs long before our records began," Lady Venhi said, turning down a narrow hall lit by low sconces. "It has weathered storms and war and centuries of salt wind. It will weather many more. Do not mind the cold. No fire is strong enough to warm every wall here."

They reached a wide staircase, its steps lined with deep velvet that dulled their footsteps. Brendolyn lifted her gown as she climbed, watching the shadows stretch and bend along the high, vaulted walls.

When they reached the landing, Lady Venhi paused beside a tall arched window. Rain streaked down the glass in slow, silvery trails. Beyond it, Brendolyn could barely see the dark outline of the trees swaying in the storm.

"This castle has two wings," Lady Venhi said. "Yours lies to the east, where the sun rises over the cliffs. Lord Loren Enzo resides in the west wing. You are to remain apart until the day of the wedding."

Brendolyn's breath caught faintly, unable to speak a word.

Lady Venhi continued walking, though her voice grew firmer, edged with warning. "You must understand the seriousness of this tradition. To be alone with him before the ceremony would be... problematic. The wise ones would question your virtue, and Rhun does not tolerate impropriety within its rites." She glanced back at Brendolyn, her expression steady. "It could lead to banishment. You must not risk it."

Brendolyn lowered her gaze and her hands tightened at her sides. She had not expected warmth, but the words settled like stones in her stomach. In her silence, her heartbeat thudded against her ribs.

Lady Venhi's tone softened slightly. "You will not be alone here. Your attendants will guide you. And when the day comes, Rhun will welcome you fully."

They reached a pair of wooden doors carved with swirling coastal patterns. Lady Venhi pushed one open, hastening inside. "These are your rooms."

Brendolyn followed.

The chamber was simple but spacious, lit by a few lanterns that cast soft pools of light. A large bed stood against the far wall, draped in cream colored linens. A washroom branched off to the right, filled with pale stone basins and a large copper tub behind a dressing screen. To the left, a wide doorway opened to a small sitting room.

She walked toward it, her gown sweeping across the floor. The sitting room held two cushioned chairs, a small table, and tall windows overlooking the cliffs. Rain continued to patter against the glass in thin rivers, turning the view into a blurred sweep of gray sky and dark sea. The storm outside made the room feel even quieter, as if the castle were holding its breath around her.

Lady Venhi stood behind her. "A girl shall be sent up to collect the gown," she said. "Tomorrow shall begin a new instruction for you, to begin learning the traditions and the language. When his high one returns from his travels, then you shall be brought before him when he is well rested."

Brendolyn nodded once.

Lady Venhi gave a final, measured bow and stepped back into the corridor, closing the door gently behind her.

Brendolyn was alone.

The bells on her gown gave a faint, lonely chime as she exhaled. Rain continued to streak the windows, the storm blurring the world beyond into shifting gray shadows. The castle's silence pressed in from every direction, vast and cold.

She moved to the window, touching the glass lightly with her fingertips.

Large doors to the main hall opened with a drawn out groan, the sound echoing too loudly for such a formal space. Brendolyn flinched despite herself as she was guided forward, her escorts moving with brisk indifference that forced her to shorten her steps to keep pace. The stone beneath her slippers was cold, even through the thin soles, and each footfall seemed to announce her smallness.

The gown she wore had never been meant for her. It had once belonged to the old duchess, a woman remembered for her commanding presence and broad shoulders. On Brendolyn, the fabric pulled and bunched, taken in hastily and without care. The bodice sat too high on her ribs, pressing tight enough that her breathing felt shallow. The sleeves stopped well before her wrists, and the weight of the skirt dragged at her hips as though trying to pull her down into the floor.

At the far end of the hall sat Loren Enzo.

The chair beneath him was enormous, its high carved back rising like a throne meant for someone else entirely. Loren Enzo occupied it stiffly, his posture careful and uncertain, as if he feared taking up too much space despite the chair's size. His hands were folded together, then unfolded, then folded again when he noticed her.

He straightened too suddenly, knocking his knee against the arm of the chair. The sound carried and his face flushed. Mihrk stood like a carved statue at his right side.

Lady Venhi moved ahead of Brendolyn with practiced grace, her silks whispering softly as she stopped at the center of the hall. She did not bow deeply. She never felt the need.

"Duke Enzo." Lady Venhi lowered herself in a graceful curtsy, motioning to Brendolyn to follow her example. Brendolyn awkwardly lowered, feeling the layers of gown pool around her, causing her to stumble. Beside her, the lady sighed. "As you can plainly see, she is quite small."

Brendolyn felt the words settle on her like weight. She folded her hands together, hiding her fingers inside sleeves too short to do their job.

Loren Enzo glanced at her, then away, then back again as though unsure where he was meant to look. "She seems," he began, then stopped. He cleared his throat. "She seems healthy."

Lady Venhi's lips curved into something not quite a smile. She stepped closer to Brendolyn and circled her slowly, her eyes tracking every imperfect seam. Her fingers reached out and pinched the fabric at Brendolyn's waist where excess cloth had been folded and sewn without grace.

"These gowns were cut for the old duchess," Lady Venhi said. "A woman of substance. Of strength. Everything here will need to be undone. Taken apart completely. There is no salvaging work meant for a body that was built to endure."

Her fingers lingered a moment too long before withdrawing.

Brendolyn's chest tightened. She kept her gaze fixed on the floor, though her thoughts raced. She felt as though she were being discussed like an object that might crack if mishandled.

"And of course," Lady Venhi continued lightly, her voice softening as though offering concern, "a frame so slight presents certain challenges. With such a thin frame, how is she expected to carry children?"

Loren Enzo shifted sharply in his seat and his hands clenched. "That is enough," he said, too quickly, the words tumbling over one another. "I command no more talk of this in my presence."

Lady Venhi turned to him, eyebrows lifting just a fraction. "Forgive me, my lord. I was only speaking of practicalities, for the future of Rhun is built upon the strength in the fortitude of lineage. We cannot think of discomfort, when this great house was built upon the blood of a birthing bed to bring the strength of male heirs to Rhun's halls."

Silence pressed in from all sides.

Loren Enzo frowned. "Call the dressmaker, toss out these hideous rags and have new gowns fitted."

The tension in the room was thick. Lady Venhi went pale, her mouth opening, then closing like a fish. Brendolyn felt her cheeks go hot.

"But, my lord, the traditions…"

Sitting forward in the chair, Loren Enzo was terse, his features shadowed by passing anger. "I shall not have my wife insulted, Lady Venhi, in regards to the choices of how she shall be compared to those that have bled for this realm. Do not insult my mother in this regard. Do not insult my intended bride with your impudent words meant to cast her aside as anything but worthy."

Brendolyn sat alone in the tearoom of the library wing, long after her afternoon tea had been cleared away. She remained by the tall windows overlooking the west gardens, watching the drizzle trail down the glass. Her loneliness ended at the sound of approaching footsteps, two sets, one measured and confident, the other a light, quick shuffle.

"Good day, Brendolyn."

Loren Enzo's familiar voice scraped at her nerves. She despised how handsome he was. Worse at how the calm warmth of his voice settled uninvited into her bones. She forced her expression into cool neutrality as he sat across from her.

His companion stood just behind him, a short woman with deep brown skin, her hair wrapped neatly beneath a silk scarf. She wore a mustard colored gown embroidered with umber flowers. Her russet eyes sparkled with mirth as she greeted Brendolyn with an amiable smile. Brendolyn returned only a polite nod.

"This is Lady Mahra," Loren said. "She has traveled from Divna. She is familiar with Rhun customs and is well spoken in all of the old languages."

Lady Mahra stepped forward. When she spoke, her voice was soft but her hands moved in graceful, familiar patterns. Brendolyn's heart tightened as she recognized the language immediately—the sacred silent speech used by the women of the southern orders, those who honored Ehnarea with vows of silence.

"Many blessings," Mahra said aloud, while her hands shaped the same greeting in the silent tongue. "May the Mother watch over you."

Brendolyn watched her elegant movements with admiration.

"Mahra has agreed to stay in Rhun," he explained. "While you remain so shall she be here, and I shall do everything in my power to learn what I can so that I can understand you completely." Loren lifted his hands and attempted a simple phrase *"I promise."*

Brendolyn inhaled sharply. She had taught herself so much through Lahrs' guidance, languages, histories, and forgotten scripts, she had not expected Loren to make an effort to meet her where she lived—in silence, in symbols, in depth.

Mahra watched her, patient and warm While Brendolyn slowly unfolded her hands. *"It is an honor to meet you, Lady Mahra, many blessings your way."*

"What did she say?" Loren asked quietly, unable to follow the rapid fluency of movements in Brendolyn's hands.

"She says she is honored by your gift," Lady Mahra replied gently.

*"You are flattering him."* Brendolyn smiled, her fingers dancing.

Lady Mahra chuckled, signing. *"Perhaps a man so eager to please you need flattery in his endeavours."*

Brendolyn blushed, turning her face away to hide her flushed look.

"You blush." Loren laughed, catching her eye. "Did I make the wrong word, tell me if I should be more careful."

"You are excellent in your languages, Loren," Lady Mahra gave a knowing look to Brendolyn, before giving her response in complete. "Perhaps it is best to let you figure out her discourse on your own." Curtsying to them both, she departed with soft, quick steps.

Brendolyn's heartbeat fluttered. For the first time since she had arrived in Rhun, she found herself alone in a room with Loren where no maids, no attendants, no escort standing between them. Lady Venhi's warning to her made her step back, alarmed, creating space between them.

Loren's brow knit with confusion before understanding softened his features.

"Forgive me," he said, bowing. "I meant no impropriety." He offered his arm then, voice gentle. "May I walk you to your chambers? It has grown cold, and they will have lit the fire for you by now."

After a long, uncertain pause, Brendolyn set her hand upon his arm. Her fingertips rested lightly at first, then steadied against the firm muscle beneath his tunic. She kept her eyes forward as they began to walk, unwilling to let her face betray anything she felt.

Her heartbeat thudded so fiercely she feared the sound might fill the hall. Their footsteps moved in soft rhythm along the carpeted floor, the woven fibers muting each step. She was still unaccustomed to such quiet. The great houses of Jorn and Corad echoed with every movement, their stone corridors carrying each sound like a whisper through the walls. Here, everything felt gentler, more confined, as though the castle listened.

Brendolyn tried to dismiss the flutter that stirred in her chest. It was foolish to feel anything for the duke. Dangerous, even. Yet she could not stop herself from glancing at him as they neared the staircase. His features were striking in the dim lanternlight, smooth skin and strong lines softened by the fall of his white hair against his shoulders. He carried the faint scent of mulled wine and winter spices and the warmth of it made her feel unsteady.

Hating him was far simpler. It kept her safe.

She took the first steps upward, placing her hand on the railing for guidance. Her thoughts swirled, heavy and unfocused, but she pressed on. She could hear Loren's footsteps just behind her, steady and measured as always.

Halfway up, her foot slipped.

A small gasp escaped her as the world tilted. Her hands braced against the carpeted stair, expecting the jolt of impact. Instead, strong arms closed around her waist, lifting her back before she could fall forward.

She drew in a shaky breath as she regained her footing.

When she turned, she found herself far too close to him. Heat rushed to her cheeks, both from the misstep and from the sudden nearness of his face. His emerald eyes searched hers, calm and unreadable, while her own felt wide with embarrassment.

Brendolyn hated him.

At least she told herself she did, even as her stomach twisted when Loren's hand steadied her at the waist. His touch was firm, holding her upright, his breath close enough that she felt the warmth of it.

"Are you hurt?" he asked, his voice barely above a murmur.

His green eyes held a flicker of worry. The staircase around them was silent, and for a heartbeat neither of them moved. Brendolyn could not bring herself to look away. Her pulse fluttered wildly beneath her ribs, the sound roaring in her ears. How could he appear so calm when she felt as though the world had slipped out from under her feet? Her hand lifted before she could stop it, pressing lightly against the front of his tunic.

"Bren." His voice dropped even lower.

The way he said her name sent a soft shiver through her. She hated that. She hated him. And yet the sensation unfurled inside her, delicate and treacherous.

Slowly, carefully, her hand traced the edge of his collar. The fabric was warm from his skin and she followed the line upward until her fingertips brushed the curve of his neck. A strand of his white hair tickled her wrist and she let her fingers slide through it, watching the silken fall slip between them. She lifted her gaze again.

Those same emerald eyes met hers. The ones she had sworn she despised. The ones she feared would undo her if she let them linger too long. He would be her husband soon, bound to her by Rhun's rites, and moments like this would no longer feel like the edge of a precipice. Still, the thrill caught her unguarded.

Heat radiated from him, easing the cold that clung to the castle walls. Her hand drifted deeper into the fall of his hair, circling the back of his neck and she felt him draw a slow breath. She wondered if he would step away, if he would remind her of the rules they both risked breaking but he remained where he stood, the hand at her waist tightening almost imperceptibly.

She hated him. But what she hated even more was the truth that she did not hate him at all. Her smile was faint, unbidden, as she leaned in. She brushed her lips softly against his, a brief kiss, delicate as a breath.

Loren exhaled when she withdrew. His eyes seemed brighter now, warmed by something she could not name. Brendolyn felt light, unsteady, as though a portion of the cold around her had melted for a heartbeat.

"Sir Enzo!" a voice echoed from the far end of the hall.

Loren's entire body tensed beneath her touch.

Brendolyn smiled, her fingers curling around the hand at her waist, grounding herself in the warmth of his palm. She lifted her free hand and lightly tapped the tip of his nose in a soft playful gesture, before turning toward the stairs. Loren let out a quiet breath, almost a laugh, and allowed her to tug him along. His steps followed hers without resistance, guided entirely by her pull.

Voices echoed from the ground floor, too close for comfort. Brendolyn quickened her pace and Loren matched her. They ran together, their clasped hands swinging between them as they fled the stairwell and disappeared down a maze of corridors. Their feet landed softly on the carpets, their breaths short with stifled laughter as they ducked beneath archways and slipped around corners.

At last Brendolyn pushed open the door to one of the unused rooms. Loren stepped inside behind her and she shut the door quietly, pressing her back to the wood. All the furniture stood beneath white sheets, ghost like beneath the muted overcast light pouring through the open windows. Dust motes floated lazily in the air, stirred by their hurried entrance.

They stood for a moment, catching their breath, chests rising and falling. Brendolyn's laugh broke first, soft and breathless. Loren's followed, deeper and quiet, warming the space between them and Brendolyn's stomach tightened with the sound. She leaned back against the doorframe, her gown clinging to her from the run. When she looked to him, she found Loren watching her with an expression that made her heart stumble. His eyes traced her face, then her throat, then the line of her shoulders. She felt the heat between her thighs grow unbearably warm.

She pushed off the door and crossed the space between them, rising onto her toes to claim his mouth in a deep, heated kiss. Loren inhaled sharply, his hands moving swiftly to steady her, one at her waist and the other sliding up her back. Her body pressed fully against him, fitting into the lines of his frame as if created for it. His mouth opened to hers, warm and eager, drawing her in with a hunger she felt echo deep inside her.

Magick thrummed through her, tightening and alive, responding to the heat of his presence. Her fingers threaded through the soft white fall of his hair, tracing the line of his neck, longing to taste the warmth of his lips and feel the pulse of his chest rising against hers. Desire coiled between them, low and urgent, an unspoken tension that neither needed words to acknowledge.

Brendolyn felt it in every nerve, knew it in the quickening of her heartbeat. She did not need her magick to sense that Loren wanted her as fiercely as she wanted him, each pulse and sigh of breath declaring it with unyielding clarity.

"Bren," he breathed between kisses yet his voice rasped with desire.

She eased away reluctantly, keeping her hands on his chest as she looked up at him. His brow was drawn, conflicted, but his emerald eyes burned with the same longing that pulled at every part of her.

"I cannot... we cannot..." He struggled, the words tripping over hesitation and need.

Brendolyn's lips curved softly. She lifted her hand and brushed her fingers along his cheek, gentling him. She leaned forward and pressed a tender kiss to his forehead and his breath stilled.

Stepping back, she let her hands fall to her sides. Loren straightened himself slowly, as if moving through water. He ran a hand through his white hair, trying to calm the heat that shimmered around them. When he looked at her again, her cheeks warmed instantly beneath the weight of his gaze.

"I should return to my duties," he whispered, though his voice still carried the remnants of breathlessness. He turned to the door, hesitating for only a heartbeat, then slipped out into the corridor and vanished from sight.

Brendolyn stood alone, the silence settling across her like a thin veil. She let out a long sigh, remembering herself and the foolishness she allowed. She hated Loren Enzo, or so she told herself, yet her heart had betrayed her once again.

She gathered her composure and stepped out of the unused office. The corridor felt colder without him. Slowly, she made her way back toward her chambers, her thoughts tangled between longing and resentment, each one pulling her deeper into the truth she refused to face.

# CHAPTER

## 29



*Divna, House of the Silent Sisters, Corad.*

S TEAM CLUNG TO THE stone walls of the kitchen as pots of boiled barley and root stews simmered quietly over low fires. The sisters moved like ghosts through the haze, faces veiled, hands busy, voices absent. Elsa stood near the chopping block, her sleeves rolled to her elbows, rhythmically slicing turnips as though the rote work might quiet the ache in her chest. Her auburn hair plaited back, away from her face that was splotched from the heat of the busy work.

A flicker of motion in the arched doorway caught her peripheral vision. Beside the crates of onions stood Eero. No armor. No sword, just dusty travel boots and a plain doublet. His short cropped hair was grown slightly, giving off the shimmer of silver, and his once hardened face looked drawn and hollowed by grief. Their eyes met and Elsa's pulse rioted, her knife freezing mid slice.

"May I speak with you?" he whispered, standing beside her.

Elsa's fingers tightened around the hilt of the knife. All around them, Silent Sisters glided on, oblivious, or ignoring his evident lack of silence. She stared at him for an agonizing moment before finally nodding, putting down the knife.

He exhaled, relief and regret at once, and gestured for her to follow. She wiped her hands on her apron and walked a few paces behind him, silent footfalls echoing through narrow corridors. They slipped through a side door into the outer cloistered gardens, where willow branches draped over stone benches and summer roses glowed deep crimson, heavy with dew.

Here, muffled from watchful eyes, they faced one another again. Eero was quiet. "I came to take you back to Corad. To protect you…"

Elsa's jaw tightened, and her brows knit into a frown. Looking around warily, looking for watchful eyes of the matrons that did not take kindly to broken rules.

"*I do not need a man to protect me.*" She did not care if he understood her, steeling herself she stepped forward to return to her duties.

His throat bobbed as he swallowed, distressed. Grabbing her by the arm quickly, he gave a great sigh, and he showed his hands. "*Elsa… you are not safe here. Alaric was seen in Denorn, two days past. He is searching for you, I came at once.*"

The garden wind stirred, lifting a curl of hair across Elsa's cheek. Her hands trembled slightly at the mention of Alaric's name… but her reply was sharp.

"*You killed Pavan.*" Her fingers struck each word like a blow. "*You broke your oath. For Bannon. And you expect me to trust you?*"

Pain flickered across Eero's features yet he didn't flinch, only stepped closer, eyes pooling with something like remorse. "*I have never forgiven myself. I believed lies. I thought I was saving Jorn. I was wrong.*" His breath hitched as he signed. "*I cannot undo what I did, Elsa. But I can still keep you alive. Let me protect you… please.*"

Silence stretched between them and somewhere nearby a dove cooed softly from the willow branches. Elsa's throat felt tight, fighting emotion she refused to let show. She began to turn away but he caught her lightly by the wrist and pressed something into her palm—a sheathed dagger. Slim and elegant with the insignia of a house she did not recognize carved into its hilt.

Elsa stared at it with widened eyes, alarmed as she whispered harshly under her breath. "What are you doing? The sisters will confiscate this if they see it."

Eero stepped closer. "Hide it. You know how. You were trained to use a blade since childhood. Keep it with you, Elsa for when he comes. Because he *will* come…" Eero leaned closer, they stood hidden beneath the shade of the tree. "Not for me, but for your own protection. Please."

Emotion surged through her chest, a war of fear, resentment, and a fragile, unwanted tenderness. She clutched the dagger.

"You cannot wash blood away by your gift." She shook her head, unable to stop the oncoming tears.

His reply was immediate. "I don't ask for your forgiveness. I beg for your safety."

"You confuse love with duty," she slipped the dagger beneath the folds of her gown, where it slid perfectly into the pocket. "The promise you made to my brother has long been fulfilled. There is little need for your declarations."

"I honor our friendship, Elsa," Eero sighed. "Your safety is my only priority..."

There was something in his manner that lingered on regret.

"You've changed," she began to understand. "Time has not been a kind friend to either of us."

Frowning, Eero bowed. "I have stayed too long, Elsa. They expect me back in Jorn before the week is out." Leaning down, he took her hand, kissing her fingers. "I take my leave, but please...keep your dagger close."

He backed away from her slowly, lingering on her for a singular glance before turning away and disappearing beyond her view. For a moment, Elsa wanted to call him back, but the weight of her fear sat too heavily upon her heart.

So she remained still beneath the willow tree, fingertips brushing the hidden dagger, praying to the goddess that she would not need to use it, but knowing that when Alaric came, she would not hesitate to make him bleed.

The road to Jorn Castle was long and rain slicked, the hooves of Eero's horse striking the cobblestones with a steady rhythm. The pale banners atop the towers came into view through the mist, each embroidered with the sigil Jorn, swaying against the gray sky. The scent of wet earth and pine followed him into the outer bailey where guards recognized him and waved him through without question.

The keep's great doors opened to the familiar warmth of torchlight. His boots left faint trails of water across the flagstones as he walked through marbled halls lined with tapestries of past monarchs. It had been only a week since he'd stood here, but the air felt unchanged, rich with the faint fragrance of rose oil and old stone.

A guard's voice carried softly in the corridor. "Princess Fiona awaits you in the east sitting room, Sir Eero. She commanded I give you notice upon your arrival."

He found her there, bathed in the pale light filtering through the arched windows. The room was adorned with soft velvet drapes, a crackling fire in the hearth, and the faint rustle of her gown as she shifted in her chair. Fiona sat with a small embroidery hoop in hand, stitching fine gold thread into a pattern of leaves and vines. Her dark hair caught the firelight as she glanced up at him, eyes bright with mischief.

"You're back," she said, her voice carrying the kind of ease that came from knowing she was never ignored.

Eero inclined his head, hands clasped behind his back. "I am, Your Highness. My charge remains unchanged."

Fiona's lips curved in a smile, but her attention returned briefly to her needlework. Still, he could feel her gaze drifting toward him every few moments, the air between them laced with something unspoken. "Must you stand like a statue?" she teased softly. "Come, sit. You've ridden far."

"My place is here," he replied, steady, keeping his weight on the balls of his feet. "I cannot lower my guard."

She set her sewing aside, silk threads pooling in her lap. "Lower it for a moment," she murmured, leaning toward him. "The other ladies have gone back to their rooms. We are alone. No one would think your oaths compromised if you took some respite."

Her tone was playful, but the undercurrent of sincerity made it dangerous and Eero's shoulders tensed. "It is not my oaths that would be questioned, princess," he said, his voice even but quieter now.

She rose, skirts whispering against the floor, and stepped closer. Her perfume was faintly floral, with a note of crushed herbs. Without breaking his gaze, she reached for his hand, her fingers warm against his. "Then sit," she urged gently, guiding him toward a nearby cushioned seat.

Reluctantly, he let her draw him down. The firelight caught the fine gold of her gown as she knelt before him, resting her hands over his. The weight of her touch brought with it an ache in his chest, an echo of something long buried.

A memory surfaced unbidden. He was young again, sitting in the parlour of his boyhood home, speaking to his mother as she put silver pins in her white hair. He had told her of a dream of a girl with green eyes, his fated match, her laugh bright as spring. She had smiled, smoothed his hair, and said he would know her when he saw her.

Now, looking at Fiona's beautiful face, her green eyes bright with expectation, he felt guilt press heavily into his ribs. He could never tell her the depth of it, nor the dangerous affection growing like a slow ember in his heart.

His voice was low when he finally spoke. "I was unable to fulfill my promise."

Her fingers tightened over his, a faint shadow of disappointment crossing her features before she masked it with a smile. "But you are too good to give up so easily," she whispered.

Eero gulped, emotion welling in his chest. "I promised to bring Brendolyn to the steps of the castle, I promised to be with her in that strange land. Now, she is beyond our customs, beyond the reach of those who know her... who understand."

Fiona's hands rubbed his, smoothing over his wrists, reaching up delicately to caress the line of his stubbled jaw, her softness radiating the room. "Brendolyn shall not resent you this act, Eero. I know her heart to be endearing."

Tears welled, his resolve to remain blocked off was breaking, everything that had happened came rushing forward as Fiona's hands held his, unable to contain the agony of betrayal, or heartache and he wept in his grief.

"Oh, dear heart," Fiona murmured, her voice softening into immediate concern. She rose at once and gathered him into her arms, settling beside him as she cradled his head against the curve of her neck. Her hands moved gently through his hair, already threaded with more silver than he'd had time to shear away.

"Do not bury your pain, Sir Eero," she whispered. "Left hidden, it grows sharp and turns to bitterness."

Eero pulled back as the storm of tears eased, his face flushed from weeping. Fiona regarded him with calm acceptance, brushing the last remnants of wetness from his cheeks, her fingers lingering in quiet reassurance. The intimacy of it struck him suddenly, and he recoiled a little in shame.

"Forgive me, Fiona," he said, lowering his gaze. "I must be more worn from travel than I realized. In the future, I will better prepare myself... so I may serve you properly." He moved to stand, but Fiona's hand gripped him firmly.

"Do not shy from my sight, Eero. Do not guard your heart." Fiona's voice was gentle as her fingertips rose to his cheek. The tender touch brought a flush to his skin. When she leaned forward, her breath mingled with his and her lips brushed his own in a soft kiss that stole the air from his lungs.

He drew back, the sweetness of her kiss torn from him by duty and the moment shattered as quickly as it had formed.

"You flatter me, Your Majesty," he said softly. "But I cannot indulge in your childish fansies."

"It is in Ehnarea's blessing that I dreamed of your heart beside mine," Fiona said, her cheeks still warm. "You cannot deny what has been placed before us."

Eero shook his head as he rose to his feet, creating distance between them that felt colder than the space itself. "I must deny what is improper. I refuse to torment you."

Fiona stood as well, her face shadowed with disappointment. "It is not torment to love, Sir Eero. I am no longer a child."

"I watched you from a cradle, Fiona. In your first years you clung to my legs when your father first visited you in Brac." A low, bitter sigh escaped him and his fingers dragged through his silver hair, settling at the back of his neck as if to steady himself. "You are young, in time this idea of loving me shall fade. When you take a husband you shall laugh at the foolishness of ever giving your attention to a knight of the old ways."

Fiona regarded him quietly. A small smile curved her lips, gentle and disarming in its calm. It unsettled him more than anger would have.

"You push and push, yet not once have you said that you do not love me," she said. "I hear only restraint, and I honor the wisdom in it. And the honor within you."

Eero eyed her closely, "My duty remains in guarding you with my life, Fiona, nothing more."

She stepped closer and extended her hand. "Take my hand, Sir Eero. Stand at my side, as the one I trust above all others. I do not fight against your vows. In time, we shall grow dearer still."

Her offered hand waited in the soft candlelight, steady and patient, as if she already knew he would take it.

# CHAPTER

## 30



*Castle Caerh, Rhun.*

THE GOWN WEIGHED MORE than it should.

Brendolyn felt it before she ever saw the hall, felt the pull of silk and muslin at her shoulders, the high waist cinched just beneath her ribs, the many layers whispering against one another as she walked. Lady Mahra's hands had lingered this morning, adjusting seams that did not quite know what to do with a body so slight, smoothing embroidery at the edges—fine vines stitched in silver thread, leaves curling in patterns meant to suggest abundance. The gown was beautiful. It was also armor she had not learned how to wear.

Her steps were short, she was acutely aware of that. The hem has been shortened twice, yet it still threatened to swallow her feet. She kept her hands folded carefully, fingers pressed together.

The doors to the dining hall opened and sound rushed in first, chairs shifting, the low cadence of conversation already begun, and voices layered and confident. The hall itself was vast, the ceiling arching high enough to swallow breath. Long banners hung between stone pillars, the colors of Rhun muted with age and smoke. Candles lined the table in careful symmetry, their flames steady, untroubled by drafts. Everything about the space spoke of permanence but she did not.

Loren was already seated at the head of the table. He looked up when she entered, his expression softening for the briefest moment before composure settled back into place.

He rose, not fully, but enough to acknowledge her presence, and gestured for her to come forward.

"Lady Brendolyn," he said in common, his voice measured and warm. "You honor us."

The others looked at her. Five men, three women, all of them dressed in the heavy silks and tailored coats of influence, guild masters, scholars, and magistrates. Their gazes moved over her without lingering, the way one looks at an object whose purpose is unclear.

Mahra guided her to her seat with a hand light at her elbow. She sat beside Brendolyn, close enough that their sleeves brushed. Brendolyn exhaled slowly as she settled into the chair, grateful for the solid back against her spine. The table edge sat high, almost at her chest where she adjusted herself, smoothing her skirts again.

Plates were served. The scent of roasted herbs and rich sauces curls through the air, heavy and unfamiliar. Brendolyn's stomach tightened, not with hunger, but with the awareness that she would be expected to eat, to perform normalcy.

Loren cleared his throat.

"If we might," he began, his gaze moving deliberately around the table, "I would ask that tonight we speak a language shared by all present."

There was a pause. Not an awkward one but an intentional one.

Then one of the men, broad shouldered and silver haired, answered in the tongue of Rhuneal. His words were fluid, clipped at the edges, and carrying a cadence Brendolyn had never learned to follow. Another responds, and then another, conversation resuming as though Loren had never spoken.

Loren's jaw tightened almost imperceptibly and he tried again, more gently.

"For the sake of inclusion," he said. "We have guests."

A woman near the center of the table glanced at Brendolyn, then away, and replied, again in Rhuneal. There was a faint smile on her lips, polite and final, but she used the only word that Brendolyn knew—*Veshari*.

The message was clear.

Brendolyn lowered her eyes to her plate and the food blurred slightly. She counted her breaths. Mahra's hand moved into her lap, subtle and precise. Brendolyn felt the familiar comfort of language returning to her body, not through ears, but through sight.

*"They refuse."* Mahra signed. *"They say it is improper to abandon tradition."*

Brendolyn nodded once and her throat tightened.

*"Do not look at them,"* Mahra added, gentler now. *"You are doing well."*

The conversation continued around them, laughter blooming and fading while references were made to matters Brendolyn could not follow. Once, a man gestured with his fork, nearly striking her sleeve, and yet he did not notice. Another time, a woman's gaze flicked to Mahra's hands and lingered, brows drawing together in faint disapproval.

Brendolyn tried to eat but the fork felt too heavy. She managed a few bites, chewed carefully, but was aware of every movement. She imagined herself from above, small, swallowed by fabric and furniture, an ornament placed where a person should be.

Loren watched her more than once and each time their eyes meet, he looked as though he meant to say something but does not. Her chest began to ache, a slow, spreading pressure. She shifted, fingers curling into her skirts and turned slightly toward Mahra.

*"I cannot stay,"* she signed, her movements restrained but urgent. *"Please."*

Mahra studied her face for a moment, then inclined her head.

Brendolyn lifted her gaze and caught Loren's attention. She rose carefully, chair legs whispering against stone.

"Forgive me," Mahra said aloud, her voice a firm current. "Lady Brendolyn is unwell and wishes to retire to her rooms."

Loren stood this time, fully. "Of course," he replied. "Lady Mahra—"

Mahra was already on her feet, offering a brief, but formal nod to the table. No one responds and they leave without further comment.

The corridors beyond the hall were cooler, quieter and Brendolyn's breath came easier with each step away from the dining room, though her limbs still trembled faintly beneath the layers of her gown.

Once inside her rooms, the doors closed, and the silence pressed in, but it was a kinder silence.

Mahra helped her out of the gown, layer by layer. With each piece removed, Brendolyn felt as though she was shedding not just fabric but expectation. At last she sat on the edge of the bed in a simple nightdress, shoulders slumped, and hands limp in her lap.

"You were brave," Mahra told Brendolyn in a soft tone, a brush in hand to untangle the set of Brendolyn's long curls.

Brendolyn shook her head. *"I was small."*

Mahra cupped her cheek briefly, and then said, "Rest. Tomorrow will come whether we wish it or not."

Brendolyn allowed herself a thin smile and when she led down, exhaustion pulled her under faster than she expected. In a moment her eyes were closed, and when she opened them again, she was elsewhere.

*Brendolyn stood in snow.*

*It was red streaked, the white broken by veins of blood that snake outward from her feet. Trees rose around her, tall, twisted things with bark the color of dried wounds. From their branches hung strips of cloth she recognized dimly, fluttering though there was no wind. She tried to move, but her feet sunk.*

*Lord Bannon stepped from between the trees. His face was wrong, too still, and his eyes were dark hollows. Blood seeped from the corners of his mouth as he smiled.*

*Behind him, the ground sloped downward, and there was Pavan.*

*He laid on his back in the snow, eyes open, and unseeing. Blood pooled beneath his head, spreading slowly, impossibly bright against the white. It spilled from his mouth in thick, silent waves.*

*Brendolyn screamed, but no sound came.*

*The trees began to bleed from their bark, from their roots. Blood poured down, soaking her skirts, her hands, her chest. She waded toward Pavan, every step a struggle, her gown dragging, dragging—*

Brendolyn woke with a sharp inhale, fingers clawing at the sheets, and her heart racing as though it might tear itself free. Her room was dark, familiar, safe but the image of red on white lingered behind her eyes, vivid and unrelenting. She curled inward, pressing her face into the pillow, and waited for the dawn.

The gardens were bright, thriving from the thick rains that constantly kept the grounds wet and lush. In the dry of the morning, Brendolyn took a walk, as the sun had dried most of the walkways. She avoided the muddier paths, but it wasn't long before the hem of her pale muslin gown was soaked and grimy. She hoped no one would notice when she snuck back into the house.

Turning a hedgerow, she froze, because walking towards her was Loren Enzo and the elf who always remained at his side, Mihrk. Caught without a way out, Brendolyn approached the two men. Dipping in a slight curtsy, she forced a smile. Loren bowed, and his eyes caught sight of her hem. Maybe it was her imagination but he smirked and was relieved when he said nothing.

"Good morning, Brendolyn. Did you sleep well?" His voice was a touch amused, crossing his hands behind his back, emerald eyes watching her closely.

Brendolyn nodded when in truth she did not sleep well at all. Her nights were plagued with nightmares, but there was hardly a time of chance to explain it. Would she even burden Loren with the things that have haunted her days and nights?

After a moment, Loren motioned along the path where Brendolyn was heading. "Do not let me intrude on your walk." He smiled, allowing Brendolyn to walk on.

She walked, keeping to the path she had been on, smiling when Loren stepped in line beside her. They walked in silence for a time, with Mihrk some paces behind them. Hearing the birds that sang not far upon the nearest clump of trees, Brendolyn took in all the plants and trees so foreign to her country or that of Jorn.

"It is unforgivable that those of this court speak out of turn."

"*I am an outsider,*" Brendolyn tried to reason, hoping her slowed movements were enough for him to understand. "*Veshari.*"

"That is no excuse for their ignorance. They have learned the error of their ways, after your departure I informed them of my displeasure..." He paused, looking sideways at Brendolyn for a moment before he continued. "But that is not the only apology I must make. I must beg your forgiveness again."

"*For what?*"

Loren smiled, scratching his neck, pausing in the lane to look down at her. "You are tempting..." His face turned a shade of pink. "I should have been more respectful and not allowed myself the temptation when I am alone with you. I do not want to cause you any scandal."

She placed a hand gently on his arm. "*You will be my husband.*" Her sign was far from elegant, she felt foolish, hoping that he would understand her.

"That is true, but even then," he continued on, taking the walk through the path of trellises. "It is not the life I am sure you have envisioned, living in such a vastly different world than Corad, or Jorn..."

She slowed her steps, an ache forming in her chest to hear Loren speak.

"Rhun is known for their rituals and dedication to the traditions born of their ancestors," he continued, his voice gentle. "Marriage ceremonies are no different. It could be months, or years..."

"*When shall we be married?*"

His expression fell, but he did not release her from his grasp. "We wait for the letter from King Barrow to condone the match, your father has consented but as a Lady of Jorn, by law he must give his as well. It seems he has made use of his own words. Rhun stands upon ceremony and shall not waver to allow us to be married unless Barrow gives his signed decree."

Brendolyn felt her whole body grow cold and heavy. Of all the things, this was a nightmare. She did not imagine Barrow would relinquish her so easily after that night in Jorn, when Barrow had been so possessive, so demanding. She disliked the man Barrow has become. At last, she locked eyes with Loren. Signing slowly, her mind racing.

"*If we marry without his consent? Would your people accept an outsider if I have no king?*" This question caught a smile from the white haired man, and he glanced at her with blazing eyes.

"If we go against King Barrow..." Here he smirked, and Brendolyn caught the hint of humor in his eyes. "He could declare war upon Rhun for your lack of decorum and duty to the namesake returned to your family. But with the entreaty acts in place between Rhun and the north and southern realm he would be in more detriment than would be worth."

Stepping forward, she smiled, daring to reach up and touch his tunic.

"*And your people?*" she signed, her fingers moving between them.

"They would take you as you are, Brendolyn. Because you would be my wife."

"*Marry me. Do not wait for his consent we know would never come.*"

Loren smirked. "You would go against your king?"

"*He is not my king. Nor do I need a king to be happy.*" Brendolyn was warmed by the radiance of heat that pulled between them. A dangerous mix of trepidation and longing. A danger whispered in her bones as she raised up on her toes to bring their lips together.

"Enzo," a warning tone from the elf behind them who stood near to the lane.

Loren hissed, impatience grating his teeth together. Drawing back from Brendolyn, he took her hand in his, kissing the curve of her knuckle instead. She at once felt the ache within her, a mixture of throbbing between her thighs and the loss in her heart to see him pull back from her touch.

"I shall send a letter to your father at once." He nodded.

# CHAPTER

## 31

Birds chirped, their song resonating through the pergola where Brendolyn sat. She marveled in the music and the brightness of the sun that peaked through the large rolls of clouds high above her head. Today was the day she would marry Loren. Against Barrow, who she knew would never give his consent. She smiled, welcoming the rebellion that was to come when the scene was set. As she sat and waited, the gardens were being set up for the simple ceremony.

A shift of branches brought her attention beside her where Mahra emerged from the hedge row. She smiled a welcome, bowing and Brendolyn nodded.

"The preparations are almost complete, my lady." She spoke slowly and gently, while her hands moved gracefully before her.

Brendolyn made no effort to respond and Mahra stepped closer towards where Brendolyn sat, her stiff skirts swishing around her.

"You look nervous." Mahra sat beside Brendolyn on the long stone bench.

Lifting her eyes to the dark skinned woman, Brendolyn tried to force a smile but could not. Finally, she nodded and the woman took hold of Brendolyn's hand, giving it an affectionate squeeze.

"There has never been a simpler ceremony than the one Lord Enzo has fashioned. No crowds, nor will there be any long speeches to remember as the traditions of Rhun have come before. You shall stand in the gardens together, where your vows in the presence of

Ehnarea shall be enough. Do not be afraid to give your heart to him, my dear. From all that I have seen it is clear as glass that he loves you." These words took Brendolyn's breath away. Looking at Mahra as she spoke, disbelief rang through her.

*"Can I give myself to another when I have loved already?"* She was afraid to ask it out loud, but Brendolyn felt uneasy. This felt wrong, so wrong when her heart was still breaking.

"Young love is never easy, not when it is torn asunder before the bud could even bloom. Think not on what is past, think now to the world before you. A man who shall love you with every waking breath. These people of this city who shall adore you." Mahra spoke and even as Brendolyn listened she could hardly believe them for herself. "Think on it, and I shall send for you soon, my dear."

Brendolyn felt a tightening in her throat, watching the woman walk away slowly. Bannon has succeeded in his promise, starting with Pavan. A warning to her that he held all the cards, that he was stronger than the king himself. She could not go against the word of the eye witnesses who had seen Pavan fleeing the crime. And for what... he was only there to rescue her. Pavan had only come to take her away from that place. Now he was dead. Pavan was dead because she was afraid.

"Brendolyn?"

She opened her eyes, unaware that she had ever closed them. Her eyes drifted around and Mihrk stood at the steps leading to the garden, his hopeful grey eyes taking her in.

"Lady Mahra came to fetch me," he said, as he neared her on the bench. Brendolyn looked down at her hands, suddenly feeling foolish as the elf sat beside her. "You need not shy away from me, Brendolyn. You are troubled, I can sense it."

He could, and Brendolyn knew it.

She understood this sense more than anyone as Lahrs often expressed it. He could sense when she was upset without having to hear her express it. Brendolyn took in a shaken breath, exhaling slowly.  And then finally looking up to meet the gaze of the elf.

*"I am afraid."* Brendolyn signed, unsure if the elf even knew what she meant.

"Afraid of what, Brendolyn?" His tone was gentle but Brendolyn was unsure of how to reply. Timidly she raised her hands.

*"Just afraid. Once I was fearless and now I am afraid."*

"The safest place now is here. Loren shall keep you safe. I do not mean to speak out of turn, my lady... your fears are valid... if you cannot tell me or Mahra your fears..." Mihrk spoke but he paused, looking to the gardens for a moment before he began again. "You can trust him."

*Him.* Brendolyn knew who he meant—Loren Enzo.

She had grown to like him these few months she lived in Rhun, but her hatred of him was still lingering. How could she love someone else now after the hurt she had felt from the life she had before? Barrow was once her only thought and feeling, now she could not think on him without a pit of anger welling inside at the heartless man he had become.

Loren Enzo was nothing like Barrow. Loren Enzo was nothing like any man she had ever met...and yet when she looked into his eyes she was reminded of her fear. She was reminded of the regret and hate she felt. When she looked into Loren Enzo's eyes she saw Pavan's eyes. When she heard Loren Enzo say her name she heard Pavan's voice. Every thought of Pavan gave her fear, knowing Bannon had won. Living this way was a new punishment, one she knew she deserved for not standing up sooner.

*"He is the only one I will ever trust again."* Her sign fell flat and she let her hands fall to her lap without looking at Mihrk.

There was a pause of time and Brendolyn felt warm, the sun now shining across her skin. As she basked in its rays, she could faintly hear Mihrk move beside her, she peeked out to see he held a small pair of embroidery scissors in his thin hand.

"Might I cut a lock of your hair? We braid a lock from you and he into the silk braid for the binding of hands." He twisted the small shears hesitantly, awaiting her reply.

Slowly Brendolyn nodded, pulling down a thin strand from her carefully braided hair that wound the crown of her head to keep it off of her neck, turning slightly as the elf leaned in to cut it from her. He was quick and efficient, tucking the long curl of hair in a handkerchief before tucking away the scissors.

"It is nearly time, you should go up to dress. Mahra has set out your gown." Without another look he was off, leaving Brendolyn to sit and reflect.

She stole one more glance at the bird upon the tree, watching it skitter off, before standing to return to her rooms. She would dress and then she would be married.

Brendolyn stood looking at her reflection in the large mirror. Mahra was delicate as she draped Brendolyn in the thin layers of silk, tucking and folding it down, pinning it into the shape of the gown, one that Brendolyn has never worn in her life. She was aware of the elegant elven garments, but never up close. With a low scooped neck over her chest, dipping over her shoulders, leading down to floor length sleeves and a long drape of skirts, she felt divine. The silk woven with flecks of gold to illuminate and make Brendolyn's skin glow. She watched Mahra take her hair down from her braid to fan out over her back, reaching down below her waist in waves.

Mahra oiled her hands to run her fingers through the ends, adding small braids here and there with added strands of silk made of gold. Trinkets of small golden metal beads clasped throughout her hair made music as she moved around the cushioned seat where Mahra set her. Tears prickled in her eyes as Brendolyn missed Elsa fiercely.

"Your feet shall be bare," Mahra spoke softly, working off Brendolyn's shoes, rolling down the stockings to expose Brendolyn's feet.

Brendolyn was shocked. *"Bare feet?"*

"To be close to the heart of Ehnarea is found through the grass and the flowers themselves. A ceremony as this, is designed by her hand. Many of Rhun take influence from the great religion of Ehncarda, and in doing so they honor the elven heritage of the realms. Lord Enzo is the first of his forefathers in a hundred years to return to his roots here. At least that is what I am told." Mahra smiled, taking up again her hands to oil Brendolyn's arms. The smell was warm and floral, fresh like the gardens and woodsy.

When her hands were free Brendolyn ventured to ask, *"An elven ceremony?"*

Mahra helped Brendolyn to her feet, walking her back to the mirror to get a good look at herself. She sighed approvingly at her handiwork.

"You are shining, Brendolyn. Tonight, will be about you, enjoy yourself and be free."

Brendolyn forced a smile, glancing at herself one last time before turning towards the door. Walking the length of her room to the door, she moved beside Mahra in silence as they descended towards the gardens, where she knew Loren was waiting.

The cold stone under her feet and the gentle breeze shifting through the light silk dress as she approached the doors towards the gardens brought chills to her skin. She took a deep breath to steel her nerves as she stepped out into the sunlight, her dress shimmering as she treaded across the path leading throughout the gardens.

"Keep your chin up." Mahra smiled, reaching out to touch up Brendolyn's jaw.

Doing as she was told, Brendolyn sighed.

"Breath slowly and allow your muscles to relax." Mahra's light voice gave her ease, calming Brendolyn as they neared the center of the gardens, where the curve of vines ran up the trellises, flowers blooming in the warm sun giving a colorful path leading towards the burbling fountains.

Her breath caught, remembering to breathe with a staggering breath as she saw the circle before her just a few yards away. Brendolyn began to shiver as in the grass below was a circle fashioned of flowers and leaves and twined rickets and sticks. At the head of the circle standing just outside it, stood Mihrk, dressed in a silver brocade tunic, his long blonde hair flowing about him.

Brendolyn stopped.

"Bren." That voice made her shiver and she looked over to see Loren standing within arm's reach. He was stunning, dressed in a long white tunic, embroidered with gold. His hair braided back at the sides and clasped with a golden metal piece. He smiled, his eyes drifting over her before settling back upon her eyes.

"You are stunning," he whispered, offering her his arm.

Brendolyn took it, as they walked side by side towards the circle. Nearing it, she felt a sense of calm fall over her, stopping as Loren did when they reached the edge of the circle.

Mihrk smiled. "Favor find you."

"Favor find you," Loren said out loud, looking at Brendolyn with a gentle smile.

Brendolyn froze but quickly signed with her hands. "*Favor find you.*"

"As Ehnarea stands witness, your blessing is accepted. Please, enter the circle." Mihrk's voice was sure, a tone Brendolyn had never heard from the elf before.

Taking his cue, she stepped forward, watching her feet pass over the circle, just as Loren did the same, his equally bare feet falling into the cool damp set of grass beneath them.

"Do you come to this circle of your own free will to make these vows of union?" Mihrk asked, his eyes coming first to Brendolyn.

She nodded quickly and beside her, Loren chuckled, also nodding his consent.

Loren turned to face her, his eyes a brighter green. The smile lit up his face, creasing around his mouth with a flash of teeth. Brendolyn blushed—he was gorgeous and she couldn't look away. Taking her hands in his, her stomach fluttered.

"Blood of my blood, and bone of my bone. I give you my body, that we now be as one. I give you my soul, until my life is done. I give my love to only you and promise where I stand, you shall want for nothing... while we be hand in hand. I promise with every breath in my body I shall forever endeavor to deserve you. From this moment on... I promise." His words came surely and elegantly.

She stood breathless and Brendolyn could only blink up at him.

Loren squeezed her hands gently. "No rush, Bren. Speak from your heart."

Her hands fell free, fumbling through her words. "*I promise to you my devotion. I offer you my hand and my heart. Love me as I will love you. For every night and moment hence.*"

Smiling, Loren caressed Brendolyn's cheek, taking one of her hands in his hand and then finally looked over at Mihrk. As he did, the elf presented a glinting rope made of braided silk.

Without breaching the circle Mihrk reached between Loren and Brendolyn, slowly wrapping the rope around their joined hands.

While he did, he spoke, "Take these vows that bind you together. From this day, for the rest of your days, Ehnarea blesses you. Favor find you."

Every inch of Brendolyn's hand began to warm as it clasped in Loren's. Her fingertips tingled and she sighed at the touch. Looking up to meet his gaze, where his green eyes gleamed brighter than ever, Brendolyn felt lightheaded, her body weightless and her chest warm. His mouth was moving, but she could not hear his words.

But he smiled, guiding her with their bound hands, and helping her step over the circle around them. At once the warmth was gone and Brendolyn returned to herself, blinking back the foggy sleepiness that began to wash over her. Glancing over to Loren, who stood so near, it appeared as if he were looking into her very soul.

"Come this way," he said, his hand held over hers, and he guided her away from the circle, away from the eyes of Mihrk and Mahra.

Brendolyn did not notice when the rope had been removed, or what had happened when the vow was finished, but she felt at peace. Her heart was warmed as she walked hand in hand with Loren Enzo. Her husband.

They walked until they reached the outer reaches of the garden. It was somewhere Brendolyn had not explored and she gazed around as Loren walked her through the tall metal gate, to the rolling hills of trees in neat rows. It was an orchard. But her eyes found the view from just beyond, the evening had worn on and she could see far across the distance as the sun began to set, the golden hues basking the village of Rhun in a fiery blaze.

"Lady Enzo." Loren's voice sent a shiver up Brendolyn's back and she looked up to his tender gaze as he whispered, "Bren."

Leaning close, Loren brushed his fingers along Brendolyn's cheek, as though she were something fragile. Her breath caught the familiar flutter of butterflies waking in her belly as his lips dared to close the distance. He kissed her softly, reverently, drinking her in. She rose on her toes, one hand eager for his shoulder.

They parted only when the sun drowned beneath the horizon, surrendering the sky to twilight's silvery blue.

Music lilted down the once darkened corridors of Castle Caehr like spun silk, the laughter of guests echoing beneath chandeliers ablaze with candlelight.

Brendolyn paused on the threshold of the great hall, watching the revelers twirl and clap in celebration of her marriage. Lavender hung from every archway, wine shone like rubies in raised goblets and in a quieter corner of the room, Loren sat with Mihrk, the two murmuring in earnest conversation.

Her heart tightened with uncertain curiosity, of standing amongst those that bowed as she neared them, whispering in murmurings of devotion to her. Some of the women even braided ribbons in her hair, a tradition she had learned from Mahra to honor Brendolyn with good luck and prosperity in the union.

Keeping a watchful eye upon her husband, where he sat in wrapped conversation, Brendolyn began to make her way towards them, weaving through the well-wishers, hearing the wonderful music played by the musicians that filled the hall with beautiful melodies Brendolyn had never heard before.

Mihrk rose the moment he saw her approach, offering a deep bow before slipping back into the crowd. Loren's gaze lifted to her with soft warmth and Brendolyn extended her hand which he took at once.

Together they crossed the glittering floor until they stood amongst the dancers. As the musicians swelled into a lilting tune, Loren drew her gracefully into his arms. Brendolyn laughed, the joy of it lighting her from within. Around them, couples spun beneath the chandeliered stars, but her world remained fixed on her husband's face.

Within his emerald eyes she found something that made her stomach tighten and her skin thrum with heat. Want bloomed low and sweet inside her and her fingers wove into his, gently tugging him from the hall. They slipped away together through an arch, laughter trailing behind them until they reached the cool hush of an empty corridor.

Before Loren could speak, Brendolyn pressed her body to his, capturing his mouth in a kiss laced with urgent longing. His arms immediately wrapped around her, responding in kind, until desire pulsed between them like lightning. She wanted to whisper his name against his lips, needing to be nearer to him.

But he broke the kiss with a ragged breath, cupping her cheek and pressing a tender kiss to her palm. "Bren," he whispered hoarsely.

She swallowed, disappointment flickering. Breathing in his scent, she felt the thud of his heartbeat against hers. Her throat ached, wanting to demand he take her.

"I shall come to you, when the time is right." He smoothed a hand over her hair, touching the tied ribbons he found there. "But not now, not while the celebrations are at hand."

"*I want you.*" Brendolyn shook her head, keeping her finger movements slow so he could understand her.

Grasping tightly to his tunic, Brendolyn brought herself up to meet his mouth again, feeling the growing restrictions of her gown as she wrapped her arm around his shoulder, tangling her fingers in his white hair. His mouth was hot against hers and she cursed the clothes that separated them, knowing this was right. But being in his arms was where she was meant to be.

Loren sighed heavily, his large hands lost in the depths of her hair, holding onto her bodice, holding her to his body. She began to feel the height of his desire, her magick coiling tightly around them, like a fire burning within her. A desperation to have him, to give herself into his arms overwhelmed her.

Reaching between them, Brendolyn grasped Loren's straining manhood through his trousers, pleasantly delighted. Loren gasped, his body tensing, and suddenly she felt a thrill run through her, wondering if he had ever been with another woman. In the same moment jealousy rushed through her veins, gasping into Loren's mouth as she reached for his laces.

"Bren." It was a warning and his hand shot out, their breath coming in gasps, holding her wrist tightly.

She looked up into his emerald eyes that were now nearly black. He was flushed and she could feel the restraint of magick he used to hold back, it was thick and palpable, like the magick he held in the corridor when he pulled Barrow free of her. But this was stronger, this was deeper, he wanted her, she could feel the straining desire pressed against her belly, but there was something else. Something more than just his desire he was holding back.

"*Come to me.*" She pulled herself free of him. "*When everyone has gone to bed. Come to me.*"

# CHAPTER

## 32

MIHRK ENTERED LOREN'S CHAMBERS to see the man pacing the length of his offices. He knew the duke was far from easy, knowing that his heart was burdened.

"Have I done what is right?" Loren muttered, running a nervous hand through his hair, turning on his heel to venture the other way and taking no notice of Mihrk, but the elf knew that Loren was aware of him.

"She is safe. And her safety was desired above all else," Mihrk stated.

But the white haired man growled, unceasing of his pacing. "She expects me tonight. She expects a man to bed her on her wedding night... I cannot." Loren stopped, pressing the palms of his hands into his eyes.

"Brendolyn shall understand your reasoning if you only explain..."

Loren threw his hands down, looking pointedly towards Mihrk. "I was there with her in the corridor. Beneath my hands I felt her magick calling to me..." He paused, and Mihrk could see the tension in the man before him.

He could sense and feel Loren's pain thick in the air.

"You are leaving, aren't you?" he asked, but they both knew the truth.

Regretfully, Loren bowed his head.

The tall man groaned, falling his large frame into the nearest chair, letting his head lull, covering his face with his hands. Mihrk knelt before him, placing a sure hand upon his shoulder. Magick rolled over his hand, magick that was hard and coarse. Angry. Mihrk sighed, venturing to place his other hand along the top of Loren's head.

"Breathe, be easy." Mihrk sighed, feeling magick connect between them.

Loren lifted his head, allowing the connection to form between them. Mihrk was glad, sighing as he watched the man before him ease back. His face shifting as his true form emerged, the glamour of Loren Enzo melting away. Before the elf now sat his master and friend.

*Pavan.*

"I cannot hurt her," he dared to speak out loud. "Her magick calls to me… I can feel it whenever she is so near. Whenever she is so willing." Pavan shut his eyes. "I wanted to take it, to draw from that forbidden magick and take her soul."

Mihrk pressed back the magick that danced around Pavan. "You didn't, Pavan… you are more than your magick."

Tensing, Pavan reached up and grabbed hold of Mihrk, but the elf could feel the ripple of magick as he knelt between his knees.

"I have left her alone, to walk this realm without company." Pavan shook, his hand coming up to rest above the dip of Mihrk's throat. "Am I so heartless to not have thought of it sooner, to leave her without a friend, a companion."

"You have already made plans to retrieve Elsa, Pavan… for now you must rest."

Pavan scoffed, leaning closer to Mihrk until their lips were nearly touching. Mihrk could smell the hint of wine upon Pavan's lips, the scent masking the sweet tang of desire. Mihrk gulped, trying to forget the draw towards the man before him, trying to forget the thick legs that bracketed his hips as wanting desire coiled in his gut.

"You must sleep."

Slowly, the larger man began to fade, falling back as sleep overtook him. Mihrk stood at last, giving one last look over the man sleeping there and retreated from the room, returning to his usual place, the one where he would sit outside the doors of Loren's bedchamber so no one would enter or intrude.

He was gone and Brendolyn hated him for it.

Without warning Loren Enzo left her there in Rhun to fend for herself. Left her with a household of servants, gardeners, and cooks who could not understand her when she used the old silent language. Mahra had gone away, and Mihrk had gone with Loren.

It was the seventh day after his unexpected departure that Brendolyn ventured from her rooms again, walking the corridors she had memorized weeks ago and taking the turns and stairs she remembered. Finally, she emerged in the high tower that looked out over the vast lands of Rhun and even in her anger she calmed at the beauty before her.

This stretch of land from the foot of the mountains, across the plains and through the old marsh lands to the west, Brendolyn could see the farthest reaches of the fields of Thourns. It was a span of ground once scorched by dragon fire long ago, now being the place of ground where many have battled.

A gentle breeze found her, shifting about her like a dance of magick. She took in a deep breath to smell lavender and sage, two earthy smells that brought her peace and comfort. Brendolyn gazed across the fields and gardens but there was no evidence of the source of the smell. Her eyes shot out to the horizons and the vast lands beyond.

Brendolyn ventured down to the library, where she spent most of her days, pouring over the old leather books that sat untouched upon the shelves, but this day she sat, her eyes lost upon the pages of endless scribblings. Brendolyn slammed the book closed, tapping her fingers on the table, trying to ignore the silence that fell around her. She longed to sing. Her chest ached for it, her throat squeezed around the familiar muscles that refused to produce her music.

A tear sprang to her eyes.

Pain. What once brought immense joy produced the worst pain she has ever known. A fiery burn that never quite went away. Brendolyn wiped her cheek and pushed back her tears. She was not willing to allow Lord Bannon to win this fight. She refused to play his game of pity. She would not fall into the darkness of her loneliness or fall into the despair that tried to take her.

Standing as the candles grew low, Brendolyn walked the uninterrupted path to her chambers, but she stopped.

Instead, she turned down the familiar corridor, but never once dared to path towards his chambers, to his bedroom where he slept and made a fortress for himself. She knew no one came here but Mihrk or Loren himself, not even a maid or any other servant to tend to his needs but he was not here now.

Curiosity got the better of her and she pushed into the room where the mystery was held.

His rooms were plain. No ostentatious design upon the wall nor a decorative vase in sight. She noticed no mirrors nor portraits, only books littered the shelves. Brendolyn took one down and opened it, scoffing when she found it was blank. Replacing it to take down another—blank. And another. And another.

Every book within this room was blank.

Brendolyn walked the length of the room to the desk where a fine line of dust had settled upon the top. She ventured to inspect the drawers, all empty. She turned to the room, advancing on the wardrobe to throw it open. Here she found the tunic he wore the day they married.

It was all that was there.

There was no evidence he ever stepped foot into this room. She even examined the bed yet it was untouched. Not a crease or dip formed upon the mattress where one would imagine a person had once slept. She took another turn around the room. Then again, her eyes taking everything in, every expanse of table and chair, hearth and shelf. Loren left no evidence of himself anywhere.

She left the room as she found it, taking the small hall to the room across, where the office sat. A wall of books evenly spaced upon the shelf, with a line of glass bottles upon the other. Brendolyn turned to find a large hearth with evidence of use, and a chair seated near it. Her hand fell upon it, letting her fingers find the dip across the back. She looked around her, here was where Loren slept and made use.

It was smaller than her bathing room, smaller than the wardrobe that kept the multitude of gowns made for her while in Rhun.

Loren Enzo slept in a chair and kept no possession of his own.

Slowly, she walked the path to her room, her eyes gazing up at the high ceilings and the painted murals there. To the design on the carved bedposts and her ornately designed dressers and vanity and desks. Her vases painted in bright colors. Brendolyn looked around the expensively decorated room, a room that reflected most of the castle. This newfound fact irritated her. She always disliked her room, the opulence and propriety of being in so much since childhood while many around her went without food, or clean water, or shelter.

A fit of malice filled her, and Brendolyn picked up a vase and shattered it upon the stone floor. She waited, listening for the rush of servants to come to her, but no one did. She was alone in this part of the castle.

Her heart raced, looking at the broken pieces on the floor.

A sob broke free and Brendolyn clamped a hand over her mouth, her throat aching as the tears began to fall. Trapped within her was the voice and anger she wanted to shout to the world. But the pain gripped her, curling in her gut, as Brendolyn crumpled to the floor, kneeling before the broken vase. Broken into pieces just like how she felt—helpless in her fear, her loneliness. She cried freely. Her hot tears falling from her eyes and scorching fiery paths down her cheeks.

# CHAPTER

## 33



*Divna, Corad.*

THE GARDEN HAD NEVER felt so narrow.

Elsa stood just beyond the archway where ivy crept along pale stone, her breath shallow, and every sense sharpened to the scrape of gravel and the whisper of leaves. Dusk pressed low over the estate, the light turning the roses bruised and dark. She had been told there was a visitor. No name. No explanation. Only urgency.

Her fingers closed around the dagger at her side. The hilt was worn smooth from habit, from nights spent waking to imagined footsteps and days spent pretending she was still safe. Alaric's shadow lived too close in her thoughts and every summons carried his shape. Every unexpected footstep sounded like betrayal returning to claim its due.

She did not step forward when she saw the man waiting near the fountain.

Her stance was careful, knees slightly bent, blade still hidden but ready. The figure turned at the sound of her breath, and for a heartbeat fear flared sharp and white. He was tall, broad shouldered, dressed in dark traveling clothes that marked rank without spectacle.

Then she saw his face—it wasn't Alaric but her grip tightened anyway.

"Elsa," his voice was steady, low. "I thank you for agreeing to meet."

She did not answer at once, instead she studied him the way she had learned to study men. His posture was open, his hands visible, his gaze direct without pressing. *Too controlled*, she thought. *Control was not kindness.*

"You are Duke Loren Enzo," she said at last. It was not a question.

He inclined his head. "I am."

The name carried weight, and with it memory of last being in Rhun and then being taken from there to this place.

"You should not be here," she said. "If Barrow learns of this meeting, you place us both at risk."

"I am already at risk," Loren replied. "So is my wife."

The word wife landed heavily between them and Elsa's jaw set. "Your marriage was not set until the solstice."

"Yes," he said, and something softened briefly in his expression. "We went against those wishes, and in doing so, she renounced her claim on Augusta. Our marriage was not sanctioned. Barrow did not warrant it and never would have."

Elsa's fingers flexed around the dagger.

"I did not come to defend politics," Loren continued. "I came because I want what is best for her. And for those she loves."

Suspicion stirred hot and familiar. "You ask me to believe that now, after everything. After knights who swore oaths and broke them as easily as breath." Her voice shook despite her effort to keep it level. "I trusted Sir Eero, and he went against his word. Against his vows. Against *me*."

Loren did not interrupt. He listened, and that unsettled her more than any argument would have. When he spoke again, his voice was quieter. "I shall tell you something, Elsa. I shall reclaim your honorable opinion of Sir Eero."

She laughed once, sharp and humorless. "You presume much."

"I presume necessity," he replied. "There are truths bound by blood and silence that you have not been told." He stepped closer, slowly, giving her time to retreat.

She did not, though every instinct screamed caution.

"May I," he asked, gesturing faintly toward her hand. "Touch you. Only your wrist. So that you may know I do not lie."

Her heart hammered. This was foolish. This was dangerous. Every lesson she had learned urged refusal. Still, something in his eyes held her. It was not a command, it was resolve, and beneath it an urgency that felt painfully familiar.

She hesitated, then extended her hand, the dagger still held tight.

His fingers closed gently around her wrist. The contact was warm, grounding, and then the world shifted. Not violently, not with spectacle but recognition bloomed like a wound reopening. She gasped, her breath catching as she saw the man before her as he truly was, no pretenses, no glamour to hide his face.

"Pavan," she whispered, the name torn from her chest.

Loren did not release her. "I swear to you," he said, and now his voice carried the weight of oath and truth intertwined, "that nothing shall come to harm you. Nor her. I swear it by the name you know me by, and the one I have hidden."

Tears burned her eyes and rage followed close behind, hot and uneasy. "You let us believe you *dead*."

"I had to," he said. "To survive. To protect what I could not shield openly."

Silence stretched between them, thick with all that had been lost.

At last Elsa nodded. Her voice was unsteady but resolute. "I will go with you to Rhun."

Relief crossed his face only briefly before urgency returned.

Footsteps broke the moment and Mihrk burst into the garden, breathless, a letter clutched in his hand. He crossed the space in hurried strides and thrust the parchment toward Loren without ceremony. Loren read it once and then swore softly, viciously, under his breath. He looked back to Elsa, grip tightening briefly on her wrist before releasing it.

"I shall have my men come for you," he said. "You will leave this land. You will not delay."

"And you?" she asked, fear rising again.

"I must return to her," he replied, voice fierce with promise. "Do you understand?"

Elsa swallowed, then nodded.

# CHAPTER

## 34

*Field of Thourns, Rhun.*

Pavan pulled his horses' reins up, bringing them to a slow trot as they neared the great gates of Rhun. They had rode hard through most of the morning, and now in the lateness of the day the sun began to set beyond the towering spires of the castle just visible over the tops of the high walls. Eagerly dancing about, the horse beneath him grew impatient as the gate swung open enough to let them through.

Villagers paused in their routines, craning their necks to get a good look at their duke who had returned without notice, some were eager to get a good view of them, but Pavan had no patience, spurring his horse on through the growing crowd. Behind him, Mihrk was held up, as the villagers who pulled a cart, blocked the path.

Pavan pulled his horse around, pushing up on the stirrups to get a better look.

Mihrk shook his head. "Do not wait for me, my lord," he called over the crowd.

Turning before the crowd surrounded him, Pavan kicked his horse into action, the hooves clattering on cobbled streets as he wound with speed through the narrowing street, around the corners leading up and up until he came to the iron gates, now creaking open on old hinges. He drove his horse through, and ignoring the men that stood guard, he galloped the path leading around to the front steps of Castle Caehr.

Two men rushed out to meet him as he dismounted, breathlessly pushing past them as Lady Venhi emerged from the front doors. "Oh, Lord Enzo, you are here!" she exclaimed.

"Where is she, what happened?" he demanded, untying his gloves and tossing them aside, vaguely registering a footman stepping forward to retrieve them. Next, unclasping his jacket as he hurried into the castle.

Lady Venhi hurried to keep pace beside him. "It started three nights ago when Lady Brendolyn refused to leave her room and barricaded the door. No one could enter, so she refused to eat."

"Has Lady Mahra spoken to you about the matter?"

Lady Venhi faltered, making Pavan stop and glare at the lady who began to go pale. "Lady Mahra was dismissed shortly after you left, my lord."

Seething fury emanated from Pavan. "Who has been attending her these last five days?"

An uncomfortable silence followed.

"You dismissed my wife's attendant without first consulting me on the matter?" There was impatience in Pavan, they stood at the base of the steps, but he could not proceed if this woman should follow.

"She made the servants uncomfortable in her familiarity with the duchess, as well as her disregard for our customs." Lady Venhi stood tall, proudly denying fault.

"Lady Mahra was here for one reason. Where is Bren now?"

"This morning she was screaming like a howling wolt. We tried to calm her, my lord, but she refused to let anyone touch her. She's been to the upper chambers and in the tearoom smashing all the portraits and many of the books have been torn to pieces."

A scream from a maid echoed through a distant part of the castle, making the hairs on Pavan's neck raise. "Where is she, Lady Venhi?" His voice lowered to a growl.

"The library, my lord."

He did not wait for her. Pavan ran, his lungs burning and his muscles tired, but he pushed on, taking the steps and rounding the corridors and halls to come full stop into the library. He saw two maids flanking the outer shelves, and a gardener standing on a table. Pavan's heart was racing, every inch of him fueled by fear and adrenaline as he looked up to the sight of Brendolyn.

She stood out of reach to the gardener who beckoned her down from the tops of the shelves, barefooted and dressed in her silk chemise, her hair falling wild and free around her. Papers were torn and thrown down from her height, fluttering down around them. Pavan approached, seeing Brendolyn now sign the same words over and over again—*hate.*

His chest began to hurt as he looked upon her. The gardener, seeing Pavan approach, stepped aside slightly.

"She won't come down, my lord. Excuse the boldness—she is immodest but I cannot see her fall to harm." The older man kept his eye on her.

"You have done well, sir. Allow me." Pavan looked back at Brendolyn, taking the place of where the gardener stood. "Brendolyn," he addressed her, but she threw a book down from her perch. Pavan dodged it, the book clattering beside him.

"*Hate you.*" Her hands signed as she locked eyes with him. Her skin was pale and dulled. Pavan knew something was wrong, he could feel the darkened magick permeating the air around them.

"Come down please, talk to me," he said, reaching his hands towards her, inching closer to where she stood.

Brendolyn pulled herself away from his reach.

"*This place is suffocating, I hate this place. I hate your home. I hate you.*" She signed, her hands shaking. He could see her fingers were covered in small cuts caused by ripping through the old books that were now scattered about the library.

"Yes." He reached for her again. "Hate me. Hate my home. But please, come down from there. You are unwell." His voice broke as he spoke, urgency sharpening into desperation. He could feel it now, the presence of servants gathering, drawn by the disturbance, their whispers pressing in from the edges of the room.

Brendolyn stood like a wild thing cornered, a creature caught between flight and fury. The light cast her in a pale, ethereal glow, her silk chemise clinging to her form. Her long onyx curls fell in tangled waves around her shoulders, once carefully kept, now frayed and disordered. She hesitated, amber eyes darting toward the servants who watched in uneasy silence, then back to him, wary and fierce.

Pavan stepped closer. Then closer still. Slowly, carefully, he reached out, his fingers brushing her wrist with a tenderness that contrasted sharply with the chaos of the moment and her golden eyes shimmered as they met his.

"You are unwell," he whispered, his heart pounding so loudly he feared she might hear it. When he slid his hand to her waist and gently guided her down, she did not resist. Her feet met the solid stone floor beneath them, and for a breath it seemed as though the storm had passed.

Then she struck him.

Her palm slammed against his chest, driving him back a step. Her face twisted with raw, feral anger, grief spilling unchecked. She struck him again, harder this time, then again, her fists landing against the flat of his chest and his middle. The force drew a sharp breath from him, but he did not stop her. He did not raise his hands to defend himself. He stood firm and let her strike him again and again until her strength faltered and tears broke free at last.

Her hands fisted in his tunic, clutching him as though he were the only thing keeping her upright.

"Forgive me," he murmured, his voice heavy with remorse as he pressed a kiss to the top of her head. He wrapped his arms around her, holding her close, shielding her quaking form from every eye in the room. "I shall never leave you again."

"She has gone wild, my lord," Lady Venhi huffed, breathless from her hurried ascent, her gaze taking in the disarray of the library. She stepped forward as if to explain herself, as if explanation might save her.

Pavan lifted his head, his expression turning cold and unyielding. "You are unfit for my service, Lady Venhi," he said evenly.

The room fell into stunned silence.

"I entrusted her to your care, and you betrayed that trust. You will take leave of Castle Caerh at once. Your belongings shall be delivered to your lodging beyond the gates."

Lady Venhi stammered, her face draining of color as the weight of his words settled upon her.

"And let this be known," Pavan continued, his voice carrying through the chamber with a rare and commanding authority. "If there are others who have fostered this cruelty or followed this mentality, consider your time in my court ended. My mercy will not be extended a second time should I hear of Duchess Brendolyn's suffering again. Do I have your oaths?"

No one spoke at first.

Then the gardener stepped forward, bowing his head. "Aye, my lord. Your word is just. As before, so shall I follow you."

Pavan nodded once. He bent and lifted Brendolyn into his arms, holding her close against his chest, her face hidden against him. His gaze shifted to the gardener.

"Take this woman to the gate. Lord Mihrk will be there. Inform him of her transgressions. When your duty is done, return to me. What you have shown my house tonight shall not go unrewarded. Your family will be honored."

The gardener bowed deeply and turned, escorting Lady Venhi from the library as the doors closed behind them, leaving only the hush of consequence and the quiet rise and fall of Brendolyn's unsteady breath.

Brendolyn slowly settled, the force of her sobs ebbing until they softened into shallow, exhausted breaths. The sharp tremor in her shoulders eased, leaving behind a fragile stillness. Around them, the maids and footmen remained respectfully distant, their eyes lowered, their presence hushed as if even the air feared to disturb her. Pavan gave a subtle command, and they withdrew without protest, their footsteps fading until the library was left in quiet solitude.

Pavan gathered Brendolyn into his arms, careful and deliberate, as though she might break if held too tightly. He carried her through the winding corridors, past towering stone walls and familiar tapestries that blurred in his periphery. The hall they passed through had always felt grand and secure, but now it seemed too vast, its echoes too loud for someone so worn and small.

When they entered her bedchamber, the scent of lavender and clean linen greeted him, a faint reminder of another time. He lowered her onto the mattress, easing her back against the pillows. She did not resist or protest. She simply lay there, her body yielding as though it no longer had the strength to argue. Pavan drew the blankets down and then carefully pulled them up again, tucking them around her, trying to offer warmth where he feared there was none.

Her eyelids fluttered as if sleep were calling to her from a great distance, and she was struggling to answer. Pavan reached out and brushed a lock of hair away from her face. His fingers lingered when he saw the change in her. The healthy glow she once carried had faded, replaced by a dull gray pallor that made her appear almost unreal. Dark circles bruised the delicate skin beneath her eyes, evidence of too many sleepless nights and too much unspoken pain. The sight tightened something in his chest.

Fear lodged between his ribs and heart, convinced he was the cause of her illness, feeling the writhing pain etched deep into her sorrows where he was unable to reach them. He straightened, turning to leave so she could rest, telling himself that sleep was what she needed most, but before he could take a step, her hand lifted weakly and closed around his wrist. The touch was light, barely there, yet it stopped him completely.

Pavan looked down at her.

Her golden eyes were open, fixed on his with a quiet intensity that stole the breath from his lungs. In them he saw exhaustion, fear, and something else, something unguarded and searching. His breath caught as their gazes held, the room seeming to narrow until there was nothing but the two of them.

Pavan sat upon the edge of the great bed, touching her cheek tenderly. "You should sleep. We shall talk in the morning."

"*I cannot sleep, when I sleep, I dream of him...*"

"See who, Bren?" he whispered, his voice barely louder than breath.

He lifted his hand and gently wiped the tears from her cheeks, his thumb traced the damp tracks left behind. Her fear pressed in around him, thick and suffocating, as though the very air had turned heavy. Every muscle in his body tightened in instinctive response as her magick stirred, reaching for him without conscious intent. It called to him like a cry in the dark, desperate and unrelenting.

He wanted to take her pain. He wanted to take everything that hurt her, everything that kept her wide eyed in the night.

"*Bannon.*" She moved her hands gently. "*I am afraid. I am afraid.*"

Pavan's breath caught sharply, a painful knot forming in his throat. The name struck him with the weight of a blade, cold and merciless. He gathered her hands in his, rubbing warmth into her chilled skin, then traced slow, grounding circles along her arms as though he could anchor her to the present by touch alone. He murmured soft assurances she barely seemed to hear, willing her fear to loosen its grip, but it was far too strong and she was consumed by it.

The room felt altered, saturated with anguish so dense it seemed to fog the space between them. Pavan forced himself to slow his breathing, drawing each breath deep into his chest, steadying himself as he focused inward. He reached for the familiar thread that bound them, the invisible current of magick humming beneath his skin. It answered him immediately, warm and dangerous, alive with intent.

He knew this was dangerous and he knew he should leave.

Yet the thought of walking away while she lay shattered before him was unbearable. Pavan could not endure seeing her in pain, not when he had the power to ease it. His fingertips grazed over her skin, and a sharp tingle raced up his arm as her magick flickered beneath his touch, reactive and raw. It danced like lightning just beneath the surface, unrestrained and aching to be soothed.

*Just a small portion*, he told himself.

His eyes closed as he opened himself to it, welcoming the bitter tang of pain as it bloomed on his tongue, metallic and sharp. It flooded him all at once, searing and immediate. He felt it sink into his bones, into his chest, into the deepest parts of him that already knew suffering too well.

Brendolyn's breathing slowly evened as the tension bled from her body, her brow smoothed and her fingers loosened their grip on the sheets. Pavan watched as sleep claimed her, heavy and merciful, her lashes resting softly against her cheeks. Only then did he allow himself to pull away.

The moment he severed the connection, the weight of what he had taken fully descended.

He staggered back, barely catching himself before sinking into the chair nearest the bed. The pain burned in his fingertips, crawled up his arms, and lodged itself deep within his chest. It felt like razor blades dragging through his heart, each breath scraping raw as it entered his lungs. Breathing became laborious, as though the air itself had thickened in protest.

Loneliness crushed him, vast and suffocating, filling him from head to toe with a hollow ache that left him shaking. He sat there in silence, shoulders hunched, and eyes fixed on Brendolyn's sleeping form. She looked peaceful now, untouched by fear, and the sight both soothed and destroyed him.

He let the pain course through him without resistance.

Tears stung his eyes, blurring his vision as he remained there, keeping vigil, bearing her suffering so she would not have to.

# CHAPTER
## 35

H ER SKIN BURNED. NOT a single place spared. It was red hot and itching, alive with a thousand tiny pinpricks that shivered across. The sensation crawled and flared all at once, as though her body no longer belonged to her. Brendolyn wanted to scream. She wanted to claw the thoughts from her mind, to tear away the fear and the memories until nothing remained. But no sound would come.

Her throat clenched tight, seized as if caught in a vise. Each attempt to swallow only made it burn more, swelling with the pressure of words she could not speak. Her breath became shallow and erratic and hot tears spilled freely, tracing the soft curves of her cheeks and dripping down to her chin, unchecked and relentless.

"Breathe."

The voice reached her through the chaos, deep and steady. It cut through the heat like cool water poured over flame. The sound alone was a balm, grounding and impossibly calm against the storm raging within her.

Brendolyn forced her eyes open. Her vision swam, blurred by tears and pain, but slowly the shape before her sharpened. A man knelt at her level, close enough that she could see the tension held in his posture, the careful restraint in his stillness.

Loren Enzo.

Fury surged through her, sharp and sudden. She recoiled, trying to pull away from him, from the man who stirred too many emotions she could not bear to name. She shoved at his chest with what little strength she had left, her palms striking firm muscle beneath fine fabric but he did not move and the immovability of him only fed her panic.

Her breath fractured into quick, shallow pulls as another wave of emotion crashed over her. Sobs tore free, raw and broken, her body shaking beneath their force.

At once, Loren reached for her.

His hands came up gently, cupping her cheeks with a tenderness that startled her into stillness. His touch was sure but careful, thumbs brushing lightly against tear soaked skin. She froze, no longer pushing him away, her anger dissolving beneath the weight of her sorrow. Slowly, reluctantly, she lifted her gaze to his.

Green eyes held hers, steady and intent, filled with something quieter than fury and far more dangerous. "Breathe, Brendolyn," he said again.

His voice wrapped around her, low and resonant, guiding her as she drew in a trembling breath. Then another. The tightness in her chest eased, just enough to keep her from breaking apart. Yet the fire beneath her skin still burned, restless and unrelenting.

Loren's hands fell from her cheeks, lingering only for a heartbeat. His fingers brushed the bare skin of her shoulder, sending a shiver through her before trailing slowly down the length of her arms. He gathered her hands in his, enclosing them fully, anchoring her. One by one, he lifted them and pressed a kiss to her knuckles.

His hands were cold and his mouth was even colder. Against her burning skin, the contrast was shocking and Brendolyn gasped, her breath hitching sharply.

His eyes lifted to hers as he leaned closer, closing the distance by mere inches. One hand rose to cradle her cheek again, while the other settled at the curve of her hip. The chill of his touch sent another shiver racing beneath her chemise, gooseflesh rising where his fingers rested.

Her breath quickened, but this time it was different. The fire within her changed, no longer only pain. Something new sparked and bloomed beneath her skin, spreading warmth in a way that left her unsteady. He was too close. She could smell him now, musk and earth, something dark that chased away the ache in her stomach and replaced it with a flurry of sensation. Butterflies erupted within her as wild as the beast in the old forests.

Wanting him, suddenly and desperately, terrified her more than the pain ever had.

"Do not be afraid," he murmured softly, as though he had reached directly into her thoughts.

Brendolyn shivered beneath his hands, caught between fear and longing, her body responding even as her heart wavered, the heat beneath her skin burning brighter still.

Brendolyn shook her head, dark hair loosening and dancing around her shoulders with the movement, the strands catching against her damp cheeks. Loren's hand remained firm at her side. He shifted closer, careful not to crowd her, and placed his palm at the small of her back. The warmth of it seeped through the thin fabric of her chemise, holding her even as her thoughts scattered.

His chest rose and fell with heavy breaths as he searched her face, as though memorizing every tremor and flicker of doubt. When he spoke, his voice was low and earnest, threaded with restraint.

"Trust me. Let me help you."

The words echoed in her mind, slow and indistinct, as if spoken through water. She struggled to grasp their meaning. His nearness intoxicated her, the weight of his attention making her dizzy. She wanted to pull him closer, to feel his certainty wrap around her and drown out the noise in her head.

Before she could stop herself, she reached between them.

Her hands brushed the open lapels of his tunic, fingertips grazing the rough weave of the fabric beneath. The texture was real and solid. She inhaled sharply at the contact, then pulled back just as quickly, shaking her head again as if to banish the impulse.

Loren exhaled slowly, a quiet sound of patience rather than frustration. His hands twitched once, then stilled as though he were restraining an instinct. When they moved again, it was gentle. His palms traced slow, deliberate circles along her sides, creasing the fabric of her chemise, never demanding, only asking. Her heart began to race, each beat loud in her ears.

She finally dared to look at him.

His eyes were clear and green, unflinching, watching her with an intensity that made her breath catch. Those eyes she claimed to hate most, because they saw too much.

"You are in so much pain," he said softly. "I can feel it. Show me your memories. Open your mind to my touch, and I will feel them with you. Let me see through your eyes the horrors that haunt your dreams and every thought that brings you fear."

His words flowed like poetry, measured and reverent. They slipped past her defenses and took hold of her heart like a familiar song. Hope stirred, fragile but undeniable, blooming where despair had taken root. For the first time, she wanted to trust him, like she had trusted one other before him.

Loren lifted the hand that rested warm against her cheek. With the first two fingers, he touched her temple, feeling the steady pulse beneath her skin. A soft sigh curved from his lips as his eyes closed, his focus turning inward.

Brendolyn felt it then.

Cold traveled through her, gentle at first, then spreading like a numbing tide. It soothed rather than startled, easing the fire in her nerves, quieting the ache in her chest. Her limbs grew heavy and the room blurred at the edges as her eyes fluttered closed, the world slipping away from her grasp as she fell.

Downward and deeper, into a vast, waiting darkness, surrendering to it as it swallowed her whole.

Welcoming its soothing comfort through her burning skin as it blanketed every moment of her life. She saw her memories flashing, like a single blink of the eye she saw as every moment of her waking moments passed before her. Each early memory, from her first steps in her nursery, a stumble, growing taller, learning how to ride a horse. She saw herself holding her first sword. Scaring Lahrs while he read.

Brendolyn drifted in and out of the moments of her life, each memory unfolding around her with startling clarity. She felt every laugh as though it were happening anew, every fleeting joy, every tear that had once fallen. She moved through the visions like a dancer, light and unanchored, spinning through happiness until it grew overwhelming, until the sweetness turned sickening.

Then it stopped and time froze.

The world stilled, and Brendolyn found herself standing apart, peering through a veil at what lay beyond. Mud clung to her boots as she stood upon a narrow road at the edge of a bustling city square. People hurried past her, unaware of her presence, their voices and footsteps flowing through her as though she were nothing more than air.

Her breath caught. The sights were achingly familiar. The sounds. The smell of damp earth and smoke. A sharp twinge curled in her stomach but Brendolyn could not look away and her gaze remained fixed on the scene before her.

"This memory has drawn you," a deep voice murmured beside her.

"It was the day I met him." The words left her without intention, her thoughts given voice. She gasped softly at the sound of it, at the resonance of her faie voice echoing through the space.

Loren Enzo stepped closer, coming to stand at her side.

"There," Brendolyn said, lifting her hand. She pointed toward the edge of the square where a small iron cage stood. Inside it knelt a man, broken and bloodied, yet still defiant. "Do you see him?"

Silence followed and she glanced up at Loren. His eyes had not left the vision, pain etched itself into his expression, creasing the corners of his eyes even in profile.

"I cannot explain it," she whispered, turning back to the memory. She watched herself kneel before the cage, her younger self meeting the man's gaze without fear. "From that moment, I knew I would never forget him. He was so fierce, even caged like an animal."

"But you saw him again," Loren said quietly.

The memory shifted.

Fading away, the city noise and grime unraveling into light. Stone streets softened into pale flagstones warmed by the sun, and the air shifted, heavy with the scent of greenery and incense. They stood now in the cathedral gardens, a place of quiet reverence and ordered beauty. Tall hedges framed the paths, trimmed with careful hands, while climbing roses spilled over white stone arches. Sunlight filtered through the leaves, dappling the ground in shifting patterns of gold and shadow.

And there he was.

The same man stepped into view, yet he was transformed. No iron bars held him in now. No blood or grime marked his skin. He stood straight and unbroken, his posture proud, his expression clear and alive. The strength in him was unmistakable, no longer muted by suffering but honed by it. The sight struck Brendolyn with such force that she forgot to breathe.

She watched herself approach him, her younger form moving slowly, cautiously, as though afraid the vision might shatter if she drew too near. She circled him once, then again, studying the angles of his face, the familiar lines of his jaw and brow now free of shadow. Her disbelief was written in every step, in the way her hand hovered just short of touching him, in the tilt of her head as she searched for signs of the broken man she had known.

A flush crept across her cheeks as recognition dawned. Brendolyn felt the ache of that moment deep in her chest, the shock of seeing him restored, alive, and impossibly real, standing in the open sunlight as though he had never been caged at all.

"He denied it was him," she said softly. "I never understood why he would lie."

The vision changed again and she saw herself hurry away, calling for Elsa, laughter and confusion tangled together. Then the world rearranged itself once more.

They stood in another garden, one softer and less ordered than the last. The air was heavy with the scent of damp earth and flowering vines, the ground uneven beneath her feet. Pale lantern light glimmered between climbing leaves, casting long shadows that stretched across the path like reaching hands. At the far end of a trellised walk stood Pavan.

He did not move; he simply waited.

The sight of him struck Brendolyn with quiet violence. Her chest tightened as though a band had been drawn around it, stealing the air from her lungs. She watched herself approach him in the memory, hesitant and hopeful all at once. When he smiled, gentle and familiar, it pierced straight through her. The expression was so achingly known, so unchanged, that her eyes filled before she could stop it.

"You are drawn to these moments," Loren murmured beside her, his voice low and near. "They weigh heavily on you."

"No matter how my life changed after that," Brendolyn whispered, her gaze never leaving the scene, "he always found his way back to me."

A tear slipped free, burning as it traced the curve of her cheek. She wiped it away quickly, almost angrily, and turned from the vision. She could not endure the sight of him standing there, alive and smiling, not when the ache in her chest threatened to tear her open. Her breath came unsteady, each inhale trembling.

"It brings you great pain," Loren said.

She turned to him. His hand lifted, brushing her cheek with a gentleness that made her flinch and then still. Where his fingers touched, a cool shimmer spread, easing the frantic tremor beneath her skin.

"He was kind to me," she said, her voice breaking despite herself. "There were so many moments when he showed me how gentle he could be. How careful. But his light was taken from him. He saved my father. He saved so many lives." Her words tangled as grief surged. "And the one man I thought I loved could not see past his own grief, could not look beyond the loss of his father long enough to see the truth."

Her throat closed and she squeezed her eyes shut as the emotion swelled, pressing hard against her ribs, threatening to split her apart.

"I did not know," Loren said softly.

His voice sounded distant, as though it came from far away, yet his presence was solid and unyielding. Brendolyn leaned into him without realizing it, grounding herself against the strength of his frame, clinging to the only thing that felt real.

"Oh, Bren."

The way he spoke her name resonated through her, intimate and aching. It stirred something deep within her, something she was not ready to face. She tried to pull back, to escape the pull of memory and the echo of Pavan's voice that haunted her thoughts.

She lifted her gaze to Loren but the vision around them shifted.

When she turned back, her breath caught violently in her throat. The world lurched, and she stumbled backward as though struck.

She saw herself kneeling on cold stone, King Beaumont cradled in her arms. His body was slack, his skin pallid, his breath coming in shallow, ragged gasps. Blood stained her hands and the weight of him was unbearable. A sob tore free from her chest as the memory closed in, sharp and suffocating.

"This is not..." Her voice rose, shrill with panic. "I cannot think of this day."

Tears spilled freely as she shook her head, eyes squeezed shut, her body curling inward as though she could shield herself from the sight.

"I am here," Loren said, his voice close now, steady and unwavering.

Yet the sounds would not fade. She could still hear the king's labored breaths. She could still hear her own singing, raw and desperate, her voice cracking as she tried to hold him to life. Then another sound cut through it all—Pavan's voice.

She felt him arrive again, felt his arms around her as he lifted her away from the horror, just as he had on that day. A long, shuddering breath broke free from her as the memory loosened its grip.

"I am afraid," she whispered, the admission barely audible.

"You are fearless," Loren murmured near her ear, his touch sending a shiver through her.

"He was killed," Brendolyn said, her body shaking as the truth pressed in from all sides. "I saw Beaumont. It was not Pavan. It was not him."

Her eyes remained tightly shut as she struggled to pull free of the visions, her heart pounding violently as the truth clawed its way toward the surface, refusing to be silenced.

*Slap!*

She flinched as the memory surged forward without warning, sharp and invasive. Her hand flew to her cheek as though she could ward it off, even as the scene unfolded before them with merciless clarity. She heard Barrow calling her name, his voice strained with urgency, but the sound only heightened the panic clawing up her throat. She turned away from it, burying her face against Loren's chest, clinging to the solid warmth of him as if it were the only thing anchoring her to the present.

Darkness swallowed the vision, and the memories began to shift and fracture, dancing around her in disjointed fragments. Then she heard it. The voice that froze her blood where it flowed. Her body shook violently as dread coursed through her, and she could not bring herself to open her eyes.

Bannon's voice slid into her ear, soft and intimate, sickening in its calm. It carried promise and threat in equal measure.

She heard the struggle again, the scrape of her feet against stone, the memory of her breath tearing from her lungs as his hand closed around her throat. The burn returned, vivid and choking, as though it were happening all over again. Tears blurred her vision even with her eyes shut as she heard Bannon's low, cruel laugh, felt the phantom press of his lips against her temple.

"He cannot touch you now," Loren said firmly, his voice cutting through the memory like a blade through fog. "Bannon cannot reach you here. Not with me. I promise."

"You left me," Brendolyn whispered, the words barely more than breath.

"Never again," he murmured. His breath was warm against her neck, sending involuntary shivers up her spine. "If I leave, you will be with me. Until you feel safe again, I will not leave your side. I swear it."

The memory loosened its grip and the darkness softened, reshaping itself and easing her gently into a new vision. Warmth spread around her, steady and comforting and when she opened her eyes, a quiet sigh escaped her lips.

She stood in an empty bedchamber, the space peaceful and undisturbed. The hearth burned low, embers glowing and crackling softly. She moved closer so she could feel the heat against her skin, grounding her, real and present.

"It was my fault," she said, the words heavy with regret. "I should have told Barrow the truth. Maybe then…" Her voice faltered, her eyelids growing heavy as the warmth pressed in around her. "Maybe then Pavan would still be alive."

"You place the weight of his death upon yourself?" Loren asked gently.

A strained laugh escaped her, brittle and aching while tears burned behind her eyes. "Is it not mine to carry? I was the only one who saw the man who killed Beaumont. I was afraid then." Her voice fluctuated. "Now I am terrified of losing everyone. He started with Pavan. He chose him first to prove his power. Vasco was one of the best, but he vanished, and no one seems to remember he existed. Then Elsa was sent away. He is powerful, Loren." Her breath hitched. "You believe me, don't you?"

She turned, ready to face him but he was not there, the room remained unchanged, silent and empty.

"I shall always believe you." Loren's voice drifted through the chamber, faint yet certain.

"Loren?" Her voice echoed softly, blooming through the room.

"Forgive me," his voice answered, soothing and calm.

Her heart began to race as she stepped deeper into the chamber, searching for him, but the space remained hollow.

"Loren?" she called again.

The room shifted subtly, the air thickening as though the veil itself had begun to stir. Then, slowly, a figure took shape near the edge of the firelight. He stood shrouded in shadow and Brendolyn took a cautious step forward. The firelight stretched, illuminating him inch by inch and she stopped short.

"I wanted to tell you," the man said softly.

He stepped toward her, hesitant, then halted. Her breath left her in a silent gasp because the man before her was no longer Loren.

He stood as she remembered him, dark hair falling loose about his shoulders, angular features etched with familiarity. The curve of his mouth was unchanged. His green eyes, achingly familiar, watched her with a tenderness that pierced straight through her chest.

A tear slid down her cheek as she stared, unblinking, afraid the vision would vanish if she looked away.

"Pavan," she breathed, the name leaving her before she could stop it.

"Brendolyn," he answered softly as he drew nearer.

Something inside her snapped and anger surged up from deep within, hot and sudden, forcing breath from her lungs. Her chest heaved as she shoved him away, fury and heartbreak colliding as the memory refused to release her.

All at once, the darkness receded, dragging her back with it, leaving her gasping for air. Her chest heaved, lungs burning as if she had run a mile, and the world came rushing in with a dizzying jolt. Blinking rapidly, her limbs heavy and uncoordinated, as every muscle ached as though she had been pulled apart and stitched back together.

Her eyes opened, and she saw him, or at least what she thought was him. Loren Enzo had fallen back onto his backside, wide eyed and startled, a flash of surprise etched across his features. But it wasn't Loren. Her stomach twisted violently as she took in the truth.

The man before her wore the familiar white hair and the tailored clothes of the duke, but the face was Pavan's. Her heart lurched, a thunderclap of disbelief striking her ribs. She reached out instinctively, her fingers in the air, but stopped short.

Pavan winced at the hesitation. His eyes, once the deep green she remembered, had flared to a ghostly white, as though some part of him resisted the light of her gaze. Time seemed to stretch, her stomach churning, every instinct screaming at her to flee and yet to close the distance at once.

Slowly, he straightened. The color returned to his eyes, settling into the familiar, piercing green that she had not dared hope to see again. Brendolyn recoiled, sliding back against the pillows, her legs curling beneath her as she glared at him, fury and disbelief warring in her chest.

"*Liar,*" she signed with shaking hands, clenching her teeth with the words she so desperately wished to scream. Her jaw hurt from the tension, her throat aflame.

"Yes... I lied to you," Pavan admitted, his voice low and thick with anguish. Tears welled in his eyes, glimmering with the same misery she felt thrumming through her own chest. Brendolyn could see every second of it, the guilt, the regret, the unbearable weight of months lost.

She shut her eyes tightly, chin quivering. For months, she had believed him dead and had resigned herself to a life she barely wanted. And yet here he was, alive, standing before her, not daring to move closer. She recognized the hesitation in his posture, and a strange relief mingled with the anger. She wanted him to stay away. She wanted to grab him and never let go. She wanted to punch him for leaving her.

"*You promised,*" her hands shook uncontrollably as she lifted them to push him away.

Pavan's brow furrowed, confusion shadowing his features. He did not understand her panic, her fury, or the chaotic storm of longing and resentment that burned inside her.

Frustration wound tighter inside her chest. She wanted the strength of her voice back, but exhaustion pressed down on her. Her throat burned, raw and screaming, and she buried her face in her hands, trying to stifle the storm of emotion that threatened to undo her.

"Brendolyn..." His voice, that same haunting, familiar timbre, whispered against her consciousness. She hated it. She hated *him*.

"*Get out*!" she finally tore out, her own voice breaking and reverberating around the room, fierce and raw. It was her voice, her faie voice, yet even as the words left her, her body froze, rigid with shock and the ache of sudden emptiness.

Her hands fell away and the space before her was empty—Pavan had vanished. Panic flickered briefly, but she exhaled a shuddering sigh, sliding back against the pillows. Exhaustion pulled at every fiber of her body, and she let herself collapse, feeling the sheets cool beneath her skin.

A single tear escaped, soaking the linen as she clutched at her neck. Each breath gradually eased the fire in her throat. Her fingers found the ribbon still tied loosely there, tracing it absently, clinging to it as though it were a tether to something solid. Anger and betrayal churned in her gut. She hated that he had lied.

For months she had believed him dead, had resigned herself to a life with a man she barely knew, Loren Enzo—the polite, gentlemanly duke whose portraits had charmed her. Loren had been kind, honorable, offering to step aside if she loved Barrow. Brendolyn knew she might have grown to love him in time. But it had never been Loren. It had always been Pavan.

It had been Pavan who had danced with her in Jorn. It had been Pavan who had given her the choice to choose Barrow, even when she had feared the consequences.

She sat up sharply, gasping, her chest heaving. Memories flooded her, sharp and vivid. Pavan had intervened when Barrow had not yielded. She had felt the darkness rolling from him, a thick and heavy magick. Power. But it had been restrained, purposeful. *Protective.*

She felt it before she reached the door, a pull, a heaviness pressing against her chest, the way the air seemed thicker here, darker. Her hand hesitated on the wood, then she knocked softly. The hollow echo seemed to mock her; there was no response. A chill slid through her, a creeping darkness that pressed into her chest and into her heart.

Brendolyn swallowed hard and opened the door. The room was dim, shadows stretching long across the floor, the candlelight flickering faintly as though afraid to linger. There he was. In the same worn, tired chair she remembered, Pavan slumped back, eyes shut. His shirt hung loose over his frame now, the fabric soft and threadbare, a pale contrast against the lean strength beneath.

He looked peaceful, almost serene, but she knew better. She could feel the lingering pain, the echoes of despair, the bitter tang of darkness hanging in the air like smoke. She stepped forward cautiously, each footfall muted on the old floorboards. Her fingers twitching slightly as she lifted her hand and brushed against his cold jaw, tracing the lines she had memorized from memory and longing.

"You shouldn't be here," he murmured, low and rough. There was no anger in the words, only loathing, a quiet malice that rumbled beneath his voice. His jaw tensed under her fingertips, a subtle ripple of muscle, a warning and a confession all at once.

Brendolyn let her hand fall, tracing the line of his shoulder, the soft linen against the firm muscle beneath, feeling the warmth of his body despite the pallor of his skin. She let her fingers drift until she took hold of his hand, pressing it gently against her cheek. Her eyes met his, catching the familiar green that still held a shadow of the man he had been.

She kissed his palm lightly, a reverent gesture. His lips parted with a soft sigh, and his eyes opened wider, meeting hers. Her fingertips drifted to the inside of his wrist, feeling the faint, steady pulse beneath the skin. Then her gaze fell to the thick, jagged scar that marred the smooth flesh, a dark line that told its own story of pain and survival—a deep secret of his past.

Pavan recoiled slightly, his face a mask of panic and guilt. She saw it all in him—the misery, the despair, the weight he had carried alone. And she felt it too, that deep ache that wrapped around her chest, pressing and twisting.

Without thinking, Brendolyn slid onto his lap, letting her body lean into his. She took his hand again, her palm now resting over the old scar. A tear slipped free and fell onto the rough fabric of his shirt. Beneath her, Pavan shivered, she could feel through the thin material.

"*I shall keep you safe,*" she signed softly, her hands steadier now as she let him feel her intent. He shook his head slowly, a bitter, broken motion.

"I cannot be saved," he whispered, voice raw and brittle.

Brendolyn lifted the ribbon from her other hand and wrapped it carefully around his exposed wrist, securing him to the moment in a tangible way. She leaned in closer, brushing a loose white lock of hair from his face. Her hands cradled his head, warm and steady against the cold lines of his jaw.

"*Safe from yourself,*" she murmured, her voice low and her chin quivering as the words burned through her.

"I don't deserve you..." Pavan exhaled, his hands cupping her jaw gently, his touch both hesitant and reverent.

Relief coursed through her, rich and burning, filling the hollow in her chest with warmth. Her lips pressed against his in a soft, deliberate kiss, tender yet unrestrained. Pavan exhaled sharply, caught off guard by the sudden intimacy, but a gnawing ache drew him back.

"I can go no further, Bren..." He shook his head forlorn.

# CHAPTER
## 36

"ID YOU SLEEP WELL?"

Brendolyn looked up into the face of Loren Enzo, his long white hair falling about his shoulders. She looked into the green eyes, knowing now it was Pavan who looked back at her. Her night after he left her was full of dreamless slumber. In the morning she awoke rested, but her body ached. She dressed herself and stole down into the kitchens to eat.

Now she walked the gardens until the sun rose over her head and that is when he found her. He walked beside her for a time, allowing them to be near each other before he dared to even speak. When he finally did, his voice gave her chills.

Brendolyn did not dare to the use of her faie voice again, relying now to communicate how she had before.

*"A night full of dreamless slumber."*

Pavan nodded, his hands still clasped behind his back. He nudged a smile on his lips, the lips that were the dukes. Brendolyn stopped, looking him over. He caught her eying him intently, a quirk of his lips and she was blushing.

"It is best I remain as I am... does this form bother you?" he asked, keeping his distance from her.

She reached up, touched his cheek and shook her head.

He took hold of her hand, walking down the path for a time together, before letting her go. Brendolyn felt the loss of his touch but noticed the pained look on his face.

"Forgive me for leaving you alone..." he began, his hand reaching up to rake his white hair back from his face. "I had thought it was best, but I know it was wrong to not explain it to you."

Silence followed and together they walked side by side for a time. Brendolyn waited for him as he walked worrying, his hands behind his back, and then suddenly he stopped.

"In time everything shall be clear, I promise."

Brendolyn gave a nod, looking up at him, waiting.

"My family lineage is a long and complicated one... there was never really a chance to talk to you before about my magicks. Nor did I feel at liberty to do so for fear of discovery."

Brendolyn moved her hands. "*You are an Ehlfern.*"

He nodded. "An old magick bloodline. Until very recently it has taken many years to learn control over that part of me. It is a harsh and unyielding magick. One I had not been raised to acquire or use."

"*There is not much known about your magick?*"

Pavan smirked. "As known only to the world through stories, and within those stories are the horrors. They were once believed to shepherd souls into the Veil. Some older religions still believe it is true, and the only chance to receive Ehnarea's blessing to be welcomed into the forest of gold is by honoring the Ehlfern, to honor them as gods.

"We live and die, just as all creatures must. But these religions do not give up hope of the Ehlfern returning to them, even if it is impossible... the remainder of my people have all died away."

Brendolyn's eyes widened. "*You are the last?*"

He swallowed, his features darkening as dread filled him. Brendolyn felt the harshness of his depression like it was a heavy weight upon her chest. Quickly she took his hand in hers and those otherworldly emerald eyes looked up to meet her.

"Do I frighten you?"

Brendolyn shook her head, pressing her palm into his hand.

A smile etched at the corner of his lips. She blushed, her cheeks growing warm to see him like this, the face of the duke, but the eyes of the man she knew he was.

"Do you find me cold... abrasive?"

Again, she shook her head and then leaned up on her toes to reach his mouth with hers, pressing a kiss there. He sighed into her. His hand pressed to her lower back, holding her to his chest. It was warm there in his arms, welcoming. Brendolyn kissed him deeper, but the familiar pull made her shiver. It tugged at her heart, like an invisible string tethering herself to him.

Pavan gasped, clutching to her waist when Brendolyn at last pulled away, resting his forehead to hers.

"I shall need to teach you how to resist that pull, Bren... you are irresistible." Pavan's voice was deeper, sending shivers through her bones and caused her skin to rise in gooseflesh.

"*We are fatebonded.*" Her hands danced, leaning into him.

"Yes. I believe we are, but there is a deeper pull... one I cannot control. My body craves magick... it craves to take it from every living thing. Yours is the sweetest. Yours is the most tender. But I cannot possess you Bren. I cannot steal your magick from you, nor can you give it freely." Pavan shook his head, his hands flexing delicately over the contours of her hips through the pleats of her gown.

Brendolyn bit her lip, wishing nothing more than to kiss him deeper, to feel his strong body pressed to hers. Her dropped eyelids flicked over the race of his reddened lips.

Pavan took a breath, his cheeks turning a shade of pink, unable to meet Brendolyn's gaze. "I cannot bed you, Bren. There is more than the Vow of the Aenarii, if we are joined, it would kill you."

Heat flushed through her. His fingers danced along her waist, his smell enticing her, enveloped in his whole being as his words made her gut twist. To never have him. To never claim him as hers.

"I cannot risk harm to you," he said after a long moment, breathing in heavily. "It is not that I expect it of you... that is, I had not believed you would desire me, but you deserve to know the truth of everything. If I pull away, or deny a simple touch..."

Her hand shot up quickly, covering his mouth with her fingers.

"*You are not a monster.*"

Pavan looked at her sharply, quirking his eyebrow as Brendolyn smiled. Brendolyn took his hand in hers and she marveled at the size of it in her grasp as they took the path further through the cultivation of trees. It was serene, taking this walk with him.

She paused to look up into his green eyes. They were so close again, she could feel the rapid beating of his heart under her hand pressed firmly against his chest. The familiar twinge of pain in her throat happened again and she swallowed her fear to open her mouth.

*"Having you, is something very new. You at my side, my fears subside."* Her faie voice sung softly, her words drifting between them with the melody of a song.

Pavan smiled, touching the contour of her cheek.

"Well, this is an improvement. Do you feel alright?" he asked her, looking her over.

Lightheaded, Brendolyn nodded. Gripping his arm for support, Pavan held her with the flats on his palms against her sides.

He smiled. "You are fearless Bren... I see such strength in you. Even Bannon's power cannot quiet you."

He walked her along the length of the estate. Coming to the front, Brendolyn was curious, watching as a carriage could be seen making its way up the lane.

"I have a gift for you."

As it neared, she did not recognize the driver, but the carriage stopped. As the back was thrown open, the passenger jumped out showing a familiar head of auburn hair.

Brendolyn gasped, tears sprung to her eyes, and she released Pavan's hand. She ran, pure joy making her legs and feet move as she embraced her dearest friend. Elsa clung to her, holding to her tight.

# CHAPTER
## 37



*Divna, Corad.*

Alaric arrived in Divna at dusk when the bells of the convent were fading into silence and the air carried the scent of cold stone and incense. He passed beneath the arched gates with a confident stride, his cloak dusted from travel, his expression calm and assured. In his hand he carried a sealed letter stamped with the crest of King Barrow.

At the receiving hall the Sisters gathered around him. They read the letter slowly, their hands flowing in delicate movements as they spoke to each other. As the final lines were reached, the color drained from their faces.

"Lady Elsa is not here," one of the Sisters spoke in a calm, quiet manner.

For a moment Alaric's eyes hardened, his jaw tightened, and something sharp flickered in his gaze. "She is my obligation, Sisters. By rights of the king, you can read that she is already mine."

One by one the Sisters quietly bowed away, unable to help him, leaving him standing with one of the elder Sisters who had spoken before.

"It is beyond our power to tell you where she has gone, but perhaps when she is settled she shall send word to you, Sir Alaric."

Alaric let the anger pass from his face like a shadow crossing water and bowed his head politely. Then he turned away and stepped into the open courtyard, where ivy climbed the pale walls and the fountain whispered beneath the evening sky.

There he saw her.

A young sister stood near the cloister garden, her robes newly pressed, her hands clasped around a basket of herbs. She looked up when he approached, her eyes wide and uncertain.

"Favor find you, Sister." His words were gentle, his tone warm, his smile easy.

She shifted her hands, looking around nervously, but Alaric took her soft hand in his, stilling her movement.

"There is little need for that, Sister. We are quite alone out here, they cannot reprimand you for speaking to a traveler not in your own customs."

She gulped, looking around before she answered. "You are on errand from the king?"

"I am," he sighed heavily, looking forlorn. "I have come a great distance for not and now must travel back without reward. Perhaps you can take me to your chapel and give me up in prayer to the goddess to give safe passage on my journey."

After a moment's hesitation, she nodded.

She led him through narrow corridors where candlelight flickered along the walls. Their footsteps echoed down the cooling stairway, deeper and deeper into the quiet heart of the convent. At last they entered the lower chapel, where rows of Sisters knelt in silence at the front of the room and the statue of the goddess watched from her alcove of carved marble.

Alaric lowered himself beside the girl, nearest to the back of the chapel. His hands folded, his head bowed. Around them the Sisters' hands moved with their prayers, without the use of their voice, it left a great hum of silence safe the shifting of fabric and the chime of bells that hung from their sleeves. Beside him, the girl began to move her hands, her own bells chiming slightly .

Slowly, almost imperceptibly, Alaric turned his head toward her. His presence seemed to close in on her like a tightening circle. The girl stiffened, her breath catching. When she looked up, he raised a finger lightly to his lips and nodded toward the elders nearby, reminding her of the eyes that surrounded them.

His hand closed around her wrist.

He rose to his feet and drew her with him, guiding her from the chapel as though it were the most natural thing in the world. No one noticed. No one spoke. They moved through the corridor in silence until he opened the door to a small storage room and ushered her inside. The door closed softly behind them.

The girl's hands quaked. "Sir, I beg you to let me return."

Alaric's expression changed, his smile thinning, his eyes bright with something cold and deliberate as he leaned closer.

"What would the elders think, should they find you here with me? I come in search of answers and you shall give them to me." The words fell gently from his lips, but they carried the weight of iron and the girl fell silent.

Alaric studied her for a long moment, as though measuring how far her fear could be stretched. Then he spoke again, his voice low and intent. "You knew Elsa," he said.

Her eyes widened.

"Tell me how you knew her."

Wild eyed, the girl nodded. Alaric began rucking up her garments, exposing her bare legs beneath the thin white cotton chemise below him. "Where did she go?" He ran his hands over her thighs.

"There was a man…" she whispered, trying not to make a noise. "He… he came and took her away."

Alaric smiled, his fingers dangerously close to the hot place between the girl's thighs, she whimpered. Afraid. "What man? Do you remember what he looked like, his name, his origin?"

Tears flooded the girl's eyes, "Please, sir… I can't."

"His name," Alaric ordered impatiently.

She wept, shaking her head. "I don't know."

Alaric drew his dagger, the new dagger he was gifted to from Lord Bannon after slitting Sir Vasco's throat and placed the tip of the blade against her pale skin. It could be only one man. "Did he have a shaved head? Did he wear armor?"

She shook her head. "He wore nobleman's clothes… with an elven servant. His hair was white as the western sands."

"Rhun," he seethed, repocketing his dagger. Alaric yanked her hood from her head, exposing her long red hair and his blood flooded hot, dazzled. "I was going to let you go, but how can I leave a beauty such as yourself here without my seed to swell her belly?"

Pushing down his trousers with little difficulty, he pushed the girl back against a barrel, entering her forcefully, shoving the fabric of her hood into her mouth. She screamed, clawing at him, but Alaric laughed, spending himself within her in hastened urgency.

The girl wept, holding herself, broken. Releasing her, Alaric sneered, standing to his full height and rearranged his clothes.

"You leave me disgraced, sir," she whimpered and Alaric stopped.

"I have given you a gift. If your belly should swell, and you give me an heir, I shall come for you... if you birth a bitch... best to drown her and yourself for no man shall have you after my claim upon your cunt."

Leaving her in tears to travel into the forbidden lands of Rhun.

*Denorn, Realm of Jorn.*

The curtains had been drawn for hours, blocking the last breath of twilight from entering the study. Denorn's heavy air clung to the stone of the large estate like mildew, dense, old, and unyielding. The fire in the hearth crackled low, casting a  glow upon the room's walls, lined with ancient tomes, relics of forgotten rites, and the lingering scent of charred herbs.

Simeon Bannon stood with his back to the hearth, one hand braced on the carved mantle, the other at his side. He was a gaunt figure in shadow, shoulders rigid beneath his black doublet, his breath short, and eyes half glazed. His fingers twitched and sweat had collected at his brow, but it was the silence that disturbed him most.

For days now, her voice had been absent.

The connection he once drew from like a wellspring, that twisted, sacred channel forged in blood and oath and desire, had gone still.

"She has abandoned me," he muttered through clenched teeth. "Or she is testing me." He stared at the crimson thread of blood trailing from his nostril, dabbing it away with the cuff of his sleeve. It wasn't the first time the bleed had come during his attempts to reach her.

Far from him, Leuthere knelt stiffly in silence, armored only in posture now that his tunic lay discarded over the chair by the door. He had not spoken since entering, not when Simeon dismissed the other guards, when the door locked behind them, when he was ordered to kneel obediently at the center of the chamber.

"She is silent," Simeon whispered, more to the shadows than to the man. "I fed her my life, my marrow, and yet nothing. I have unraveled Barrow's mind, I have poured myself into the seams of his soul. And Eero..." His lip curled. "Eero is a fortress behind that devotion of his. I have seen the flicker in his eye when Barrow speaks. There is no fear, no questioning. He would die for him, and that makes him untouchable."

He turned sharply toward Leuthere, voice rising. "But you are not. You swore fealty to me, Leuthere. You brought me Vasco, spilled his blood, took the covenant."

The knight did not look up. His back bore the story of his service, long scars from years past, ridged and pale across sun dark skin. But the old wounds did not move, and the knight knelt tight with anticipation.

Simeon's hand went to the cane resting against his chair. The cane whistled through the air before it struck flesh with a resonating crack. Leuthere did not cry out, his broad back meeting another blow, then another.

Tightening his grip, the next blow drew blood, hearing a gentle rasp of an inhale from Leuthere, but the man did not change his stance, letting his head fall back slightly. Catching his breath, Simeon stretched his fingers, holding onto the sweaty hair on Leuthere's scalp.

"Speak to me," he whispered, though it was not Leuthere he spoke to, his nostrils inhaling the mingling scent of blood and sweat. "I have given. I have bled for you."

Desperation curled in his chest like a fever. Pulling back his fingers, he clenched tighter to the cane, drawing his arm back to strike another blow. Blood trickled from Simeon's nose now, mingling with the sweat at his upper lip.

"I have silenced the council. I have brought the boy to his knees. And still, you do not speak..." His hand faltered, the cane slipping from his grasp. The blood on the floor was not just Leuthere's anymore. Simeon wiped his face, staring at the red smudge on his fingers as if it were unfamiliar.

Ringing in his ears brought the man to his knees, the candles flickered in defiance as the whispers of magick coiled tighter in the air around them.

# CHAPTER
## 38



*Castle Caerh, Rhun*

THE GARDENS OF CASTLE Caerh stretched golden under the waning sun, the breeze slipping gently through the hydrangea groves and whispering past the white limbed birches that edged the palace terrace. Elsa moved through the stone path slowly, her fingertips grazing over the tops of peonies heavy with bloom. She hadn't spoken in hours. She didn't need to, here, silence was gentler than words.

The sky above was pale, brushed with lavender, and the air was cool and laced with the scent of mint and elderflower. She exhaled through her nose, trying to steady the ache still lodged in her chest since leaving Divna to return to Brendolyn, like a great weight had been lifted.

A shadow moved and her breath caught, hearing footsteps too heavy to belong to a gardener. The all too familiar footsteps. Her heart seized and the tightness beneath her ribs became nearly unbearable.

Alaric stood at the edge of the garden path, his silhouette thin and dark against the soft color of the blooms behind him. His wheat colored hair was tousled, damp by sweat, and his eyes were fixed solely on her.

Elsa took a step back before she realized it. Her throat dried, lips parting, but no sound came.

"Elsa," he rasped, his voice a crack in the serenity, outstretching his hand. "I have come for you, my love."

Her limbs locked but before she could summon the will to speak, another figure emerged swiftly from the darkness from the arch behind the garden's wall.

Loren Enzo.

The duke of Rhun moved like a shadow cleaved from the fading light, and stepped between her and Alaric, his green eyes hard and gleaming. The garden, moments before a peaceful haven, now crackled with tension.

Loren's jaw tightened, shielding Elsa without hesitation.

"While she stands upon the soil of Rhun," he said, voice taut with steel, "while I have breath in my lungs... you shall not claim any part of Elsa Laronn."

"She is mine," Alaric sneered from the gravel path, voice sharp with desperation. "I have claimed her." The moment hung in silence. Then Alaric moved in wild, reckless, lunging.

Elsa shrieked, her body reacting on impulse as the man that still ravaged her dreams came at her but Loren was faster.

He met Alaric's charge with a brutal precision, pivoting his weight and slamming him down into the gravel and dirt. The crack of impact jolted the air and dust rose while Alaric gasped as Loren's knee pinned him.

With one hand, Loren ripped open Alaric's tunic, baring the pale, scar laced chest underneath. A new scar Elsa had never seen before. His other hand came down in a flash, the tip of his finger pressing flat to the center of Alaric's sternum.

Alaric screamed. His body arched, spasmed, his fingers clawing at the stone.

"I can finish his work, Alaric," Loren said through clenched teeth, his voice low and chilling. "I can feel it. The curse, the part left undone. The one that still writhes in your blood like rot waiting for breath to come alive and eat upon your flesh, waiting until there was nothing left."

Elsa's breath hitched. Her limbs had gone numb and the mark upon her ribs began to burn in agony as whatever magick embedded itself into Alaric began to seize her too.

The air itself had grown cold and unnatural. Flowers around them seemed to shrink inward, and the shadows deepened. Her blood turned to ice in her veins as Loren's body seemed to hum with magick, frost crawling at the stone near Loren Enzo's feet.

Alaric's cries became guttural.

"Loren—!" Elsa's voice rang through the frozen haze.

He stopped.

His chest rose with a sharp gasp as if he had surfaced from beneath dark waters. Slowly, he lifted his face to her. His eyes had turned white, as she had seen them only once before. But at the sound of her voice, his focus returned. His gaze flicked to her, and color bled back into his irises, their unnatural green gleaming once more. Loren stood slowly, not taking his eyes from Alaric's cowering form.

"Leave this place, Alaric. Return, and I will end your existence."

Alaric did not speak. He scrambled away, clutching his chest, vanishing into the trees like smoke burned from the light.

Elsa stood unmoving. Only when Loren turned to her, his expression softening slightly, did she realize her fists were clenched and her cheeks streaked with tears she didn't remember shedding. Outstretching his arms, offering himself to her embrace she ran to meet him there in the empty path.

"You're safe," he murmured.

The candles burned low in their sconces, their golden light flickering against the smooth stone walls, casting long shadows across the tapestry that hung upon the wall. She sat in the cushioned seat, her knees drawn up, a blanket draped over her legs, the hem barely brushing the floor. The garden outside was quiet now, night had blanketed the scene in darkness, but her mind remained loud.

As the door creaked open, Elsa knew it was Pavan without needing to turn her head. She bristled slightly to draw her arms closer around her middle as the tall man approached.

"Alaric entered through the western gate, taking the dress of a shop keep. My guards have been notified, he shall not enter these streets again."

Elsa could say nothing.

He sat across from her, close enough to feel the warmth of her presence but not close enough to touch. His hands were folded in his lap, pale and tense, and his shoulders curled slightly inward.

He spoke softly, but each word felt deliberate, like the soft tread of someone stepping over broken glass. "I can't take the bond from you, Elsa. It's stitched too deep." His gaze flicked toward her, then away. "But I can lessen the pain."

Elsa's eyes shone. Her lips parted, breath catching on the edge of resistance.

Pavan gave the faintest of nods. "I understand your reservation, Elsa. You do not wish me to see your memories, that you cannot trust me."

"I trust you," she whispered, though a flutter lingered in her voice. "There are few men whom I can ever trust again, it is only..."

"I will not think less of you, Elsa." Pavan looked at her, those green eyes piercing straight through her, taking her breath away. "You have endured the unthinkable. Being held at the mercy of another simply because they thought you weak."

She swallowed thickly, her throat tightening, willing herself not to cry. This impossible man before her sat so decidedly still, but there was something in his look, the hardness in his green eyes that made Elsa think of Eero, to think of the fierce protectiveness that the knight embodied. Now, Pavan looked at her, waiting for her to give him the permission to help her, to show her a kindness she could never return.

"You owe me nothing," Pavan breathed as if holding his breath. He reached out, one hand hovering near her temple, then paused. "May I?"

She closed her eyes and tilted her head forward, giving permission.

With gentle fingers, Pavan brushed against her skin, and the room slipped away.

Catching her breath as the darkness unfolded around them like a room with no ceiling. Pavan moved in the darkness, his magick weaving through her mind, like following webs of string he began to sift through her memories. Each one that held remnants of Alaric were gently embraced, her pain in each one lessened until the searing heat in her side became a dull throbbing sting and then finally a slight tickle. She began to feel Pavan's magick like a cool balm, each memory he touched, without looking into began to shift, lessening in pain and connection to Alaric.

And then, Pavan stumbled.

It was the smell of tea that first enveloped them, then the tang of copper, and the burrowing etching of confusion that burned in her mind. Pavan turned and saw a memory trying to bury itself beneath layers of hurt. Elsa's presence flared beside him, panicked, trying to pull him away.

"Not that one," she said sharply, her voice tense. "Please."

But he caught her hand before she could retreat.

"We're already here," he said gently. "I cannot leave without tearing it from your mind. Don't be afraid, you can show me…"

And the memory opened.

Elsa stood there, pale in the dimming light, her hair braided tightly. Her fingers were clenched before her as she clung to the handle of the kettle. Leuthere stumbled back, one brow split and bleeding. He chuckled as he advanced, and Elsa began to retreat down the corridor behind her.

And then, from the shadows, a figure snatched her into the alcove, clamping his hand over her mouth. It was muddled, shifting, terror seized Elsa as she tried to hide from the memory, but Pavan stood near her, trailing a hand along the shift of shadow.

"Your memory was changed," Pavan noticed, his hand retracting from the darkness as he smoothed his fingertips. Elsa could see nothing but the danger that held her.

"There was someone there, they made me forget… but they didn't hurt me." Elsa shook her head, unable to remember and looked at the darkness like a faded dream.

Pavan turned away from the memory, focusing on Elsa, looking deeply into her eyes. Elsa saw the depth of his green eyes, his unsettling deep eyes that were like a doorway in this dream scape. She had heard Brendolyn describe what it was like, but to experience it herself, this was not what she expected. Being the first time Pavan had looked at her directly, she felt fear crawling through her skin.

"They altered your memory, Elsa. Who was it?" Pavan's voice was a deep and guttural growl.

She breathed, shaking her head, attempting to look away, but unable to keep her eyes from his. "I can't…"

"Concentrate." Pavan placed his forehead to hers. He smelled of sulfur, and lavender making her nose tickle. "The magick was not deep, you can see the face. Leuthere cannot reach you here, but the alcove saved you, someone pulled you in."

Taking a breath, it was cold and sudden, drenching Elsa in calm. Slowly, she turned, her eyes focusing on the darkened alcove.

"Shut up girl," the voice trickled into her ear, knowing it was faie magick. Her breath hitched. "I'm not going to hurt you."

"Thad." She saw the familiar copper haired faie who held her close to his chest, shielding them in the darkened alcove as Leuthere lumbered off down the corridor in a terrifying fright.

Elsa sighed and Pavan had stepped back, his face white as ash. Around her, the memory went cold and stagnant. They watched as the scene unfolded, just as Elsa remembered before Thad had stolen the memory, making her forget. In the darkness of the alcove, Elsa waited, watching the faie slip away.

A sudden shift engulfed them and Elsa felt her head swimming, being pulled through the memories and into a long dark corridor. Beneath her feet was white marble, but noiseless in the smooth walled corridor, filled with flat oak doors. She spun, alone in the unfamiliar corridor. Her heart hammered in her chest as unease settled in, realizing this was not her own memory.

"Pavan," she breathed, her breath catching in her throat.

There were voices, followed by a low light. Following it, Elsa approached the doorway, taking hold of the handle, it gave way, opening with a rush of cold air. Taking her breath away, this cold was unlike any she had experienced in Jorn or Corad.

"Pavan," she called again, entering the memory, her bare feet stepping onto a rigid forest floor. She visibly saw her breath around her, but the cold felt different, it felt stagnant locked in the clutches of the memory.

Voices muttered again, reaching her ears. Elsa turned, the door was gone, and in its place was a young boy with dark hair and large green eyes. He stood in the darkened forest, shivering and Elsa stepped forward.

"Pavan," she whispered. He looked past her, his skin paled with fear. "Pavan, you need to come back with me." Not knowing if this was the memory or the man who had brought her here, she reached out a hand. Touching the boy's dark hair, it was soft beneath her fingers.

"He's gone." His little voice was scared. Elsa lowered herself, kneeling before him so they were closer to eye to eye. "Thad is dead."

"Yes, Pavan." Elsa tried to steel her aching heart. "He is gone to the Veil... but we must return now."

The little boys' eyes shimmered, unshed tears welling in the small eyes. A sadness enveloped her, dragging through her bones, Elsa realized it was his grief. Pavan was grieving, a little boy was *grieving*. Her smile fell and mirrored tears fell down her cheeks, swiping away the tears from his splotched cheeks as his little face scrunched in the preemptive wail that would soon follow.

His little voice was heart wrenching. "Why did mummy have to die?"

"Your mummy loved you, Pavan." Elsa swallowed thickly around her words. "There are so many who love you."

"Why do they all leave me?"

Elsa fought her heartbreak, grasping the little boy's hand tightly in hers and kissing it fiercely as she looked into those swimming green eyes. "I am not leaving you, nor is Bren."

Standing to her feet, the little hand was solid in hers. She looked down at their joined hands and in a flash the hand grew, large and trembling. Blinking through her own tears, she looked up at the Pavan she had come to know. His white hair was unkempt about his shoulders and his eyes looked down at her with such tenderness, it made Elsa blush.

"Let's go back." She was stern, squeezing his hand.

Fading from the mind scape was easy, like waking up from a long night's slumber. Wincing as the sleepiness as the room came back into her view, Pavan sat beside her, as he had looked the second they had joined their minds. Elsa sniffled, wiping her nose on the blanket that remained over her lap.

"Forgive me, Elsa," he said hoarsely, eyes wide.

A faint smirk curled her lips. "Always so willing to help others, but never willing to see yourself helped." Her brow lifted slightly. "Brendolyn was right when she told me you were stubborn."

His face broke with the ghost of a smile, quickly smothered by weariness. "I cannot change the past," he said, voice low and cracking.

"No," Elsa sighed. "You cannot change the past. No more than I can, Pavan. But if you run from what happened in your past forever…" She shook her head. "You will let it fester in your mind. It will rot you from the inside, even if your magick does not."

He didn't answer at first. His eyes had gone distant, shadowed by memories too sharp to touch. "I can't go back there," he whispered.

"Not alone," she said gently. "But you should."

# CHAPTER
## 39

LEADING HER INTO THE darkened room, Pavan felt the flutter of nerves. There was so much he wanted to tell her, but a fear began to grow as they walked deeper into the cathedral, her hand small in his grasp.

"This is a great place of magick," he whispered. "You have heard many of the rumors in Rhun, but this was once the home of Sanna."

She paused, her eyes widening as the room they entered became clearer. Sensing Pavan's magick, the shimmering stones that were nestled in the stone wall began to glow, illuminating the long hall. A glimmer of the stars mirrored in the still waters of the pool that stretched out before them.

"*This place.*" Her fingers began to sign. "*I can feel the magick in this place.*"

"Dragon glass has been imbibed into the pool, the shimmer that looks like the stars is moon stone to heighten the strength. The waters have been purified by the centuries of stillness in this cavern at the heart of the cathedral." Pavan spoke, his mind whirling where they stood so near to the pool's edge it looked as if they stood in an endless void of starlight.

"*Beautiful.*" She lowered her hands.

"I would like to show you my past, where I come from, who I was before I was Loren... before I was Pavan..." His breath stilled, but his heart beat hard in his chest as he dared to look down at Brendolyn.

Her eyes were glossy and her cheeks flushed in the heat of the room. It would be cold soon under the temperature of the dark waters.

"*Mind as one.*" Her fingers moved in one quick movement.

Pavan turned to her, reaching up to trace the line of her soft cheek, he could sense her magick, it's pull, her longing for him and it made Pavan shiver.

"It will be safe in the pool, it calms my magick, there I shall show you everything." He traced the line of her lip. "Anything."

Nodding, Brendolyn reached up, pulling the first lace of Pavan's tunic. His heart fluttered, allowing her to pull the garment free. He made quick work of removing his boots, setting them aside. Unlacing his trousers to pull them down, he stood before Brendolyn in only his linen pants. Her eyes widened as she gently traced her fingertips along the length of the scar upon his chest. Their eyes met and Brendolyn blushed.

Taking away her hand to pull at the ties of her bodice, Pavan tossed the garment aside. Her fingers loosened the ties of her petticoat and the material fell around her feet.

Pavan waited patiently, watching Brendolyn as she turned, pulling the length of her hair to the front, exposing the laces of her stays. He hesitated, touching the curve of her neck, then the secured twisted coil of the ties. They came free, pulling them apart until the length of the crossed fabric could be removed with little effort, leaving Brendolyn standing before him in a thin chemise.

Taking her hand again, Pavan pressed a kiss to her palm. Leading her after him, Pavan stepped down into the stillness of the pool, the ripple making the stars around them shift. Slowly, he stepped again, his feet finding the lowest step before he turned back to Brendolyn where her hand remained in his and he helped her step in after him.

The water was cool and it crept up the length of his body. Leading them deeper into the pool until his thighs were covered, he turned to see Brendolyn watching intently, her chest heaving slightly at the chill.

"Don't be afraid," he whispered, taking both of her hands, and bringing them up to touch each side of his face, her fingertips just beneath his temples.

Leaning into his magick, Pavan blinked as the room spun, his body slowly tilting back and falling into the icy depths of the water. Her hands remained on his temples and he saw her shift through the rippling water.

"Pavan..." her voice followed.

"Hold on to me."

His breath caught, emerging into the lines between their minds, shivering as the magick was dulled. Standing in a long narrow corridor of a hospital, Brendolyn's arms were wrapped around his middle where they were dressed in ashen colored scrubs.

"Pavan?" Brendolyn looked down the corridor, her eyes wide as she blinked up at the fluorescent lights. "What is this?"

"I was born in February of 1976, in a place called London... I was born with my brother, Henry. My name was Isaac Maison." The hallway came alive, shifting from a muted grey to a dance of fleeting colors, as fragmented memories of people came and went through the doorways. Pavan's breathing quickened and he held Brendolyn's hand tighter.

"This is a hospital where those who are sick come to get better by healers called doctors and nurses. There is no magick here, nothing like Lahrs who can heal bones and close wounds. It takes longer here, it takes patience and a chance."

He didn't focus on one memory as they faded in and out through the doors, but instead stepped forward, opening the first door in front of them.

"It is not a world like yours." They stepped into the room together and laying down on a hospital bed, attached to tubes and wires, was a boy with sallow skin and dark wild hair surrounded by machines beeping rhythmically. "Does this frighten you?"

He could see the worry in her, the terror in her eyes as she neared the bed, looking down at the pitiful boy beneath the muted blue covers. Gently, she reached forward, touching the small hand wrapped with bandages and glanced at the leg pulled up in a cast.

"Is this you?" she whispered, unable to look away from the boy.

"I was six." Pavan stood at the end of the bed, glaring at the broken boy that lay upon the bed before them. "My femur was broken. Sorry, the large bone in your leg..." He placed a hand on his thigh.

"What happened?" Brendolyn reached forward, brushing the hair out of the boys eyes, in his sleep he stirred, but did not wake.

"My father pushed me down the stairs."

Brendolyn's eyes snapped up, looking at Pavan with such intensity, it looked alarming to see her golden eyes intense with such fury.

"How could he—"

The door opened, and they both looked as a timid woman entered the room, holding herself close as she neared the bed. Pavan held his breath, watching his mother, her long dark hair hastily braided, her cardigan thrown over her shoulders as she neared the boy who lay upon the bed.

Watching intently as the woman neared the light, Brendolyn stepped back, gaping at the woman, her eyes widening as the woman sat at the edge of the bed, taking the boy's hand.

"Queen Eleanore…" Brendolyn whispered, looking up to Pavan who hadn't taken his eyes off his mother.

He touched his mother's cheek, his fingers tracing the tears from her warn face and then letting his hand fall to her shoulder, as another hand melded through his own. He knew who had entered the room, who comforted his mother.

"Ellie… you can't stay with him…" his uncle urged.

Pavan turned quickly, his eyes shimmering as he suddenly shifted the memory, turning away from the room as they returned in a heave of breath to the empty corridor, staggering to grip himself on the wall.

"Sorry," he muttered, covering his eyes, unable to shake the unease in his hands. "Sorry, I need a moment."

But then there were arms wrapped around him, drawing him close. Brendolyn embraced him, touching his hair and kissing his temple. "Take all the time you need, Pavan… I am here…"

He stood straighter as the second memory wrapped around them like a vice. "I used my magick to take our family to Entheas, when me and my brother were nine years old. My father had tried to hurt our mother, had tried to hurt her to get to me… in my anger, I took us to Entheas…" Around them a familiar room of dark stone and a warm fire.

Brendolyn gasped, stepping forward to kneel before the younger Beaumont who sat playing with one of the two identical boys in the room. Together they played a strange game with smoothed stones that were carved with elven runes.

"Come have a round, Isaac." Beaumont smiled, looking up to encourage the boy who sat at the window but there was a fall in the young boy's shoulders. "Your mother is safe with Meilyr. They speak of difficult things."

"He's killed people, hasn't he?" Standing from his seat near the window, Pavan watched his younger self shut the book he held and then knelt beside his brother on the floor.

Beaumont was quiet for a time, playing with a smooth stone in his fingers. "Your father is troubled, Isaac... he will answer for his crimes."

Looking away, Isaac frowned. "I wish I had killed him the first time he struck her."

A large bronze hand reached between them as Beaumont gently placed a hand on Isaac's clenched fist. "You are calm, Isaac, you are safe here."

Isaac glaring up at Beaumont from beneath the curtain of black hair, his eyes gone white. Hot tears trickled along his pale cheeks but beside them, Henry whimpered, curling into himself as he covered his ears. Not flinching away, Beaumont was quick to kneel, drawing Isaac into his broad chest.

"Calm the storm, Isaac... I am here. You mustn't be afraid..."

"Pavan," Brendolyn whispered, holding tightly to Pavan's hand, her eyes shimmering with unshed tears.

"My mother was Eleanore Aubin... Beaumont took her and my brother from this place, married her... Fiona is my sister."

She smiled, touching Pavan's cheek as he gave a sad smile. "What happened to you? Where did you go when they entered Jorn?"

Pavan sighed, waving his hand and the memory shifted, letting the waves of thought trickle through, emerging into the corridor again, the empty hospital wing fading as they entered through another door.

"Isaac!"

Smirking, he turned, they stood upon the old stage of his uncle's theatre. Seeing the fine suit his uncle wore as he glared up at the stage, the lights illuminating the worn wood. Quiet hushed over the stage, those Pavan could not remember the names of, but the familiar brunette who giggled at center backstage with rosy cheeks and an infectious giggle made Pavan shiver. He had forgotten how beautiful Anthony had been, how he made his heart thunder and his palms sweat.

"Benedick, didst thou note the daughter of Signior Leonato?" Anthony said loudly, getting them back on track, waiting.

"I noted her not, but I looked on her."

Anthony laughed. "Is she not a modest young lady?"

"Do you question me as an honest man should do, for my simple true judgment? Or would you have me speak after my custom, as being a professed tyrant to their sex?" Isaac rolled his eyes, shoving a hand in his pocket as he pushed back the fall of his greasy dark hair.

Anthony, drawing closer to Isaac, touched his arm. "No, I pray thee, speak in sober judgment."

Isaac shouldered him off, scoffing a little as he looked out to the non-existent audience. "Why, in faith, she is too low for a high praise, too brown for a fair praise, and too little for a great praise. Only this commendation I can afford her, that were she other than she is, she were unhandsome, and being no other but as she is, I do not like her..."

"Come on." Pavan took hold of Brendolyn's hand, trudging across the stage as the scene went on, ignoring the raising of hair upon his neck as he pulled them forward through the side of the stage, into another memory.

"Was that... another of your lovers?" Brendolyn questioned, keeping up with Pavan's long strides.

"Anthony... he was Penelope's brother, one of my best friends, but yes..."

They came through another of the memories, Pavan winced as the wooden floor gleamed, wall to wall mirrors bringing everyone into view. None of the other dancers looked his way, but together he and Brendolyn saw the memory playing out nearest to the outer wall, where a girl poised with elegant lines practiced at the barre.

"Penelope," Brendolyn breathed, stepping forward to stand on the opposite side of the barre near the young girl who raised on her toes, extending her arm. Brendolyn mimicked her, following the motions almost perfectly. Pavan gulped, unable to stop her admiring the grace. "She is extraordinary, Pavan."

"Took you long enough." Penelope smirked over her shoulder at the boy who wore a white shirt and black tights and danced dangerously close behind her. His dark hair was tied back in a low ponytail and he winked, keeping his attention on the teacher who made her rounds nearby, but when the teacher walked on the other side of the room, Isaac leaned closer to Penelope's ear.

"I am going to France next week."

"Well, perhaps you can learn from your experience and gain some true talent." Penelope kept her composure following through with her footwork as her arm swept back. Young Isaac touched it, his fingers trailing along her inner arm.

"Brendolyn." Pavan reached out, beckoning Brendolyn towards him. She stopped dancing, stumbling towards him as he pulled her through the memory, exiting through a side door, and into another room.

In a smaller, dingier stage, they entered into the wildly loud set of playing with the band, *The Jacked Pistols*. Pavan gulped, maneuvering around the set of drums, catching sight of Anthony out of the corner of his eye as he pulled Brendolyn along behind him. Her eyes locked solely upon the leather clad Isaac, strumming the electric guitar as his sweaty hair fell into his face, droning into the microphone.

He wanted to get out of there, his skin beginning to crawl as they hurried through the backstage, but the memory shifted, walking in between Anthony and Isaac arguing off stage. A distance grew between the lines of Pavan's memories as they went through the green room door. Stepping out onto the vibrant colors of a skating ring there was no music, but the sound was muffled by the pounding in Pavan's head. He stopped at the center of the rink, his mind narrowed in on the two figures who came into focus.

"Our first date, Penelope and I..." he muttered, rubbing Brendolyn's hand as they watched the two fumble, laughing after Penelope elbowed Isaac in a blundered maneuver.

"You look happy." Brendolyn nodded as they watched while Isaac laughed, smiling as his younger self looked at the girl with dark hair.

"I was happiest when I was with her," Pavan muttered. Turning, he watched the scene continue. They walked closer to the darker part of the skate rink, seeing the pair sit at a booth while Penelope dabbed ice at Isaac's nose.

"ISAAC!" a voice shouted in the memory, jarring into Pavan that stole his breath.

Thudding pounded like the rhythm of his heartbeat, but when he pressed a palm to his chest, there was nothing. Around them the memory faded before Penelope's lips kissed his younger self. Shifting as the voice grew more insistent, louder, drawing Pavan deeper into his mind and further into the pain.

"Isaac!"

Pavan turned, his breathing coming in short as he felt the palpations of his blood, the churning in his stomach as his veins felt on fire.

"Pavan, what have you done?" Brendolyn was shaking, her eyes searching wildly, looking around them as the memory faded into existence.

They stood at the center of the greenroom behind the theatre his uncle owned, in the room that Pavan once used as his dressing room. Pavan stumbled back, his skin hot to the touch as he backed further away from the hunched frame at the vanity.

"She is dead," his younger self muttered. "You've killed her... you mean nothing. Nothing. Nothing."

Stepping forward Brendolyn desperately grabbed at his younger self, holding his shoulders as she began to cry. Taking his arm to still his hand, she pried at his fingers, but it was useless and she watched in horror as his younger self swallowed the handful of pills.

"No, no, no..." she whispered, agony raking through Pavan as he felt her anguish.

Pushed back, Brendolyn stumbled aside, crying desperately as she knelt beside his younger self when he fell to the carpeted floor. Pavan closed his eyes, knowing what was coming, feeling the bile rising up in his own throat as his younger self began to choke on his tongue, violently convulsing on the floor.

"Please," she whimpered.

Opening his eyes, he couldn't move, his body felt frozen. Flinching as the door burst open with a loud bang, he watched a familiar ginger haired youth stumble in, assessing Isaac before rushing forward. Brendolyn scampered to the other side, wide eyed as she watched the stranger turn young Isaac onto his side and shove his fingers down his throat. It was repulsive as the contents of Isaac's stomach spilled onto the floor.

"Not today, Isaac," Thomas grit through his teeth, hastening to lay him flat, beginning chest compressions.

Darkness shrouded them, fading the man in the distance as the room twisted and turned, changing into a dark, dangerous room that smelled of sweat and death. Brendolyn wept, andPavan could feel it like it was his own.

"Run Isaac... you must run..."

Flashes of the nightmare coiled hot within his mind and Pavan winced, grabbing his head. The memories flooded back, dread coursing through his veins as he tried to shut them out, trying to regain control as ice crept along his spine. Hearing a voice shouting, muffled by the loud nightmare that tried to consume him, warmth enveloped him, breathing in and out, his dread fading as he began to breathe slower.

Raising his head to see Brendolyn in front of him.

Gasping, Pavan spit out water, breaking the connection in a violent pull, splashing against the waters as he regained his footing. Standing in the darkness of the cathedral, the chill of the air was palpable, seeing their breath coiling around them in little puffs of vapors.

"I'm sorry." He shuddered, water dripping down his body. He saw Brendolyn shivering in the darkened waters, wiping away her tears in earnest.

"*He saved you.*" She trembled as she signed. "*That man in your memory saved your life.*"

"Thomas..." Pavan hated himself, hated the lies he told to protect his friend, but it was that very man who saw him at his lowest. "I could never allow myself to thank him... to apologize..." His throat thickened.

"*He knows. That is not a man who asks for thanks... he loved you fiercely.*"

Anger foiled his bones and magick burned beneath the surface. Wading to the edge, he pulled himself up, Brendolyn came swiftly after him, her under dress dripping on the stone floor as she followed closely behind him.

Grabbing his arm to pull him back, she clapped her hands together.

"*You are a selfish child, Pavan,*" she scolded him, her fingers signing vigorously. "*To believe no one else can love you so deeply, they sacrifice for your goodness.*"

"I am not worth saving, not by him, not by you..."

She shook her head, reaching up to touch his cheek tenderly. He felt the warmth of her hand, the sweetness of her magick ease into his skin, soothing the raging agony. Pavan breathed a sigh, leaning into her touch and his anger subsided.

"*You are the soul I'd brave the Veil, the love hearts share can never fail.*" Her voice was a song, echoing through the shimmering hall like starlight, catching Pavan's breath. He reached up to sooth away the tears that fell on her cheek.

"I love you, Bren," he whispered, bringing his lips down to meet hers.

# AFTER

P AVAN STUMBLED INTO THE shadows of his bedchamber, the air thick with the scent of smoke and cold stone. His fingers fumbled at the knots of his tunic, loosening the ties with a weary, uneven pull. He sank into the same worn chair where he slept every night, never the bed in the adjoining room.

Down the hall, Brendolyn slept in her own separate chamber. He could feel the faint flicker of her magick like candlelight through the dark. Elsa's presence lingered with her, a second flame, steady and watchful. Relief loosened the tightness in his chest. She was safe. She was not alone.

In the half light of his chamber, the hearth smoldered low, its fire reduced to a bed of embers that pulsed faintly with each breath of the draft. Sleep tugged at him... but so did another pull.

*Isaac.*

The name came like a whisper in his bones, a sound without breath, echoing in the cavern of his mind. Pavan shivered, shifting in the chair, fighting the call. He should not follow that voice into the dark but he was unable to stop his heavy eyes from drifting closed.

*Isaac.*

The room fell away.

Hal's eyes snapped open, Irises burned red as a blood moon. He dragged in a breath so sharp it rattled his ribs and black silk slid from his bare shoulders, pooling at his waist.

His pale, unmarked chest gleamed under the spill of moonlight seeping through the open balcony doors. A looming silhouette of black marble that continued from floor to ceiling in one seamless line.

The dream clung to him like ice but it wasn't a dream.

He tore the sheet away and lurched to his feet, the night air biting against his skin. The wind poured in, carrying the scent of the sea and the faint copper tang of the poisonous mist of the blood trees seen for miles beyond the walls of the great black castle.

"Your Majesty," came a deep voice from the shadows.

Hal barely glanced toward the guard standing at the edge of the black marble floor. The moon spilled a silver column between them, making the guard's presence feel distant, unreal.

"I can see him, Davyn," Hal whispered, his mouth curling into a laugh that carried no joy. "I can see Isaac… I can see my brother." Images bleed through his mind of golden halls, a forest in flight, and his mother's last gaze.

Behind him, the guard straightened. "I advise you to bed, King Halvar."

Hal's head turned slowly, the hiss of his voice cutting through the space. "To bed?" He began to stalk toward the man, each step deliberate, the marble cold under his feet. "The foolish man orders his king to bed."

The guard's eyes flickered with fear. "The Queen Mother would not be pleased."

Hal's sneer deepened, his attention dragging inward as memories twisted tighter, gnawing at his mind, each former memory bleeding and blending together with the new—*No*. He struck the side of his head with his palm, then again, harder, trying to beat the visions out, the running, the screaming, the blood. Hatred and disgust churned in his gut until he could almost taste it.

"King Halvar," Davyn said softly, almost pleading.

Hal ignored him. He turned toward the chamber's doors, pushing them wide, the iron handles freezing beneath his touch. The corridor beyond was a yawning black void. His breath came loud in the stillness as he moved, bare feet soundless against the stone, until he reached the next chamber's balcony.

Moonlight washed over him, turning his sweat slick hair into strands of shadow and silver. He spread his arms, feeling the cold wind tear through him, welcoming its bite. Somewhere behind, Davyn's footfalls followed.

"Think of your actions, my king. Think of the Queen Mother," the guard urged, his voice quaking now.

Hal's laugh was sharp as glass. "No one knows how much I think of her, Davyn. It is her magick that bleeds within me, her taste that lingers on my tongue. I cannot close my eyes without thinking of what she has done to me, what she has taken from me."

He stepped onto the marbled ledge, toes curling over the drop.

"You can't!" Davyn lunged, grabbing Hal's arm.

With a flick of unseen force, Hal hurled him back. The guard slammed into the wall with a crack, sliding to the floor, a dark smear of blood running down his temple. He groaned, struggling to lift his head. "If you are dead, she will bleed me dry, Halvar!"

Hal's grin sharpened.

He turned toward him, stretching out his hands, his voice was almost tender. "She will bring me back. She *always* brings me back. And by your blood, she shall renew my life. By your sacrifice, I shall be stronger."

Then he stepped over the edge, surrendering himself to the void, falling into the black and falling to the cold stone far below with a sickening crack.

# PROPHECY

Two brothers, born hand in hand,
*Beirt deartháireacha, rugadh lámh i lámh,*
Will stand upon the marble grand,
*Seasfaidh siad ar an marmair gan cháim,*
Where cold and black the slab is laid,
*Áit atá dubh, fuar, gan solas is scéal,*
In Nyr, where light has slipped away.
*I Nyr, áit nach lonraíonn an réalta ar bith.*
Beneath their feet, the maiden lies,
*Faoi na cosa, luíonn an mhaighdean chiúin,*
Of ancient blood and magick wise.
*De shliocht ársa, cumhachtaí fighte i sruth.*
With hand and blade, their fates combined,
*Le lámh is lann, snaisc a ndán,*
The fate of worlds is thus designed.
*Ag cruthú cinniúint do gach aon chríoch.*
When red runs freely on the stone,
*Nuair a ritheann fuil ar an gcloch,*
And breath is lost, and souls are sown,
*Agus imeíonn anáil, is greamaítear an t-anam,*
Then Venora shall rise with grace,
*Eireoidh Venora, i ngreim na feirge,*
Wearing the immortal's darkened face.
*Ag caitheamh aghaidh na síoraíochta.*

# Family of Maison

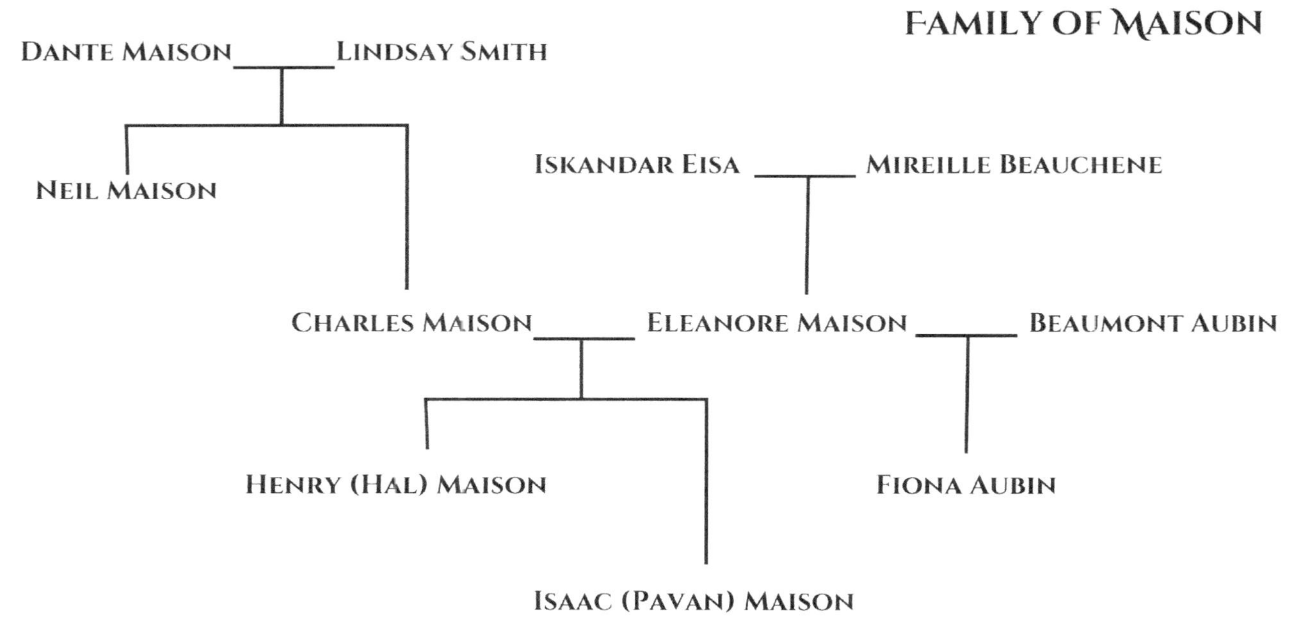

# FAMILY OF AUBIN

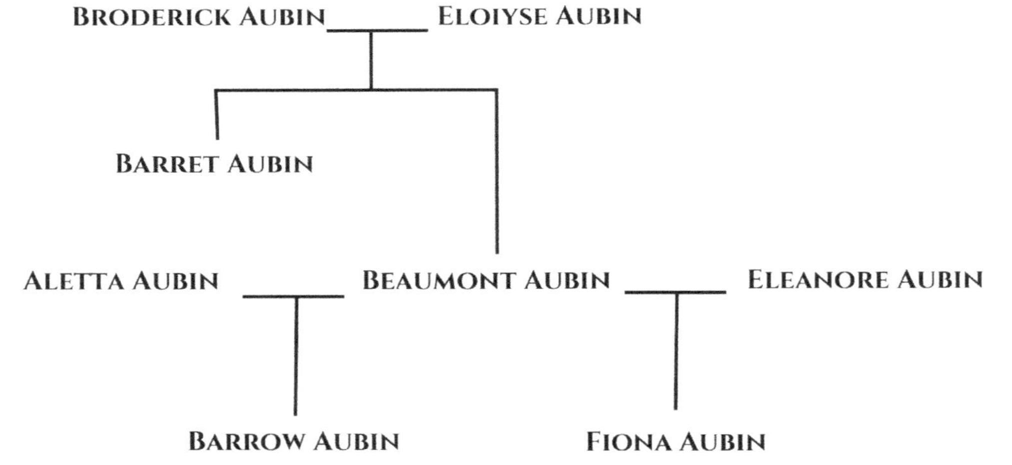

# FAMILY OF MOREAU

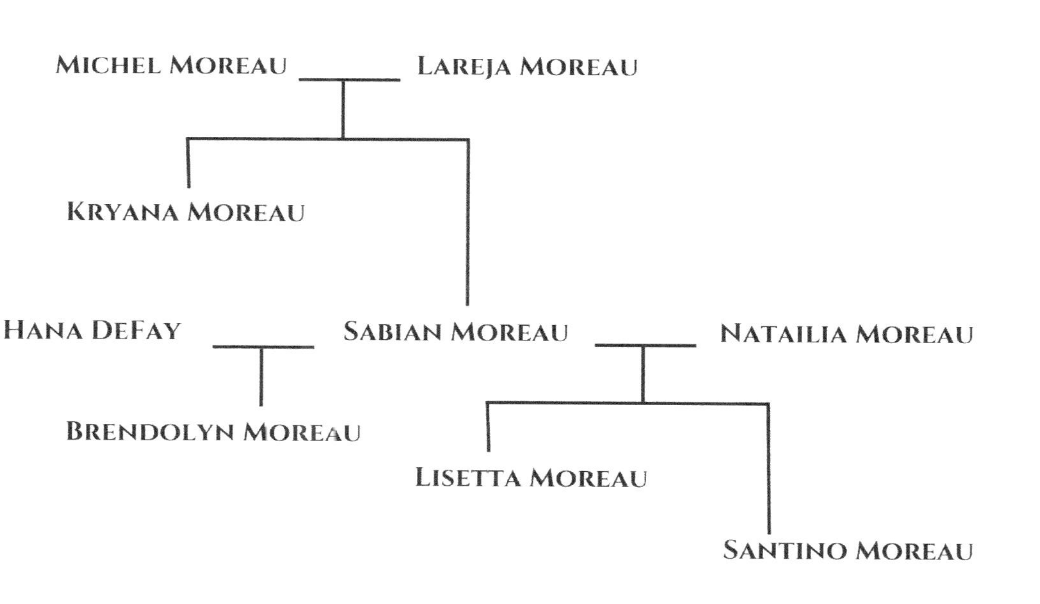

COMING SOON....

*FATES OF VEILORE BOOK FOUR*

# FATE
## OF
# MAGICK

## IRELAND LYDON

*AN IMPRINT OF VEILORE PRESS*

*London, England. 2000.*

"You didn't." Isaac's voice was a low growl, the kind that cut through the din of the bar and rooted itself in Thomas' chest.

"Oh, please—just one song. They'll love it!" Thomas' excitement spilled out in a rush, his cheeks flushed, the warmth of three fast gulps of beer rising to his head.

Across from him, Isaac's expression hardened, turning grey and stony. The light drained from his face so quickly Thomas felt his stomach drop. Isaac pushed back from the table, muttering, "I have to go."

"I'll talk to him," Malcom said quickly, already half rising. He threw Thomas a tight, apologetic smile, as though this sudden fracture was somehow his to mend. "This is on me."

Heat rose in Thomas' face, shame burning hotter than the alcohol. He felt the weight of curious eyes from the nearby tables, the air thick with whispers he couldn't hear but felt all the same. The buzz of the beer curdled, leaving only hollowness. He fumbled for his wallet, dropped a few bills onto the table, and shoved his chair back. As the emcee called up the next act, Thomas slipped out into the cold, bracing air.

The night air bristled over his skin, sharp enough to bite. Just a few feet from the door, he spotted Isaac hunched beneath the amber glow of a streetlamp, Malcom leaning close, whispering into his ear.

"Isaac?" Thomas called, breathless.

Isaac straightened instantly, face smoothing into something guarded and cool. The shift cut into Thomas, sharp, merciless. The vibrancy that used to radiate from Isaac, the easy warmth that had once lit entire rooms, was gone. All that remained was a shell, a reflection in a darkened mirror.

"I'm fine. It's just...been a long time since I've had this much to drink." Isaac lied, and Thomas knew it. Isaac hadn't touched his glass inside.

A lump rose in Thomas' throat, sobering him faster than any cold wind. "If it's about the play—"

Isaac shook his head. "You're the best actor we have, Thomas. I'm glad you'll be the one to replace me."

"Can I help? With anything?" The words cracked out, raw, desperate. He wanted to bridge the gap between them, to fight against the widening chasm that seemed impossible to cross.

"It's late." Isaac's head dipped in dismissal.

Thomas' frown deepened. "Will you call me for coffee?"

"I can't do that."

The rejection made Thomas rake a trembling hand through his russet hair, his chest caving inward. "Right. Right."

The silence between them was unbearable, heavy with a cold finality. Pain throbbed in his temples, though he fought to keep his voice steady.

"Coffee, next Tuesday." Isaac's voice turned unnaturally bright, brittle with forced cheer. "You can ask me whatever you like about Othello." It was the same voice he used on stage when the mask slipped over his true self, when he had to pretend everything was fine.

"I have to go," Isaac blurted suddenly, and before Thomas could speak, he turned sharply on his heel.

Isaac strode quickly down the walk, shoving his hands deep into his denim pockets. Malcom lingered a beat longer beneath the lamp, his face shadowed by worry.

"I'll have him call you, Thomas," he said with a half smile that didn't reach his eyes, then hurried after his friend.

The bar door swung open behind Thomas, spilling laughter and music into the night before closing again. Alone under the light, Thomas stood shaking, his hands trembling as memory flooded him. He remembered that night.

The greenroom. The locked door. His fists hammered against it until the skin split across his knuckles, the sharp ache barely felt through the rush of panic. Then came the muffled sound, words he could not make out, the broken cadence of a voice that chilled him. A thud followed, heavy and final, and Thomas' stomach dropped as though the floor had given way beneath him.

He threw himself against the door until the lock gave way, stumbling inside. The sight carved itself into him. Isaac lay crumpled on the carpet, body convulsing, lips already darkening toward blue. For a heartbeat Thomas froze, terror rooting him to the ground, the air sucked from his lungs.

Then instinct seized him. He fell to his knees. His hands were slick with sweat as he forced his fingers down Isaac's throat, gagging as the acrid stench of bile and chemicals filled the room. He fought against the jerks of Isaac's body, heart racing so fast it drowned out every other sound. There was no space for thought, no space for fear. His body moved before his mind could catch up, driven only by the need to keep Isaac alive.

He remembered the taste of salt on his lips from his own tears, the smear of vomit on his shirt, the way Isaac's chest barely rose beneath his hands. Every second felt like an eternity stretched taut, waiting for the breath that might not come.

And still, he had not thought. He had only moved, driven by desperation and the raw, aching terror of losing him. Forcing chest compressions as he heard the oncoming steps of others along the hall.

"Wait." His breath spilled white into the night, his fists clenching so tight his knuckles ached.

He bolted forward, the familiar urgency propelling his steps. Rounding the corner onto a cobbled side street, his chest heaved as his eyes searched the shadows. Empty. The road stretched silent before him. Only the cold pressed against his ribs, dragging him downward, leaving him hollow.

"Fuck." The word hissed from between his teeth, sharp as the wind.

# Acknowledgements

This book would not exist without the love, support, and encouragement of so many incredible people.

To my husband, Austin, who continues to put up with the late nights, as well as the countless ramblings.

To my best friend, Kat, who always encourages me through every stage of my chaotic writing process.

To my editor, Stacey, who has been such an amazing support in keeping all the words that tumble from my heat in a straight line.

To the amazing Indie Lantern Community, with Ash at the forefront, who has cultivated the growth of community and passion that has helped guide this path that would otherwise be torn asunder.

To every reader who picked up my first few books, who saw something in this world worth holding onto, and who encouraged me to continue—this is for you. Your excitement, your words, and your support have meant everything. Thank you for giving this story a home in your hearts.

# Author Bio

Ireland Lydon lives in Northern Utah, where she balances the beautiful chaos of everyday life with her passion for storytelling. Between the whirlwind of schedules and the ever-growing list of creative ideas, she finds solace in writing, bringing new worlds and characters to life. Fueled by a love for fantasy and an unshakable determination, she continues to weave stories that have been years in the making—one page at a time.